SOMEONE ELSE'S DAUGHTER

A love story, a mystery and finding yourself when you thought there was nothing left to find.

"An empowered and formidable heroine." *Kirkus Reviews*

"Highly charged and emotional… Read it with tissue from the very beginning." Pamela Mason.

"It was a great read, honestly couldn't put it down and can't wait to read the next one." Cathie - Sydney, Australia

"Miranda Steele is one ballsy lady who lives through hard times, has her heart broken and still has room left over for love. And she makes a great PI. I loved it! She's what I'd call 'one HOT pepper!'" Diane Kratz - crime fiction writer

She doesn't need a man.
He wants to find a killer.
Together, can they save a thirteen-year-old girl?

THE MIRANDA'S RIGHTS MYSTERY SERIES

Someone Else's Daughter
Delicious Torment
Forever Mine
Fire Dancer
Thin Ice

THE MIRANDA AND PARKER MYSTERY SERIES

All Eyes on Me
Heart Wounds
Clowns and Cowboys
The Watcher
Zero Dark Chocolate
Trial by Fire
Smoke Screen
The Boy
Snakebit
Mind Bender
Roses from My Killer
The Stolen Girl

OTHER BOOKS BY LINSEY LANIER

Chicago Cop (A cop family thriller)
Steal My Heart

THE PRASALA ROMANCES

The Crown Prince's Heart
The King's Love Song
The Count's Baby

For more information visit www.linseylanier.com

PROLOGUE

Some women sit around in bars after they get dumped, complaining about the jerks who treated them like yesterday's dog squeeze. Miranda Steele didn't go to bars. She didn't have friends to complain to. But she did have the dog squeeze beat out of her regularly by the jerk she was married to.

That was until one cold wintry day when the jerk decided to dump her and throw her out in the snow.

From the floor where Leon had left her, Miranda lifted a shaky hand to her mouth to stop the blood oozing from her cut lip. "What are you doing?"

"What I should have done the night your bastard was conceived. What I've wanted to do for months." His voice shook with quiet rage.

He jammed the suitcase shut, grabbed her by the wrist again and dragged her back downstairs.

"What are you doing?" Miranda screamed the words this time, as he wrestled the front door open.

"Purging my house." He hurled the suitcase into the snow on the front yard. It broke open and her clothes tumbled onto the snowy grass. Then he gave her a hard shove.

She stumbled outside onto the cold concrete porch. Her feet were bare. She was still in her bathrobe.

"Leon," she begged. "Let me back in. What will the neighbors think?"

"They're at work. Besides, no one cares about you. They know what you are." He pushed her again.

She staggered off the stoop and landed with a hard thud on the ground next to her clothes.

He grabbed her purse from a chair and tossed it into the snow beside her. "Take this and go, Miranda. Go away from me." His words pulsed with a dark rage. "I never want to see your face again." He turned and slammed the door so hard, it made her eardrums vibrate. She heard him turn the key.

Her chest heaving, she tried to catch her breath. As she sat on her bruised butt in her front yard in Oak Park, Illinois, dressed in only her PJs and bathrobe, staring up at the cheery, pink stucco two-story she'd lived in for seven years, Miranda didn't wonder whether her "Lord and Master" had beaten her up and chucked her out because she hadn't gotten the crease in his police uniform just right. Or because she'd mouthed off when he'd complained his steak was a bit singed last night.

She knew exactly why he'd done it. She had dared to lunge at the great, the powerful, the all-holy Leon Groth, with her nails bared.

And why had she done that? Not because he'd said she was stupid. Not because he'd called her a filthy whore. Not because he'd told her she was tainted, ruined. She was used to that.

Because early this morning, he'd snuck out of the house with her three-week-old daughter and given her up for adoption.

Adoption.

"Don't worry. They assured me she'd go to a good home. A family who'll never know her true origin. I'm not a monster, after all."

Amy. Her baby.

How had Leon pulled it off? He must have forged Miranda's signature on whatever documents he needed. As a cop, he was connected. He had friends on the force who'd turn a blind eye for a favor owed. He knew court clerks, judges.

The cold seeped into Miranda's bones. Angry tears welled up in her throat. Amy. Her baby.

Get her back. I want her back.

She's gone, Miranda. They took her away and neither of us will ever know where she went. You'll never find her again.

She should have known Leon would do something like this. He'd been pressuring her to give the baby up for adoption since she got pregnant. She should have known he'd meant it when he said he couldn't live under the same roof with "it" any longer. He always referred to Amy as "it." He hated her. He said Miranda had no right to keep her.

Amy wasn't his, after all. Leon was unable to have children after a bout of measles during their first year of marriage. The child had come from Miranda's "unfortunate incident," as he called it. The nightmare last February when she'd gone out late at night to get him ice cream.

The memory of those hands grabbing her, that nameless hooded face hovering over her, hurting her, still filled her nights with terror and emptiness. The examiner at the hospital said she had been lucky. Hard to believe one woman could be so lucky when it came to men.

She squeezed her eyes shut, trying not to see the empty crib she'd found this morning.

Her baby. Where was her baby? Was she hungry? Cold?

She laid her head against her knees, wanting to cry. Daring the hot tears to run down her face and sear her cheeks. She wanted to sob forever. Her nose ran, her stomach was ready to heave, but the stubborn tears refused to come. They would later.

She lifted her head, batted at her wet lips with her sleeve.

Her jaw ached where Leon had smacked her. There'd be an ugly bruise on her cheek soon. Her wrists and shoulders were sore from being yanked down the stairs and across the floor. But she'd gotten in a nice nick on his chin, before he'd grabbed her arm and whaled the tar out of her.

Standing up to Leon, even for just a moment, had felt pretty good. She'd like to feel that way again.

She gazed at the concrete porch he'd shoved her down, the front door he had carried her through when they were first married.

Her toes began to burn. Her things were strewn all over the yard. She found a pair of socks in the snow and pulled them on. Crawling on her knees, she packed her clothes back into the suitcase Leon had tossed out with her. It refused to close. The latch was broken. Giving up, she struggled to her feet.

It started to snow, the soft flakes falling against her cheeks, wetting her wiry, dark hair.

Go back. He'll forgive you. He always does.

Leon would go off to work soon. She could go inside, get warm, start making preparations for a beef stew dinner, his favorite. Women like her always went back. Or so she'd heard on *Oprah*. He'd come home from work, they'd sit down at the table. Everything would be all right.

Women like her always went back. She should do something about that. Slowly, she shook her head. *Go back?* Not this time.

Disoriented, numb with pain, she reached for the broken suitcase and hobbled down the driveway. Her mother was gone, her father had left when she was little. She had no siblings, no close friends, no idea what she would do or where she would go. But just now, a seed of determination was breaking through the hard years of pain. Would it take root and grow? Why not? At twenty-three, her life was far from over.

Yes, that seed would grow. One way or another.

One way or another, she'd survive. One way or another, she'd learn not to be afraid. One way or another, she'd make herself so strong, no man would ever hurt her again.

And one way or another, she would get her daughter back.

CHAPTER ONE

Thirteen Years Later

"Go. Go. Go. Go."

Nothing like a chorus of burly fellow construction workers cheering you on to boost your ego. Miranda looked around at the half-demolished building, with its backdrop of modern skyscrapers and older structures against the gray, Pittsburgh sky, then she picked the bright green jalapeno off the paper plate that sat alongside the ham sandwiches and soda cans on the wooden slab that served as the crew's lunch table.

She waggled it under Dombroski's nose. "Number five, Dumbo."

"That's right, bitch," he sneered. "Number five. I say you can't do it."

Dumbo. That was her affectionate name for this baldheaded bruiser with the big ears who'd made her life on the wrecking crew hell for the three months she'd been in Steel Town.

Miranda pulled at her leather jacket, took a whiff of the cool March air, and curled a lip at Dombroski. "Oh, do you?"

"That's right."

She leaned over the table. "I should have taken you down at Luigi's last night."

Little Jake stepped between them. "Hey now, we made a deal." It had been the skinny twenty-year-old who'd talked her out of belting that bastard in the bar when he'd called Jake a whore-loving fag—which didn't even make sense. At the moment, Miranda couldn't think what had made her agree to this pepper-eating contest instead. Some things were worth fighting over. Oh, yeah. She didn't want to risk getting carted off to jail and losing this job.

"Number five," Miranda repeated.

"That's the record," said Nye, the quiet black guy with ham-sized biceps she admired.

Cassidy, the resident big guy on the crew at over three hundred and fifty pounds, shook his jowls. "Naw, the record's seven. Some dude in Chambersburg set it."

Miranda nodded toward her opponent. "Doesn't matter. Dumbo here's already out."

"Don't call me that," he snarled. "You mean you're out, don't you, Steele?"

"Not on your life." Years ago, she'd discovered she had high tolerance for capsaicin. Dumbo didn't know who he was talking to.

Dramatically, she lifted the pepper to her lips, opened her mouth, and crunched down on it hard. The raw skin snapped between her teeth, burned like the Lake of Fire. She took a couple more bites, then put the whole thing in her mouth. She fought with the fiery seeds, forced back the tears behind her eyes, and finally got it down.

She spat out the stem and held her hands up to the rest of the crew. "Nothing to it." Good thing she got the words out before her tongue started to swell.

They gave her a rousing round of applause for her efforts.

She took a bow then pushed the plate toward Dombroski. "Your turn."

His eyes flashed like a police siren as he picked up his fifth jalapeno. "Take this, cunt."

It took all the control Miranda had not to deck him. Might be worth a night in jail.

She leaned over the makeshift table. "Go ahead, Dumbo. Show me what you've got."

"I said, don't call me that." It looked like smoke was already coming out of his elephant ears. But he bit down hard on his pepper.

For a minute, Miranda thought he might get it down. Then he grabbed his throat and started to sputter like a broken lawn sprinkler.

"Hell. Damn," he coughed, getting to his feet. His face turned the color of a stop sign. He grabbed a can of soda and started guzzling.

Little Jake patted him on the back in alarm.

Nye chuckled. "Looks like you lost, Dombroski."

Dumbo tried to answer, but all he could manage was a low, gurgling sound.

Miranda couldn't keep a straight face. She burst out laughing. Cassidy giggled, and soon the whole crew was guffawing. All but Dombroski, who was still choking and chugging down soda.

"What the hell's going on here?"

Cassidy's large face went deadpan. "Uh oh. The Super."

Charging toward them, the seven-foot man in the suit and blue hardhat looked like a steam cruiser. He went by the name Sherlock. As in, no shit.

"We was just having a little game during lunch, boss," Cassidy said, as the man approached.

"Lunch time's over," Sherlock barked, glaring at Dombroski. "What's wrong with him?"

"He'll be all right," Nye said.

Miranda picked up her hard hat and nonchalantly sidled back to the bucket she'd been filling with the concrete debris.

Sherlock caught up to her and tapped her on the shoulder. "Hold it, Steele."

She turned to face him. "Jeez, boss, we were just having some fun." Was she going to get fired again?

He shook his head. "Never mind that. There's a call for you."

She stared at him, taken off guard. "A call?" Nobody called her.

"You can take it in the office." He gestured toward the small trailer that sat on the corner of the lot. "Or ignore it and get back to work."

Might as well see who it was. "I'll take it. Thanks." She trotted over to the makeshift building.

Inside, the tight space was empty of people and held only a couple of filing cabinets and a metal desk crowded with papers.

Gingerly, Miranda picked up the line. "Hello?"

"Is this Miranda Steele?"

"None other."

There was a pause, then what sounded like a determined snort. "Ms. Steele, my name is Barbara Thomas. I'm with The Seekers. The adoption reunion organization? You registered with us online?"

Miranda's knees wobbled. The Seekers? Yeah, she'd registered with them. Along with every other adoption reunion agency she could find. She'd done that thirteen years ago on advice from a counselor at the battered women's shelter she'd escaped to after Leon threw her out. And she updated her records every time she'd moved so they could contact her. But no one ever had. After all this time, Miranda had given up hope of ever finding Amy.

She smirked in disbelief. "You mean you people actually look at that information?"

After she left Leon, she'd tried to find Amy. With everything she had. She talked to counselors and social workers and clergy. Most of them thought she was lying about what he'd done. They believed she'd given her daughter up for adoption and changed her mind. She'd even petitioned the courts to open Amy's records. The judge thought the same thing as the others and denied it.

The woman on the phone hesitated a moment as if she didn't know what to say. "Ms. Steele, my manager would like me to speak with you."

She looked at the receiver. "You're speaking with me now."

"I mean in person. Are you available this Saturday?"

Miranda's heart started to race. She thought she might hyperventilate. Did this stranger have information about Amy? Did The Seekers know where her daughter was? "What's wrong with right now?" Sherlock would give her an hour or so. She hoped.

There was a pause. "I'm a volunteer. I won't be in the office until the weekend."

It was only Tuesday. Miranda wasn't going to wait all week to hear what this woman had to say about Amy. "Can't we meet somewhere? A coffee shop maybe?"

Another pause. Miranda wasn't sure if it was pity or annoyance in the woman's breathing. "You can come to my apartment. I don't have to be at my regular job for another hour."

She exhaled in relief. "Thank you—what was your name?"

"Just call me Barbara." She gave Miranda her address.

"I'll be there in fifteen."

CHAPTER TWO

Nerves somersaulting down her spine, Miranda knocked on the door of Barbara's apartment. She heard scuffling then the door opened.

"Ms. Steele?"

"That's right."

"Please come in, Ms. Steele." The occupant opened the door wide. "May I take your coat?"

"Sure." Miranda stepped inside the cheery living room, half-expecting to see a dark-haired, thirteen-year-old girl standing in the middle of it. But that was her mind playing tricks on her.

She pulled off her scarf and leather jacket, and handed them to the small, trim woman. Probably in her fifties, Barbara had graying brown hair cut in a short, demure style, and brown, inquisitive eyes. She was dressed in a peach-colored wool business suit that had a sterile look to it.

Her place was clean and well kept, with plants, needlepoint pillows, and pretty curtains on a window where the afternoon sunshine spilled in. It had a sort of grandmotherly feel. As did its occupant, who was trotting across the floor, straightening things that didn't need straightening, as if Miranda were the Queen of Sheba.

"Thanks for seeing me. Don't go to any trouble." She was feeling a little guilty for forcing herself on the woman.

"Oh, it's no trouble, Ms. Steele. Won't you have a seat?" Barbara indicated a flowery couch with a small coffee table in front of it.

"Thanks." Miranda sat down. After carefully placing her coat on the back of a dinette chair, the woman settled next to her.

No sign of other life. Barbara must live alone. Miranda hoped her reason for solitude wasn't like her own. She wouldn't wish that on her worst enemy, let alone someone who might know something about Amy.

The woman reached for a stack of files on the coffee table and began to sift through them. "I apologize for being a little disorganized. As I said on the phone, my manager wanted me to talk to you, Ms.—may I call you Miranda? Oh, would you like some tea?"

"Yes, you can call me Miranda. And no, I don't want any tea." This lady could use a self-confidence course. Or maybe a shift with the wrecking crew.

Barbara nodded and kept sorting folders, her expression solemn.

Miranda watched her a moment. She wasn't going to wait until the whole stack was alphabetized. "What is it you have to tell me, Barbara?"

She stopped shuffling and gave Miranda a pained look, her brown eyes darting back and forth, as if she were looking for some lost secret. "I'm sorry, Miranda. I'm new at the agency and your file has just come to me. I have to perform some, uh, formalities."

Miranda shifted her weight. "O-kay."

Barbara selected one of the folders, took a paper from it and picked up a pen from the coffee table. "Let's see. You've registered with us a number of times." Her voice took on the singsong quality of an interviewer.

"Yes, every time I moved." Maybe that wasn't the best thing to say.

Barbara read from her sheet. "You're originally from Oak Park, Illinois."

"That's right."

She turned a page. "But you've worked in several states. And several jobs."

Yeah. So what? Since she'd left Leon, she'd welded girders on a skyscraper in New York, harvested crab on a fishing boat in Maine, done odd jobs on an oil rig in Texas.

She rubbed her hands against her jeans and laughed it off with a shrug. "Some people think I'm obsessive about physical jobs. Not only does it give you muscles, it thickens your skin." A therapist once told her she was sublimating repressed feelings about her affectionate ex-husband and should talk about them. What did shrinks know?

Barbara seemed interested. "Oh, is that important to you?"

Was she being screened? Was Barbara trying to determine if she was fit to meet her daughter? "You know how it is, Barbara. A woman can never make herself too tough or too strong." Or too street smart. She laughed awkwardly and waved a hand at the file in her hostess's lap. "Most construction work is seasonal. We all job hop."

But that didn't explain the restless urge that had made her pick up and go, aimlessly roaming the country taking jobs here and there, making casual acquaintances, leaving them behind. Always moving. She didn't want to admit Leon's specter still haunted her after all these years. She'd told herself Amy could be anywhere, so why not go to a new place? None of that made her…unfit.

Barbara smiled sweetly. "And now you're here in Pittsburgh, working for Norris Wrecking Company."

"Right." Miranda resisted the urge to tap her foot. "I've been with them about three months."

Barbara's eyes grew soft. "You say your daughter was placed thirteen years ago?"

Placed? Miranda nodded. She'd been purposely vague about the adoption. Most people didn't believe what Leon had done. They thought she had simply changed her mind after signing the papers.

Barbara pursed her lips, shaking her head. "Such a sad story. So your daughter would be a minor, wouldn't she?"

Annoyed by the comment, Miranda stiffened. "The legal age being eighteen, or twenty-one depending on the state, that would make her a minor, yes."

"Oh, dear. I'm not doing this very well. I apologize." Barbara set the folder down on top of the stack. "Let me get you some tea."

"I don't want any—" but the woman was already heading for the kitchen.

Her heart sinking, Miranda sat back and listened to her hostess bang around a few minutes and fought with the stupid tears that were suddenly stinging her eyes.

Leaning forward for a tissue on the coffee table, she spied the corner of an envelope sticking out of the folder Barbara had been reading from. She glanced toward the kitchen. The woman was still rattling away. Wouldn't hurt to take a look. After all, it was her file.

She slipped a finger under a corner and nudged it out. It was a letter addressed to The Seekers headquarters here in Pittsburgh. The handwriting didn't look like an adult's. There was no return address. The postmark was from Buckhead, Georgia, wherever the hell that was.

Cautiously, she peeked inside and found a piece of notebook paper. Her fingers trembling, she slid it out, unfolded it. She stared down at the childish handwriting. Her whole body went rigid.

Dear Seekers,

I'm thirteen years old. I was born in November in Oak Park, Illinois. Now I live in a big mansion in Buckhead, Georgia. My mom's an executive and my dad's always away. They are never home.

I think I'm adopted. Can you help me find my real parents?

Someone Else's Daughter

Miranda gasped out loud.

"Oh dear." Barbara was in the middle of the living room, looking as if she were about to drop her tea tray. Quickly, she dashed to the coffee table and set the china down, shaking her head. "You weren't supposed to see that."

Miranda glared up at her. "Why not?"

With a sigh, Barbara laid a hand against her graying brown hair. "Oh, Miranda. My manager wanted me to tell you in person there's nothing we can do for you. We don't handle situations like yours."

Miranda blinked at her. "Really?" She held out the letter. "And what about her? Can you help her?"

Barbara shook her head sadly. "There's nothing The Seekers can do to help that girl, either. She's underage. We work with adult children. Adoptees who are of age and are looking for their birth parents."

For a moment, Miranda couldn't even speak. She knew adoption reunification agencies worked only with adult adoptees. What had she expected? Certainly not this. She waved the little girl's letter. "What were you going to do with this?"

"Why, keep it in the file in case the girl ever contacted us again." Barbara shuffled to the couch and sat down wearily. "We received it several months ago. When you registered with us, we matched it to your records. But there's nothing we can do until she's an adult. Even then, there's not much information there."

Miranda held out the page. "The girl who wrote this is thirteen. My Amy's age. And she was born in November. In Oak Park. Like Amy."

Barbara straightened her skirt. "Yes, but—" She lifted her hands. "It was only in your file because we didn't know what else to do with it."

Miranda released the breath she was holding and ran her hand through her wiry, dark hair that some people called curly. "What are you saying?"

Barbara exhaled slowly. "An adoptee wouldn't necessarily know her true birthplace."

"She might. Some parents are very forthcoming about such details."

"True, but only a few of your facts match this letter. It could be a coincidence. We didn't want to give you false hope. That's why my manager insisted I not show you that letter. Oh, dear. She's going to be very upset."

False hope. Was there any other kind? But false hope was better than no hope at all. Miranda reached out and patted the woman's hand. "Don't worry, Barbara. I won't tell your manager."

"You don't understand. It's against policy."

Ignoring her, Miranda read the letter again.

My mom's an executive and my dad's always away. They are never home.

Had Amy written those words? Was she being neglected? Miranda had always told herself her daughter was in a loving, caring home. She'd go insane if she let herself think otherwise.

"I'm so sorry, Miranda," the woman moaned softly. "We don't have any legal authority here. We can't do anything to help you find your daughter."

Slowly, Miranda put the letter back in the envelope. "Maybe you can't, Barbara. But I can." She pointed to the postmark. "Buckhead, Georgia. Where's that?"

"An area near Atlanta."

"Atlanta." Could her daughter really be living in a mansion in some place called Buckhead? Must be some hick town near the city. How many mansions could there be in a place called Buckhead? She even had the zip code.

She got to her feet.

Barbara's eyes bulged. "What are you going to do? You can't be thinking–"

"Don't worry about me, Barbara. I wouldn't want your manager to get upset. By the way, she sounds like a bitch." If she had time, she'd go down to the office and tell her so.

"But, Miranda, you've just come to Pittsburgh. Don't you want to settle down here?"

She scoffed. "Settle down?" What was that?

"Perhaps you could meet a nice young man. You could fall in love and have—" she stopped herself.

"Children of my own?" It wasn't the first time Miranda had heard that. "Amy *is* my child, Barbara." And as far as falling in love, it would be a cold day in Hades before she let herself be so vulnerable again.

The woman began to stammer. "But there's no return address on that letter. Nothing more than what's on that paper. Almost nothing. We have no idea who this girl is, who her adopted parents are."

"Like I said, Barbara. Don't worry about it."

"You don't understand."

"I think I do." She crossed to the dinette where her coat was waiting.

Barbara shot up and followed her. "Miranda, think. That letter could be a crank. Some lonely child angry with her parents, who decided to get their attention by pretending to be adopted."

Miranda turned to the woman, that familiar numbness of disappointment stealing around her heart.

"Children do that, especially with their access to the Internet these days." Barbara's voice was gentle, motherly now, but her words stung like razors.

She had a point. Any kid could google adoption reunion agencies, find The Seekers' web site and write to them. She thought a moment. "Do you get a lot of letters like this one?"

"No. But that doesn't mean you should get your hopes up. I fear you'll end up very disappointed."

Miranda smirked. Disappointed? Her hopes had been dashed plenty of times over the past thirteen years. She was used to it. Besides there was a chance the letter could be real. This could be Amy. She had to try.

She reached for her jacket and scarf. "Thank you, Barbara." She held up the letter. "Can I keep it?"

The woman waved a hand as if giving up. "Oh, I suppose so. I have a copy."

Tenderly Miranda put the letter into her pocket and moved to the door. She had a couple hundred in her bank account. That ought to get her to Buckhead and put her up until she could get another job. She'd pack today, say sayonara to Sherlock and the wrecking crew and be off.

"Thank you, Barbara." She extended a hand toward the woman.

As if she were taking the hand of a priest to ask for atonement, Barbara shook it. "I don't know what for. I couldn't do anything for you."

"You've done more than anyone else has up to now." Miranda resisted the urge to hug her.

The woman half-smiled. "Call me if you want to talk."

"Sure." Miranda turned and went out the door.

She glanced at her watch. Almost two. She'd swing by the demo site, then head for her place. If the landlord didn't give her grief about her deposit, she could be on the road before rush hour. Hugging the letter in her pocket close, she sprinted down the hall to the stairs.

Was the tide finally turning? After years of frustration and disappointment and dead ends, could this piece of notebook paper lead her to her baby? The little girl Leon had stolen from her? The child he said she had no right to keep?

The stubborn hope that had risen from the ashes of her heart so many times before began to rise again. Suddenly, she felt more alive than she had in months.

CHAPTER THREE

The music was classical, tasteful, sedate. The wine was white Bordeaux. Dry, rare. The caviar was Black Russian. Crisp, tasting of the ocean. And the women…ah, the women. Glamorously dressed in their latest designer gowns, the ladies were as alluring as they were lovely.

Wade Parker leaned against a tall Ionic column near the grand staircase of the Georgia Governor's mansion and sipped from his champagne flute. Beneath the Italian chandelier, an elegantly coiffed redhead smiled at him. Near the portrait of George Washington, a blond winked. Under the archway to the hall, a brunette cast him a flirtatious glance.

Parker chuckled to himself. Were they all after the man that audacious reporter for *The Atlanta Journal-Constitution* had dubbed the town's most eligible forty-four-year-old bachelor?

His gaggle of admirers amused and wearied him at the same time. As beautiful and enticing as they were, not one of them could replace Sylvia, the love of his life. It had been three years now since cancer had stolen her from him. His heart ached at the thought as if it were yesterday.

But then, he wasn't here tonight to flirt. Or for the mid-April fundraiser.

His gaze drifted across the room to a thin and pale man standing alone near the great fireplace, nervously fingering a drink. His name was Thomas Jameson. The Governor's steering committee would have thrown him out, if Parker had not persuaded them to honor the invitation he'd wheedled out of a member.

Not a hair out of place, Jameson was impeccably dressed in a fine Gucci suit, but it was all a veneer. The scoundrel was lower and more revolting than the bird droppings the servants had to scoop out of the fountain in the front yard.

Tonight, Parker would prove that by catching him in the act.

One of Parker's devotees glided across the floor toward him, and he braced himself as her perfume waylaid his nose.

"You seem bored, Wade," the attractive redhead said, low laughter in her voice.

"Do I?" *Focused* might be a better word.

She inhaled. "These affairs can be as dry as the champagne."

He nodded, sipped from his glass. "An understatement, Patricia."

She gestured at the crowd of Atlanta's most well connected personages. "Everyone loves coming to this historical Greek-Revival house with its sprawling lawns, drawing rooms, and fine Federal Period furniture. But I'd rather be outdoors."

Parker smiled. "I'm sure you would." Patricia raised horses and was rather good at it. They'd ridden together as teens.

She gave a little yawn. "Besides, if you've seen one Buckhead luxury home, you've seen them all. In fact, it's a tad smaller than the one you grew up in, isn't it?"

Parker's gold-digger alarm would have gone off, if he didn't know Patricia was independently wealthy. "My father would be delighted to hear that observation."

"Ah yes." She wrinkled her face and feigned a newscaster's voice. "'Wade Russell Parker, junior, Atlanta's most prosperous real estate developer and son of Wade Russell Parker, senior, one of our city's most renowned judges.'"

He shook his head. "I wish I'd never given that interview."

"But now everyone knows you're 'Atlanta's ace detective.'"

He felt a muscle in his jaw tense. He didn't want to admit he'd been pleased when he'd read that. "Everyone was well aware of my profession before the article was printed." Many of his peers tonight had become clients over the years.

Her laugh was musical. "You're too sensitive about it, Wade. How is your father?" Her lovely blue eyes widened. "Why isn't he here?"

He was glad to change the subject, even if the topic was his father. "He had a heart attack recently. He's had to move into a nursing home." Though the old gentleman had seemed fine the last time he spoke with him. The man was a notorious flirt and Parker suspected an ulterior motive.

"I'm sorry to hear that. I know he's sorry to miss this fundraiser."

"I imagine he is." And sorry to miss charming the ladies away from his son, as if it were a competition. His father thrived on social affairs. While for Parker, they were mere obligations. But he'd learned to work such occasions to his own purposes. As "Atlanta's ace detective."

Some called him obsessive. He preferred the term thorough. He didn't see himself as some sort of savior. He'd merely discovered at a young age that it was in his nature to right wrongs, to protect the innocent and apprehend the guilty. It was his calling. A calling that drove him, spawned as it was by a deep, shadowy need, a dark episode from his past that had plunged him into a career both his father and grandfather had disapproved of.

Patricia smiled coyly, trailing a finger around the rim of her glass. "It's such a beautiful night. The dogwood and cherry trees are in full bloom. Maybe we could go for a walk?"

Moving in for the kill? "Perhaps later."

"Or," her voice took on a sensuous note, "we could leave early and go to my place for a nightcap."

Parker grinned, noted the plunging neckline of her sequined, ruby-red gown, her round breasts rising and falling beneath the fabric. Tempting. But he had business to attend to. He turned his eye to Jameson again. The man hadn't budged.

Parker watched Jameson's deep-set eyes carefully scan the room. His straight features, his curled lip gave him a surly look that made him even more disagreeable.

About a month ago a young woman named Elizabeth Kinkade had contacted Parker's firm after someone looted her upscale apartment, stealing thousands of dollars in jewelry. She'd broken off an affair with Jameson recently and swore he'd robbed her for revenge. After tailing the suspect for several days, Parker discovered revenge wasn't Jameson's motive. It was simple greed.

Jameson had a string of ex-girlfriends all over town. His M.O. was to romance the ladies until they let down their guard, then abscond with their valuables. He had been at his game for about six months now, responsible for a run of thefts the police hadn't been able to solve. Tonight, Parker suspected, he would attempt something even more shameless.

Parker had gathered an abundance of evidence against the man but not quite enough for an arrest. Tonight, he hoped to seal the case. His jaw tightened as Jameson set his glass on the mantelpiece and made his way along the wall to the grand staircase, which was now deserted.

Parker watched him ascend.

"So what do you say, Wade? Shall we make our apologies to our hostess?"

Parker turned, forced a grin. "Perhaps some other time, Patricia. If you'll excuse me." He wasn't pleased with the shock on her face at his ill-mannered behavior, but he had no choice. He headed for the stairs.

It was quiet on the mansion's third floor and the lighting was dim. Parker caught the tail of Jameson's suit just as he slipped through the entrance to the master bedroom. The insolent bastard. Silently, he moved to the door, put his ear to it. Nothing. He waited a moment, then slowly inched the door open.

Movement. Barely perceptible. Another inch and Jameson's dark figure came into view. He stood at the dressing table, his back to the door, a fistful of sparkling jewels in each avaricious hand. Evidently, during his short career, the thief had learned that wealthy women tend to keep their valuables in plain sight, feeling secure in their own private quarters.

Parker slipped inside the room, reached for his lapel pin and snapped several shots with the microscopic camera hidden in it. Jameson was still unaware of him.

He cleared his throat. "Stealing from the governor's wife? How politically incorrect."

Jameson spun around, shock peppering his face. "Who are you?"

Parker smiled casually. "A very, very bad dream."

Fumbling with the gems, Jameson tried to put them back where he'd found them. "I'm not doing anything wrong. I— I lost my contact lens."

Parker chuckled. "On a lady's dressing table covered with jewels? How convenient."

"It's true. I swear."

"And how do you explain the things you took from Elizabeth Kinkade? Sarah Smith? Tamara Johnson?"

Jameson looked as though his eyes were about to pop from his head.

"I'm afraid your career as a jewel thief has come to an abrupt end."

Jameson glanced toward the window.

"I wouldn't try it." Parker slipped a hand into his pocket.

The thief froze. His eyes bulged even more as Parker slowly drew out a small metallic object.

Parker couldn't hold back a chuckle as he flipped his cell phone open and pressed speed dial. "Hosea, you're still downstairs, aren't you? Having a good time? Well, I have something on the third floor that will make your night. Yes. The master bedroom." He closed his cell and turned to his subject. "That was Lieutenant Hosea Erskine of the Atlanta Police Department."

Jameson took a step toward the window.

"Uh uh," Parker scolded him. "You don't want to risk finding out what I have in my other pocket."

Looking as though he might soil his slacks, Jameson stood without making another move until Hosea and several other members of the APD who were downstairs, burst into the room.

While his men placed Jameson in handcuffs, Hosea narrowed his eyes at Parker. "Have you been meddling in police business again, Mr. Detective Man?"

Parker chuckled. Hosea hated it when he one-upped him. "Merely serving my client." He reached into his jacket pocket.

"Look out," Jameson cried, struggling against the cuffs. "He's got a gun."

"Our perpetrator seems a bit paranoid." Parker drew out a slip of paper and handed it to Hosea. "I believe you'll find the stolen goods in this safe deposit box at the Freedom Bank on Peachtree Street."

With a huff, Erskine snatched the paper from his hand.

Satisfied, Parker left the room and made his way down the hall, wondering if Patricia was still below. A case closed called for a celebration.

Before he reached the first stair, his cell rang. He flipped it open again. "Parker."

"Wade, thank God we've gotten hold of you."

The urgency in his friend's voice made Parker stop dead in his tracks. "Jackson. I thought you'd be here tonight."

"Here?"

"At the Governor's mansion. The fundraiser—"

"I completely forgot about it. The most dreadful thing's happened…" His voice broke.

Parker's spine went rigid. He'd known Jackson Taggart since high school. As Chief of Staff at Saint Benedictine Hospital, he was no stranger to emergencies. He never panicked. "What's wrong?"

"It's Madison. Our little girl."

God, no. Parker knew that desperate tone. "What about Madison?"

"She's disappeared." He broke off, stifling a sob that tore at Parker's heart.

Knowing he had to be calm, Parker forced himself into professional mode. "What makes you think she's disappeared, Jackson?"

There was a pause, he could feel the insult through the phone, and then the anguished words gushed out. "Last night Madison spent the night at Tiffany Todd's house. She was supposed to be back this morning. She never came home. When we checked with Tiffany, she said Madison had left hours ago and walked home. She never got here."

The news hit him like a jackhammer. Madison was just thirteen. First step, keep the parents from panicking. Or rather, keep the panic from festering. "Calm down, Jackson," he said as gently as he could. "Is there anywhere else she could be?"

"We called all her friends. No one's seen her. She's simply gone. Cloris is beside herself."

The mother always suffered the most. "What time did she leave Tiffany's house?"

"Eleven this morning."

"Have you argued with her recently?" It was a hard question but important.

"No. We've been closer than ever."

Parker's mind raced through the possibilities. Runaway. Kidnapping. Possibly for money. If that were the case, the Taggarts might be contacted soon. "Have you called the police? The Special Crimes Unit—"

"Yes, but they haven't done anything. I want you, Wade. Both Cloris and I do. We know you can find her."

He was flattered, humbled by his friends' trust. He'd do his best. "Very well, Jackson," he said. "I'll be right there."

He clicked off, glanced at his watch as he raced down the stairs, his heart sinking. It would be a long night. Twelve hours since Madison Taggart was last seen and no word from any kidnappers. Not good. He would have his work cut out for him, but he would do all in his power to find her.

With all his heart, he wished he could bring the girl home to Jackson and Cloris tonight. But experience told him it could be days or weeks before that happened. If she were still alive. The world could be a dangerous place for the young, even in the shelter of well-to-do Buckhead.

CHAPTER FOUR

Miranda sat at a small granite table in one of the hip nightclubs along Buckhead's strip, called The Gecko Club, sipping a beer. She shook Tabasco onto the lame excuse for a Thai roll she had ordered and took a bite.

Buckhead, Georgia, she'd discovered, wasn't a hick town. It wasn't even your average suburb. No, Buckhead, Georgia, had turned out to be one of the swankiest damn spots in the nation. The freakin' Beverly Hills of the South. There weren't just a couple of mansions in Buckhead, Georgia. The whole place was littered with them. Ritzy subdivisions tucked away among the lush trees and rolling hills, with highbrow names like Mount Paran and Brookhaven and Peachtree Heights West and Tuxedo Park. All chock-full of elegant homes.

So which one did "Someone Else's Daughter" live in?

After three weeks, Miranda hadn't had a clue. Driving through those upscale neighborhoods hadn't turned up anything. Trying to get a job at one of the hoity-toity middle schools, so she could learn about the kids in the area, had been a bust. Her current approach of starting up conversations with thirteen-year-old girls in the mall hadn't worked either. She'd learned a lot about the funkiest styles in clothes, the coolest hair-dos and the hottest rap singers, but nothing about a girl who was adopted and who'd written an anonymous letter to The Seekers.

Her first bit of luck—if you could call it that—had happened today. It was the end of spring break and she'd been wandering around Phipps Plaza before she had to be at her new second shift job on a local road crew, when she'd noticed a group of teenage boys lounging near a fountain. She'd eavesdropped on their conversation and found out one of the boys had a girlfriend.

The girlfriend had a sister. The sister was in middle school and had a best friend. The best friend…was adopted. Her name was Ashley Ingram. She lived in a subdivision called Mockingbird Hills. Bingo.

And it got better.

The girlfriend was on the outs with her parents. They'd caught her and the boyfriend going at it hot and heavy on the living room couch, had grounded her, and forbidden the boy to come over again. Tonight, girlfriend was sneaking out to meet boyfriend after dropping sister and Ashley at the Ingrams.

Miranda set down her beer and stared at the map she'd printed off her laptop that afternoon. Thank God for the Internet.

Mockingbird Hills. 111 Sweet Hollow Lane. A red star marked the spot where a family named Ingram lived.

Opportunity knocking? Or a long shot?

So much could go wrong. The girlfriend might change her mind. The parents might discover her plan and put a stop to it. But if the kids did show up, if Miranda could just get a look at the adopted girl, for just a moment—Hell, if she were really lucky that girl might turn out to be—Would she even recognize her Amy after all these years?

"Need a refill?" a black-clad waiter pointed at her beer, shaking her out of her thoughts.

Miranda took a last swig and handed him the bottle. "No, thanks." He took it, along with her empty plate and left. She glanced at her watch. The two young lovers were supposed to meet at the Ingrams' at midnight. She had almost forty minutes to get there through the Buckhead party traffic. Couldn't be late.

As she stood and dug in her pocket for some cash, a female voice from the table behind her floated over the jazzy music and crowd noise. "Isn't it terrible about that missing girl?"

Miranda stiffened. *Missing girl?*

"Why, it's just the most dreadful thing I've ever heard," another voice agreed. "She's barely a teen."

Stunned, Miranda turned and spotted a skinny, middle-aged woman with large, chartreuse earrings, who was shaking her head.

"You've been following the story on the news, haven't you?" she said to her dinner partner. "She's been gone almost a week."

The short redhead next to her frowned solemnly. "Her parents must be beside themselves."

A young teenage girl from Buckhead had been missing a whole week? Damn. Why hadn't she heard about it before? That's what happens when you live in your car for two weeks, then rent a tiny studio apartment with no TV. She hadn't noticed any flyers when she'd been through the neighborhoods, but that was when she first got here.

The woman with the earrings opened her purse to leave a tip, then patted her friend's hand. "They'll find her. Wade Parker's on the case. He's the best."

The friend smiled, reassured. "Not to mention the sexiest." They rose from their table.

Wade Parker? Who the hell was Wade Parker? Miranda shoved her map into her pocket, got to her feet, and followed the women toward the door.

"Excuse me," she called out after them, shoving her way through the waiters and the patrons waiting to be seated. "What were you saying about that missing girl?"

But the women were gone.

Disgusted, Miranda turned back and scanned the room. A piano stood in a dark, empty corner. By contrast, a noisy, interracial mix of designer-clad yuppies, businesspeople, and moneyed local college kids were jam packed along a gleaming, salmon-colored bar that swept the opposite wall.

She had a few minutes to spare. Maybe the bartender could tell her something. She hurried over and tried to get his attention, but he moved to the other end, busier than a one-armed paperhanger with psoriasis, keeping everyone's glass filled.

Shit. Well, that missing girl didn't have anything to do with Amy. Right?

"Excuse me," said a soft Southern voice. It belonged to a classy-looking young woman daintily perched on the next stool, waving a graceful hand. "Sir?"

The barkeep didn't even notice.

"What a jerk, huh?"

The delicate woman turned and stared at Miranda with big blue eyes. She looked to be in her mid-twenties. A sheltered mid-twenties, in contrast to Miranda's unsheltered mid-thirties. Her platinum hair gave her a sort of Jessica Simpson look and she was dressed to the nines in a slinky, low-cut black dress. "I'm sorry?"

Miranda gestured. "That barkeep. He's ignoring us."

"Oh. Yes, he is." She seemed disappointed by the fact.

Someone vacated the seat behind her and Miranda slipped onto the stool. "Say, have you heard anything about a missing girl?"

The blond woman thought a moment. "You mean the one they've been talking about on the news?"

"That's the one. She's from around here, right?" Miranda tried not to sound like a newcomer with no TV.

"Yes. She's from Buckhead. Her father's on the staff of one of the hospitals."

So she did come from a wealthy family. The words from the letter echoed in her head, *my dad's always away*. "How old did they say she was?"

"I'm not sure. Pretty young, I think."

Hmm. That could be anywhere from twelve to sixteen. And nobody said she was adopted. No, that girl didn't have anything to do with Amy, though Miranda felt bad for her poor parents. They must be going through hell.

Just then a muscular arm slithered around Blondie's shoulder. "Pardon me," said the arm's owner, "but the little lady and I were having a conversation."

Blondie turned a little pale.

He gave her a squeeze, kind of like a python. "C'mon, now, Sweet Pea. L'me buy you a drink." His speech was slurred, his accent thick, almost artificial. But then, every Southerner in Atlanta had an accent that sounded fake to Miranda.

Blondie turned her head away.

"Tell me what you like, honey. The sky's the limit." The Southern Python was young. Big enough to be a football player. He wore designer jeans and a T-shirt with a local sports logo. Probably some spoiled college kid with an athletic scholarship and a rich daddy to bail him out of any trouble he managed to get into.

Blondie shifted nervously on the seat, like a frightened rabbit trapped by a wolf. "No, thank you. I don't want a drink."

No thank you? What was with the manners? Tell him to go screw himself.

Mr. Football Player couldn't take the hint. "Aw, why not, Li'l Cutie? Don't you know I been waitin' for you all my life?" Instead of removing his unwanted hand, he slid it up Blondie's arm. Then he nuzzled her hair with his nose. "How about you and me goin' back to my place?"

Alarm danced in Blondie's eyes. "No, thank you," she repeated.

Thank you, again? Tell him to drop dead. Miranda nodded toward the guy. "Is he with you?"

Blondie shook her head.

Miranda looked the jerk in the eye. "You got a problem with your hearing, bud?"

He studied her with an inebriated scowl for a moment, then reached over and put his hand on her knee. "Honey, don't be jealous. We can make it a threesome."

Miranda's stomach knotted. She spoke in a quiet, threatening tone. "Get your damn hand off me before I break it."

He chuckled. "I like my women feisty."

The familiar earthquake rumbled inside her. This guy didn't know who he was talking to. "You've got three seconds to move your hand."

"Baby, you're cute when you talk tough."

"Okay, I warned you." She grabbed hold of his middle finger, bent it back hard, yanking his hand off her leg.

"Yeeeoww," The creep hopped back, cradling his throbbing finger like it was a football he was carrying over the goal line.

Miranda shot her thumb toward the door. "Now get lost."

His pain turned to insult. "Who the hell do you think you are?"

"The pervert police," Miranda sneered.

Blondie's light blue eyes glowed with shock, as if no one had ever stuck up for her before in her life.

From out of nowhere, two more young men sauntered up to the bar, like sharks smelling blood. Ah yes. The buddies. They were big, too. Also sports-scholarship types, with the requisite hundred-dollar jeans and T's. The bigger one had a baseball cap on sideways. "You gonna take that, Bobby Lee?"

"I reckon not."

The stout buddy shook his head at Miranda. "This one's brazen. She needs to be taught a lesson."

She rolled her eyes. Good Lord, not now. She had to be at the Ingrams' in a few minutes. "Look, asshole, we're not interested, so why don't you and your friends go play in the street?"

"Oooh," The trio crooned in unison.

"Oh, my word." Blondie looked like she might faint.

Slowly, Bobby Lee folded his arms over his broad chest. "This little heifer doesn't know her place, does she?"

The hairs stood up on the back of Miranda's neck. Heifer? Her place? Now he was pushing her buttons. She spun around on the barstool to face them and glared. "You like comparing women to animals? Kind of ironic, coming from a jackass like you."

Bobby Lee's face turned sullen. Involuntarily, his hands balled into fists. Like him, they were big. Large enough to hold a couple of footballs. She sized up the rest of him. Six foot two. About two-eighty. Pretty drunk.

She clenched her teeth and eyed his spiky, sandy-colored hair, his thick, muscled neck. He had a baby face but was as muscle-bound as Arnold Schwarzenegger in his prime. There was a small-but-fancy-looking knife pouch on his expensive alligator belt. Probably hadn't used it for anything more than cutting his toenails.

She could take him.

His accent flattened. "I'd take that back, if I were you, cunt."

Miranda slid off the stool and leered at Bobby Lee. "Make me, prick."

Blondie squealed and scampered out of the way just as the creep swung at Miranda's head, growling like an intoxicated gorilla.

Miranda ducked and Bobby Lee's big, solid fist dragged across the bar, knocking over drinks. Haymaker. He was too smashed for a good aim.

Customers cried out in protest and moved out of the way before they got doused.

The ruckus got the bartender's attention. "Hey, knock it off. This is a classy place."

Not anymore. Miranda backed away from the bar, crouching into a favorite position she'd learned years ago. More than thirty seconds for a fight, one of her self-defense instructors used to say, and something's wrong. She eyed the size of Mr. Football Player's fists again. This one might take a tad longer.

Raising her hands, she beckoned to him. "You want some of this, asshole? Come and get it." Man, it would feel good to shatter his over-inflated ego.

He charged, swiped at her again, this time with his left.

Miranda sidestepped and he shot past her. When he caught himself and turned back around, she stepped up to him and gave the jerk a hard shove with both hands. With a stunned expression that made her heart dance with glee, he stumbled backward and fell against the bar like a bowling ball knocking down a set of pins. More fancy glass shattered on the floor, along with a couple of shiny barstools, as the air clouded with the smell of imported beer and fine whiskey.

Women in the crowd screeched. The bartender's panic bellowed over the din. "What the hell is wrong with y'all? Where's Earl? I told Frankie we needed more than one bouncer. Earl!"

From the corner of her eye, Miranda saw customers turn her way. "Y'all take it outside," somebody yelled from a table.

And end up with that knife blade across her throat?

Bobby Lee found his balance. Again, he lunged toward her. His arms went around her, going for a bear hug.

She smashed her heel down hard on his toe. She'd been aiming for his instep, but the digit would do in this case.

He shrieked in pain, loosened his grip, began hopping around like a drunken kangaroo.

Miranda pulled away, grinning.

"Damn. Did you see that move?" somebody said. "Girl's a real scrapper."

The crowd had circled around by now, and Miranda thought she heard someone taking bets.

Bobby Lee stopped hopping and glared at her, his eyes glowing like Godzilla. "Goddamn you, you bitch."

He gritted his teeth and he rushed toward her, swinging hard. Miranda swiveled, but this time, she wasn't fast enough. Damn. She'd let the crowd distract her. It wasn't a perfect hit, but her teeth crunched as his right jab connected with her jaw. She stumbled back, and he stuck out his foot and tripped her. Might have known he'd be a dirty fighter.

She crashed to the floor near the stage where the piano sat. Before she could think, he was on top of her, his knife at her throat.

Her lungs hitched and her heart began to pound. "Get off me, asshole."

His beer breath puffed over her throbbing chin. "Your old man ought to put you in your place, bitch."

"Don't have an old man," she spat through gritted teeth.

"Then I'll have to do it." The small knife blade glinted at her throat.

"I'll teach you a lesson you won't forget." Slowly, he lifted his weapon.

A lady in the crowd shrieked. "Somebody do something."

Pain from the fall on the hard floor shot through Miranda's back, clenched around her hammering heart like a tight fist. Time seemed to stand still. The speechless spectators seemed like ghosts in a dream.

C'mon, c'mon. It wasn't like this was the first bar fight she'd ever been in. Or the first time she'd had a knife at her throat. Been there, done that, wiped up the blood with the T-shirt.

Still, panic shot through her. Ancient panic. That sharp, stinging fear she used to feel years ago when Leon came at her, that terror she felt the night Amy was conceived. That wretched reflex of helplessness that could rear its ugly head at the worst times. Damn.

Bobby Lee moved the knife a millimeter closer, taunting her.

She'd be dead if her old emotions got the best of her now. More than one trainer, along with several shrinks, had told her those repressed, unresolved feelings were her biggest weakness. They could bring her down like Superman near Kryptonite.

The bartender's voice vibrated through the crowd noise, like she was underwater. "Earl. Where the hell is Earl? Dammit, I'm calling 911. Ya hear?"

Miranda heard all right. The cops. Wouldn't be the first time she'd gotten arrested for getting into a brawl. If they got here in time. Then she remembered Mockingbird Hills. The Ingram mansion. She'd be damned if she went to the slammer tonight.

By sheer will, she conjured up her power. That hard core she'd spent years forging, nurturing, molding. She forced down her fear, her pain. Miranda Groth, Leon's wife, might have been too much of a wimp to fight back, but Miranda Steele wasn't going to let this adolescent sonofabitch get the best of her.

She bared her teeth. "I don't need a lesson from you. And I don't need an old man."

She grabbed Bobby Lee's wrist, jerking the knife away from her face. She shoved her hips up hard, knocking him off balance. As he fell forward, his mouth opened stupidly in surprise. The next instant, through the opening she'd made between them, she pulled both knees to her chin and kicked against his chest as hard as she could. The adrenaline gave her legs an extra shot of power.

He went sailing.

With the look of a freshly caught salmon, he fell across the stage and crashed into the empty piano with a clang of sour notes.

The stunned crowd stood in silence a moment—then broke out in applause.

Too late, the bartender came around the bar swinging a baseball bat over his head. "Y'all are gonna pay for this damage. The police will be here any minute."

A siren rang outside. Cops. Time to vamoose.

While the spectators were still cheering, before anybody could figure out what to do, she got to her feet and shot out the door.

Slow down. Nice and easy. Adrenaline pounded in her veins, but Miranda forced herself not to run as she blended into the crowd on the sidewalk. The blare of sirens set her nerves on edge. She made herself ignore them. If she kept her head, no one would come after her. She'd get to her car, drive away, and be on her way to Mockingbird Hills in a few minutes. On her way to the Ingrams'.

The faint shouts of cops rushing into The Gecko Club melded into the music and laughter of the teeming partygoers on the streets. The festive atmosphere felt odd after a fistfight.

Don't look back. Keep walking. Stay out of trouble. Keep your nose clean.

By the time she found her car in the next block, Miranda's heartbeat felt almost normal again. Her old beat-up blue Lumina, patched together with Bondo, seemed to sparkle like a royal chariot beside the curb. As she reached for the handle, someone brushed her arm.

Ready to strike, she spun around.

"I'm so sorry, ma'am."

She balled up her fists but caught herself when she recognized the figure. Ma'am? Might have known. It was Blondie.

Miranda rolled her eyes. "What do you want?"

"I didn't mean to startle you."

Miranda bristled. "You didn't startle me."

She cocked her blond head and reached for Miranda's arm. "Yes, I did. You're shaking."

Miranda stepped away. "I am not." She'd tried to sound softer, but the woman still looked wounded by her reaction. Up close, with her fluffy hair and her slinky black dress, she seemed younger and even more fragile than she had in the bar.

She shifted her weight from one high heel to the other. "I—I just wanted to thank you."

Miranda shoved her hands in her pockets with a shrug. She hadn't meant to hurt her feelings. "You don't need to thank me."

Her big blue eyes grew round. "Yes, I do. You saved me from Lord knows what back there."

Miranda knew exactly what she'd been saved from. The kind of things brutish men liked to do to women. Things that could ruin your life. "Yeah, so?" It wasn't like they gave out medals for taking on jerks in a bar.

"I owe you."

Miranda waved a hand and scoffed. "No, you don't."

"But I do. What can I do for you?"

Was this some kind of twist on Southern hospitality? You can go home, Miranda thought, glancing at her watch and eyeing the lineup of cars along the strip. She had less than twenty minutes to get to the Ingram mansion.

The pitiful look in the woman's eyes tugged at her heartstrings. "Look, you don't have to pay me back. But you ought to take a self-defense course or something if you're going to hang out in places like that. Even the high-class ones can be dangerous at this hour when you're alone and, well, all dressed up." Miranda didn't want to mention that most men would see her get-up as a come on.

The woman stared wide-eyed. She seemed totally naive about the world she had just left. "Oh, I couldn't do that. Dexter would never approve."

"Dexter?"

"My husband."

She had a husband? "So what were you doing alone in The Gecko Club?" Maybe they'd had a fight.

She looked crestfallen. "I wasn't doin' anything wrong. I was just looking for a job."

"Job?"

"The Gecko Club is a happening place. I'm a pianist, a singer. An entertainer." She dug into her purse and pulled out a CD. "I was trying to get the bartender to listen to my demo so he'd hire me to play their piano and sing. Here." She reached into the purse again. "My card."

"Cool." Miranda took it. Pink and fluffy, with fancy musical notes all over it, it shouted girlie-girl. She read the name on it. "Coco."

"That's my stage name. My real name is Cora Beth, but that's so boring. So I changed it to Coco. Do you like it?"

"Sure. It's nice." If Coco got a job in that lounge, she'd need a bodyguard. Miranda shoved the card in her pocket and glanced at her watch again. She had to get going. "Well, Cora Beth, er, Coco, just go home and stay safe. Here's a tip. In the future, until you can defend yourself, I'd stay out of places like that. Someone like you doesn't belong there."

"You sound like Dexter."

"Do I?"

"He doesn't want me to play piano. Especially not in a bar. And not for money. He'd be really upset if he knew I was out here. But music is my life."

"I didn't mean you shouldn't play piano. You just need to be careful." Wait a minute. "Dexter doesn't know you're out here?"

She shook her head. "He's working late. He does that a lot." She laughed softly. "That's when I go job hunting."

"I see." Something sounded fishy about that arrangement. Off the top of her head, Miranda could think of a number of things. But it was none of her business.

Coco shifted her weight. "Well, I'd better get back home before Dexter does." She shivered and rubbed her arms. "I don't want to face his temper tonight."

"Dexter's got a temper, does he?" What kind of a dude was this husband of hers?

Coco put a hand to her mouth as if she'd said something she shouldn't have. "Not usually. Most of the time, he's pretty sweet. You know what I mean."

"Sure." Miranda was familiar with the pattern. Leon could be sweet at times, too.

She turned to go, then stopped. "My number's on my card. Call me if you think of anything I can do to repay you for tonight."

Miranda scoffed. "You really don't—"

"—Or we can just chat some time. You know, girl talk."

She wanted to be friends? Miranda wasn't in the habit of making girlfriends. "Right."

"Well, then. Bye-bye."

Miranda raised her hand. "Bye." She watched Coco sashay down the sidewalk and disappear into the pack of revelers. So her husband had such a temper, she had to sneak out at night to look for a job playing piano. That didn't sound good. Miranda had an urge to follow Coco home and give old Dexter a piece of her mind. And maybe a taste of what she'd given Bobby Lee in the bar.

But married people didn't like other people sticking their noses in their business. She'd tried that a few times and gotten burned. Besides, tonight she had her own agenda. Shaking her head, she got in her car and headed for Mockingbird Hills.

CHAPTER FIVE

One after another, majestic, sprawling mansions rolled into view. There was every imaginable style. Traditional, Colonial, Tudor, Greek Revival. Brick, stucco, stone. Southern castles, they were. Architectural ocean liners drifting on waves of flowing lawns, which were just as dauntingly gorgeous. Under the streetlamps and security lighting, a glut of trees, shrubs, and flowers swayed softly in the gentle wind, all perfectly manicured, artfully arranged on the sloping grounds. Elegantly intimidating.

Miranda cruised slowly down the curvy streets. She'd seen more than her share of these magnificent homes during the past month, but they still took her breath.

Here she was.

Mockingbird Hills. One of the richest neighborhoods in one of the richest sections in the entire country. She could almost smell the money.

She glanced down at her map, turned a corner, and read the number on the mailbox. 111 Sweet Hollow Lane. The Ingram place. Bingo.

She pulled over to the curb and stopped the car. For a moment, all she could do was stare.

The house was a breathtaking edifice of whitewashed stucco, decorated with elaborate chimneys, balustrades, and fancy arched windows. A sweeping drive led to a stone staircase and an ornate front door that could have come from some cathedral in Europe. The lower windows had a practical twist. They were covered with security bars. Ornamental of course, but they'd keep out unwanted intruders. No fence around the sprawling yard.

No one of her ilk lived in these houses. Could Amy really have ended up in a place like this? The thought filled her with joy and dismay at the same time. If her daughter were used to this lifestyle, what would she think of her?

She glanced at her dash. Two minutes before midnight.

With a nervous huff, she reached for a pair of binoculars and scanned the yards. She didn't need the infrared model the guy at the army surplus store had tried to sell her that afternoon. There was enough artificial illumination around the homes to take in a good bit of detail, but no one was out. The whole neighborhood was dead still.

Had she missed them?

Miranda shifted in her seat. A strange feeling came over her. Like someone was watching. She turned around and peered out the back window. Nothing. She touched her jaw.

Ouch. It throbbed where Bobby Lee had smacked her. Pulling down the visor, she studied her chin in the mirror. Not too bad, though she'd have an ugly bruise by tomorrow. She touched her neck. Blood.

Damn. The bastard must have nicked her with his knife when he had her down. She searched in the glove compartment for a cloth or a tissue. Nothing. Shoving the visor back, she rolled up the tail of her tank top and wiped off the blood. It wasn't too bad a cut. She'd tend to it when she got home.

The Seekers' letter made a crinkling sound in her pocket. She wiped her hands on her jeans and pulled it out, smoothed it open tenderly on her lap, read it over again. *I think I'm adopted. Can you help me find my real parents?*

Was it even remotely possible that Ashley Ingram was Amy?

One thing could tell her. A birthmark Miranda had seen every time she'd bathed and dressed her baby. A small, dark mark on her neck. She remembered it clearly. If Ashley had that mark…Miranda could meet her Amy tonight. A rush of excitement went through her.

Wasn't smart to get her hopes up.

She put the letter in her pocket and peered through the binoculars again. All was still, except for a light spring breeze rustling through the magnolias and dogwood. Might rain soon.

She looked at the dash again. Past midnight. If she'd missed the kids, she'd go back and kill that jerk at The Gecko Club with her bare hands.

She tapped her fingers on the steering wheel. Maybe the boyfriend was just a braggart. Maybe the grounded girlfriend was smart enough to tell him to forget sneaking out to meet. Maybe her parents caught her. Maybe Miranda was crazy for sitting out here in the middle of the night waiting to talk to an adopted rich kid. Desperation could make you do…almost anything.

Down the street, an engine purred. She sat up as a shiny silver Porsche pulled past her and into the Ingrams' driveway. She grinned.

Not so crazy after all.

Shimmering under the house lamps, the Porsche came to a stop in front of the massive garage, the engine shut off, and the doors opened. Giggles echoed into the night as three girls hopped out. Miranda adjusted her binoculars for a close-up. She focused on the tall one first. Sixteen or seventeen. Blond hair pulled back in a ponytail. She wore a denim mini skirt and a dark tee with a sequin crown across the front.

The girlfriend, Felicia Todd. Miranda had gotten both her names during the boyfriend's conversation with his buddies at the mall today. His name was Jason.

She shifted the binoculars to the younger two. They were both in stylishly frayed jeans with flowers and butterflies embroidered on the pockets. The blond one's pink tee shirt read "Everybody's Darling." Had to be Felicia's little sister. The other girl was half-hidden behind the sister, but it had to be Ashley Ingram. Miranda's breath caught. She couldn't see her neck at all.

For several minutes, the girls stood talking in the driveway.

Golden opportunity. Laying the binoculars on the seat, quietly Miranda opened her car door. From the passenger side, she grabbed the dog leash she'd bought at a pet shop in the mall today. Her alibi. She stepped out into the street, softly shut her door, and tucked the bloodstained tail of her tank top into her jeans. Taking a deep breath, she made her way across the lawn.

As she neared the trio in the driveway, she came to a stop. The fancy foliage and trees on the neighbor's lawn hid her from sight. Pretty much camouflaged her jalopy as well. Lucky break. The girls were absorbed in their conversation. Maybe she could get a few more clues from the gist of it before she tried to talk to them.

Felicia leaned against the hood of her Porsche and groaned. "Good Lord. How humiliating to be forced to babysit my own sister and her girlfriend." Her accent was that sophisticated Southern Miranda had heard at the snobby middle schools she'd applied to for janitorial or kitchen jobs.

The little blonde sneered at her sister. "We don't need a babysitter, Felicia. Momma's just teachin' you to not mess around with your boyfriend." Sharp kid.

Felicia's pretty face twisted into a snarl. "Shut up, Tiffany Todd. What Jason and I do is none of your business. Y'all go inside."

Ashley frowned. She wasn't quite as pretty as the other two, but she was still cute as a button. The girl gazed up at the big house. "Why'd you take me home, Felicia? Nobody's here."

Felicia rolled her eyes. "I told you. Your Mama called and said to bring you home."

Liar, Miranda thought. She did it so she could tell her parents she hadn't brought Jason to her own house after they'd forbidden it.

Confusion played over Ashley's little face. "But she's not here. I'm supposed to sleep over at your place."

"Yeah," Tiffany added. "Nobody's home. Ashley's brothers are away with their friends. Her parents are at a party."

"Like, she called me from the party, dumb-dumb. She'll be along any minute." Playing with fire.

Ashley dug her hands in her pockets, shook her head. "But Momma didn't give me the key."

Felicia grunted. "You're such a little whiner. Look under the mat or something."

Tiffany and Ashley shot cross the drive and skipped up the mansion's majestic front steps. Miranda studied Ashley's deep strawberry blond hair as it bounced up and down. Her heart sank. Red was dominant. No one that she knew of in her family had hair that color. But hair could be tinted.

On the top step, the girl bent down and lifted a mat. She brushed her hair back and Miranda got a good look at her neck. No mark. She chewed her lip. Birthmarks could be removed. And even if she wasn't Amy, one adopted girl might know another adopted girl.

"There's nothing here," Ashley called to Felicia.

Felicia had her back turned and was on her cell phone. Talking to her partner in crime, no doubt, from the sound of her soft, girlish giggles.

On the steps, Tiffany turned to Ashley. "Felicia's sneaking around to see Jason."

Very smart kid.

She stuck her tongue out at her sister. "C'mon, Ashley. Let's go see what Wendy's up to." Tiffany bounced down the steps and across the yard to the neighboring mansion. Ashley put down the mat and followed her.

Where were they going? Better keep an eye on these kids. Crouching behind the shrubs, Miranda scuttled along the grass to keep up with their movements.

When they got to the neighbor's house, Tiffany stopped and gazed up at a window where a light was burning.

Ashley caught up to her. "Do you think Wendy's home?"

Tiffany laughed haughtily. "Where else would she be? Nobody invites her anywhere." She put her hands to her mouth and called up toward the window. "Oh, Wendy. Wendy Van Aarle. Hair in a snarl."

Ashley joined in. "Wendy burger. Or is it Wendy *booger*?"

They fell into uncontrollable giggles.

Tiffany shouted louder. "Oh, Wendy. Are you givin' yourself a facial up there? It won't help." She picked up a pebble and threw it at the window. The small rock bounced against the side of the house. A silhouette appeared in the window for an instant, then drew the curtains.

Miranda hunched down in the bushes. That was mean. Why were they taunting some neighbor? What kind of little shrews were these girls?

"Wendy's such a loser," Tiffany said to Ashley. "Madison always said she was pathetic."

Ashley spun around, fear in her eyes. "Don't talk about Madison. It scares me. She's been gone for almost a week and nobody knows where she is."

Tiffany reached out and put her arms around her friend. "Don't worry, Ashley. They'll find her soon. Madison's father hired his friend, Mr. Parker. He's the best detective in the state. Maybe in the whole country."

Miranda froze. They were talking about that missing girl she'd heard about in the club tonight. *They were friends with her? They knew the detective who'd been hired to find her?* Miranda held her breath, her mind racing. One adopted girl might know another adopted girl? No, that missing girl couldn't be Amy. She couldn't be. Please God, no.

Ashley nodded, reassured. "I'll bet Madison ran away. She always said she wanted to go to Hollywood and become a movie star."

Felicia snapped her phone shut. "Hey, you two dweebs. Like, find the key and get inside. I'm leaving." She turned toward the Porsche.

She wasn't really going to leave them here alone?

The two younger girls ran across the yard. "Hey, you can't leave us here by ourselves."

"Why not?" Never underestimate the selfishness of a hormone-ridden teenager.

"We can't find the key."

Now was the time to make her move. These girls needed adult supervision. Miranda took a deep breath, straightened herself, and started walking toward the drive as if she'd just come from the road.

"Hey, girls," she said in as friendly a voice as she could muster. "Any of you seen a dog?" She held out the leash.

All three froze. Miranda looked into three sets of light bluish eyes, as stunned as if they'd been caught stealing the Crown Jewels. The Todd sisters stepped close to each other. In a nervous gesture, Ashley hunched her shoulders and pulled her hair up. No mark. She definitely wasn't Amy.

Felicia was the first to recover, realizing she wasn't getting caught for sneaking out. "What kind of a dog, ma'am?" She was suddenly oozing with Southern gentility.

"A black lab," Miranda decided. She pointed in the distance. "I was walking him over there and he got away from me. Guess I'll have to get one of those choke collars."

Ashley smiled. "I like dogs."

Miranda's heart melted at the little girl's innocent reaction. Her old stand-by of pretending to be a pet owner always warmed kids up.

Felicia eyed her suspiciously. "I didn't see any dog."

Miranda smiled, looking as friendly as she could. "I was sure he ran this way. It's too dark to tell for certain."

Felicia rubbed her arms. "I've never seen you around here before. Who are you?"

The trust factor was waning. This would go a lot better if it were daylight. At night, the friendliest people could look suspicious. Miranda thought fast. "Actually, I'm lost. I'm from out of town. I'm staying with a friend who lives in a subdivision just like this one."

Felicia folded her arms. "Oh? Where?"

She was cautious. That was good, actually. Miranda suddenly felt guilty for tricking them into talking to a stranger in the middle of the night. But all she wanted was a little information about Ashley. And maybe the missing girl, Madison.

She scratched her head. "Where?"

"What street does your friend live on?"

Good one. Miranda was starting to think a little better of the teen. Her mind flashed back to her research of Buckhead. "Holly Lane."

Felicia cocked her head. "That's in Crawford Chase. It's about two miles from here."

Headway. "Is it? Can you give me directions?" Smiling wider, she stepped into the light.

Suddenly Felicia glared at her and stepped back. "We shouldn't talk to strangers."

"That's right," Ashley added, sounding a little panicky. She put a hand to her mouth and whispered to Tiffany. "Madison talked to strangers."

Tiffany scowled. "She did not."

"She did. That weird man hanging around the schoolyard. She and Wendy hung around with him."

Their friend talked to a weird man hanging around her schoolyard? That didn't sound good. "I heard about that missing girl," Miranda said, trying to sound comforting and motherly. "Do you girls know her?"

Tiffany stamped her pink sneaker-clad foot on the driveway. "She did not. Madison wouldn't hang around with Wendy."

"Yes, she did," Ashley insisted. "She told me."

Felicia groaned. "Shut up, you two."

"Hey. Let's all calm down," Miranda said. Nobody was listening to her.

Suddenly Ashley glared at Miranda with a sour, fear-filled face. "I'm scared, Felicia," she whined. "Do something."

Felicia flipped open her cell. "I'm calling the police."

Miranda held up her hands. "No need for that, girls. Just listen to me a minute."

Tiffany pointed down the street. "Look, there's a policeman now."

Miranda glanced toward the lane. Sure enough, a patrol car was heading this way. Shit.

"Officer," Tiffany waved her hands.

"No, please don't do that." But it was too late. The cop had already pulled over.

Damn, this encounter had taken a bad turn. The last thing Miranda needed was a cop. Nosey cops were always asking questions when she was looking for Amy, like she was some kind of pervert. She'd scratch this idea and take off now, but that would look really bad.

The policeman got out of the car and made his way up the long driveway. "What seems to be the trouble, ladies? What are you girls doin' out so late?"

Felicia pointed to Miranda. "This woman—she just came up to us. From out of like, nowhere."

The officer regarded Miranda with serious, wide-set eyes. He seemed pretty young. Just out of the Academy? Short curly hair peeked out from under his cap. With his chin tucked in and his burrowed brow leaning forward, as if he was about to ask a question.

A dispatcher squawked through a radio on his hip. He turned it down. "Is that right, ma'am?"

Miranda shrugged. What could she say that wouldn't get her into worse trouble?

He gestured toward her. "What's that leash for?"

"I stopped to give my dog a bathroom break and he broke loose and ran away."

He didn't look like he was buying it. "We encourage the use of pooper scoopers." He frowned. "What are you doing in this neighborhood? You don't look familiar."

She scratched her head. Better stick to the story she'd told the kids. "The truth is I'm lost. I'm from out of town. I'm visiting a friend for a few days."

"A friend?"

"Someone I knew in high school. She lives in a subdivision just like this one. I must have made a wrong turn. I'm really bad with directions." It wasn't smart to lie to a cop, but what choice did she have?

He rubbed his chin. Soldier-like in his freshly starched uniform, he seemed kind of green. If he were just out of the Academy, he might be eager to prove himself. With one of the neighborhood youngsters missing, she must look awfully suspicious to him.

He peered off down the street. "Is that your vehicle?"

Miranda turned. She couldn't make out her jalopy from here. He must have seen it when he pulled up. "Yeah." She shifted her weight, tried to sound like it didn't matter. "I was trying to find my friend's house when Scruffy had to use the toilet. Uh, I'll get a pooper scooper tomorrow."

"Can I see your license and registration?"

"Uh, actually, it's my friend's brother's car. My Mercedes is in the shop." Miranda fought back a wince as she realized he'd probably already run her license plate through his database. He'd know her address then. And that she'd just lied. And that she had a record. Just a few arrests here and there for barroom brawls, but still, a neighborhood girl was missing and a strange woman with a rap sheet was talking to her friends alone at night. A new cop would be all over that—just for the bragging rights back at the station.

He held up a flashlight, blinding her.

What was this? The third degree? She shielded her eyes with her hands. "Hey, man. No need for that."

The cop's face turned to stone. "What's that?" he pointed to her shirt.

Damn. Her shirttail had slipped out when she'd scrambled next door after the girls. The officer was staring at the blood on it that she'd wiped off her neck in the car.

"How'd you get that cut? And that bruise on your jaw?"

Bruise? She touched her neck. The cut on it was bleeding again. She must look like shit. No wonder the girls freaked out when they saw her. If only she'd had time to clean up before coming here.

Nervously, she laughed, started to back away. "Scruffy must have nicked me. He can be ferocious when he wants to go for a walk."

He lowered the light. "Stay right there, ma'am."

Her vision still blinded, she froze. Was he going to take her in? If they found out she was looking for her daughter, they might slap a restraining order on her, or even charge her with stalking kids. It had happened before. No one would talk to her about the weather then, let alone adopted kids. She'd never find out who "Someone Else's Daughter" was.

Suddenly an ear-splitting screech came from the far side of the Ingrams' garage.

Everyone jumped. The girls screamed in unison.

"What was that?" Ashley cried.

Miranda's sight had cleared. Or at least, she thought it had, as she pointed to the other side of the driveway. "Something moved behind that bush." Had to be something worse than a strange woman with a leash, even one with a little blood on her.

The cop pointed at her again. "Stay put." Then he turned toward the sound and waved his light toward the garage while reaching for his radio to call for backup.

That was all she needed. More cops.

The sound rang out again. This time, it sounded like an animal. Suddenly, Tiffany ran to the side of the garage and disappeared around the corner.

"Come back here." The cop sprinted after her.

Miranda hesitated. This was her break. Her chance to get away. But she couldn't let these kids get hurt. She started toward the corner, too.

Then the screeching noise turned into—a frazzled meowing. Ashley's girlish laughter echoed into the night air. "It's just the Oglethorpes' cats. They fight all the time."

"Don't pick it up," Tiffany warned.

They were okay. The girls were okay. And she'd be okay, too.

Miranda stopped. Silently, she turned around and headed back across the lawn. The cop would see that the girls got back to the Todds' house. Everything would be fine and she'd just disappear.

She made it to the bushes just past the neighbor's window where she'd watched the girls making fun of their schoolmate, Wendy Van Aarle. Could she reach her car? It was a pretty long walk. Too risky. She'd just crouch down in these shrubs and foliage until the cop left with the girls.

She found a spot where the branches wouldn't stick up her butt and bent her knees.

A voice bellowed behind her. "Where do you think you're going? Stop." His light flashed in her direction. He started across the lawn, coming straight for her.

Shit. Panic washed over her as she straightened. Her heart pounded. She couldn't let him take her in. It was stupid, but she couldn't think clearly. She turned and ran.

"Stop," he shouted.

She glanced over her shoulder. The young cop was coming after her like the Terminator. Why'd he leave those girls alone? But she couldn't tell him to go back and take care of them. She had to get away. She couldn't go to jail. She'd lose her job, her apartment. She'd never find Amy.

She sprinted straight across the Van Aarles' spacious front lawn, dodging flowerbeds, sculptured hedges, miniature trees. If only the landscaper had been a little less creative. If only she could get to her car, but that was impossible now. She could hear the cop behind her, hear his angry snorts as he ran. Suddenly, she had a vision of Leon in their old living room, snorting and cussing at her, and pounding his fist against the wall near her head.

She shook it off and sped up. She had to lose this guy. Her heart banged in her chest. C'mon, you can hold out. You're in good shape. But the cop was, too. She looked up and saw she was at the far side of the Van Aarle mansion. She should stop. Take stock of the situation. But he was gaining on her.

Instead, she dashed around the building's corner and zoomed toward the back, hoping she wouldn't run into a fence. Relief hit her when the grounds broke out into a wide yard, clear of flowers and bushes. It was darker here, but in the distance, she could make out a wooded area that edged the property. Joy spiked in her stomach. Great place to get lost in, if she could make it there.

She started down the hill toward the trees just as the cop came around the corner and stopped. He flashed his light again, but she was to the right of its beam.

She could make it to the trees. She was too far away for him to catch up now. It started to rain. A soft rain. The kind, somebody had told her, that often came up in Georgia without warning. Beneath her, the ground sloped steeply as the grass grew wet. She slipped, tried to stifle a yelp, but it escaped her lips.

The cop heard her. His light found her. "Stop," he yelled.

Man, she was having a bad night.

But the rain slowed him down, too. She could hear him grunting and cussing behind her as he struggled down the slippery incline. She reached the bottom and the land became flat again. Almost there. She sprinted across a patch of grass to the first clump of trees. Hesitating, she stopped to catch her breath.

The bright moon cast an eerie glow on the rocks and wild growth. She'd never liked wooded areas. She thought about murders in the forest preserves where she'd grown up. She thought of stories she'd heard about snakes in the Georgia woods. She glanced behind her.

The cop's light bobbed about halfway down the hill.

No choice. Gritting her teeth, she braced herself and stepped into the tall grass. Her foot went down on a squishy surface of pine straw and matted grass, a twig snapped, but it held. She took another step, reaching out and felt tree bark in front of her. She sidestepped and moved around it. The ground was uneven and muddy. The drizzling rain fell against the leaves with a sound like soft cymbals. The air smelled cool and freshly washed. Brush tangled around her shins. Her hair and clothes were wet, but she couldn't think about that now.

She looked back again, could barely make out the cop. That meant he couldn't see her either. She'd done it. She'd escaped. But he'd be hunting her in these woods soon. Probably call out the cavalry, too. Maybe she could make it to the other side. It was part of a subdivision, after all. She couldn't remember the layout of the forest from her map.

Better move faster. She took a quick step, then another. Found a spot where the trees opened up. She started to sprint. Wrong move. Something caught her foot. Down she went. She tried to catch herself on a tree, but her hand scrapped across its bark. Her palms skidded across the muddy ground.

Damn. She didn't need this now. What had she'd tripped over? She brushed her hair out of her eyes, hoping she hadn't landed on a slithering snake.

Then she froze.

Inches away from her face, lay a shape. A familiar shape. She stared at it, her breath coming in snatches. *Was she hallucinating?* It looked like a kid's sneaker. Peeking out from a pile of wet twigs and pine straw, like it had been lost there. Or buried. She reached out and whisked away some of the debris covering it.

Her chest tightened. The sneaker had a foot in it.

She got to her knees to sweep off more dirt. An ankle. A sock. A hem of denim. Oh, God. It was a leg. A human leg. She found the other sneaker. She was shaking all over by now.

Her heart choking her throat, she crawled to the side of what she now realized was a mound. Desperately she shoved away the muck and grimy pine straw, the dreck someone had used to…she couldn't even think it…to bury someone?

Two legs appeared under her hands, clad in a pair of designer jeans. The type hip young girls liked to wear. She kept going and found the bottom hem of a fancy, girlish T-shirt. Then two young hands…tied with thick rope, clasped together as if in prayer. Oh, God. This couldn't be happening. Tears burned her eyes. She couldn't stop herself. Madly, she brushed away the rest of the dirt, and at last, the face appeared. Young. Pretty. More than pretty. Beautiful. And perfectly still.

Dead.

Miranda's mind reeled. This was the missing girl everyone was talking about. This was Madison. Had to be. But how did she get *here*?

Her whole body shuddering, she put her hands to her head. She had seen death before, knew the look of a body in a casket. An uncle she barely knew who'd passed away when she was a child, a fallen officer who'd been a buddy of Leon's, her own mother lying so still in her coffin with her hard, stony face. But she'd never seen death like this.

So close, so stark, so…undeniable.

The air had a dank smell. Long, dark hair lay damp and matted on the ground. Gnats and flies buzzed around the swollen face, glistening with the raindrops that fell on it. Instead of a childlike expression of innocence, there was the whisper of a smile. An air of superiority, as if she had felt far above whoever had left her this way.

It was the eyes that got her. Open, staring, lifeless. Looking at them, Miranda felt as though a fist had reached inside her chest and yanked out her heart.

She forced her gaze away from the eyes. Her breath caught, as her mind cleared. The girl's neck. She had to take a look at the girl's neck.

She crept closer and saw that a wide, white ribbon had been tied around the young girl's neck. What was that for? She didn't know, but she had to look under it. She shouldn't touch it. It was evidence. But she had to know.

Slowly, she reached out with trembling fingers and lifted the soft cloth, moist with the rainwater. Her hands shivered so hard, she could barely slip it down, but somehow she managed.

And then she saw it. The mark on her neck. Dark, round, distinct.

She put the soaking ribbon back in place. Her hands shook violently, shot to her mouth, her head. Her chest felt like it would burst. Tears streamed down her cheeks, mingled with the rain, dropped onto the forest floor.

This was Amy. This was her baby.

No, oh, God. No. "Please, please, no." Her ears rang with her own scream.

She crawled closer, picked up the body, brushed away more dirt. She held her daughter in her arms, rocked her like the baby she hadn't held in thirteen years. "Oh, Amy. Honey, it's your mama. I'm here. I'm finally here."

The rain pelted down on them, washed away more dirt, turned the ground to a muddy puddle, soaked the girl's clothes, as well as Miranda's. She kept rocking. Time passed. Stood still. Minutes. Hours.

A light flashed. Behind her she heard a muffled shout. The cop. She held the body close. They couldn't have her baby. They couldn't take her away again.

"Put your hands up and come out of there."

He wasn't close. Had to be at least fifty feet away and on the other side, nearer the house.

She couldn't stay here. He'd lock her up for murder. She looked around and saw she was just at the edge of the tree line. She'd gone in a circle. If she could get out and over that hill without the cop spotting her, she could make it to her car.

Gently she laid the body back down on the ground. She couldn't keep her baby, even now. "Goodbye, my darling," she whispered, put a trembling hand to her mouth, kissed it and touched her face once more. Then she raised herself slowly and turned away, her heart in agony.

She tried to move quietly, but a thick twig snapped under her foot before she could catch herself.

"Don't move. Put your hands over your head."

Miranda turned, raised her arm against the beam from the flashlight. The uniformed silhouette stood under the trees like a ghost. He'd been closer than she'd thought, or he'd moved fast. He didn't have his weapon drawn.

He swept his light down and saw the body. "You're under arrest, ma'am."

Like hell she was. She turned and shot out of the forest, lurched across the grass, heading for the hill.

"Stop. Hold it right there."

She ran as fast as her legs could move. The ground rose under her feet. She staggered, slipped. If she could just get over this hill. If she could just get to her car.

"Hold it, I said." He was on her. He grabbed her from behind.

Those hands. Thick, leathery, greedy. Cop's hands. Leon's hands. The attacker's hands that had grabbed her from behind. Suddenly, it was thirteen years ago and she was fighting for her life. Flashback. PSTD, some shrink had told her. Long ago she had been helpless. Now she could fight. Madly, she spun around, lifted her leg in a hard kick.

Her foot smacked the cop's cheekbone and he fell back, stunned. Staggering, he reached for her. She spun the other way, got him on the other side. Before he could recover, she turned and scrambled farther up the hill. Her car was parked along the street. If she could just make it to the street.

The rain poured down in sheets now, making the ground even slipperier. She slithered over the grass and mud, stumbled.

Behind her, the cop regained his balance. In two steps, he reached her again. His wet hands slipped over her arms. She swung out, smacked him near his eye. He almost fell on top of her as he grabbed her and they both went down.

"Get off me. Leave me alone." Her throat ached from screaming.

"You're resisting arrest. I'm taking you in."

"You're not taking me anywhere." She kicked out, struggling to turn around. This time, he blocked her thrust with his knee.

She pushed and groaned. Terror gripped her. "Leave me alone," she screamed. She couldn't get him off her.

"I'll have to restrain you, ma'am." The cop rolled her over, tugged her hands behind her back.

"No. Stop it."

He ignored her. "You're under arrest," he repeated, like a damn broken record.

Thin, wet plastic slid around her wrists, pulled shut. She buried her forehead in the grass, gasping for breath.

He pulled her to her feet, started to haul her across the lawn.

She twisted and kicked. He couldn't drag her away to jail. She wouldn't let him. She fought like a wild animal all the way across the yard, back through the maze of shrubbery, back to the street and the patrol car. She didn't stop fighting until he pushed her head down and shoved her into the backseat.

He shut the door. She sat there catching her breath, dripping wet, her mind reeling, an agonizing blur. Sirens moaned through the air. Slowly she realized they had sounded minutes ago. Blue lights flashed.

She stared out the window.

People were everywhere. A horde of cops was heading down the hill where she had found the body. Neighbors stood in the yard, some holding umbrellas, others in their wet pajamas, hair streaked with rain, frantically demanding to know what was going on. More cops held them back from the scene. Where had they come from?

Beneath the eaves of the Van Aarle mansion, little Ashley Ingram, Tiffany and Felicia Todd stood crying hysterically.

Miranda sat back. She'd been right. Her instincts had been dead on. Those girls knew Amy. They had been her friends. They had known her baby.

The door opened and the cop slid into the front seat. He turned around. His face was cut where she'd kicked him. "I'm taking you to headquarters for questioning, ma'am."

Numb, she glared at him. His youthful face suddenly seemed too innocent for this scene. "You have the right to remain silent and refuse to answer questions. Anything you say may be used against you in a court of law…" As he droned on, throbbing pain made her aware of how hard she'd fought him.

At last, he finished his spiel. "Do you understand?"

She nodded.

He announced his destination into the squawking radio and pulled off. The sight of horror and shock in front of the mansion faded into the night.

Yeah, she knew those lines. The so-called "Miranda Rights," named after a rapist who'd gone free because of them. Like some sick joke life had played on her. Funny, that she'd had no rights when it came to Amy. No rights on the night the stranger raped her. No rights when Leon took Amy away and threw her out of the house because of it. No rights to the years she'd lost with her daughter.

Miranda Rights. Leon told her once that she deserved her name.

CHAPTER SIX

Miranda lifted her head and looked into the husky face of the heavyset black man across the table. His dark eyes gleamed like black marbles. Mean marbles.

"One more time. What were you doing in Mockingbird Hills at 12:20 this morning?"

She raised her cuffed hands, pushed her wiry, damp curls out of her eyes with the towel they had given her. Her hair and clothes were still clammy from the rain. The room was tight, suffocating, lighted in a blue glow designed to set your nerves on edge. Two officers stood on either side of the door like dutiful soldiers.

She shivered.

"Ms. Steele?" The creepy voice echoed like Darth Vadar's.

She turned her face away. She'd been here for hours. They'd made her stand in a long line of suspected pimps, drug pushers, and streets thugs before they took her fingerprints and snapped her picture.

The man inhaled slowly. "Ms. Steele, why were you at the Ingram mansion tonight?"

That poor little girl she'd held in her arms tonight. Poor little dead girl. While she was being fingerprinted, her head had cleared and she'd decided that girl couldn't have been Amy. That mark on her neck wasn't a birthmark. It had to be something else. Probably something the killer left, she thought with a shudder. Amy couldn't be gone before she even got to know her.

"Answer the question, Ms. Steele."

Miranda turned her head and glared into those menacing eyes. "I thought I had a right to remain silent."

He sat back with a disgusted look. "Yes, you do."

But she was looking guiltier by the second. "I told you what I was doing. I was looking for my dog."

"Your dog."

She stared at the shiny silver badge on his blue uniform, that seemed as bright as the flashlight that officer had shined in her eyes. His nametag read "Lieutenant Erskine." This guy was no rookie. They'd have to bring in the big guns for a case like this.

"That's right. Scruffy."

"Mm-hmm." He narrowed his black eyes.

"I got lost on the way to my friend's place."

"A friend whose exact address you can't remember."

Miranda shifted her weight. Better to pretend to forget the street name than to give them something they could check out in a couple of minutes.

"What's your friend's name?"

"I told you. Jane." She'd had a best friend named Jane when she was a kid. Hadn't seen her in years.

"Her last name?"

She thought a minute. "Used to be Anderson. I can't remember her married name." She guessed she'd be married by now.

Sweat beaded on Erskine's brow. Stiffly, he opened a folder. "This report says that you've lived in apartment 1520 in Colonial Towers on Peachtree Street for the past two weeks. You've worked for Johnston Construction Company on a road crew during that time."

Nailed.

She rubbed her cuffed hands. There was a big mirror along the wall. Had to be two-way. She wondered who was watching. "That's right. I moved down here recently and hooked up with my friend a few days ago. She asked me to spend the night at her place."

The Lieutenant leaned forward. He wasn't buying this load of crap. "You know what I think, Ms. Steele?"

She cleared her throat.

"I think the reason you were in Mockingbird Hills has something to do with that young girl's death."

She studied the plain walls, glanced at Tweedledee and Tweedledum at the door. *Keep your mouth shut. You'll only incriminate yourself if you talk.*

"Did it start out as a kidnapping and get out of hand? Maybe you've got a boyfriend and you two wanted money. The Taggarts are loaded, aren't they? Is that why you picked their daughter?"

Taggart? Was that the dead girl's name? "You're crazy."

"Maybe you're part of a kidnapping ring. You know, child pornography. White slavery."

She bit back a curse. "You've got a great imagination."

Erskine didn't flinch. He sat back and shut the folder. "Let's see. Kidnapping. Accomplice to murder. I'd say you're looking at fifteen to twenty years. And if you're the one who did the killing..." he leaned forward. "Maybe you don't know we've got the death penalty in this state."

Miranda clenched her jaw. He was bluffing. He didn't have enough to pin the girl's death on her. She sneered at him. "Go to hell."

His eyes blazed. He gestured to the two soldiers. "Take her away."

The officers moved toward her. Miranda recoiled, trying to dodge their grasp. "You can't hold me. I didn't do anything."

Erskine slammed his hands on the table. "Think again, Ms. Steele. We've got you on trespassing, assaulting an officer, and resisting arrest. We'll see if the judge thinks there's reason to hold you for more."

"I'm not guilty of murder."

His lip curled. "Tell it to the judge." If Erskine was playing the bad cop, where was the good one?

He rose and left the room. Her mind reeled as the two officers took her by the arms, lifted her out of her seat, led her through the door and down a colorless institutional hallway.

"I'm not a murderer." She could never kill anyone, let alone a girl who might be Amy.

"Like the Lieutenant said, tell it to the judge." The cop on her right pulled on her arm to maneuver her around a corner.

She twisted in his grasp. "Hey, watch it, asshole."

The officer's face flushed with anger as he tried to control her with a firm, unyielding grip. "Don't test me, Steele. I won't put up with the crap you pulled on Officer Chambers."

Officer Chambers? "Was that the guy who brought me in?" Guess she'd ruined his reputation with his buddies on the force.

"Rookie didn't know how to handle a prisoner. We do." He gave her arm a yank and hit a bruise. It hurt like hell.

Rage shot through her. "Knock it off, jerk, if you don't want a brutality charge." She struggled to get a leg up, kicked at him hard.

"I told you not to test me."

Just then, Lieutenant Erskine emerged from another door and stepped in front of the men. "Sergeant Reed."

"Yes, sir." The officer loosened up on her arm.

Erskine leaned toward her with his hands on his hips. "Do you want another chance to tell me about tonight, Ms. Steele?"

He wasn't going to reprimand his officer? They had tried and convicted her already, hadn't they?

She gave him her sourest look. "Screw you."

Erskine's big body stiffened with anger.

"Excellent interrogation methods, Lieutenant."

Erskine, the two officers and Miranda all turned in the direction of the voice.

A tall, well-dressed man was leaning against the opposite wall, his arms carelessly folded over his chest. He wore a sublime confidence, as if he were head of the whole police department. Or president of the whole world. He looked to be in his mid forties. Dark hair, salt-and-pepper around the temples. Matching brows, thick and expressive. Eyes the color of steel. A face to die for. Just now, that face was lined with disapproval.

A couple of women officers passed by. Their heads turned in his direction, as if programmed.

Erskine's chest rumbled like a bad muffler. "Wade Parker. What the hell are you doing here?"

Wade Parker? Third time she'd heard that name tonight. So this was the investigator everybody was talking about.

The man gave Erskine a piercing look. It was clear he didn't care for the exchange he'd just witnessed. "Business," he said flatly.

"You don't have business here."

His lip turned up in a wry grimace. "Of course, I do, Hosea. You know I'm investigating the Taggart case."

Of course. He'd been hired to find the missing girl. But why was he dressed in a fancy black suit? More than a suit. Classic dress shirt. Wingtip collar. Satin vest. A tuxedo. A damn tuxedo. What kind of a man wore a tuxedo to a police station? A rich man. An eccentric man.

"I thought I might be able to help, since your progress in the interrogation room was so…minimal." His Southern accent was as smooth as silk, yet smacked with scorn. She kind of liked that.

Erskine bared a set of white teeth. "How do you know what kind of progress I made in the interrogation room?"

The steel gray eyes shined with charm and cynicism. "The suspect's behavior is a vague clue. But actually, I watched you through the two-way mirror."

Erskine stiffened. "Oh you did? Who'd you bribe for that privilege?"

The well-dressed man grinned. "Everyone has his price, as they say. What's yours for a moment with this lady?"

He wanted to talk to her?

Slowly, he turned his head and fixed those sensual gray eyes on her, drank her in like soda through a straw, as if he could see right down to her soul. She shivered. Actually shivered.

"Go to hell, Parker," Erskine barked. "I told you at the crime scene this was my case."

With a sigh, he put his hands in his pockets and shook his head. "Hosea, aren't we old friends? I seem to remember saving your life recently."

The Lieutenant scowled. "That's a matter of interpretation. The way I see it, I lost a promotion because of you."

He took a step forward. "That's also a matter of interpretation."

Erskine held up a hand. "I don't owe you anything. Get out of here, you lily white SOB."

Unfazed, the man chuckled. "You have such a way with words. I'll only need a moment with her."

"Talk to the DA."

He drew in a slow breath. "I'll do that. He owes me a favor."

With one more penetrating look at Miranda, the strange man turned and strolled down the hall, evaporating into the crowd near the desk, as mysteriously as he had appeared.

Erskine was really pissed now. He turned to her with a dark scowl. "Lock her up," he said to his men.

CHAPTER SEVEN

The heavy door clanged shut and the guards shuffled away. Miranda stared at the concrete walls, the iron bed, the dirty toilet.

She'd been locked up before. A night or two in the slammer for "disorderly conduct," which she'd deserved. Her arrest, followed by community service, after she took revenge on the courts. But never for anything like this.

Desperate for something to smack, she grabbed a flimsy pillow off the bed, gave it a couple of punches, tossed it back on the dingy blanket. Didn't help.

She flopped down on the thin mattress, her body aching from sheer weariness. She ran her hands through her thick hair and wished for a rubber band to pull it back.

Her head pounded with the charges Lieutenant Erskine had rattled off in the interrogation room. Trespassing. Assaulting an officer. Resisting arrest. Kidnapping? Murder?

She wiped her face with her hands. How could they charge her with murder? She was innocent.

She stared at the bars.

Innocent people got charged with crimes all the time. A rich girl had been killed. It was in the news. This was a high profile case. They needed somebody to blame. She had no one to vouch for her. No character witnesses. If the cops in Atlanta weren't too picky about details, she could end up doing life—or worse.

She rose and paced to the wall, pressed her face against the damp, hard concrete. Frustration erupted inside her. "Damn." She banged her fist on the cinder blocks.

She rubbed her arm. It still hurt from being bullied by Officer Reed. She squeezed her eyes shut. She could still feel the weight of that poor, dead child in her arms. Smell the damp decay on her body. Her mind raced. That girl couldn't have been Amy. The dark spot on her neck wasn't a birthmark. Or was it? Doubt stabbed at her heart. If they convicted her for murder, she might go to her death and never know.

Old memories flashed in her head. That horrible day she woke up and found Amy gone. Leon's thick knuckles against her face. The violent slam of the front door. The cold softness of the snow against her cheeks. Her old life. Her old self. The weak, sniveling woman she'd struggled to escape for thirteen years. She'd made herself strong and fearless, but she hadn't done much else with herself. A real career, a family. They weren't for her.

But would her life end like this?

She banged her fist against the cinder blocks. "Damn," she yelled, wishing she could knock a hole through the stone. "Damn. Damn."

"I don't think pounding will bring down that wall."

With a gasp, she spun around and saw the figure standing at her cell door. The crazy investigator in the tuxedo.

Annoyance fisted in her belly. "What the hell are you doing here?"

"Visiting you." He grinned at her with his too gorgeous looks, exuding that confident ease he seemed to carry with him, even into a prison. He said he was going to see the DA. Must be a fast worker.

She bared her teeth. "Get lost."

Sexy laugh lines formed around his eyes. "First my friend Hosea tells me to go to hell. Now you tell me to 'get lost.' What have I done to deserve such warm greetings tonight?"

Miranda curled a lip. "You showed up."

He chuckled and casually rested an expensive-leather-shod foot on the lower rung of her cage. "I have a job to do."

He was the best, the woman in the bar had said. "You're investigating the murder."

"That's correct." His handsome steel gray eyes shone like the sharp glint of a Magnum, boring into her as if he could read all her secrets. Her secrets were none of his business.

She made a circle with her finger. "Well, Mr. Fancy Gumshoe, you can just turn around and go back where you came from. I don't have to talk to you."

He shrugged. "Of course you don't. But I thought you might like some company."

Company? That was a good one. She put a hand on her hip and glared at him in disbelief. A few stray wisps of his styled hair fell flirtatiously over his forehead, making the air suddenly crackle with the raw sensuality of a sophisticated, Southern male in a fine black suit. He shifted his weight, making the well-formed physique beneath the elegant cut of his fancy clothes all too evident.

"You think I want company?" He wasn't getting any more out of her than the cops had.

"Wouldn't someone to pass the time with be more pleasant than being alone?" His smooth tone dripped with sweet molasses.

She smirked out loud. "Like visiting a sick aunt? Here's a news flash. I wasn't born yesterday." She took a step toward him. "Here's another one. I didn't murder anybody. So why don't you go out and find the real killer?" She pointed down the hall.

He studied his fingernails a moment. "You needn't be so defensive, Ms. Steele. I might be able to help you."

Help her to the electric chair. She let out a huff and scratched her head. What did she have to do to get rid of this guy? Curiosity got the best of her and she gestured at his fancy tux. "What are you all dressed up for?"

"This?" He fingered the lapel of his dinner jacket. "It's the spring social season. I was attending a charity event when I got the call that Madison Taggart's body had been found."

Madison Taggart. The name sent a shockwave down her spine. "If you're not going to find the killer, you should go back to your party."

"I believe it's over." He arched a dark, wickedly handsome brow. "Besides, I prefer your company just now."

Was he trying to charm her? Arrogant jackass. If only he weren't such a good-looking jackass. If only his words hadn't just put a quiver in her stomach. "Look, I'm not talking. Not to you. Not to the cops. Not to anybody."

Parker drew in a breath as he watched those lush, deep blue eyes glow viciously at him. They were fringed with the blackest of lashes. Lashes that pointed at him like sharp daggers over eyes gushing with vitriol. There were oceans of feeling behind those eyes. He studied the matted black hair, still damp from the rain, falling in knotted curls around her angled face. The clothes torn and streaked with Georgia clay. She reminded him of a poodle who'd been rolling in a tar pit.

And yet, the feisty woman produced a strange sensation in him. Curiosity, perhaps. Or fascination. Not an impression he normally experienced while questioning a murder suspect. The distraction annoyed him. He was certain she wasn't working alone. She was an accomplice to the real killer. His usual tactics weren't working on her, she saw straight through them. But he'd get the truth out of her, if it took him all night.

He inhaled slowly, shifting his weight. "Very well, Ms. Steele. I'll be straightforward."

He was visibly irritated, wasn't he? Miranda felt a small thrill of victory. "About time."

"When I spoke with Officer Chambers at the crime scene he told me he saw you touch the body."

She rubbed her arms at the memory of the child she'd held. Then sucked in her breath. Maybe he could help after all. "That's right. Erskine said you were there tonight. Did you see the body?"

"Of course."

"Did you…examine her?"

"I watched the ME examine her. Why?"

Her heart pulsed and her mind raced. "There was a ribbon around her neck."

"Yes." His eyes narrowed with suspicion. "What do you know about that?"

"There was a mark under the ribbon." Her voice shook as she uttered the words.

"Yes."

"A birthmark."

His expression turned to confusion. "It wasn't a birthmark."

"No?" Her heart stopped.

His angry gaze penetrated her like a laser. "If you killed her, you should know what the marks around her neck were."

Marks. Plural. *Around* her neck. Grief and relief tore at her. "The killer strangled her."

With a sudden violence, he grabbed the bars, jerking himself close to her. "Ligature strangulation, Ms. Steele. Strangling without the fingers or by means of hanging." His voice was dark, full of emotion. "It was done with a rope. Probably tightened with a stick. Very quickly. Very neatly. The marks went all around her neck. They were bruises, Ms. Steele. *Bruises.*"

Miranda cringed at the sickening description, put a hand to her mouth, dizzy with the image playing through her mind. "Oh, God."

"I know you didn't put those marks there. Who did?"

She blinked at him. He wasn't accusing her of murder, like Erskine. He was accusing her of being an accomplice. Well, being a PI wasn't too far from being a cop. With all the strength she had, she forced her mind to clear. Just because those bruises were from the killer didn't mean there wasn't a birthmark under them. That girl could still be Amy.

He suddenly seemed bone weary, his face flushed from his outburst. The girl's death was personal to him.

"You knew her, didn't you?" she said.

His brows shot up in surprise before he could catch himself. He paused, weighing his words, then slowly nodded. "Her parents are friends of mine."

She wanted more. "Friends?"

His steel gray eyes narrowed for just an instant as he considered whether to be open or demanding. She let out a breath when openness won out. "I went to high school with Jackson Taggart, Madison's father. I was at the wedding when he married Cloris."

"Cloris is Madison's…mother?"

"Yes."

Miranda stepped toward him, shivering. "They hired you."

"Yes. I see you watch the news."

She ignored the comment and took a deep breath. Time to bet the house. "I'll tell you what I know if you tell me something."

"What?" Suspicion was back in his tone.

"Was Madison Taggart adopted?"

At that, he took a step back, as if the bars had given him an electric shock. Confusion peppered his expression for an instant, before it turned to stone. "Tell me about her murder first."

With a grunt, she shoved her hair away from her face and marched toward the corner of her cell. "No deal."

The PI followed her, leaning close to the bars, his words an exasperated plea. "Ms. Steele, if you know anything about what happened to Madison Taggart, tell me. Think of her parents. If you could have seen Cloris's face tonight when I told her that her daughter was gone. The anger and despair in Jackson's eyes. If you had heard their sobs."

Sobs. She turned, glared at him, heartbreak flooding her. *He* was the one who had to tell the parents? She almost felt sorry for him. Those poor people. They had to be going through hell. She knew he was manipulating her, but those handsome gray eyes were filled with genuine pain. He felt their grief, too. Deeply.

If that girl were Amy, it would kill her. But she had to know. "I can't tell you anything until you answer my question."

Frustration rumbled in the deep breath he took. "Not until you answer mine." He waited a beat, then in a soft, low tone, played his trump card. "Did you strangle that girl, Ms. Steele?"

Bastard. Rage shot through her. She grabbed the bars and pulled herself near to his good-looking face, wanting to spit in it. "Fuck you," she hissed.

His lip twitched in anger.

With a snarl, she pushed away from the bars, crossed the cell to the bed and stood with her back to him, her hands on her head.

If there had been a clock in the cell, she could have heard the minutes tick away. Then softly, his voice broke the silence.

"Madison wasn't adopted."

Slowly she turned, stared at him. "Really?"

He opened his palms in a gesture that somehow made her believe him. "I was at the hospital the night she was born."

Her legs gave way beneath her. She sank onto the hard bed, put her head in her hands. It wasn't Amy. The dead girl wasn't Amy. "Thank God. Oh, thank God."

"My turn," he said quietly.

She was drained. Her resolve crumbled to pieces. "I had nothing to do with that little girl's death. I've never been in that neighborhood before in my life."

"Why were you there tonight?" The question was a gentle nudge.

"I was looking for my daughter." She put her hands to her face. Damn. She was crying. She hated feeling weak and vulnerable, but she couldn't hold back.

She sobbed.

Daughter? Suddenly, it all made sense. Parker watched her rock herself back and forth on the ratty mattress and weep. A moment ago, he'd found himself focusing on her trim, lean body, her shapely backside, and a raw, primal desire had rippled through him. Now, his heart filled with tenderness for her. He'd seen a similar reaction in many a client when a lost child was found alive. Evidently, Miranda Steele had given her daughter up for adoption and was now searching for her. For some reason, she'd thought Madison was her daughter.

Still that didn't explain everything. He couldn't let compassion override his judgment.

"Why were you looking for her in Mockingbird Hills? After midnight?" He folded his arms. "Do you expect me to believe that you went to the Ingram residence on chance? That you picked out the area where Madison's body was at random?"

Miranda gasped aloud and grabbed at her hair, feeling as if she were going insane. He wanted it all, didn't he? Defensive words began to tumble out before she could stop them. "I was living in Pittsburgh last month when a woman from *The Seekers* contacted me."

He raised a brow. "The independent adoption reunion company?"

In his line of work, he'd know about them. "That's the one. The woman had a letter from a girl about my daughter's age. It said she lived in Buckhead in a mansion. The letter was signed 'Someone Else's Daughter.' That's why I came to Atlanta."

"You came all the way to Atlanta just because of a letter?"

She held up her hands. "It was all I had."

"That doesn't explain what you were doing at the Ingram mansion."

She wiped her face, got to her feet, wrapped her arms around her waist. "I've been cruising through ritzy Buckhead neighborhoods for over a month looking for the girl who wrote that letter." She started to pace the cell. "This afternoon, I overheard some teenage boys in Phipps Plaza talking about their girlfriends. One of them, his friends called him Jason, had a plan to meet his girlfriend at midnight tonight at the Ingrams'."

"Felicia Todd."

"Yes. The boy said her sister's friend was adopted. That they'd all be there. I looked up the address on my computer. That's why I was there. I just wanted to talk to those kids. To the girl who was adopted." She bit back another sob. When would this nightmare end?

"That adopted girl would be Ashley Ingram."

"That's the name I heard."

Felicia's mother had often complained about her daughter's attempts to sneak out and see her boyfriend, Jason. There was no way Ms. Steele could have known that. She was telling the truth.

He let out a relieved breath. "You're innocent."

Miranda stopped pacing and glared at him. He believed her, at last? What had convinced him? Then she got it. "Don't tell me. You grew up with their parents, too."

He gave her a smile that was suddenly tender. "I'm close to the Ingrams and the Todds. Ashley and Felicia's younger sister Tiffany were Madison's best friends."

She nodded. "They were talking about her tonight. They thought Madison had run away to Hollywood to become a movie star."

"They told me that, too." Sadness colored his face. "Ashley is adopted, but it was open," he offered. "Her birth mother visits her every week."

Miranda shook her head. "I didn't think she was Amy after I saw her. Her hair's too red. And she doesn't have the mark."

"The mark?"

She folded her arms tightly, as if that could stop the pain. "Amy, my baby, had a dark mark right here on her neck." She touched her throat. "A birthmark."

"Your daughter's birth name is Amy?"

"Yes." Miranda's voice nearly broke.

"Her birthmark is what you were looking for on Madison's body. Underneath the ribbon."

She nodded. "I didn't know Madison's body was there. If Officer Chambers hadn't chased me down that hill, I wouldn't have found it. I swear that's the truth. I could never hurt a child. Her poor parents. Her poor mother." Cloris Taggart was Madison's real mother. She could only imagine what that woman must be feeling right now. The damn tears were starting again. She wiped her nose on her sleeve.

He reached into a pocket, held out a handkerchief to her. "How long have you been trying to find your birth daughter?"

How could he see straight through her like that? The term "birth daughter" told her he understood everything. She took the kerchief from him and wiped her face. "A long time. Years."

Miranda looked up and frowned. The PI was staring at her, his eyes filled with tenderness and admiration. No one ever looked at her like that. He believed her. Finally someone believed her. Too bad he wasn't a judge.

"Frustrating, isn't it?" His voice was low, soft.

"Way beyond frustrating." She looked at the dingy bed and wanted to collapse onto it. She was exhausted.

"Adoption cases are some of the hardest to solve." His tenderness seemed genuine. "Maybe I can help."

She stiffened. Reality check. A minute ago, he was about to pin a murder rap on her and now he wanted to help? She thought about the detective who'd shysted her out of three thousand dollars when she first started looking for Amy. Yeah. She knew how detectives worked.

"No thanks." She held out his handkerchief. "You want this back?"

He shook his head with a half-smile. "Please, keep it. Did you see or hear anything strange when you were at the Ingrams' tonight?"

She thought a moment. The whole ordeal had been strange, but it was a blur. "Not really."

He rubbed his face, gestured toward the bars. "We need to get you out of here."

We? "What do you have in mind? A prison break?"

His eyes suddenly twinkled. "Something better. I know several good criminal defense attorneys. Probable cause is weak in my opinion. And if you tell them why you were in Mockingbird Hills—"

"Hell, no," she snapped. "I don't want anybody to know that." Nobody believed the story about what Leon had done. Everyone thought she gave her baby up for adoption willingly. "They'd keep me from trying to find Amy. At the very least, I'd get a restraining order."

He rubbed his chin a moment. "Perhaps you're right. When is your pretrial?"

Erskine had mentioned she'd be going before a judge. "Nine a.m. Monday morning."

"I'll give an attorney a call on my way out."

"I don't need your help."

"You're innocent. I don't want the police wasting their time on you."

"Thanks, but I can take care of myself." She refused to be indebted to a detective, no matter how desperate she was.

Parker grinned at her in sheer delight. Stubborn, obstinate, relentless. As well as cagey and determined. Her face had a kind of jaded beauty.

Lost in thought, Miranda turned away from him. Should she tell the truth at her trial? Maybe part of the truth. If she could convince this detective she was innocent, maybe she could convince a judge. If only he didn't slap a restraining order on her. In her experience, judges weren't kind to birth mothers trying to get to their kids. Even if he did, a restraining order was better than a murder charge.

She turned back to the PI. "Don't tell your cop friends I'm looking for my daughter. They'll try to stop me."

He nodded, studied her once more. There was something going on behind those steel gray eyes, but she was too tired to figure it out. "Very well, Ms. Steele. We'll play it your way. Your secret's safe with me." He reached into his pocket. "If you change your mind, here's my card."

"No, thanks."

"Humor me."

Reluctantly, she took it, glanced at it. *The Parker Agency. Wade Russell Parker III, President, Chief Investigator.* "The Third, huh?"

"I come from an illustrious old Southern family. I was named after my father, who was named after his father."

Good for him. She shoved the card in her pocket. "What's up with Atlantans and their fancy cards?"

He frowned. "What do you mean?"

"This is the second one I got tonight."

"The second one?"

She smirked. "Before I went to Mockingbird Hills, I stopped in at a new place in Buckhead called The Gecko Club. I met a woman there who was trying to get a job as a piano player. She gave me her card, too."

"Oh? Do you have it?" There was that cagey look again.

"The guards took it, along with my other stuff, when they booked me." She gave the PI a half-grin. "A guy was bothering her and I busted his chops."

He cocked his head. "I beg your pardon?"

"I got into a fight with him at the club. Got in a few good licks before the bartender called the police. I almost wound up in here earlier. Guess that would have been better."

"I see." That was right. She could fight like the dickens. He'd heard the staff talking about the battle she'd given Officer Chambers tonight. He stroked his chin. She'd just given him the facts he needed. "Are you sure you don't want my help?"

She blew out a breath. This guy didn't take no for an answer, did he? "Yes, Mr. Wade Russell Parker the Third. I'm sure."

His smile turned formal. He nodded. "Very well, Ms. Steele. Suit yourself. Good luck on Monday." He gave her a salute and turned away.

Well, that was abrupt. Did he think she'd cry out for him to come back, like some damsel in distress? Not a chance. But as she listened to the tap of his expensive shoes fade down the concrete hallway, uneasiness settled over her.

She sank onto the bed and pressed her hands to her face. Could she really convince a judge she was innocent? Wade Parker just said probable cause was weak. That meant the cop didn't really have grounds to arrest her in the first place, didn't it? Still, cops and judges liked to press their own opinions about things.

And if she couldn't sway the judge…? She'd lose her job. Her little matchbox of an apartment. Everything. She'd do time…or worse.

She pulled Parker's card from her pocket and ran her fingers over the embossed letters. Attraction fluttered inside her. His handsome face had seemed so full of concern. That scared her worse than the idea of jail time. She'd learned a long time ago it was fatal to depend on the masculine gender. Not when it mattered.

Standing up, she went to the toilet. She tore the card into little pieces, dropped them into the nasty water, flushed the handle with her foot. She watched the off-white flecks churn and disappear. Then she went back to the bed and lay down to try to get some sleep.

She'd figure out something to say to the judge on Monday. She didn't need Mr. Fancy-Pants Wade Russell Parker the Third, Private Investigator to help her. She could take care of herself.

Miranda Steele didn't need a man.

CHAPTER EIGHT

"All rise and give your attention. The honorable Judge Orville Knight presiding."

Monday morning. Nine a.m. A chilly courtroom in Fulton County Justice Center Tower.

It wasn't the AC that produced the shivers scuttling down Miranda's spine as an officer led her through the door in the state's fashionable orange jumpsuit and handcuffs. It was the rumble of the crowd as they shuffled to their feet and murmured about the suspect in custody.

"This court is now in session," a bailiff bellowed. "The People versus Miranda Steele."

She looked into the faces staring at her. They were here to see Madison Taggart's killer. Probably had already tried and sentenced her in their minds, just like Erskine and his men had.

When they reached the bench, she turned to focus on the judge. Not much better. Suspended overhead between two tall flags on a glossy wooden structure sat a large man. His brows were thick, his hair pure white and styled in a cross between Elvis and a late night televangelist. With the gold county seal over his head, the elderly man looked like God Himself.

Man, she was in deep shit.

He shuffled through the papers before him. Acres of polished wood lined the space behind him. The entire wall was paneled with it, like a wealthy man's sitting room. Intimidating.

Miranda studied the lines in the judge's face. Were those furrows etched from frowns of sympathy for defendants over the years? Or from scowls of condemnation while doling out harsh sentences?

At last, he raised his head. "This proceeding is an arraignment, not a trial," he drawled to the assembly in a thick accent, "a preliminary hearing to determine probable cause."

He peered down at her, a weary expression in his deep-set eyes. "Do you have representation?"

She shook her head. "No."

"Do you request a court-appointed attorney?"

Was he kidding? A low-paid peon of the state would get her life. "No."

The judge eyed her a moment, as if thinking that a person who represents himself in court had a fool for a client.

"Very well." He rearranged his frame and shifted through a few more papers. "Ms. Steele, you were arrested Friday night in Mockingbird Hills near the body of one Madison Elizabeth Taggart, age thirteen. Murder victim. Trespassing, assaulting an officer, resisting arrest. Possible suspicion of murder." He turned a page. "Earlier that night, you were seen by Officer Chambers talking to three young neighborhood girls who, I might add, were out later than they should have been. You told the officer you were looking for a lost dog. Is that correct?"

Miranda shuffled her feet. "Well, not exactly, Your Honor."

"Can you tell me what you were doing there?"

She took a deep breath. She'd done a lot of thinking over the weekend. She'd played out every possibility in her mind several times. In the end, she'd decided there was only one choice.

Time for the truth. "Well, Your Honor, I was—"

Suddenly there was a commotion behind her. The crowd gasped. Miranda turned as the courtroom doors swung open and a man entered the room.

He looked to be in his early thirties. Tall and lean, he was impeccably dressed in a dark blue suit, Armani or something, with a crisp, white shirt that set off his dark skin. His hair was black as onyx. In contrast to his formal clothes, he wore it in a long, shiny ponytail that reached to his waist.

"I apologize, your Honor," he said in a Hispanic accent when he reached the bench. "I'm running late this morning. Atlanta traffic, you know."

The judge glowered like a lion ready to devour its prey. "I've heard that excuse from you about a dozen times before, Mr. Estavez. What are you doing in my courtroom?"

He smiled charmingly and gestured toward Miranda. "Why defending my client, of course."

"Wait just a minute." She glowered at this…this Estavez dude. He was god-awful good-looking, beaming with confidence. Where the blue blazes had he come from?

"You are representing Ms. Steele?"

"I am."

Like hell he was. She didn't even know him. "I didn't ask for a lawyer."

He leaned toward her and whispered in her ear with that delicious accent. "You've got one now. If you're smart, you'll take the gift, keep your mouth shut and let me do the talking."

"Gift?" she sneered.

He turned to the judge. "Your Honor, I need a moment to consult with my client."

The judge narrowed his eyes in a vicious scowl. "This is highly irregular, Mr. Estavez."

Estavez put a hand to his chest with a pleading look. "Your Honor, please forgive me if I've offended the court." If the judge had been a woman, he might have thought the lawyer was a Latin lover trying to seduce her.

The judge shook his head in disbelief, though his hair didn't move. "Very well. Court is recessed for five minutes." His gavel came down, he rose and left the room.

"Shall we?" Estavez took Miranda by the elbow and gestured toward the defendant's table like he was inviting her to have dinner with him.

She strolled around it and sat down. "Who sent you?" As if she didn't already know.

The lawyer opened his briefcase and pulled out some papers. "A mutual acquaintance." He reached into his pocket for a pen and laid the papers on the table. "I just need your consent on this form."

She surveyed the crowd. Everyone was gossiping to each other, trying to figure out what was going on. Bristling, she eyed the pen. "You mind telling me who you are first?"

He chuckled. "Certainly. Antonio Estavez. Criminal defense lawyer. My card."

Another card. She took it, glanced at the name of the law firm. *Chatham, Grayson, and McFee.* She shrugged. "You any good?"

He flashed a very white grin. "We lawyers aren't known for our humility, so I'll just say I'm one of the top defense attorneys in the city. Ninety-eight percent acquittal rate."

Damn. She folded her arms. "So you just happened to be strolling by the courtroom and decided to drop in?"

He chuckled. "I heard about your case on the news."

She'd been on the news? Great. Nothing like a little notoriety to welcome a stranger to town. She glanced at the spectators again. That's who most of them were. Reporters itching for a story. She eyed Estavez with suspicion. "Wade Parker sent you, didn't he?"

He grinned again. "Very astute, Ms. Steele. Yes. Señor Parker mentioned to me that you might need my help."

"*Señor* Parker? And he mentioned this…when?"

"I spoke to him on the phone Friday night."

Friday night? Parker had been at her cell in the wee hours. Had to be at least three in the morning when he called this guy. And he'd walked sublimely away, like he wasn't going to do a thing in the world. Sneaky bastard. "You and Parker must be tight."

"You could say that. Señor Parker saved my life."

"One of your clients pull a gun on you or something?"

"No. I don't like to discuss it."

She exhaled. "I think you owe me a little background."

He pursed his lips, then gave a quick nod. "Señor Parker pulled me off the streets when I was a teenager hitting convenience stores for drug money. He took me in, straightened me out, got me through college. If it hadn't been for Señor Parker, I wouldn't be on this side of the courtroom today."

Miranda blinked. Parker had done all that? Mighty philanthropic of him.

The crowd began to murmur again and the bailiff called for order as the judge made his way to the bench once more.

Estavez tapped the papers. "Do you want me or not, Ms. Steele?"

Miranda let out a breath. Guess a reformed street punk with a ninety-eight percent acquittal rate wasn't such a bad choice. As if she had one. Even if she told the truth, she could get locked away for a long time without decent representation. Feeling as though she were signing away her life, she skimmed the paper and scribbled her name on it.

He took it from her, slipped it into his briefcase and turned to the bench. The officer gestured for her to follow. She took her place beside him.

He was good. Really good. He went on and on, bantering back and forth with the judge about habeas corpus, probable cause, search and seizure.

But the judge was unmoved. "You make a good case, Mr. Estavez, but nothing you've said explains why the defendant was found standing over the victim in the middle of the night." He scanned the crowd. They wanted blood. Wouldn't hurt his election prospects to give it to them.

Estavez held up a hand. "I do have a character witness, Your Honor."

"Character witness, Mr. Estavez? This is just a hearing."

"I have someone who can provide an alibi. May I proceed?"

Miranda's ears started to burn. *Alibi?* She didn't have an alibi.

The judge sighed. "Very well, Mr. Estavez. But you'd better not be wasting my time."

The attorney turned and gestured dramatically to the officers near the back. They opened the doors and the witness entered the courtroom.

Miranda sucked in her breath as the blond, figure wearing a form-fitting, stop sign red party dress and matching five-inch heels, sashayed down the aisle. It was Coco. From The Gecko Club.

She passed through the dumbstruck spectators, ignoring the women with their mouths hanging open and the men with their tongues dangling to their chins. She squared her shoulders and continued to the bench with determination on her pretty face.

Estavez lit up as she approached like a Cinco de Mayo firecracker. Miranda was definitely going to have to have a talk with that girl about her clothes.

"Your Honor," Estavez continued. "This is Cora Beth Hinsley. She can testify that an hour before her arrest, Miranda Steele was with her in a Buckhead establishment called The Gecko Club where an…altercation broke out and the police were called." He handed a paper to an officer, who took it to the judge. "Please note the time on the police report."

The judge's brows twisted with suspicion. "Is that true, Ms. Hinsley?"

"It's Mrs. Hinsley." She nodded. "Oh yes, Your Honor. Is there a Bible or something I can swear it on? I will."

Now she got it. Parker must have gotten Coco's card from her things. The stuff the cops had confiscated. She whispered to Estavez. "Parker's tight with the cops, isn't he?"

He grinned. "Señor Parker, he can get anything he wants." He turned to the judge. "The autopsy report states that algor mortis, the cooling of the body, indicates Madison Taggart was killed not more than an hour and a half before she was found. That would be about eleven P.M. It was a Friday night. Ms. Steele could not have gotten through the traffic on the Buckhead strip and met Mrs. Hinsley at The Gecko Club in time. It's highly unlikely she killed the girl after she left the club."

It was close, but not close enough.

The judge put a hand to his head as if he had an Excedrin headache. He wasn't going to be the one to put Madison Taggart's killer away. At least not this morning. Angrily he banged his gavel on the bench. "Insufficient evidence. Case dismissed." Then he pointed a finger at Miranda. "Make sure you don't leave town while this investigation is going on."

She nodded. "Yes, sir." She didn't intend to.

In a small room down the hall, Miranda changed out of the orange monkey suit and back into the dirty jeans and bloodstained T-shirt she'd worn Friday night. If she'd known Coco was coming, she'd have asked for a change of clothes. But then again, they would probably be covered with sequins.

She finished quickly, stepped out into the hall, and barely had time to rub her wrists, now loose from the shackles, before Estavez rushed her and Coco through a side door and down another hall before the ravenous reporters could get to them. He took her to Processing, where she got back her map, her dog leash, and most important, her letter from The Seekers.

She was free.

Her new attorney escorted the two of them out a side door and into the lot where somebody had parked her old beat-up blue Lumina.

Feeling a little bewildered, she turned to him. "I don't know what to say."

Estavez's dark eyes twinkled. "You don't need to say anything, Ms. Steele. The pleasure was mine."

Guess he liked winning, but she was grateful for the magic he'd worked. "Thank you. Really."

"You're very welcome."

"Oh, and thank that mutual acquaintance of ours, too."

He grinned. "I'll be sure to do that."

She scratched her neck. "I don't owe you any money for this, do I?"

"Not a penny. Pro bono."

She narrowed an eye. "That's lawyer talk for 'no charge,' right?"

He chuckled. "You're quite correct."

Had to be sure. She turned to Coco, reached out to shake hands. "Guess it's my turn to say thanks."

Teary-eyed, the woman ignored her hand, threw her arms around her, and gave her a kiss on the cheek. "Oh, Miranda. I'm only too glad to help. You can always count on me. Do you need anything else?"

Jeez, no need to get so emotional. Miranda pulled away. "Uh, that's okay. I guess we're even now."

She looked a little crestfallen.

Miranda winced. She didn't want to hurt her feelings. Especially after what she'd just done. "Maybe I'll call you sometime."

She brightened. "Do you still have my card?"

Miranda shrugged. It wasn't with her stuff. Parker had it.

Coco pulled another one out of the tiny purse she was carrying. "Here."

Miranda took it. "Thanks."

"Can I drop you off anywhere, Mrs. Hinsley?" Estavez asked in his steamy Latin accent.

Coco stared at him for a moment as if she'd forgotten where she lived. Then she came out of it. "Oh, no thanks. I've got my car. I've got to get back. Dexter has the afternoon off. He's taking me shopping."

Now it was the attorney's turn to look crestfallen. "I see. I hope you enjoy it."

"I will."

"Thank you for helping us today." He held out his hand to her.

Gingerly, she shook it. She was wearing that dreamy look again. "Don't mention it. Any time." She turned back to Miranda with her big blue eyes and laughed. "Not that you'll get arrested again or anything." She glanced at Estavez once more, then stepped off the walk. "Well, I've got to run. Dexter will be home soon. Bye-bye."

"Bye," Miranda and Estavez said in unison.

Miranda looked at Estavez. He had the same kind of faraway look on his face. Hmm. He'd better watch his step. If what Coco had told her about Dexter's temper was true, he wouldn't appreciate some hot-blooded Latin lawyer ogling his wife. Might take it out on her.

"Thanks again," she said to him.

"Don't mention it." He was still looking at Coco.

As Miranda walked back to her car, she was hit by a sense of emptiness. She'd beaten a murder rap, but as far as Amy was concerned, she was back to square one. And now the cops would be watching her.

She'd better be careful searching for the girl who wrote that letter. If somebody in the neighborhood figured out who she was, she could end up back in jail for talking to kids. But she wished she could talk to Ashley Ingram again. Maybe she should buy a dog for real.

And what about poor Madison Taggart? If only she could help in some way. She'd love to do something to catch that killer. But what did she know about tracking down murderers?

As she reached her car, she glanced at her watch. It was Monday. Second shift on the road crew would be starting in a few hours. Might as well head home, shower, catch a few z's and go back to her crappy job. At least her timing was good. No one on the crew would suspect a thing about her crazy weekend.

CHAPTER NINE

Never in her wildest dreams had Miranda thought she'd be so glad to see the gnarly lot she worked with on the road crew. But when she boarded the transport rig late that afternoon to take her to the job site and plopped down next to Dupree, the heavyset roller operator, she wanted to kiss him. She wanted to give every last one of her co-workers a big, juicy smack.

Now that her weekend of terror and her fifteen minutes of fame were over, she was glad to get back to her usual work-a-day oblivion. A shower, a nap, and a sandwich had made her feel human again.

That was, until she noticed skinny Lester, the oldest screed operator, on the opposite bench reading the *Atlanta Journal Constitution.*

Deep lines furrowed his dark brow as he scratched at his scraggly brown beard. "Cryin' damn shame," he muttered in his thick drawl.

Beside him Gibbs, the paver, a big, burly guy with tattoos of roses and crossbones on his arms, scowled. "If you weren't hogging the paper, maybe we'd know what you're talking 'bout, man."

Lester slapped at Gibbs with the paper, then handed it to him. "I'm talking about what happened to that little rich girl last Friday night."

Gibbs opened the paper and Dupree peeked over his shoulder, raising his bushy brows. "That girl they found outside that mansion?"

"Yeah," Lester smirked. "All the Buckhead muckity-muck, uppity-ups are in an uproar. Worse than when they lobbied to close the bars early."

"Did they catch the killer?" Dupree asked.

Lester tapped the page. "Says right there that they took in some woman."

Gibbs pushed his sunglasses up on his bald head with the arm with the roses. "A *woman* killed her?"

"God awful," Dupree muttered.

Uh oh. Miranda cringed and hoped to God the paper hadn't mentioned her name. Guess it wasn't quite oblivion she was getting back to. She'd better watch what she said. She'd never be able to explain she was searching for her daughter to this lot.

Joan Fanuzzi, a short, dark-haired single mom from New York with three kids, and the only other woman on the shift except the foreman, sat on the other side of Miranda. She wagged a finger at Lester. "That woman didn't do it," she said in her Brooklyn accent. "They let her go this morning. I get *my* news on the radio. I heard it driving in."

Dupree shook his head. "That's justice for you. Catch the killer, then let her go."

Miranda stared down at the boards lining the truck bed. There sure were a lot of knots in them.

"She didn't do it," Fanuzzi repeated. "The mayor gave a press conference about it. I think it was one of the neighbors. Some pervert, probably."

Gibbs folded the paper and set it on the bench. "Did he say why they let her go?"

Fanuzzi gave a huff and rolled her eyes. "She. Didn't. Do. It. Alls the mayor said was that the crime rate in Atlanta is the lowest it's been in a decade."

"Political bullshit." Gibbs folded his arms across his big chest. "You'd think they'd do more in a place like Mockingbird Hills."

Fanuzzi's face took on a worried look. "Yeah, it's bad when even the rich man's kids aren't safe. Makes me worry even more about my three."

"Cryin' shame," Lester said again.

"Cryin' shame."

Everyone turned to the corner where a tall, thin black guy in his early twenties sat by himself. His name was Truman. Everyone said the construction company hired him because they had to. He had some kind of disability.

"Ya think so, Truman?" Lester asked.

Everybody said he was slow, but Truman knew what his coworkers were talking about. He shook his head. "Cryin' shame," he muttered under his breath. "What's dis world coming to?"

Next to her, Fanuzzi gave Miranda a nudge. "Whad' you think, Murray?" All the crew called her Murray.

Miranda swallowed. "Uh, I'm new in town, so I don't know the place. But I think it's awful." She thought of Madison Taggart's body in her arms.

Fanuzzi grabbed the paper from the bench and skimmed it, then gave a wide grin. "They got Atlanta's finest on the case."

"The police?" said Gibbs.

"Heck no. Wade Parker. Atlanta's most famous private investigator. He's a looker, ain't he, Murray?" Fanuzzi nudged her again and pointed to his picture.

Miranda looked at the image of Wade Russell Parker the Third. His neatly styled, salt-and-pepper hair, his knowing eyes, his confident air and handsome face, all just as alluring as Friday night in her jail cell. Idly, she wondered if he had something to do with keeping her name out of the papers. "He's okay."

"Rich as Solomon, that one. He doesn't have to work. His family is loaded. He does it anyway to fight crime. All the women want him." She grinned at Miranda.

Miranda just rolled her eyes.

"You got the hots for the private dick, Murray?"

Miranda looked up and saw the crew foreman leering at her from the air-conditioned cab. The boss lady liked to sit up there with the driver on hot days, but she kept the back window cracked to listen to her crews' conversation. Paranoid.

Her name was Clark, but everybody called her Fat Mama. She was a huge woman. Six feet tall. Almost as wide. Her arms were like hams and her legs were like tree trunks. When she moved around the job site with the gait of a stampeding rhino, everybody got out of her way.

Miranda eyed her wiry red hair that she rarely combed, her flaming eyes that nearly matched her hair, the huge mouth she liked to use to intimidate her crew. She was the typical tyrant boss. Might have taken lessons from Hitler.

She turned her head away and looked out the back window. "Not me. I stick to myself."

Fat Mama smirked. "A loner, eh? Maybe you like other girls. Or maybe you'd like to do Truman here."

The young man nodded eagerly. "Truman like Miwanda."

Miranda turned back, glowered at her boss. Why did the bitch always pick on the poor guy? Yeah, I wonder what your typical date is like. But she kept her mouth shut.

"No, sir. Wade Parker ain't no muckity-muck," Fanuzzi said, still ogling the picture. "He's always helping solve some crime or other the police can't handle."

"He's good," Gibbs agreed. "Damn good."

The truck kicked up a cloud of red clay dust as it pulled onto the job site and squeaked to a halt. Miranda felt a wave of relief.

"Ya think he'll get the killer, Les?" Dupree asked, getting to his feet.

"Hope so. The police won't."

Miranda grabbed her hard hat and hi-viz vest from off the hook and jumped down to the pavement. Behind her, Fat Mama got out of the cab and started barking out orders. Everyone grabbed tools or climbed aboard big yellow rigs and got to work.

Miranda's official title was Lute Person. That meant she had to repair any imperfections in the asphalt with a lute—otherwise known as a rake—before rolling, Dupree's task.

At Fanuzzi's direction, Gibbs's paving truck roared over the surface, laying down the hot mix, while Lester, Miranda and the others smoothed out the thick, smelly black gook before Dupree came hissing behind, perched atop the heavy, slow-moving roller.

It was a crappy job. Hot, grimy, but it paid the bills and worked her arm muscles to boot, keeping them lean and strong, as well as any fancy Buckhead workout spa. The sweat rolled down her back as she worked her rake over the sticky goo, and she wondered why she always took the crappy jobs, never went back to school, never tried to better herself. She'd taken some community college courses years ago after she'd left the woman's shelter but had lost interest after awhile. She was restless, didn't want to be tied to a nine-to-five job. She wanted freedom.

As long as she had some money in the bank, she could pick up and leave a crappy job like this anytime the urge struck. She could move on and go anywhere in the country. And she had. Right now, of course, she was broke. She'd be staying put for a while. This time, she had a reason to stay.

The Georgia sun was as hard at work as the crew. The early spring hot spell hadn't broken yet and the humidity was well over sixty. Everything was covered in fine yellow pollen dust from the local pine trees that made her nose itch—an annual symbol of spring in Atlanta–Miranda had learned.

After an hour or so, she and Lester stopped to wipe their faces with rags and drink water from the plastic bottles on their hips.

Her mind wandered to the sexy detective who'd visited her cell Friday night. Fanuzzi seemed to think he was the best PI on the planet. If Wade Parker was as good as everyone said, he'd have the real killer behind bars in no time. After that, she could look up Ashley Ingram and the Todd girls and explain what she'd been doing at the Ingram mansion last Friday night. She imagined them all laughing together about it and little Ashley rattling off a list of friends who were adopted.

Well, they couldn't be that gleeful in the wake of Madison Taggart's death.

What had happened to the poor girl whose lifeless body she'd held in her arms? Having seen it, touched it, Miranda was even more outraged about the murder than her crew. If there was anything…anything in the world she could do to help put the killer away, she would. But there wasn't.

She slid her bottle back in place and turned to Lester. "You ready to go after it again?"

"In a minute." He wiped his skinny arm over his tanned forehead and stared out at the road.

She followed his gaze. They were resurfacing a stretch of I-85 just south of Freedom Parkway. The interstate was one of Atlanta's busiest and most dangerous. They had to cut traffic down to two lanes to work, and the drivers didn't like it one bit. Cars started to backup, then zoomed ahead when the road cleared. Not the safest way to drive near a road crew.

"Motorists are antsy today."

Miranda shrugged. "I don't blame them for being cranky." But she worried about Truman, who was limping back and forth alongside the work area, an orange stick in his hand. As the Flagger, he was trying to make the drivers slow down. Because of his disability, he had an even crappier job than she and Lester had.

She could hear him muttering to himself, which he did when he was nervous. "Fat Mama say Truman, hold de flag. Truman, slow those cars down. It dang'rous out here."

Poor guy. He was harmless and he'd always been nice to her.

A car whizzed by. Truman waved his hands up and down trying to make it slow. It didn't. It was dang'rous trying to control Atlanta drivers. They drove like bats out of hell. Another car zoomed near the workers, wavering through the lane as the driver realized he was in a construction zone.

Miranda thought about the stories of fatalities she'd heard. "Look out, Truman," she shouted to him.

As the car passed, she caught a quick glimpse of the occupants. The driver was shouting at a woman in the passenger seat. She thought she recognized the blond head. Coco? Naw, the sun must be getting to her.

Truman's voice rose above the rush of the traffic. "Slow down. Cars won't slow down. Truman scared."

Miranda handed her rake to Lester and jogged over to him. "You having a bad day, Truman?"

His head bobbed up and down. He was rattled. "Cars won't slow down. Truman gots to sit down a minute."

Miranda glanced over at the grassy stretch along the highway where they had been dropped off. Fat Mama usually made rounds to keep an eye on everyone, but today she was engrossed in a conversation with the guy who drove the refreshment truck. Discussing the size of his sandwiches?

She turned back to Truman. "Why don't you take a break? I'll hold the flag for awhile."

"No, Miwanda." He always had trouble with her name.

"C'mon. Let me have the flag."

He wagged his head back and forth. "Fat Mama not like it."

"I'll handle Fat Mama. Don't worry. It'll be okay."

He hesitated another moment, then handed her the stick. "Thank you, Miwanda, thank you," he muttered and shuffled off to the side, sat down on the cement divider at the edge of the road.

Gibbs said he was born with that bum leg. Her heart went out to him.

She turned toward the traffic and waved the flag back and forth with big strokes, but the cars only slowed a little. Must be the pollen count or the heat making the drivers extra crazy today. They weren't paying much more attention to her than they had to Truman. Then she noticed a couple of the work zone signs had fallen over down the way. Hell.

Waving the flag aggressively at the drivers, she jogged over to the signs and stood them back up one by one.

There, she thought, returning to her place. The drivers started to ease off now. Maybe that would make it better for Truman. The pavement was drying and she had to get back to her rake.

"You ready to come back, Truman?"

He didn't answer.

She'd give him another minute or so. Then she saw a shadow behind her. She turned around.

Fat Mama stood with her big fists on her hips, staring at her, red eyes flaming. "What the hell you doin', Murray?"

"Just helping out. Truman needed a break."

The veins in her neck were sticking out. A puff of smoke might have shot out of her nose. Definitely not a happy camper. She slapped her chest. "I'm the one that calls for breaks around here."

Miranda took a deep breath to hold back her temper. "He was rattled. A car nearly hit him."

"So? If he can't take the heat, he doesn't need to be working here."

And you're a shining example of qualifications? It took all Miranda had not to spit out the words. The woman would love to fire Truman, but with his disability, she'd bring a lawsuit down on the construction company. So she settled for making his life hell. The bitch.

Fat Mama gestured toward Lester. "Get back to your rake. The asphalt's drying."

It would in a few minutes, but there was still a little time. "Just give Truman another second or two."

A rumble came from her chest. "Just who do you think is the boss on this shift?"

"Look, he only needs—"

Her eyes flamed. "I don't need a no-count good-for-nothing like you telling me how to do my job." She reached out and pushed her. "I said, get back to your rake."

Miranda's fist went back instinctively. It was all she could do to keep from driving it through the woman's skull. But she needed this paycheck. She forced herself to hand over the flag to Fat Mama.

The big woman gestured to Truman. "Hey, asshole. Get back to work, if you want to keep your job."

Truman looked like a lost puppy as he hurried back to the side of the road. Fat Mama stuck the flag in his hand. "Don't leave your post again."

"Yes, ma'am," he nodded. "Truman won't leave."

She stood over him, watching his every move.

Gritting her teeth, Miranda went back to her spot and retrieved her rake from Lester, who just shook his head.

The heat burning down her neck, she raked away at the asphalt, trying to control her rage. Her hair was pulled back in her usual ponytail, but her thick mane stuck to her neck. Annoyed, she brushed it away. If she could just get that bitch alone in an alley some night.

Everything was all right for a while. Gibbs inched forward in the roaring paver, Dupree hissed and rolled along. They were making progress. The traffic backed up and the drivers had to slow down.

But after another few minutes, it thinned out and they sped up again. A kid in a Buick whizzed by. Truman jumped.

"Coward," Fat Mama was behind him, still micromanaging.

"Truman scared, Fat Mama," he pleaded.

She folded her big arms and shook her jowls. "Shows how unfit you are for this job."

Looking wounded, Truman bowed his head and feebly waved the flag. Another car whizzed by.

"What kind of a pussy are you?" She marched up to him and gave him a shove.

He stumbled and stepped into the lane. An oncoming Audi blared its horn and swerved around him.

Miranda stopped raking.

Fat Mama must have felt her glare. Slowly, she turned her head. "Get back to work, Murray. This ain't your concern. Rake that hot mix. I'd like to see you do something right for a change."

Miranda straightened her back. Enough was enough. Some would have reported the incident to the higher ups, but she'd never been one to go through conventional channels. "Ya know what I'd like to see, Fat Mama?"

The woman's eyes narrowed and her big nose wrinkled like a rotten prune. "What?"

Miranda cocked her head and lifted the tool in her hand. "How far I can ram this rake up your ass."

Slowly, the mountain of bitch swiveled around, Mount Vesuvius erupting in her eyes. "You wanna take me on, Murray?"

"Yeah, I think I do."

She laughed. "I'd like to see that."

Miranda grinned. "It's your lucky day."

Gibbs's paving truck squealed to a halt. Dupree stopped the roller and jumped off. "Hey, what's going on?"

With a guttural belch, the huge woman stripped off her orange vest, handed it to him. "Stay out of my way."

Lester stepped back, while Miranda tossed down her rake, pulled off her own vest and chucked it to the side. So much for this job.

Fat Mama moved in and crouched down. Miranda bent her knees and squatted into her favorite version of *mabu*, the horse stance that every sensei she'd trained with had drilled into her. She raised her fists to her face.

For several moments they glared at each other.

Everyone on the crew stopped working and gathered round in a circle. Nobody said a word. The only sound was the traffic cruising along the road.

Suddenly, screeching like The Creature from the Black Lagoon, Fat Mama lunged. Hurtling toward her, she stretched out her thick, burly hands like two big crabs, aiming straight for the throat.

Miranda kept her eye on the massive bulk, forced herself to keep still, to breathe. Then, just as the monster-woman reached her, she slipped her arms between the claws and snapped them apart like a nutcracker.

Hah. Self-defense 101. She stepped away and the momentum carried Fat Mama right past her and into a row of orange road barrels. The woman went down with a noisy clatter and an "oomph."

"Hot damn," Lester cried.

Gibbs trotted over to pick up the barrels. "Why don't you give it a rest, Fat Mama?" he said, helping her to her feet. "We've got work to do." He always was an ass kisser.

Fat Mama pushed him away. "Shut up, Gibbs." She glared at Miranda. "I'll make you pay for that, Murray."

She curled a lip. "I don't think so."

"Oh, yeah?" Her face filling with an impossible degree of hate, she stomped the ground like a bull in a Spanish ring. Then she charged again.

Miranda tried another side step, but Fat Mama had learned her lesson. This time, she adjusted her aim and her thick palm smacked Miranda on the shoulder with full force.

Her clavicle stinging, Miranda stumbled backward into the lane of traffic. She knew it was too early to celebrate. A sedan came to a screeching halt only a few feet away. Bitch didn't care if she killed somebody, did she? Her heart pounding, Miranda regained her footing, glared at the car. The driver took off, not wanting any part of the ensuing chaos.

She centered herself. *Strength, mental strength, was the key.* She wasn't the weak groveling woman she'd been years ago. She never would be again.

She stepped back onto the tarry surface. That was the problem. The ground was too sticky to move well.

Before she could figure out what to do about it, Bull Woman stampeded again. This time, as she reached her, Miranda spun away and shot her leg up in a low kick that landed on the bitch's thigh.

Fat Mama stumbled, caught herself. But the kick hardly fazed her. She reached around Miranda's waist with one hand, grabbed her by the ponytail with the other and yanked her head back.

"Hey," she yelped. "That hurts."

"I'll bet it does." Fat Mama yanked harder.

"Knock it off."

"Make me." Another tug. The sky rocked above her. Floaters danced before her eyes. She felt like she would gag, but maybe that was from the woman's sweaty body odor. Still, Miranda wondered if the bitch could break her neck this way. Dizzy, she focused on the ugly snarling face above her, saw the sagging flesh under the jaw wagging back and forth. That was it. Clear shot.

Slowly, she drew back her arm. "Fat Mama, I'd never guess you fought like a girl." With a laugh, Miranda brought her fist up hard, landed the punch square on the target, knocking back all of the woman's chins.

She staggered back and into the tire of the paving truck.

"You go, girl," Fanuzzi shouted from the sidelines.

Miranda dusted off her jeans. "Okay, Fat Mama. That's enough. Time to admit defeat."

The big woman shook herself as if coming out of a deep sleep. "Defeat?" she sneered. "You call that defeat?"

She raised her hands. "Hey, I didn't hit you with all I had. If I broke your jaw, who'd humiliate the workers?"

It should have been over. But the woman couldn't admit a loss. "I'm not through with you, Murray," she screamed.

"Oh, yeah?"

"Yeah. And after I finish with you, I'll take apart that dickhead over there." She pointed over at Truman.

Truman? She'd dare attack defenseless Truman? Rage flashed over her. Flamed up inside her. That uncontrollable fury that could blast through her brain like a hurricane, obliterating her senses. Forget breathing. Forget strategy. Forget control.

She opened her mouth and let out a *kiai*. That guttural shriek of empowerment. Her battle cry.

With the cry in her throat, she ran headlong across the asphalt, rushed the woman, jumped her, felt her knees scrape the pavement as their bodies thudded onto the tarry surface. Straddling her, she raised herself up, and with all her might, pummeled the bitch's cheeks. The look on her fat face was as much shock as pain. Miranda didn't care. She just kept hitting. Hitting. Hitting.

Gradually, she became aware of voices around her. Shouts. Someone grabbed her arms. She fought, struggled, twisted, her blows churning the air. But she couldn't stop whoever it was from pulling her to her feet.

"Clark? What's going on?" It was the chief supervisor.

One of the super's lackeys knelt down, cupped a hand under Fat Mama's head. "Are you all right?"

Her eyes were swollen, her lip bleeding. She looked a little like Rocky after his fight with Apollo Creed, but she wasn't saying, "Yo, Adrian." Shakily, she raised a finger, pointed it at Miranda. "I was telling this worker to do her job when she went berserk and attacked me."

The man turned to Miranda. "Is that true?"

Not exactly. But if she mentioned Truman, it would only be worse for him. "She was harassing me."

"I never harass my workers. Not if they do their jobs. I can't work with her, Harry."

Harry and his subordinate helped Fat Mama to her feet, then took her aside for a confab.

Miranda turned to the crew. They looked back in stunned silence. Everybody could guess what Fat Mama was telling the chief super. The woman was in thick with her superiors.

After another minute, Harry came back. "Sorry, Steele. I have to send you home."

"I'm fired?"

"Suspended. We'll see if we can find another position for you in a couple of weeks."

Right. Nice CYA job. She'd heard that one before. "Thanks for nothing." But she hadn't expected anything less. She turned to Fanuzzi. "Watch over Truman, will you?"

Fanuzzi nodded.

Her sense of victory fading into oblivion, Miranda grabbed her gear and headed for the transport.

Wade Parker sat in his neutral-colored Mazda on the raised parking lot near the university and exhaled the breath he'd been holding since the fight broke out on the Interstate. He lowered his binoculars, put down his cell phone.

He'd been about to call the construction company's headquarters to file a complaint about their treatment of disabled employees when the altercation started. Then he'd wanted to call Hosea, call 911, scale down a tree and come to her aid. But she hadn't needed him. He wasn't quite sure what Miranda Steele was doing to his sense of Southern chivalry, but he couldn't help being impressed.

Damn, what a woman.

Though her boss was huge, she had used her size against her. She'd held her own, outmaneuvered her, would have finished her off if the men hadn't pulled her away. Obviously she'd had training. She was light on her feet, graceful, even if overemotional in her attack. Rarely had he seen a woman with such courage, such daring, such conviction.

She'd willingly sacrificed her own job to defend the unfortunate young man with the limp. Admiration welled up in him.

Miranda Steele was amazing.

Friday night in her jail cell, when she turned the tables on him and peppered him with questions, he'd felt disconcerted. Chagrined she'd gotten information out of him first. Then he'd realized what he'd found.

She was creative. Bright. Perceptive. Instinctive. With the tenacity of a rabid bloodhound. Qualities you couldn't teach.

True, his background search on her revealed she had a record, was a drifter with a spotty work history. Facts that usually eliminated a prospect. But he'd decided to waive that rule in her case. He knew talent. He aimed to recruit the best. It was how he'd built the Parker Agency into the best investigative firm in the state, possibly the country.

He had to have her. As a recruit, that was. Miranda Steele would make an excellent trainee.

He couldn't have been prouder of Antonio for his work in the courtroom if he were his own son. After the skillful defense attorney called this morning to tell him the charges against her had been dropped, he'd wrestled with the idea awhile, then decided to visit the irascible Ms. Steele to discuss a position with the Agency. He'd found her here and decided to observe her working for a bit, wait until she took a break.

He'd observed her, all right.

Once more, he raised his binoculars and watched her leave the job site. Her stride was decisive, confident. Not at all like someone who'd just been dismissed from a position. She'd lost her hair band in the fracas and the breeze played with her wild, dark curls, brushing them against her face as she walked. Her lean, trim muscles were shiny with sweat. Her dark tank top revealed the outline of firm breasts. Despite her bravado, she had a touch of feminine air about her.

He thought of her search for her daughter. In the prison, he'd seen the letter from The Seekers she'd told him about. In his opinion, it had been written by an angry child to get back at her parents. He'd worked missing persons cases and found them enormously frustrating. Finding an adopted thirteen-year-old was…impossible. His heart went out to her. He'd make a few inquiries, just to satisfy himself, and he'd put the Agency's equipment at her disposal.

Across the street, he watched her climb aboard the transport truck. The determined look on her face moved him. Even Antonio might not have freed her if it hadn't been for the character witness she'd rescued at The Gecko Club.

Yet another case of defending the defenseless.

Was that trait, that inability to leave well enough alone, the reason Miranda Steele had been in so much trouble over the years? A warm feeling stirred inside him. He'd been in trouble himself for similar actions. She was something of a kindred spirit, then.

What could she be with a little training? The thought made his heart smile. A bright spot after Sylvia's death, after Madison's murder and the sense of failure that haunted him just now.

The lumbering transport truck took off, spun around the job site, and pulled into traffic.

Parker turned the ignition, backed out of his parking spot.

She'd be heading home, no doubt. He had her address from the police report. He'd beat her there. He was sorry she'd lost her job, but at the same time, he was relieved.

Now she had no reason to turn him down.

CHAPTER TEN

Miranda turned off Peachtree Road and into the Colonial Towers parking lot, pulled her old blue Lumina into a spot and turned off the car. Feeling a little lost, she sat awhile, staring at the neatly trimmed hedges of the yard, the sun teasing out their bright green color. Things weren't really that bad, were they?

It didn't really matter that she was broke. That she'd just gotten fired for beating up her boss. That she'd been arrested three days ago on suspicion of murder. That she'd held a dead girl in her arms. That after more than a month in Buckhead, she'd gotten nowhere in her attempts to find Amy. It was just another ordinary week.

Somehow, she wasn't convinced.

With a groan, she pulled her keys out of the ignition and got out of the car. It wasn't as if the job on the road crew was her life. Like most jobs she'd held over the past thirteen years, it was pretty boring. Just something to keep a paycheck coming in. To prove she could survive.

She would survive. She always did. And somehow, somewhere, she'd find Amy.

First things first. She locked her car and looked up at the tall, red brick towers of her apartment building. Rent was due in a couple of days. She had to get another job soon.

She headed down the sidewalk, positioning her door key firmly between two fingers, an old habit a self-defense instructor had taught her. Turning the corner, she sensed a presence. Nerves on edge, she looked up, stopped in her tracks.

Dressed in a light tan suit, looking just as suave and confident as he had in his tuxedo the other night, was Wade Russell Parker the Third. Arms crossed over his broad chest, he stood leaning against the tall, white, Southern-style column at the entrance of her building, just as casual as in the jail where she first laid eyes on him.

What did he want? She sucked in her breath, irritated she had to pass him to get inside, and started up the steps. "You lose something around here, Mister?"

His brows shot up, then he straightened his shoulders, as if welcoming her challenge. "Good afternoon to you, too, Ms. Steele. Actually, I was wondering if I could discuss something with you."

Now she got it. "Pro bono," her ass. Parker had footed the tab for the lawyer this morning. He was here to collect. That was all she needed.

She turned to face him. "How'd you know where I live?" Probably got it from his cop buddies or Estavez.

"I have my ways." He nodded toward the building. "Nice place."

"It was the cheapest I could find in the area." As in, *I don't have any money*. She sorted out her keys. Should have known she couldn't trust a lawyer.

He stepped toward the doorway, partially blocking her access, and frowned. "I didn't think Colonial Towers allowed pets."

She looked up into that determined face, took a step back. "Huh?"

"You know, the one you lost the other night. What was his name? Scruffy?"

Man, he knew how to rub it in. She went to the steps and sat down, put her face in her hands. She was grateful, after all. "Okay. I owe you for sending the defense attorney to court for me."

"Don't mention it." He sat down beside her.

Well, she'd never dealt with a better-looking, sexier bill collector. She blew out a breath. "How much do you want?" He'd have to take installments. Low ones.

"Want?"

She turned to face him and thought of Joan Fanuzzi drooling over his picture in the paper. Couldn't blame her a bit. God, he was handsome. "To pay for the mouthpiece this morning."

"Ah." He chuckled, then regarded her with those intense gray eyes. "I thought we could work out an arrangement."

She tensed. "What do you have in mind?"

"I thought you might be able to do me a service."

Her chest rumbled. Just because he was rich and good-looking didn't mean he could take whatever he wanted from her. She curled her lip at him. "Look, bud. I don't care how much that fancy Latin lawyer cost. I don't pay for favors with my body."

He blinked, then his lips twitched as he tried not to laugh. "Not that type of service, Ms. Steele. The fact is I was impressed Friday night when you told me about your search for your daughter. I could use someone with your persistence and ingenuity in my office."

She blinked back at him. "You want to *hire* me?"

"That's right." He leaned a little closer. "Are you looking for work?"

Something in his tone made her wary. "I don't type. I don't really like office work."

Parker studied the way her dark hair framed her angular face. Her long, sharp lashes, those deep blue eyes. The defiant way she held her chin. He sensed vulnerability in her, despite her bravado. His gaze swept over her throat, the muscled contours of her arms, the way her tank top hugged her breasts. And he was overcome with the urge to cup them in his hands. His own reaction irritated him. He didn't fondle employees.

He inhaled, shook his head. "Not an administrative position. As it happens, I'm short an investigator. One of my associates has just left my agency, and I'm promoting another to a case I was working on."

"So?"

"So I have an entry level slot as a detective open."

Miranda stared at him, her mouth open. What was he smoking? Was this his idea of a joke? "Thanks, but no thanks," she sneered.

His classically shaped brow rose. "Then I assume you're happy in your current job?"

She eyed him with distrust, watched a wisp of salt-and pepper hair fall over his forehead, which made something below her navel twitch. Which really annoyed her. He might be able to get her address from his cop friends at the station, but he couldn't know she'd gotten fired. It had just happened.

"You want to hire *me* as a private eye?" She snorted. "Right."

"I've never been more serious."

She gave him a scowl. Now why in the world would Wade Parker want to hire her as a detective? The only experience she'd had was watching CSI and reading a couple Spenser novels. If this were a real job, no doubt, he'd have her filing case files. "I'm not the type for office work. I can't sit behind a desk. I have to be outside."

"Oh, a nature girl?"

"Something like that."

"Blue skies, fresh air?"

"You got it."

"Is that why you chose a job on the Interstate inhaling gas fumes and asphalt all day?"

She glowered at him. "How do you know what I breathe in all day?"

He smiled. "Conditions in my office are much more comfortable. But many of our associates spend quite a bit of time on the street."

His evasiveness was pissing her off. "Answer my question. How'd you know what I do?"

He just grinned.

"You saw it on the police report at the station, right?"

His smile widened. "You've got raw talent, Ms. Steele. And from what I just saw on I-85, you've got a lot of intestinal fortitude, as well."

Intestinal fortitude? "I-85?"

"You took on a bruiser of a woman twice your size. You almost had her. Would have, if the supervisor hadn't pulled you off of her."

He saw what happened on the road crew? Her jaw clenched. "You spied on me?"

His sexy smile was as sugary as peach pie with a glass of sweet tea on the side. "Covert surveillance is one of the techniques you'll learn when you come to work for me."

Anger flushed through her. "Nosiness run in your blood, Mr. Fancy-Ass PI? You've got a lot of nerve, buster." She got up, stomped up the stairs, fumbled with her keys.

He rose and put his hands in his pockets, chuckling. "It probably does. I'd say it's in yours, too. Spying on young girls late at night to find information." He clucked his tongue.

He really knew how to turn the screws. She spun around, ready to spit out a string of cuss words. Was that admiration dancing in his eyes?

Whatever it was, it disarmed her. "Look, I'm not a detective."

"It's a trainee position. You'll learn to be one."

She didn't want training. That sounded like ties, like something that might keep her here for years. Why couldn't she find the key to the door? "I only take physical jobs. I like to stay in shape."

"We have a gym. In fact I require regular workouts. My team has to stay in top condition."

She smiled sweetly at him. "Then it shouldn't be much effort for you to walk back to your car and go away. I'm tired of your jokes."

"It's no joke, Ms. Steele." His voice was dark and low. With a determined expression, he leaned toward her. "You could look for your daughter."

Now he had her attention. "Look for my daughter?"

"We have state of the art computer equipment, lightning fast Internet connections, access to databases that you don't know about."

"Yeah?" She eyed his expensive suit. Okay, this detective was a little more successful than most. Maybe this job of his could help her find Amy. Plus he had all those fancy rich friends. He could be a regular database of information himself.

But what would he want in return? "I don't think so. Wouldn't work out." She reached for the door handle. God, she still didn't have the right key. Where was it?

He pointed to the silver one with the hexagon head. "I believe it's that one." His face turned cold. "Very well, Ms. Steele. You certainly don't have to take this job. But the more time I have to spend looking for a recruit, the less I'll have to find Madison Taggart's killer."

Her hand dropped to her side as the image of the poor dead girl flooded her mind. She thought of her grieving parents. She wanted to help put that murderer away.

"I hope I can do that before he strikes again."

What did he say? She glared at him. "Strikes again?"

He gazed out onto the street where cars were passing, his face hard as flint. "The placement of the body, the ribbon around her neck, everything points to a ritualistic murder. A signature. A serial killing. Madison was his first victim. There will probably be more."

Anxiety prickled her whole body. Her mind raced. Amy could be out there in one of those mansions. If that killer were targeting girls like Madison Taggart, none of them would be safe until he was put away.

And what about Madison's poor mother? She felt for the father, too, but the mother's grief really got to her. Miranda'd had thirteen years of heartache, but nothing like the finality of death. She'd do anything to ease that woman's pain.

She held up a hand. "Okay. That's enough." She still wasn't interested in being a detective, but if she could do something to help put that killer away, she'd give it a whirl. "Since I'm in a bind and you seem to want me so badly, I'll take your stupid job."

He smiled sincerely. "I've never been more flattered." He reached out for her hand.

His strong fingers slipped around hers, and for a moment, she thought he was going to kiss it, like some aristocratic archduke from the last century. Instead, he just shook it, lingering with a sexy gleam in his eye. It was the most sensual handshake she'd ever experienced in her life, a seductive jolt akin to sticking your finger in a light socket.

"It's been a pleasure doing business with you, Ms. Steele. Be at my office nine sharp tomorrow morning."

It took a moment to find her voice again. "Great. Where's your office?"

"It's on my card," he whispered as he let her hand drop.

Miranda resisted the urge to cradle her palm. "Your card?" She laughed with a shrug. "I kind of tore it up and flushed it down the toilet. Sorry."

A scowl of displeasure crossed his face as he reached into his coat pocket. Then stopped, stood there with challenge dancing in his attractive gray eyes.

"You were going to give me another?"

"Another card?"

"Yeah." What else did he have in mind?

He shook his head. "No, I don't think so."

"No?"

He grinned and turned away. "It won't be hard to find my office. Consider it your first test."

Leaving her with her mouth open, he walked down the sidewalk, got in his car.

Dumbfounded and still a little dizzy from his charm, she stood on the steps and watched him drive off.

Damn if that wasn't the strangest job interview she'd ever had. Shaking herself, she turned and reached for the apartment house door, inserted the hexagon key in the lock.

So now she was a detective. She wondered how long that would last.

CHAPTER ELEVEN

Of course it wasn't hard to find. She wasn't a nincompoop, after all. The Parker Agency had a small, tasteful site on the Internet with a phone number for a private consultation. She called it and got the address from a recorded message. Fifteenth floor of the Imperial Building.

Just before nine the next morning, she stood in a crowded parking lot on Piedmont Road gazing up. The Imperial Building wasn't in the seedy part of town she'd expected. It was right in the middle of Buckhead's posh commercial center. Constructed in steel and swanky aquamarine glass, the fancy structure rose to a cloudless blue sky, about to the height of the stack of bills she had coming due.

If she were lucky, maybe she could hold onto this job for a couple of weeks and pay some of them before Parker realized she was no detective and kicked her out. And maybe in the meantime, she could learn something about local adopted thirteen-year-olds who lived in mansions.

She raked her fingers through her hair, which she'd worn down. That might have been a mistake. Already, the humidity was playing havoc with it. This morning, she'd gone through her drawers and found some makeup to wear, gone through her closet and put on the fanciest tank top she had. A light blue print with spaghetti straps and a Y back. Okay, it was a little tight. And it had a stain, but only a small one and it was on the side. Her jeans were a little frayed at the knees. But that was the style, wasn't it? She'd even found some old hoop earrings.

She looked down at herself. Well, this was as good as it gets. Mustering her courage, she took a deep breath and headed for the silver revolving doors.

On the fifteenth floor, the elevators opened with a soft ping and Miranda stepped out. This was Parker's office? She was expecting some cramped hole-in-the-wall with bad furniture, like in a dime detective novel.

Instead, the fancy décor sang out wealth and success. The building's color scheme echoed in the satiny blue-and-gray tones of the carpet, the walls, the paintings. Tall potted palms sat in the corners. At the far end was a huge rosewood counter, semi-circular, where a lone receptionist sat. Big silver letters on the wall over her head read, "The Parker Investigative Agency." Guess she was in the right place.

She made her way to the desk, feeling like she was about to audition for a part in a movie.

The receptionist was young and thin with the figure of a fashion model. Done up like one, too. Her hair sported several shades of brown and auburn, and was pulled back in a sleek do with fancy bronze barrettes. Her chic, silky blouse mirrored the décor. Silver beads dangled from her earlobes. Miranda could smell her ultra-expensive perfume.

The mouthpiece of a headset curved along her cheek. Busy answering the phone, the woman ignored her. "Good morning. The Parker Agency," she said mechanically. How did the callers tell her from the recording? "I'm sorry, he's in a meeting. Can I take a message?"

She typed swiftly on a computer. "You're welcome." Next call. "Good morning. The Parker Agency."

Business must be good. Miranda waited about five minutes.

Finally, the model-receptionist turned to her. She blinked as if she hadn't noticed Miranda standing there. She cleared her throat. "Good morning. How may I help you?"

Miranda shifted her weight. "Uh, I'm here to see Wade Parker."

"One moment please." She turned back to the phone. "Good morning. The Parker Agency."

This could take a while. Miranda wandered over to a coffee table and flipped through a magazine. The articles were about weight loss and plastic surgery.

After another five minutes, the receptionist spoke to her again. "I'm sorry, ma'am. Mr. Parker doesn't take walk-ins."

Miranda scowled. "Walk-ins?"

"You'll have to make an appointment," she said stiffly.

"I'm here about a job."

She blinked again, recovered. "We don't have any openings right now, but you can fill out an application." Gracefully she reached for a clipboard with papers and a pen attached and pushed it across the glossy desk.

Miranda stepped up, glanced down at the clipboard and pursed her lips. No openings? After all that arm-twisting yesterday? Maybe she'd failed the test. Maybe she had the wrong Parker Agency. Atlanta was a big place after all. "This office belongs to Wade Parker, doesn't it?"

The receptionist looked up from her keyboard. "Yes."

"Mr. Wade Russell Parker, the Third?"

She frowned in confusion. "Yes, of course."

"Just checking." She tried to keep her tone steady. "Mr. Parker was the guy who hired me. He told me to be here today."

The receptionist blinked again, robot-like. The phone rang. She pressed a button. "Good morning. The Parker Agency."

Hmph. She knew it was too good to be true.

She strolled back to the coffee table, spotted a newspaper. She flipped through it and found the job section. The least he owed her for her trouble. She tucked it under her arm and moved toward the door.

"Excuse me, Miss."

Miranda turned around. It wasn't the receptionist who had called her this time. It was a tall, thin woman standing in front of a side door that led to the inside. She had short blond hair and was dressed in a severe black summer suit and a starchy white blouse with no frills.

Miranda grimaced at the receptionist. "No need to call Security. I'm leaving."

"Did you say Mr. Parker hired you?" The blond woman studied Miranda with dark, suspicious eyes.

Now it was her turn to blink. "Yeah, that's right."

"Mr. Wade Parker?"

She was still pretty sure that was the name on the card she'd flushed in her jail cell. "Yeah. The Third."

Her eyes narrowed, growing more guarded. For a minute, Miranda thought she was back in the courtroom. "Your name?"

"Miranda Steele."

"Wait here one moment, Ms. Steele."

The security woman stepped into a small room on the side and closed the door. Miranda tiptoed up to it. It had a glass window on the top. She peeped through it and saw the young woman on the phone, her mouth going a mile a minute. She seemed really irritated.

After a minute, she hung up and opened the door.

Miranda turned away and pretended to admire one of the paintings.

The woman glared at her with a very fake smile. She looked like she had just swallowed an ice cube. She took a few steps, grabbed another clipboard off the desk, and opened the door she had come out of. "Come with me, Ms. Steele."

The door led to a wide, open space filled with a large bank of office cubes covered with canvas in a variation of the blue-and-silver of the reception area. The blond woman led her down a long stretch that made a sort of corridor with the wall.

As Miranda hustled to keep up with her escort's quick steps, she could hear muted voices, phones ringing softly, and keyboards being tapped. They turned a corner, which held another potted plant, went down another long passage along another set of cubes.

How many employees did this guy have? He was a private eye. She didn't think he owned a freaking corporation.

Finally, the woman came to a halt at a cube in a corner facing a row of windows. She gestured. "Take a seat in here."

Miranda peeked inside. There was a plain desk, a chair, some empty bookshelves. "Sure." With a shrug, she stepped into the small space and plopped into the chair.

The blonde examined her as closely as marble-eyed Lieutenant Erskine had back in the police station a few nights ago. "What's your background?"

"Background?"

"Your job history. What qualifications do you have?" With her black suit against the light, she looked even more severe.

Okay, she wasn't Security. She was HR. Miranda lifted a shoulder. "For the past ten years, I've mostly worked construction jobs."

Confusion washed over her face. "What kind of construction jobs?"

No reason to fib about it. "A little of everything. Road crews, demolition, sheet metal fabrication, brick masonry."

"In Atlanta?"

"Heck no. A lot of places. Pennsylvania. Alabama. New York. I was on an oil rig in Texas a few years back."

The woman swallowed. "Any certifications?"

"I don't care for schools and tests." She watched the blonde's lips twitch. Yep, that's right, lady. I'm a dyed-in-the-wool underachiever. Didn't need fancy pieces of paper to boost her self-esteem.

She shoved the clipboard she'd grabbed from the receptionist desk in front of Miranda. "You'll have to fill this out."

Miranda took the pen with a great lack of enthusiasm. "Okay."

The woman tapped her foot, then turned. "I'll be right back." She headed down the corridor in a different direction.

With a sigh, Miranda printed her name on the top line of the form. It would be good practice for the next place she tried.

Parker stood at the table in his office staring down at maps, interview transcripts, crime scene photos. Precious few pieces of a puzzle that, so far, led nowhere.

Yesterday evening had been heart wrenching. He'd re-interviewed Jackson and Cloris, witnessing again his friends' agonizing pangs of grief that he couldn't assuage. He had gone through Madison's room again, her closets, her bed, her computer, hoping Hosea and his team had missed something. There was nothing. The girl hadn't been conversing with anyone but close friends over the Internet lately. He spoke with Tiffany Todd and Ashley Ingram again, but they had nothing to add.

He picked up a photo of the scene. Compared to the many murders he'd investigated over the years, the killing had not been particularly gruesome. With a sharp twist of a rope, perhaps with a stick of some sort, she'd been strangled, the life snuffed out of her small body in a matter of seconds. Had she been awake? Had she felt pain? How long had those last few minutes seemed to her?

Such questions always haunted him. Now more than ever.

He thought of Jackson's frantic voice on the phone last week, telling him his daughter was missing, begging him to do something. Along with himself, the Special Victims Crime Unit and the GBI had been called.

They had all been too late.

He ran his hands over his face. The funeral was tomorrow. It would be a tearful, heartrending affair. He was too involved emotionally. He needed distance. He'd have to dig up some objectivity somewhere. Fast.

The door to his office opened. Without looking up, he recognized Gen's footsteps. She stopped at the end of his table and stood there, tapping her foot. She'd never been the patient type.

He glanced up and smiled at her with tenderness. A scowl spoiled her pretty face. "What is it?"

Her mouth twisted back and forth for several moments. She paced to his desk, raised her arms in exasperation. "Far be it from me to question my father's decisions, but what the hell are you doing, Dad?"

He chuckled. "And you would be referring to…?"

"You know very well what I'm referring to."

He looked down at the autopsy report. "I'm a good detective, but I'm not clairvoyant."

She huffed. "I'm talking about that woman you told me to put in a cube. Miranda Steele."

"Ah, Ms. Steele." His heart brightened. His reluctant trainee had shown up. So the challenge of finding his office hadn't kept her from backing out after all. "I'm glad she's here."

Gen smirked. "Here in all her glory. Ratty hair, frayed jeans, a flimsy tank top, and hoop earrings. Sybil said she looked like a streetwalker who'd come to take advantage of your generous nature."

He stiffened. "Our receptionist is quite presumptuous."

"She's perceptive. I trust Sybil's judgment."

Parker shook his head and laughed quietly at his only child's irritation. He'd brought in Gen to manage new recruits just two years ago when she earned her MBA. She was perfect for the job, but she could be a little rigid at times. She still needed to learn there were occasions for bending the rules. "I wouldn't let Ms. Steele's dress habits bother me."

"They do bother me."

He picked up one of the transcripts of an interview. "We'll clean up her appearance."

"It's not just her appearance. Where did you meet her? How long have you known her?"

"In the area. And not long."

Gen's eyes flashed at his evasive answer. She moved to the window and let out a frustrated grunt. "Dad, she has no qualifications. No police work, no military experience. What are you thinking?"

Parker turned the page of the transcript. "Ms. Steele has qualifications. They just aren't readily apparent."

"Such as?"

"Raw talent. Guts."

Gen groaned. "Dad, she's worked constructions jobs. Where in the world did you meet a woman like that? Why is she filling out an application for an Investigator in Training?"

"Because I recruited her." He set down the papers and met her worried gaze. "Are you questioning my judgment, dear?"

Her dark eyes narrowing, she moved toward him and pointed a finger in his chest. "Don't tell me you've got the hots for her. Isn't it enough that I have to put up with the social climbers who chase you all the time?"

The hots? Parker glanced over at the picture he still kept on his credenza. He smiled tenderly at the dark blond beauty with the haunting eyes that he'd fallen in love with so many years ago. Sylvia. His wife. He hadn't quite forgiven her for the hole she'd left in his heart when she died. But it took time to heal after twenty-two years of marriage.

Gen favored her mother a bit in her features, but not in personality. Sylvia had been quiet, intellectual, well-bred. The feminine type. She had taught English Lit at Agnes Scott College. No one was like Sylvia. No one could live up to her standard. If there was a woman who could match her, he hadn't found her yet. Gen needn't fret. No one could replace her mother in his heart.

He leaned over and kissed his daughter on the cheek. "You have nothing to worry about, Precious."

She smiled but brushed her cheek. "Not in the office, Dad."

"Give Ms. Steele a chance. You were upset when I brought the young Antonio Estavez home years ago and now he's like a brother to you."

"Tony's not like—" she stopped. "Is that it? Is she a charity case? Sybil was right. She's twisted you around her little finger already."

He raised a brow. "No one twists me around their finger, Genevieve. My relationship with Ms. Steele is purely professional. And don't let her hear you call her a charity case. Or Antonio, for that matter." He picked up another photo of the crime scene. "What's our new recruit doing?"

"Still filling out the paperwork."

"Bring her back as soon as she's finished."

She put her hands on her hips. "To see you? Really, Dad—"

"Need I remind you that this is my company?"

He watched her eyes flash. Gen liked running things her own way. She didn't relish the reminder that she wasn't in complete control. "Okay. But don't be surprised if she doesn't make it here." With a huff, she turned and went out the door.

Age, optional. Thirty-six.

Education. High school dropout. Okay, she'd gotten her GED and had some college, but why complicate things?

List residences for the past five years.

Miranda thought a moment, put down a date, then wrote, "Central Park Zoo." A couple of years ago, she'd spent a night there on a bench when she was between jobs and couldn't pay her rent. It was pretty safe for New York.

She looked up and saw a pair of dark brown eyes peeking around the cube's opening. "Hi there."

Another pair of eyes, green ones, joined the first. "Howdy, ma'am."

The green-eyed owner stepped out of his hiding place. He was a tall, fairly young guy dressed in a lightweight navy blazer with tan slacks, plain blue tie. His brown hair was combed to the side. He shoved his hands in his pockets and turned his head away, like he was afraid someone would catch them. "Are you a new recruit?" he whispered.

More or less. "Yeah," she whispered back. "Who are you?"

He straightened his tie and let his voice return to normal volume. It was deep, with an accent that sounded Texan. "I'm Curt Holloway and this is Dave Becker." He pointed to the brown-eyed one, a short man in a gray suit, maybe a couple years older than the green-eyed guy.

His brown eyes were big and expressive, accompanied by thick eyebrows and a big nose. He wore his dark hair in a crew cut that made his nose look even bigger.

"We're a team," said Becker in a nasal-sounding voice that could have been annoying, but right now sounded kind of cute. He shot his thumb toward Holloway. "Started on the same day, me and him."

"You don't say." She held out a hand. "I'm Miranda Steele."

They both shook it.

"Glad to know you," Becker grinned.

"We've been here a couple of weeks now," Holloway said, glancing over the cubicle wall, like a lookout. "We're IITs."

"IITs?"

"Investigators in Training. Newbies. Also sometimes affectionately known as IdIoTs." He punched the letters as he spoke the word. "But we haven't started formal training yet."

"I see."

He reached for his lapel. "Me, I did a stint in the Marines. Becker here, he was in Collections a couple of years."

The short guy smirked. "Two years waist deep in mind-numbing bull hockey waiting to get into the Parker Agency. It was worth every minute."

"No shit?"

Becker made a coughing sound. "Sure. The waiting list to get in this place is as long as your arm."

It was? Miranda stiffened.

"What's your background?" Holloway asked.

"Uh." She shifted her weight and thought about her conversation with Parker on her doorstep. "Lately, I've been doing surveillance."

"Really? What kind?"

Talking to kids late at night and getting arrested for murder. "Private."

Becker's eyes glowed. "Tell us about it."

She leaned back in her chair and cleared her throat. "Well, I couldn't do that. You know, then I'd have to kill you."

"Oh, right." He nodded, trying to look professional.

"You're gonna love it here," Holloway smiled. "The Parker Agency has one of the best training programs in the southeast for PIs. A lot of people go on to work for the CIA, the FBI. But then a lot of them stay with the Silver Fox."

"Silver Fox?"

"A nickname they call the old man."

"Old man?"

"The man himself. Parker."

She nodded like she'd heard it before. "Oh, right."

"Did Gen give you your schedule yet?" Becker asked eagerly. "I saw her bring you in."

"Gen?"

He squinted. "The tall lady with the short blond hair and the face like a bulldog?"

Holloway laughed. "That's Gen, all right. Her name's Genevieve. We call her The General. She's as tough as my old drill sergeant."

"I kinda gathered that."

Becker waved a hand. "Don't let her scare you. She just doesn't want us to think Parker plays favorites. She's Parker's daughter, you know."

Miranda had to keep her chin from dropping. Parker had a daughter? That usually implied a mother. She looked down at her application. Suddenly she wanted to tear it up and stomp out the door. What did this fancy pants gumshoe want with her, anyway? If he tried any monkey business, he'd find himself pretty sore between his legs.

"Don't you two have some phone calls to make?" The bark came from down the corridor. Gen.

Holloway nearly jumped out of his skin. "Yes, ma'am," he said in a voice that had suddenly gone up two notches.

Becker saluted. "We'll get right on that, Ms. Parker." He whispered to Miranda. "Talk to you later, Steele. Glad to have you aboard."

Then the pair scurried off down the corridor.

Gen scowled after them, then turned to Miranda. "Come with me," she growled.

"Where we going?"

"You'll see."

CHAPTER TWELVE

She didn't expect Gen to take her to see Parker. The "Old Man." The "Silver Fox." It kind of felt like being sent to the principal's office. But Miranda changed her mind after her escort dropped her off and stomped away in a huff, and she stepped through the door.

This was no schoolhouse.

Parker's workspace was huge. Her whole studio apartment and maybe part of her neighbor's could fit inside it. The floor-to-ceiling windows that ran along two walls showcased a breathtaking view of the city, with the sunlight flooding in, shining on the glassy furniture, making everything sparkle like diamonds. Done in the same blue-and-silver décor as the rest of the floor, the place had an unearthly glow. Like a little slice of Heaven.

And there was Michael the Archangel himself, staring at her, his hair perfect, his arms folded over his chest, wearing a blue cashmere suit and a silk tie. "Silver Fox," huh? This angel had horns.

His expression seemed dazed. Admiration? Regret? Or was he just horny?

He shot her that sexy grin. "So you decided to show up."

"Yeah." For another minute, she gawked at his place. Computers were everywhere. On the wall was a huge map, projected from a machine hooked to a laptop on the table. An aerial view of trees and houses.

"Welcome aboard. How's your first day so far?"

She ran her hand over the transparent surface of his desk. Smooth as glass. It was glass. "Peachy. It's just that daughter of yours thinks I don't belong here."

He chuckled to himself. "You've already discovered she's my daughter."

"Yeah, and I kind of share her opinion about me."

He turned away, pressed a key on the laptop.

"Look, Parker, I don't know what you want, but—"

He gestured toward the map on the wall, which he'd just enlarged. "Do you recognize it?"

She stopped talking and squinted at the projected image, noticed the outline of the streets. The landscaping seemed familiar. She made out the curves of Sweet Hollow Lane. "Mockingbird Hills."

"Precisely. The crime scene." He picked up a laser pen from the table and pointed it at the map. "The Ingram mansion is here. The Van Aarle place here. And the body was found here." His deep sigh echoed with grief and frustration.

Miranda squinted at the map. It looked funny from overhead, but she recognized the tree line and the small clearing at its edge. "I found her right there." She shuddered, remembering the feel of Madison Taggart's cold body in her arms.

"Yes." His voice had turned grim.

She gestured to the papers piled on the table. "What's all this?"

"Evidence. What we have so far." He put down the laser pen, picked up a few files, handed them to her. "These are the dossiers on Madison's friends."

"You want me to look at them?"

"Please."

Gingerly she took them, opened them one at a time. There were statements from Tiffany Todd and Ashley Ingram, assorted notes, school photos. She scanned them, recognized the young faces she'd seen in the Ingrams' driveway. Then she opened the third file. There was another picture. She held it out to Parker. "Who's this?"

"Wendy Van Aarle. Ashley Ingram's neighbor. They all attend Dogwood Academy, where Madison went to school."

Dogwood Academy. One of the ritzy private schools where she'd tried to get a job when she first got to Atlanta.

And Wendy Van Aarle. The girl who lived in the mansion where Madison was found. The girl the other two were taunting that night. Miranda studied the photo. Wendy was all in black. Must be into one of the fads that appealed to kids her age. Dark hair, dark clothes, dark makeup. Sad, hollow eyes. A surly look on her cheerless face.

She stared at the picture, and a sledgehammer hit her in the chest.

Wendy looked a lot like…herself…. *Amy?*

She scrutinized her throat. It was covered with black lace. Why was every girl's neck covered?

She forced herself to exhale. It didn't matter. Wendy couldn't be Amy. That would be too easy. She could just imagine the look in Parker's eyes when he told her, no, Wendy wasn't adopted. She didn't bother to ask.

She closed the files and set them down on the glassy table.

"The girls' testimonies corroborate each other," Parker said. "Madison went to school as usual on Friday a week ago. That night she and Ashley Ingram went to Tiffany Todd's house for a sleep over. She left the next morning and walked home by herself."

"And then?"

"She never got there. Cloris Taggart, her mother, came home from shopping early that afternoon, expecting to find her daughter. She wasn't in her room or anywhere in the house or the yard. Cloris called Madison's friends. They told her they hadn't seen her since that morning."

"That's when they called you?"

"They called the police. Later that night Jackson Taggart called me." Parker picked up another document and handed it to her. "Have you ever seen a coroner's report?"

Miranda shook her head. "Uh-uh." She'd always been curious about such things. Long ago, when Leon got his job on the police force, she'd asked him about autopsies and such, but he'd always said she was too stupid to understand them.

She took the paper, scanned the pages. It was mostly medical mumbo-jumbo. She winced when she saw the cause of death, remembering that the poor little girl had been strangled with a rope.

"Non-contributory drugs present," she read. "GHB? Isn't that a date rape drug?"

Parker nodded. "It's easy to get. The killer probably used it to sedate her. There was no sign of sexual assault."

Somehow that news gave Miranda some relief. But how could that sick bastard use a date rape drug on a little girl?

She read more. The report described the clothes Madison was found in, the state of her body. The rain had washed away any fingerprints, including hers, she supposed. "It says there was a substance on her face, neck and arms." That was right. She'd forgotten it till now, but she'd felt something sticky on the girl and had wondered what it was.

"An ointment of some sort. Thank God, there was just enough left on the body after the rain for the lab to analyze."

"Cooking oil mixed with sea-salt, rosemary, sage," she read, then looked up at Parker with a grimace. "Sounds like a salad dressing."

"Guess again."

Her mind raced. "Some kind of ritual?"

"A purification rite of some sort, perhaps. As though it's the first in a series. Or made to look like one, along with the ribbon around her neck."

The ribbon that covered the bruises on her neck that had made Miranda think she was Amy. She put the paper down. These details were giving her the creeps.

She held up a hand. He'd gone far enough. She'd better set him straight and get out of here. "Look, Parker. I don't know what you want with me, but let's just can the shop talk."

He eyed her with a penetrating look. "You don't believe I'm serious about your job, do you?"

She glanced away to avoid his gaze and spotted a woman's picture on the credenza. She moved to it, picked it up. The woman was beautiful. Her soft, expressive brown eyes seemed to speak to her from the photograph. "This your wife?"

He stiffened. "Yes."

Pretty bold to keep a picture of her around while he was intending to cheat on her. "You're married. So what do you want with me?"

He came around the table, stopped before he got too close. Her stubborn distrust of him irritated him. "Do you think I brought you here under false pretenses, Ms. Steele?"

She pointed toward the door. "I just met two guys out there, one with military experience, the other who'd done collections or something. They told me there's a long line of folks waiting to work for you. You don't need me. Why did you bring me here?"

"You have a rather low opinion of your own talents, don't you?"

She blinked at him. She could handle a rude sexual slur, a comment you'd hear in a bar. She didn't know what to do with a compliment in an office. No boss had ever told her she had talent. But it wasn't a question of talent. It was a question of experience. And of inclination. "I know who I am," she told him flatly. "And what I'm not."

"I think you're wrong." He took the picture out of her hands and gently set it down. "And as for this photo, this is my *late* wife. She died three years ago. Ovarian cancer."

Parker watched her, letting the impact of his words sink in, studying the light from the window play with the color of her dark hair. Her brows knitted with a mixture of embarrassment and sympathy. She had a sensitive side, for all her toughness. Seeing it touched him.

Miranda flinched. Parker's words had hit her like a punch in the chest. "I'm sorry." It was all she could think to say.

"It was a natural mistake." He put his hand gently on her shoulder. It was the most sensual touch she'd ever felt. Maybe she was the one with the problem.

He stepped back, folded his arms and studied the aerial photo on the wall again. "Now that we understand one another better, let's get to the business at hand. We can't get the whole picture from this image. I'd say a visit to the crime scene is in order. Would you like to join me?"

He wanted to take her back to that place? "What for?"

"More clues, of course."

She grimaced. "I don't know anything about looking for clues."

"You're here to learn. And you could help. Something there might jog your memory. You might be able to think of something you saw or heard the night you found the body. Something the police missed."

She held up a hand.

He studied her with tenderness. "You don't have to go if it's too much for you."

Well, she wasn't a wimp. She gave him a sharp look. "Am I on the clock?"

"On the clock?"

"Am I getting paid for this?"

He chuckled. "Of course. I hired you. I don't break my word."

She hesitated. "When do I get to use your Internet connection? Your databases?" As soon as she had that kind of access, she could start looking for Amy again without drawing attention to herself. It would be worth it to stay.

"Soon. Would you accompany me to the crime scene?"

She ran her hand through her hair, scratching at her scalp. This whole thing was crazy. She wasn't any more a detective than the man in the moon. But if Parker wasn't trying to get in her pants, he must be bent on making her one.

She shifted her weight. Miranda Steele, private eye. Hmm. Not a bad ring to it. It wasn't like she had anything else to do. And she was getting paid.

Plus there was the off chance of doing something to help Madison Taggart's grief-stricken mother.

She turned to him with a shrug. "Sure. Why not?"

CHAPTER THIRTEEN

In mid morning traffic, it took only about twenty minutes to get to Mockingbird Hills. As they rounded the corner onto Sweet Hollow Lane in Parker's silver Mazda, the two mansions and their lush, rolling lawns came into view. In broad daylight, the bright colors of the weeping willows, dogwood and azaleas were dazzling.

Parker nodded toward a shiny red Jaguar in the Van Aarle's drive. "Look's like Shelby's home."

"Who?"

"Shelby Van Aarle."

That name sounded familiar. "The golf pro?"

"The same."

So the mansion was owned by that Van Aarle. "Did you grow up with him, too?"

Eyes narrowed, Parker perused the house. "No. The Van Aarles moved here several years ago."

She thought of the little girl with the sad, hollow eyes in the picture. "So Wendy Van Aarle is…"

"Correct. Shelby's daughter." Slowly, he rolled past the driveway. "Must be between tournaments."

She didn't see any activity. Van Aarle must have been inside polishing his trophies.

Parker pulled the car to the curb. "We'll head across the yard from here."

Guess Parker didn't want to be seen.

Miranda got out and followed him up the hill. Circumventing the landscaping, they made their way up over the crest and down again, until they came to the woods bordering the property, the place where she had tried to escape from Officer Chambers a couple nights ago.

The memory made her shiver, but now the grounds were as quiet as the eighteenth hole on a championship golf course. Or a cemetery. Birds sang in the pines and oak trees, as the boughs swayed back and forth in the gentle breeze. On the grass, a lone piece of yellow tape fluttered where the police had sectioned off the spot.

Miranda walked up to it and stared down at the bare patch under the trees. Though she didn't even know her, in her own way, she grieved for Madison Taggart. "Why would anyone kill a child?" she murmured, half to herself.

"That is the question, isn't it?" Parker said, sadness in his voice. He bent down. He had a silver carrying case with him. He laid it on the ground, snapped it open, took out some equipment, a pad, a pen. Then he rose and began to pace along the trees in a systematic line, stopping now and then to take a note.

Miranda followed along beside him, rubbing her arms. She watched him, amazed at the serious look on his handsome face. He was intent, focused. And a little bit driven, she thought. "The motive had to be money, right?"

"When Jackson called to report his daughter was missing, ransom crossed my mind." He trekked on.

Miranda took a step to catch up to him. "Lieutenant Erskine said the Taggarts are loaded." Like everybody around here.

He stopped, then moved another few paces, studying the ground. "They're fairly well off. Jackson is Chief of Staff at Saint Benedictine Hospital. Cloris comes from a prominent Atlanta family."

Chief of Staff. Wow. "And money was the motive?"

Parker shook his head. "Kidnapping for ransom is rarely committed these days due to stiff penalties. Madison's killer never even contacted her parents."

Oh. "So the motive for nabbing her was murder from the get go?"

"It looks that way."

But that didn't tell them the motive for the murder.

He'd gone several yards along the tree line by now. In the daylight, Miranda could see a small brook flowing through the undergrowth. If she had gone in there the other night, she might have been in Jackson Taggart's hospital nursing snake bites instead of being arrested for the murder of his daughter.

She watched him pace off the area, bend down, looking closely at the ground, rise again. After a few minutes, he stood still and stared across the water.

"What are you doing?"

"Looking for evidence."

"What kind of evidence?"

"Anything. Tracks. Broken glass. Jewelry. Anything the police might have missed and the rain didn't wash away." He put his hands on his hips. "Nothing worse than a contaminated crime scene," he muttered in a frustrated voice.

Guess she'd messed up some clues when she picked up the body, too. That thought didn't make her feel good.

"Keep your eyes open. See how sharp they are." He turned around. "Let's go over here."

She followed him, squinting at the grass, trying to see something that might not be there. Seemed like a waste of time.

When they got to the bare patch with the bit of yellow tape, he bent down and carefully ran a hand over it.

She crouched beside him. "It doesn't look like Madison was killed here."

He glanced up, surprise on his face. "Good observation. There are no signs of struggle. The knots around her wrists and ankles support that. They were too carefully tied to subdue a fighting victim."

"She'd been drugged with GHB."

"Correct." He seemed pleased she remembered that from the autopsy.

Miranda gazed around the area. "How did she get here, then?"

"Excellent question."

He stared into the forest. "These trees stretch on for about three acres until they reach the next neighborhood. What do you think? Did the killer come through the woods? Or from the street?"

She turned around and surveyed the hill. "The street seems more likely. He could have driven over the lawn."

"There were no tire tracks. Even the rain wouldn't have washed all of them away. That means she was probably carried."

"Or dragged."

"Perhaps. The killer, if he was working alone, had to be strong enough to lift, or drag, a ninety-pound thirteen-year-old. Most women aren't."

Miranda smirked. "I am."

He chuckled lightly. "I imagine you are."

"But it's at the top of my limit." She thought a moment. "What if he wasn't working alone?"

"A possible theory. But a serial killer would be unlikely to have an accomplice."

Sounded right. Again, she gazed up the hill toward the street. The murderer must have parked along the curb up there, where she'd been that night. Maybe he'd thought these woods were a good spot to dump the body. "So the killer was a man, working alone. He killed Madison somewhere else and carried her here."

"It may have happened that way," he corrected.

She frowned. "Didn't we just prove that?"

"It seems apparent. But what's apparent can be deceiving. It's important to stay open."

Stay open. Okay, she'd try to remember that. "Seems like he didn't hide the body very well. Anybody who came down the hill would have found it sooner or later."

Parker's face took on a pensive look. "He might have been interrupted. Or…"

"He wanted the body to be discovered."

He nodded. "For the attention." He reached for his carrying case. "A serial killer's profile can have many variables. Abusive childhood, violent or criminal history, belief in supernatural abilities. The reasons for their crimes range from experiences in prison to voices in the head telling them to do it. Possessed with a need to dominate their prey, they choose the vulnerable, the weak. There's usually a cooling off period between victims. After the fix wears off, they look for another."

She'd heard most of that on crime shows, but it all seemed different after holding the victim. So they might have a little time before he struck again. She rubbed her arms again. Parker's words were giving her the creeps.

Still crouching over the patch, he regarded her intently. "Do you remember anything from that night?"

She stared at the ground, then closed her eyes, for a moment reliving the horror she'd felt when she'd found Madison Taggart's body and thought it was Amy. The wetness of the rain against her, the feel of the twigs and pine straw as she pushed them away from the girl's clothes, the faint smell of scented oil. Shivering, she shook her head. "Nothing we don't already know."

Grimly, he nodded, then opened his case and took a small vial, lifted the lid.

"What's that for?"

"A dirt sample. The police have already found unidentified fibers on Madison's clothes. There may be more here."

"Oh."

He regarded her a moment. "You seem to be the type who learns by doing. Be my guest." He put the small bottle in her hand.

"Huh? What do I do with it?"

"Just dig around in the dirt and get a scoop. Enough for our lab to analyze."

"Your office has a lab?"

He nodded. "Not as large as the police department's or the GBI's, but we make do."

Might have known. It was good to be rich. She pointed to the ground. "Anywhere?"

"Anywhere that looks promising."

It all looked the same to her, but she picked a spot and skimmed the bottle along the earth until it was full.

"That's enough. Excellent work."

Guess she'd passed Playing in the Dirt 101. "Thanks." She handed the bottle to him.

As he reached for it, his fingers went around hers. She looked up and their eyes locked. Miranda's heart skipped a beat. Why did he have to be so good-looking? Her gaze wandered to his lips. What a sexy mouth he had. No wonder she had to fight the melting sensation every time he smiled at her. It was more than that. They shared an outrage over this crime, a desire to find the killer, that united them in a way she'd never known with another person.

"Good morning."

The shout came from the hill, the direction of the house.

With a start, Miranda let go of the bottle and struggled to get to her feet. She turned in time to see a figure at the top of the lawn's crest that led to the mansion.

Parker rose in one dignified move. "Shelby," he called out. "How are you?"

Shelby Van Aarle cantered down the hill, jogged over to them. "Parker, is that you?"

The two men shook hands like they were old buddies, but their body language told Miranda they didn't really like each other.

Van Aarle crossed his big, muscular arms over his broad chest. He was in good shape and wasn't a bit winded, but he seemed upset. "What are you doing here?"

"It's nice to see you, Shelby," Parker drawled in a neighborly air that dripped Southern hospitality, without answering the question. "What are you doing home this time of year?"

Van Aarle grinned and eyed Parker up and down. The dark, wavy hair framing his angular face was styled and tinted blond at the tips, like he'd just come from a session with Vidal Sassoon. To Miranda, his smile seemed as fake as a used car salesman's.

"I cancelled one of the events in my PGA Tour schedule when I heard what happened." He wiped the grin off his face, as if on cue. "I had to come home to be with Wendy. She's very upset."

Parker nodded. "As are all Madison's friends. It's difficult for young children to go through something like this. Is Iris home, too?"

"No. She's in Paris. Tied up in important meetings."

"I see." Parker turned to her. "Mrs. Van Aarle owns Iris Rose Cosmetics."

"Don't say." Miranda had seen commercials for the pricey makeup and lotions on TV but had never paid much attention. Dolling up with expensive powders and lipstick wasn't her thing. Guess a murder in her backyard wasn't enough to interrupt business.

"Excuse my lack of manners, Shelby." Parker gestured toward her. "This is Miranda Steele, my new associate."

Van Aarle reached out a hand, reluctantly, it seemed. But he kept his face in that TV interview expression. "Glad to meet you."

"Likewise." She shook his hand and watched his eyes. They had the same dark, deep set look of his daughter's. His hand was soft but felt dexterous. A golfer's hand. She thought about Fanuzzi saying it was one of the neighbors. She thought of Parker's question. Had the killer come from the woods or the street? Or had he come from…the house? With his athlete's body Van Aarle could certainly carry ninety pounds.

"So what are you doing here, Parker? The police were here all day yesterday. They already got everything they need."

Open, she told herself. Stay open. But Miranda saw a gleam of suspicion in Parker's eyes. "The Taggarts hired me when Madison disappeared a week ago. They asked me to stay on the case. Of course, our police department is thorough. I'm just double-checking their work."

Van Aarle grinned at Miranda. "Parker likes to one-up our chief police detective. You really get on Lieutenant Erskine's nerves, you know."

"Just a concerned citizen helping out."

Van Aarle shifted his weight. He seemed even more nervous. "Still, I'm going to have to ask you to leave."

Parker raised a brow. "Oh?"

"I'm having some business associates over and I don't want to call attention to…all this."

"We won't be in the way."

"Humor me. I'm a little superstitious."

Really? Did he hear voices in his head?

"I'm not known for bringing bad luck to the innocent, Shelby," Parker drawled.

He fidgeted. "C'mon, Parker. This whole thing is damned embarrassing. I just got rid of the last of the reporters yesterday."

Parker turned and eyed the wooded area. "You know, I grew up in this neighborhood, but I'm not sure where the property line is exactly."

Parker grew up here? No wonder he knew everybody.

Van Aarle inhaled stiffly. "It's my property, all right. I had a dispute with the Thompsons over it years ago when we first moved in. It's on the books, if you want to look it up at the courthouse. Your company does that sort of thing, doesn't it?"

Parker smiled and flipped his notepad shut. "I'll trust your word."

"So if you don't mind, my guests will be arriving soon."

Why was he in such a hurry to get rid of them? How could Parker let this guy push them around like that? Miranda had had enough. "Look, Van Aarle. We're investigating a crime scene."

Parker nudged her. "I think he knows that, Miranda."

"A little girl is dead."

"Excuse me." Gently, Parker took her by the arm and led her a few steps away. "We're not the police."

"So? He's still obstructing justice, isn't he?"

Parker shook his head. "We have no jurisdiction. If we stay here, he can have us taken in for trespassing. Would you like another night in jail?"

She rolled her eyes.

He turned back to Van Aarle. "We'll be happy to leave, Shelby, at your request. However I must point out that lack of cooperation can often be construed as guilt."

Van Aarle guffawed, struggling to keep his face camera-ready. "What are you saying, Parker?"

"I'm merely pointing out the facts."

His expression went blank. He slapped a hand against his chest. "Do you think *I* did it? Do you think I'm crazy enough to kill a neighbor girl and leave her body in my own backyard?"

Parker didn't blink. "Perhaps you were hoping for an insanity plea."

Van Aarle's perfect face turned into a red growl. "Get out of here, Parker. Now."

As smooth as silk, Parker packed up his things and guided Miranda back over the hill to his car. They got in and drove off.

Miranda squired in her seat. "We're leaving? Just like that?"

"Not quite."

In the next block, he circled around and drove back. Then he pulled over down the street from the mansion, just past a small bridge over the creek that ran through the area.

"Hand me those binoculars from the glove compartment."

Miranda grinned with glee as she opened the slot. "Now I see there's a method to your madness."

"Always is." He gave her a sexy wink and adjusted the binoculars.

After about ten minutes, a black BMW pulled up. A man in a dark suit got out.

"That's Edward Hayden. Investment Banker at CK&G."

Just as he got to the big front door, a white Lexus pulled up. Another suit got out.

"Oliver Chatham. One of the partners at Chatham, Grayson, and McFee. Antonio's law firm." Estavez, her new defense attorney.

At the doorstep, the two men shook hands and went inside.

Miranda cleared her throat. "Is there any rich, successful person in Atlanta you don't know, Parker?"

He lowered the binoculars pensively. "I can't think of one. I've found my connections to work to my advantage over the years."

She bet they had. And his sexy charm didn't hurt either. She wondered how many ladies he'd used it on since his wife's passing. She wondered why the thought made her suddenly uncomfortable. She dismissed it and stared at the house. "So Van Aarle's line about business associates was on the up-and-up. What's he meeting with an investment banker and a lawyer for?"

"There could be many reasons a man with a ten-million dollar annual income would meet with those types of professionals."

Miranda whistled. "Any of those reasons have to do with murder?"

"Indeterminate."

She turned to him. "You think Van Aarle's guilty, don't you?"

Parker's steel-colored eyes glowed with years of experience. "I suspect everyone. And no one. Right now, it's just fact-finding. At the beginning of any investigation, you can get lost in a sea of information. Each detail could be relevant or mean nothing. It's important not to let yourself jump to conclusions."

Sounded like it took a lot of patience. That had never been her strong suit. "He sure was in a hurry to get rid of us. Seemed suspicious to me." She had instantly disliked the man, but she didn't know why. That didn't make him guilty of murder.

"Perhaps. But according to what he just told us, Van Aarle wasn't in town over the last week."

"So he says."

"That's easy enough to check. But he doesn't fit the profile we have so far."

True. Except for the remark about being superstitious, Van Aarle didn't seem like a serial killer. "So why did he want us off his property so badly? We wouldn't have disturbed it."

"Another good question."

She studied his face. "You're being professionally objective, but personally, you don't care for this golfer dude, do you?"

His expressive brows raised in surprise. "You have good instincts." Then with a sigh, he confessed. "Neither Van Aarle nor Iris spend enough time at home, in my opinion. They tend to neglect their daughter."

Neglect their daughter? Miranda swallowed. Slowly she expelled a breath as words from the letter she still carried echoed in her mind. *My mom's an executive and my dad's always away. They are never home.*

She thought of the punch in the gut she'd felt when she'd seen Wendy Van Aarle's picture that morning. The girl's coloring and expression had reminded Miranda of herself. But that had to be coincidence. Wendy looked too much like Van Aarle not to be his biological daughter.

Parker handed her the binoculars "Van Aarle's business meeting appears to be legitimate."

"There are more questions than answers to this detecting business," she grumbled as she put the specs back in the glove compartment.

"Sometimes." Parker turned the key in the ignition. "Let's mull them over at lunch. Do you like Mexican?"

"Spicy Mexican?"

"If you prefer. I know the perfect place."

A man after her own heart. And she was hungry. "Love it," she smiled.

CHAPTER FOURTEEN

Parker's perfect place was Ay Chihuahua! A festive little shop done in bright oranges, greens and reds, located just off Peachtree Road near the strip.

Inside, Cuban Salsa music thumped from speakers overhead, as Miranda followed a waiter in a poncho to a table near the back. Dotting the walls were mosaic tiles, hanging plants in colorful ceramic pots, and pictures of a large, happy-looking Hispanic family. A mom and pop business?

She slid into the booth across from Parker and eyed one of the photos. Looked like there was a mom, but no pop. Next to a matronly woman in a plain white blouse and dark skirt, stood a handsome young boy with dark Latin eyes and a proud look. A look she'd seen not too long ago.

A small, dark-haired woman with a round face and a compact body came to their table. "Hola, Señor Parker," she smiled broadly.

"Buenos días, Carlota." Parker took the woman's hand and shook it as if they'd known each other forever.

"It's so good to see you again."

Miranda glanced back at the photo on the wall. The matronly lady was a younger version of Carlota.

"How is your family?"

"Very well, Señor Parker," the woman smiled. "Dulcea is an honor student in her high school class and Belita is going to start first grade next year. They both want to do as well as their brother."

Brother? So that was why Parker chose this place.

"Excellent. And how's business?"

She raised a shoulder. "*Bien.* We're doing well enough."

"Is there anything I can do to help?"

Carlota held up her hands. "You have done enough already, Señor Parker." She pulled a pad from her pocket. "What would you and your guest like to drink?"

Parker gestured across the table. "Carlota, this is my new associate, Miranda Steele."

"Welcome to Ay Chihuahua! Ms. Steele," said Carlota, shaking her hand warmly. "Any friend of Señor Parker's is an honored guest here."

"Thanks," Miranda said.

She took their drink orders, then with a friendly bob of her head Carlota went to the back.

Miranda eyed Parker and nodded toward the photo. "That's Estavez's family, isn't it? Our waitress is his mother, isn't she?"

Parker gave her a wry half-grin. "I told you that you had raw investigative talent."

"Wasn't too hard to figure out."

"It was a good observation." He gazed at the photo tenderly. "We've become friends over the years. Carlota helps me keep an eye on this neighborhood. I keep my friends on the police force informed of anything she sees going on."

"I see." But that didn't explain everything. "Estavez told me you rescued him when he was a kid."

He shrugged. "You could put it that way."

Carlota brought out tall glasses of sweet iced tea and set them before them, then set down silverware wrapped in paper napkins. "Are you ready to order?"

"Miranda?"

She opened her menu and skimmed it. "Is the Chilaquiles Mexicanos spicy?"

Parker's brows rose. "Very."

She handed the menu to Carlotta. "I'll have that. Extra hot."

"It's pretty spicy as it is," Carlota warned.

"I can handle it."

Parker gave her his menu as well. "I'll have my usual."

"Very good. It will be out shortly. Now I will leave you and your associate alone. I'm sure you have important business to discuss." With a nod, she turned and made her way back to the kitchen. Nice lady.

Miranda looked at Parker. "So what's your version?"

"Of what's too hot to eat?"

"Of how you got involved with Estavez."

Parker reached for his glass of tea. "We met when I was on a case downtown late one night and happened onto a convenience store robbery. I went inside and found him holding up the clerk."

"You 'met' him robbing the store?"

He nodded and sipped his drink. "I caught him red-handed. He pulled a knife on me."

"Feisty kid."

"Extremely. You would think it would have been easier to wrestle a seventeen-year-old to the ground, but Antonio had a lot of fire. He gave me a few scars I have to this day."

Nice way to make someone's acquaintance. With his background, she supposed Parker had to be a good fighter. She had to respect that. Still, the image of him wrangling with a hot-tempered Hispanic kid with a knife made her smile. The man had guts. "So you turned him around? Set him on the straight and narrow?"

"I saw promise in him. Wasted talent. Carlota had thrown him out of the house for his gang activities. She told me she couldn't do anything with him. So I thought I'd give it a try." He sipped his drink and studied her closely.

"You brought him to your house?"

"Yes."

"Bet your wife was thrilled. And what about Gen?"

His lip turned up. "There were adjustments on all sides."

"So Antonio turned over a new leaf? Just like that?"

Parker played with his straw. "Not right away. It wasn't easy, but after a while, we came to see eye to eye."

Had to be a lot more to it than that. She thought of the admiration in Estavez's voice when he'd mentioned Señor Parker.

Miranda shifted in her seat. Did Parker think of her in the same way as that kid? She didn't need a savior to rescue her. "Is that why you became a detective? To help people?"

He gave her a wry look and put a chip in his mouth, chewed thoughtfully. "That's why I became a cop."

Miranda stiffened. Parker had been a cop? Not her favorite people.

"Here you are," Carlota sang out, coming from the kitchen with two piping hot plates. She set them before her guests with great care. She retrieved a large pitcher from a tray and refilled their glasses. "Be careful, Señorita," Carlota said to Miranda as she set the tea in front of her. "Caliente. Very hot."

Undaunted, Miranda picked up her fork, cut off a bit of the cheese-covered, tortilla-wrapped meat and put it in her mouth. It stung a bit, just the way she liked it. She was in an adventurous mood.

"Mmm. Delicious. Do you have any chopped peppers?"

Parker's eyes grew round. "Carlota makes some very hot dishes. I wouldn't add anything to it."

"I like spicy. Don't think I can handle it?"

He sat back. "Be my guest."

Carlota said something to another waiter in Spanish. The man hurried back to the kitchen. In a minute, he returned with a small plate of sliced peppers. "Be careful, Señorita," Carlota repeated. "Muy caliente. Very hot."

"Thanks," Miranda smiled and popped a slice in her mouth. Didn't even make her eyes burn.

Parker stared at her. "She means it. Those are hot."

"I'm fine."

Wide-eyed, Carlota shook her head and disappeared toward the back again.

Miranda turned back to Parker. "You were saying you were a cop?"

"You don't want to hear about it."

"Sure I do."

He shook his head. "It might spoil your lunch."

Now she was curious. She leaned forward. "I can handle it, just like I'm handling these peppers." She put another slice into her mouth and crunched down on it. Only stung a little.

His eyes flashed with admiration but grew serious as he picked up his napkin. "My senior year in high school, a girl I was close to was raped and murdered. They couldn't find the killer. I wanted to do something about it, so I joined the police force when I graduated."

Miranda put down her fork. Parker had based his career choice on a girl who'd been…raped? She looked away, fidgeting with her napkin. She could have used somebody like that years ago. He must have been a good cop. Not like Leon. Leon became a policeman so he could arrest people. Especially hookers.

"And did you?" she asked finally. "Get to do something about it?"

He regarded her intently a moment, as if he were harboring some dark secret. Miranda wondered what he meant by "close to." Had the murdered girl been special to him?

"More or less," he said at last. "I solved the murder a few years later. Despite the regulations and procedures."

Good for him. So he didn't like to be hemmed in. She could relate to that. "Your parents must have been proud."

He smiled grimly. "Not really. My father…" his voice trailed off.

"The one you were named after?"

"Yes, Wade Russell Parker, junior. My father is in real estate. He owns several hotels and large corporate buildings as well as some upscale residences around the area. His dream was for me to take over the family business. When I became a cop, he disapproved. Actually, he disowned me."

"Disowned you?"

"Told me to leave his house. Cut off my trust fund. We didn't speak for years."

Not exactly the rosy past she had imagined he'd lived. "Sounds like a real hard ass."

He chuckled. "That's a good way of putting it. He's quite bullheaded. He thought police work was beneath anyone with the Parker name."

"A bit of a snob?" Parker's father must be a mean sucker.

"An elitist. It was partly my fault. He was only threatening me to make me change my mind. But I'm just as bullheaded as he is. I told him to keep his trust fund and walked out." He was quiet a moment. "That's all behind us now, thank the Lord."

"How'd that happen?"

He seemed uncomfortable, like he didn't want to talk about all this. Then he got a faraway look in his eyes. "When I met Sylvia, she refused to marry me unless I quit the force. She was afraid of ending up a widow. By then, I was disillusioned about being a policeman. Frustrated that the guilty could slip through your fingers while you were filling out paperwork."

Good point. "So you started your own PI agency. And that made your father happy?"

He nodded. "To my father's mind, the Agency was much more prestigious than being a police officer. He was so delighted not to have cop in the family any longer, he sent every business contact he had my way. I had requests for subpoena services from every top law firm in town, surveillance work from every insurance company, as well as personal cases. I had to hire extra help from the beginning. That's when I started my training program to fill the vacancies. And we've only grown since then."

"So you became a teacher and a business man."

"You could say that. The work was clean, safe. I studied for a law degree at night. Sylvia finished her doctorate and began teaching."

She thought of the picture of the brown-haired beauty in Parker's office. "Your wife was a teacher?"

"College English professor."

Classy. Man, this guy was out of her league. How'd she ever wind up across a table from him at a Mexican restaurant?

He continued. "Gen came along. Sylvia was happy. My father was happy. Then after a few years, someone came to me with a kidnapping case. His daughter had disappeared. Later she was found dead in the trunk of her car. He suspected her husband had done it. I proved he was right."

And then Parker was happy, she bet. The case sounded familiar. She thought a minute. "The Logan murder?" She remembered hearing about it when she was a teenager. She reached for another pepper, put it in her mouth.

"That's the one." Parker eyed the saucer of jalapenos. "I wouldn't overdo it if I were you."

"They don't bother me." She crunched down on it, her taste buds burning like the *Disco Inferno*. "Want one?"

He sat up, challenged. "Why not?" With an elegant move, he reached for a slice with his fork and put it to his lips. She watched his eyes widened just a bit. He refused to wince.

"Pretty hot, huh?"

"Not too bad."

Typical male ego. "Have another." She pushed the plate toward him. Nothing like a good old pepper-eating contest.

He took another slice.

"Is that red I see along your collar?" She smiled and idly wondered how hot this sexy PI would be between the sheets. Not a safe thought to have about your boss.

He gave her a dark stare. "Not at all. You're right. These peppers are pretty mild." He wiped his mouth and leaned forward. "Now it's my turn to ask some questions."

She stiffened. "What do you want to know?"

He fixed her with those deep gray eyes. "Why construction jobs?"

Note to self. Never play Twenty Questions with a PI. It'll only come back to bite you on the ass. She picked at her chilaquiles. "They were there. They were physical. I wanted to prove I could make it. They didn't tie me down."

"Why did you move so much?"

"I wanted to see the country. And, like I told you before, I was looking for my daughter."

"So you just picked places at random?"

"More or less."

"And hoped to find your daughter by sheer dumb luck?"

She pushed one of the tortilla strips in her chilaquiles around in the sauce. "It was the only kind of luck I had." She didn't mention that there had been long periods when she'd sink into a funk and do little but work and drink at night. And keep in shape. And fight. She always made sure she could fight.

Parker didn't seem to buy it. "You're intelligent. Why didn't you go to school?"

He was sure liberal with the compliments. Leon always said she was stupid. Before him, her mother had often told her she wasn't smart enough to go to college, but Miranda had always wondered whether she was talking about herself. A cleanup lady at a nearby hospital, she was a cold, stern woman with little feeling. Miranda's father had been a happier person. She remembered laughing together as he bounced her on his knee before he left. She never knew why he'd gone. Except he'd probably gotten tired of her mother's grimness.

Over the years, she'd gotten her GED, piddled at a few courses here and there at community colleges. Her grades had told her she was anything but stupid, but she'd never found anything she wanted to stick with. Brains weren't that important. People with brains could still get the shit beat out of them. People who were strong, who knew how to defend themselves, didn't.

"Miranda?"

He'd called her by her first name. She shrugged. "Didn't appeal to me."

Carlota passed by with the water pitcher. Miranda waved and pointed to the saucer of peppers. "You have anything hotter?"

Her free hand went up in the air. "*Santa Maria.*"

"How about some serranos?"

She shook her head. "Oh, *Señorita. Caliente. Caliente!*"

"Bring us a dish." She turned back to Parker. "I learned to like really hot Mexican food when I was in Phoenix."

"I see," he said with a knowing look.

After a moment, Carlota reappeared and set another saucer in front of them. Muttering something in Spanish, she moved toward the door where a couple of customers had come in.

Miranda looked down on the shiny, finely diced red-orange pieces, shoved the saucer toward Parker. "You game?"

He shoved it back toward her. "You go ahead."

She used her fork to put one in her mouth. Now that had a kick. She fought back the urge to yelp. "Your turn."

He eyed the plate. "One more question."

"What?"

"Why did you put a cherry bomb in the courthouse men's room in Oak Park, Illinois, ten years ago?"

She bristled. His question stung as hard as the pepper in her mouth. "You been snooping into my past, detective?"

"It's customary to do a background check on one's employees."

"It's customary that they agree first."

"Consent was implied the moment you walked in the door."

If it was anyone else, she'd ask what was implied if she put her foot in his face. But his features were too charming to ruin. "I was under duress."

His penetrating eyes smiled at her. "Your mind has a legal bent, Miranda. That's a good trait in an investigator." His voice grew tender. "That explosive had something to do with your daughter, didn't it?"

She nodded. "Payback. The court refused to open her records for me."

He sat back and sighed. "A typical response. The court's, that is."

Okay. The act was pretty immature. But the court's heartless decision had enraged her at the time. She had to get him off this subject. She shoved the serranos toward him. "Chicken, aren't you?"

His eyes narrowed. "Of a pepper? Hardly." He put two pieces in his mouth.

Miranda had to stifle a laugh. To be fair, she took three and forced them down. Her eyes watered. Now that was a burn. "Kind of like putting a wasp in your mouth, huh?"

"Yes." Parker winced, coughed, but got his peppers down without looking like too much of a weakling. He gazed across the table into those deep pools of blue. Only a tear or two shimmered in those eyes. What a woman.

How well aligned her features were. Nose, brows, cheekbones. And well formed, too. She probably had no idea how pretty she was. And yet, he could see there were secrets behind those eyes. And pain. He remembered the raw, sensual urge he'd felt the night he met her. Once again, he heard that siren song, felt its strange exotic pull. It wasn't just his mouth she had set on fire. What was it about a woman like Miranda Steele that he found so alluring? That made him want to reach under the table and run his foot up her shapely leg? A decidedly unprofessional move.

She had natural observation skills. She seemed to have a knack for asking questions, as well. Her technique was a little blunt, but she'd just gotten more information out of him than he'd shared with anyone in a long time. He'd definitely made the right decision to bring her aboard. She could go far.

Miranda pushed the saucer toward him again. "Want another?"

He shook his head. "I've had plenty. Let's get going."

They returned to Mockingbird Hills, then visited the area where the Taggarts lived in the next subdivision. Miranda watched Parker interview all the neighbors. He'd already talked to them all, the night Madison went missing. They had nothing to add. Madison was a sweet, popular girl. She came from a perfect family. All the spring break parties were over. No one had seen anything unusual around her house or the Ingram mansion.

Once more, they had come up with nada. Detective work was darned frustrating.

They got back to the Imperial Building after five. Parker showed her a back way up to his office and Miranda was glad to bypass the lobby and the fashion-model receptionist. As she followed his attractive rear end up the stairs, she noticed her mouth wasn't the only part of her still burning from lunch.

They went to his office and he moved behind the desk where the afternoon sun glistened against the glassy surface. He beamed at her. "You've done well for your first day."

She looked at the map of Mockingbird Hills still projected on the wall. She'd never had a boss give her so many compliments. This was some first day. They hadn't accomplished much, but she'd kind of enjoyed herself. This was the first job she'd ever had that didn't bore her out of her mind.

She looked back at Parker. The light from the window gave him that unearthly glow. Maybe this was a dream and she'd wake up back in that jail cell.

He grinned and took a step toward her. "Do you think you'll stay on?"

She watched the glow in his steel-gray eyes, dared to take a step toward him. He reached for her arm, touched it so lightly she could barely feel it. But it sent another one of those electric currents down her back. Her mouth definitely wasn't the only thing on fire. *I think I will*, she was about to say when a harsh growl made her jump.

"What are *you* still doing here?"

Miranda turned and saw Gen standing in the doorway, papers in her hands, fists on her hips.

Parker moved away. "Good afternoon, dear," he said tenderly.

She scowled. "Please, Dad."

Affectionate daughter.

She glared at Miranda. "I thought you left. Where have you been?"

Parker folded his arms. "Ms. Steele accompanied me on my investigation of the Taggart murder. At my request."

"You're kidding."

"That's not something I would kid about. You know me better than that, Gen."

She stomped into the office and laid the papers she was carrying down on his desk. "Why are you making this so difficult for me?"

"Difficult?"

"If she's going to stay on, and I don't recommend it, she has to start at the bottom like everyone else."

Parker's look grew dark. "Need I remind you I started this company when you were in diapers?"

"Dad," Gen snapped.

This was getting testy. Miranda didn't want to be in the middle of a family feud. Especially if it was about her. "Hey, maybe I should take a walk."

Parker raised an arm toward her. "Stay where you are."

Gen picked up a paper and pointed at her, too. "If she's going to work here, she has to follow the rules."

Parker got to his feet. "As you know, I still run this company. I'm the head of employee training, darling."

"Then you should know, Daddy dear, that I can't have you showing favoritism."

"This isn't favoritism."

"What else would you call it?"

"Training."

"Oh? And what'll the other trainees say when they find out Steele gets special treatment? You're creating a morale problem and I'm the one who has to handle it."

Parker exhaled slowly. In the past, he'd taken a new hire under his wing, but not since Sylvia's death, before Gen came on board. Showing Miranda special treatment now might make it harder for her. He looked at her apologetically. "She has a point."

"Hey, no skin off my nose. If I'm not wanted, I'll find something else. I've had shorter stints." She moved toward the door.

"Wait just a minute." Parker beat her to it, put his arm against the post to block her path. "You're not getting off that easily this time, Miranda Steele."

Who the hell did he think he was? "Your manager doesn't want me."

"Gen thinks you're perfect for the job, doesn't she?"

"What?" Gen squeaked.

"I'm sure she recalls she can't hire or fire anyone without my approval."

Miranda looked at Gen. She was turning beet red.

"Yeah, so?"

"Gen doesn't want you to go. All she means is she wants you to participate in our formal training program."

Miranda grimaced. "Huh? What are you talking about? School?"

Gen's eyes narrowed. She had to be thinking of what Miranda had said earlier about not caring for academics. "That's right. Training classes. Study. Books. Tests."

Good Lord. "I don't know about that."

"And we have a dress code."

Miranda raised half a lip. "Dress code?"

"No jeans in the office. Dress slacks or skirts only. Simple jewelry. No earrings—anywhere. A watch is mandatory. And a cell phone."

"You didn't mention a blouse. Is it required to go topless?"

"Pressed dress blouses," Gen spat through gritted teeth. "No tank tops." Gen eyed the getup Miranda was wearing.

Miranda turned to Parker. "Sorry, Park. I don't have the cash for a new wardrobe. Guess I'm outta here."

Gen's eyes blazed. "Park?"

Miranda bent to scoot out under his arm.

He sidestepped her and blocked her way with his whole body. "One moment, Ms. Steele."

She was close enough to smell the scent of his skin. Fresh, clean. Way too close. She stepped back.

He turned to his daughter. "Genevieve, advance our new employee two weeks' salary to upgrade her wardrobe."

Huh? "Thanks, but I'll need that for my rent."

"You'll find that's already been taken care of."

What? "Look. I don't need charity." Now she was really pissed. If she weren't so desperate for cash, she'd knock him on his sexy ass and stomp right out of here. And if this day hadn't been so interesting. And if it weren't for Cloris Taggart.

He folded his arms. "Who said it was charity? Ten percent will be deducted from your paycheck each week until the advance is paid."

She squealed out loud. "Ten percent? Make it five. And what about the computer? You promised me access." If she couldn't look for Amy, the hassle wasn't worth it.

Gen attempted to step between them. "No computer use until training."

"I know how to use a computer," Miranda snarled at her.

"Really? For what? Surfing for porn?"

"None of your business."

"Ladies, enough." This was all he needed. A catfight between his daughter and his new protégé.

Gen stood a moment grinding her teeth, then she stomped over to the desk and grabbed a sheet of paper. "Very well, Mr. Parker. Here's your new trainee's schedule of classes." She shoved it in Miranda's face. "You've already missed a day. You'll have to make it up."

"Look, you." She wanted to belt the sassy wench.

"We value discipline here. You'll do what I say, when I say, how I say."

No wonder Becker and Holloway called her The General.

She shoved the schedule into Miranda's hand. "Be at classroom A at nine a.m. tomorrow morning." Then she turned on her heel and stomped out of the office.

Miranda looked into Parker's face.

"Well?" He wanted an answer.

Was she going to stay here and take that? She glanced down at the paper and grimaced. This detective thing was going to be tougher than she thought.

She looked him in his sexy gray eyes. "I'll think about it." She tucked the paper under her arm, shoved past him and headed for the exit.

CHAPTER FIFTEEN

It must have been Fate, or some other cosmic force—like the need for cash, that made her show up for classes the next morning. And the morning after that. And the one after that. Before she knew it, Miranda'd had two weeks of elementary PI training under her belt.

So far, she'd learned that Allan Pinkerton was the first US detective, skip tracing could include looking for your old flame, and in this state, a gumshoe could get a permit to carry a concealed .38 Special. She'd even aced her first exam. Not bad for a high school dropout.

By her second Friday at the agency, though, Miranda was getting antsy. She hadn't seen Parker since her first day and there was still no computer access. If she couldn't help solve Madison Taggart's murder and she couldn't use the Parker Agency's resources to look for Amy, what the hell was she doing here?

She looked around the huge, high-ceilinged room of the Fulton County Justice Center Tower, the nine-story behemoth where she'd been arraigned last week. Across the large table, Becker and Holloway sat, working away. She'd been teamed up with them for a field trip after today's lesson in courthouse record searches.

When the group of newbies from the Parker Agency had arrived an hour ago, their instructor, Detective Kay Carson, a short, tough-looking broad with ten years of service to her credit, had pointed out the reference books, handed out a five-page assignment, and left them alone. Miranda had been grateful none of the clerks at the counter had recognized her from her arrest.

She stared down at the tiny print of the plat book in front of her. Land titles and deeds were boring with a capital B. This wasn't her thing. She tapped her fingers on the table. So what was she still doing at the Parker Agency? she asked herself for the umpteenth time this week.

There was the dough she owed Parker. God only knew what had made her blow it on a new wardrobe. She told herself she had to adhere to the company's dress code but that might be stretching it. The outfit she had on today had a split up the side and was accented with a leather belt, studs and chains. When Gen got a load of it this morning, she'd had a fit.

Miranda chuckled to herself, remembering The General's face. "A detective ought to look tough, right?" she'd told her. She liked the idea of looking tough, but she didn't have to stay at the Agency to do that. Or to pay Parker back. She could get another job.

Then there was all this study. Oh yeah, that sure was a reason to stay. Some of it was interesting, but some was a pain in the ass. Like manual record searching at the courthouse. And she still felt she didn't fit in with the experienced people, despite Parker's compliments.

And then there was Parker himself. Her mind wandered back to her first day two weeks ago. She smiled as she remembered Parker's sexy face at Ay Chihuahua's, forcing down hot peppers. She thought about the incident that had started his career. A young woman who'd been raped and killed. Horrible.

She remembered his last touch in his office that day. The intense look in his steel-gray eyes. She was sure he'd been about to kiss her before Gen barged in.

Oh yeah, then there was Gen. She had to be the reason Miranda had stayed on. Gen must have gotten to Parker with that business about playing favorites. That was why she hadn't seen him for almost two weeks. Miranda couldn't help feeling resentful. Not that she wanted a fling with the boss. That would be crazy. But if it hadn't been for Parker's tight-ass daughter, she'd still be working on the Taggart case.

So…maybe she should start using her lunch hour to look for something else. She sighed and turned a page of the big book.

All this time, the clues had been buzzing around in her brain. Tiffany Todd. Ashley Ingram. Wendy Van Aarle. The sleep over at the Todds' house. The date rape drug in Madison's system. Ligature strangulation.

Who had a reason to choke a thirteen-year-old, smear seasoned cooking oil on her, tie a ribbon around her neck, take her body to the woods behind the Van Aarle mansion, and cover it with sticks and leaves?

She exhaled. No idea. But she wished she could help find the girl's killer. If she could stop a madman from killing again…might be the best thing she'd ever done in her life.

Maybe she should start investigating the murder on her own. But how?

Across the table, Becker cleared his throat.

Miranda looked up from her plat book and frowned at her two cohorts. Becker and Holloway were staring at her like hungry puppies.

"What? My blouse on backwards or something?"

Holloway leaned forward and whispered. "We heard you went out with the Silver Fox the other day."

Silver Fox. A.k.a. Parker. Crap. Guess Gen had a point after all. Now the only buds she had at the agency were going to hate her. She shrugged. "Don't know what you mean."

"It's all right," Becker said. "We know you can't divulge any secrets or anything. Just tell us what he's like."

"Like?"

Holloway looked around in that sneaky way of his. "We know you got to go with him because you've got experience."

"Yeah," she shifted her weight uncomfortably. Okay, so maybe they weren't ready to boil her in oil. "Uh, the boss just wanted my ideas on a case. Turned out it wasn't quite my expertise."

"So what's he like?"

"Parker?"

"Yeah."

Sexy. Strong. Kind. Damned aggravating. "He's pretty sharp. You guys know he's one of the best." They talked about the cases Parker had solved all the time.

They looked at her like two kids waiting for their mommy to give them an ice cream cone.

She rolled her eyes and leaned toward them. "This is strictly hush-hush. Gen would really get upset if she heard you talking about this."

Their heads wagged like bobble-head dolls. "We understand. We won't say anything."

"Parker said he was impressed with the new crop of trainees." Well, he probably would say something like that, she imagined.

"Really?" Holloway beamed. Becker's chest poked out like a rooster's.

"Sure. Say, how did you find out about me and, uh, the Silver Fox?"

Holloway put his hand over his mouth and leaned toward her. "Smith saw you come in the back door with him."

Who was Smith? "Tell Smith to keep a lid on it."

"We will," Becker nodded eagerly.

Maybe Holloway and Becker were cool with it, but if rumors about her and Parker spread through the office, there'd be hell to pay. Might be the last straw that would make her decide to quit. Wait. Hadn't she just decided to quit?

Better change the subject. She pulled out her cell phone from her pocket. Everyone in the class had been issued one this morning. "Hey, Holloway, you know how to work this thing?" She'd never had one before.

"We're supposed to keep them on at all times," Becker said. "In case someone wants to contact us."

Holloway shook his head. "Not in the courthouse."

"Doesn't matter. Put it on mute."

"Yes, it does. Okay, just turn it on for a minute." Holloway reached across the table and pointed. "Press that button."

"Thanks." She pushed it. It beeped and jingled, and people turned to scowl at her as it came on. Ignoring them, she put the phone to her ear. "No messages," she told Becker and Holloway. "Guess the president didn't need my opinion on the latest crime bill."

Becker's mouth fell open. "The President?"

Holloway nudged him.

"Oh." He forced a laugh.

Might as well check her phone at home. Not that she was expecting anything there either. She dialed the number, waited for the beep, pressed another button.

There was a message. Her heart stopped. News about Amy?

Then Fanuzzi's New York accent rang in her ear. "How ya doin', Murray?"

Miranda had forgotten she'd given her former co-worker her number.

"Just wonderin' if you found a job yet. Hey, we got something to celebrate. The gang's having a party at Truman's place tonight and you're invited. Be there at eight. Can't wait to tell you everything." She rattled off the address and hung up.

Miranda pressed the button. Celebrate? Party with her old gang on the road crew? Drinking brewskies and telling stories about Fat Mama? Why not? A lot better than sitting around here. She looked up at the clock on the courthouse wall. Almost five. Quitting time.

She closed the book. "I'm outta here for today, guys."

"Hey," Holloway called out. "We're supposed to follow Detective Carson back to the office."

She turned off her cell and headed for the door. "Tell Detective Carson I'll find my own way back."

As she navigated down the side streets of Decatur looking for Truman's address, Miranda smiled at the rows of little bungalows huddled together close to the road. Small porches, plain trim, cinderblocks, vinyl siding, paint jobs that needed a little touching up. Undersized lawns with just a few hedges and trees, brown spots where grass wouldn't grow. Homey, down-to-earth places. Much more familiar than the swanky digs she'd been dropping in on lately. More like the place she'd grown up in. She liked the area.

Worn reflective numbers on a mailbox told her when she reached Truman's place. Gibbs's Firebird sat in the yard. Fanuzzi's station wagon, with Barbie dolls and toy robots in the rear window, was along the curb. She parked her old jalopy behind it and got out.

When she rang the doorbell, Fanuzzi answered and gave her a hug she wasn't expecting. Then she shoved a beer in her hand. "C'mon in, Murray. I was afraid you wouldn't make it."

In the small living room, her old gang was crowded around a coffee table filled with refreshments. Lester, Gibbs, Dupree. Truman was on the couch, clapping his hands to the music that was playing from a CD player on the TV in the corner. When he saw Miranda, he jumped up and hobbled across the room to her.

"Mirawada." She got another hug. "I'm so glad to see you. Come in. Have some food." He pointed to the coffee table piled with chips, popcorn and plates of desserts. "My mama makes de best sweets in de world."

Gibbs shot her a toothy grin, got up and gave her a high-five handshake. "Murray. I had a bet with Fanuzzi that you wouldn't make it tonight. Glad I lost."

"You owe me two beers," Fanuzzi said to him.

Lester waved from his chair. "Good to see ya, Murray. What you been up to?"

"Yeah," Gibbs said, reaching for a chip. "We all wondered what happened to you after you gave Fat Mama what she deserved."

Deserved? They must have all been cheering for her that day. "I got a job in Buckhead," Miranda shrugged.

Fanuzzi took a swig from her bottle. "That was fast. You waiting tables in one of those fancy restaurants?"

"Naw. Office work. It's pretty boring. What's up with you guys? What's the celebration about?"

Gibbs punched Lester on the arm. "You tell her."

He punched him back. "You tell her."

"I'll tell her," Fanuzzi turned to her, moved her squat shoulders back and forth in a kind of a dance. "Fat Mama's gone," she announced with glee.

"Gone?" Oh, God, Miranda had killed her. "Is she…dead?"

"Hell, no," Fanuzzi laughed. "She checked into the hospital after the bruising you gave her, but when she got out, the chief super moved her to another crew."

Now Miranda had to grin. So her fight did some good after all. "Cool."

"Gibbs is foreman over us now."

He smiled, rubbed his bald head, and stuck out his big chest. "Ya'll just call me 'Boss'."

Dupree reached for a handful of popcorn. "Only on the site."

Miranda sat down in a chair Fanuzzi had pulled up for her. "Congratulations, Gibbs. Way to go."

"Thanks." He eyed her. "So I'm short a Lute Person. You know anyone who'd want the job?"

He was asking her to come back? Jeez, she hadn't expected that. She scratched her head. "Gosh, Gibbs. I don't know what to say."

"You like your boring office job better than our company?"

She squirmed a little. She hadn't gotten anywhere with her search for Amy at the Agency. She'd probably never see another piece of evidence in the Taggart case. If she quit tomorrow, Parker probably wouldn't even know she was gone.

"Give her some time to think it over," Fanuzzi said. "Hey, Truman wrote a song for you. He plays the bongos."

"You do?" Miranda spotted a pair of drums in the corner.

Truman seemed embarrassed. "Aw. It nothing."

"It's cool," Fanuzzi insisted. "Play it for us."

"Y'all want me to play?"

Lester got up and got the bongos for him. "Yeah. Play that song you made up in honor of Miranda after she stood up for you. It's pretty cute."

Dupree turned off the CD player while Lester set the drums down in front of Truman. With his deep-set eyes, Truman studied the skins a moment, took a deep breath, then began to beat away.

Thump de thump thump. Thump thump. He was pretty good, sounding out a funky, kind of Caribbean beat. Thump de thump thump. Thump thump. Soon everyone was nodding heads in time to it. As he started to sing, Miranda noticed his lisp had disappeared.

Mir-aaahn-da. Mir-ah-aaah-ahn-da!
Oh, she smart. She tough.
She got what it takes.
Oh, yeah. She fast. She mean. She know de stakes.
She been around the block. De thump thump.
And if you cross her, oh, oh, man…she ready,
To clean your clock.
She Mir-aaahn-da.
Miranda Stee-hee-heele!
Look out, for Miranda, all you home boys.

He finished with a flourish and everyone clapped and patted him and Miranda on the back. She did something she never did. Blush.

Hiding the embarrassment, she took a swig of beer. "That's nice, Truman. Thanks."

"Everybody all right in here?" A big black woman came into the room carrying a plate of brownies.

"Dis is my mama, Miwanda."

The woman turned to her. "You're the one that song's about? Thank you for looking out for my boy."

"Don't mention it, ma'am."

"Call me Mama Ruby. All my chilluns do." She held out the plate to her. "Have one."

Brownies. They smelled good. Warm, rich, gooey. Miranda's mouth watered. "Thanks, Mama Ruby." She picked one up and took a bite. The warm chocolate oozed out. She wiped her mouth. "Man, that's good."

"My mama's de best cook in the world."

"Now, Truman. He always likes to brag about me."

"You are. She work at de school. They all love her cookin' dere."

Mama Ruby set down the plate on the coffee table and waved her hands. "I like to think I give those chilluns a better meal than their well-off folks do."

Well-off folks? "Where do you work, Mama Ruby?" Miranda asked.

"Why, I'm the head cook at Dogwood Academy."

Miranda's brownie froze halfway to her mouth. Dogwood Academy? Truman's mama worked at Dogwood Academy? Madison Taggart's school?

As everyone started pigging out on the treats, Mama Ruby watched them a moment with a satisfied look. "Now y'all enjoy yourselves. Call me if you need anything," she said over her shoulder as she went back into the kitchen.

Miranda swigged down the last of her beer, held up the bottle. "Think I need another one." She got up.

"I got one here," Fanuzzi said.

"I'll get it." Miranda turned and headed straight for the kitchen door.

In the homey kitchen, Mama Ruby was already at work at a plain table, mixing up another batch of brownies. She smiled at Miranda as she entered. "Would you like to taste the batter?" She held out the bowl.

"Sure." Feeling like a kid, Miranda ran her finger around the edge, got a wad of chocolate, put it in her mouth. Yum. "You really are a great cook, Mama Ruby."

She grinned. "Thank you, Ms. Steele."

"Call me Miranda."

She nodded. "Miranda. I can't thank you enough for comin' to Truman's rescue. I worry so about him on the job."

"I bet you do."

"If there's anything I can do in return."

She hesitated. "Well, there may be."

Mama Ruby stopped stirring and gave her a serious look. "Name it."

Miranda shifted her weight. "I didn't want to tell the others, but I'm working at a detective agency."

"That's wonderful."

"Yeah. They're working on a murder case. A little girl who went to Dogwood Academy?"

Mama Ruby's big brown eyes grew round. "Madison Taggart."

"Guess you know about it."

She nodded and began to stir the batter again, her movements fueled by indignation. "Everybody knows about it. They closed down the school for three days for her. Had a memorial service for her in the gym this week. Grief counselors everywhere. I never heard such crying from chilluns, the poor babes."

Miranda was touched. "Did you know Madison?" she asked softly.

She shook her head. "Not really. She wasn't the type to talk to the kitchen staff. I used to see her coming through the lunch line. She always had a lot of friends around her."

"She was popular."

Mama Ruby nodded. "Seemed to be."

Miranda scratched her tangled hair. "I was just wondering…"

She stopped stirring again. "What, child? Just say it."

She blinked. No one had ever called her child. "I was wondering if there was some way I could get into the school. You know. Look around. Talk to some of the kids, maybe. Just for a day."

"To help solve Madison's murder?"

"To try."

Mama Ruby rubbed her chin. "Can you cook?"

She shook her head. "I can wash dishes."

Mama Ruby nodded. "I can put you to work washing dishes for a day."

She let out a breath she didn't know she'd been holding. "That would be great."

"Be there nine o'clock Monday morning. I'll have an apron ready for you."

"Thanks, Mama Ruby." Cool. Wouldn't Parker be proud?

She tapped the spoon against the bowl and wiped her hands. "Least I can do. Specially if it helps figure out who killed that poor little girl."

Guess she wouldn't be taking Gibbs up on his job offer just yet. She had to see how this would turn out first.

Grinning from ear to ear, Miranda turned to leave. Then she froze.

Fanuzzi was standing inside the doorway. "You dirty dog, you."

"What?"

She came up to her and grabbed her by the arms. "You're working for Wade Parker, aren't you?" She must have heard everything.

"Well, yeah?"

Fanuzzi gave her a shake. "You went to work for Wade Parker and you didn't even tell me?"

It wasn't like they were best friends or anything. "I lost your number." From the corner of her eye, Miranda saw Mama Ruby chuckling as she smoothed her brownie mixture into a pan.

Fanuzzi let her go. "What's he like?"

Did everyone in Atlanta want to know what Parker was like? Jeez. "He's just a guy. I don't see him much."

"Wade Parker ain't just a guy. Out with it, Murray." Fanuzzi pushed Miranda down into a chair at the kitchen table, grabbed a beer from the counter, shoved it into her hand, and sat down beside her. "Tell me everything."

"Like what?"

"Like how'd you get the job? What have you been doing at his agency? Is he just as handsome close up as he is in his pictures?"

Miranda sighed.

While Mama Ruby hummed knowingly to herself and cleaned up the kitchen, Miranda gave Fanuzzi a half-smile and started to talk. It would take a lot to satisfy her curiosity about Parker.

This was going to be a long night.

CHAPTER SIXTEEN

Early Monday morning, Miranda pulled on a pair of sweatpants and a tank top, called in sick at the Agency, and headed for Dogwood Academy. Mama Ruby met her at the door and put her straight to work, introducing her as temporary help.

No one on the staff questioned her. They were all too busy. The friendly hostess from last night suddenly turned into a taskmaster. Amidst the noisy clatter of knives, braising pans, and metal carts, she shouted out orders like a ship's captain. First, cut up enough carrots and potatoes for four hundred hungry mouths. Next, get the pots ready for boiling and baking. Then, time to cut the meat. Fried chicken on the menu today. Don't mix the cutting boards.

Everyone worked like galley slaves They had to, to be ready for the first lunch shift. The clock on the wall was ticking and Mama Ruby wasn't putting up with any mutiny or backtalk.

As the other workers got busy boiling, frying, and baking, Miranda grabbed a sprayer at the huge stainless steel sink and washed the pots and pans as the others finished with them. She smiled as Mama Ruby hummed an old gospel tune, and her mouth watered when someone pulled the best-smelling biscuits she'd ever inhaled out of the oven. Then a loud bell clanged and the kids started lining up.

Mama Ruby tapped her on the shoulder and nodded to a spot behind the serving line where she could watch them as they went by. Miranda wiped her hands and got into position.

Dogwood Academy's students ranged from first graders to junior high children. The school was so prestigious, only the wealthiest kids in Buckhead were allowed to attend. The crème de la crème. They looked pretty normal to her, even with their designer clothes and fancy book bags.

The little ones came first. Grades one through five. Eager young faces eyed what the staff had prepared. Impatient fingers reached for the desserts, but the staff knew to put the solid food on their trays first. Next came the sixth and seventh graders. They were much more sophisticated, especially the girls. Some were watching their weight and made careful selections. At their age.

Miranda caught sight of redheaded Ashley Ingram, the adopted girl, and blond Tiffany Todd, with her superior air. The pair laughed and talked together in that animated way of young girls, as if they didn't have a care in the world, even though their best friend had just died. Funny how easily kids could bounce back from tragedy. They passed close by but didn't even look at Miranda.

After lunch, she was back at the sink, finishing up the trays and plates. She'd forgotten how grungy cafeteria work could be. Years ago when she first got to the women's shelter, she'd had a job in a school kitchen cleaning nasty leftovers off the trays and plates the kids had used. She'd hated it then. Time hadn't changed her opinion. What a detective had to do for a cover.

So far, she hadn't learned much and felt frustrated. Mama Ruby drained a pot into the other sink.

"Any place where I might get a chance to talk to some of these kids?" Miranda asked.

The woman nodded, whispered softly. "The middle school children are outside in the playground now. Why don't you go see what they're up to. I'll finish up here."

"Thanks, Mama Ruby." Miranda wiped her hands, took off her apron and handed it to her.

Outside, Miranda leaned against the school's brick wall pretending to be on a break. Back in her IIT classes, Detective Judd had said that a good PI always kept his eyes and ears open. You never know what you might discover. Sometimes the truth is right in front of you.

She scanned the grounds. The place had all the amenities. Football field, baseball field, badminton and tennis courts. If it weren't for the huge swing set where a few of the little kids were playing, Miranda would have thought she was at a fancy resort.

Some of the younger students were playing Keep-Away on the wide pavement. Watchful teachers were stationed here and there. Everyone seemed so happy and carefree. Is that what childhood had been like? She barely remembered her own. She envied the innocence that sheltered these kids from the harsh realities of life. Except that with the murder of their classmate, they had been introduced to it too early.

Over at the courts, she caught sight of Tiffany Todd, dressed in smart jeans and a T-shirt with a big pink heart. Her blond hair was pulled back with a headband, she was playing volleyball with her classmates. Must be the captain of her team by the way she ordered everyone around. Red-headed Ashley Ingram stood beside her. Every so often they'd laugh and point at the other girls, who returned the dirty looks. So much for youthful innocence.

Miranda was just about to hatch up an excuse to go over and talk to the girls when she sensed someone beside her.

"Who are you?" an adolescent voice sneered.

She turned and saw a young girl standing near the side of the building a few feet away. She must have just come around the corner. Thick black eyeliner, caked mascara, dark eye shadow, blood red lipstick.

Wendy Van Aarle.

Miranda shrugged, trying to look casual. "Nobody. Just the kitchen help."

"What are you doing out here?" The girl seemed defensive, as if she were protecting her private property.

Miranda studied the dark hair and eyes that had given her such a start when she'd first seen her picture. Except for the makeup, she did look a lot like Miranda had at that age, but so would any dark-haired girl in a Goth getup with an attitude. She definitely had Shelby Van Aarle's angular face. Absently, Miranda wondered if Wendy's makeup was from one of the Iris Rose Cosmetics collections.

"I could ask the same thing of you." She gestured toward the playground. "Why aren't you out there with your friends?"

Wendy folded her arms and leaned against the bricks. "Friends? They aren't my friends." Her long, black satiny skirt hung around her booted calves in an uneven hemline. Her dark blouse had flared sleeves accented with a bit of purple. Around her neck was a lacy black choke-collar necklace. A small silver skull dangled from the center of it. Her weird outfit probably came from some ritzy boutique. Might have cost a couple hundred dollars. A drop in the bucket for her folks.

"You don't have a cigarette, do you?"

"Cigarette?" Miranda knew better than to give her a lecture. She shrugged indifferently. "Nah, I quit years ago. So you don't like volleyball?"

The girl lifted her lip in a sneer. "It's a stupid game. I've got a right not to participate. You gonna turn me in or something?"

Miranda shook her head. "No skin off my nose. I just work here. Just started today, in fact."

The girl rolled her eyes. She wasn't interested.

Miranda wasn't getting anywhere with this chitchat. Might as well go for the gold. "You must be awfully broken up about your classmate."

Wendy glared at her, as if caught off guard. "Classmate?"

"That girl who was killed a few weeks ago. She was a student here, wasn't she?"

Slowly, Wendy nodded. "Madison Taggart."

"Yeah, that's her name. I heard about her on the news. I thought you'd know her. They said she was popular."

She groaned out loud, then spoke in a mocking tone. "The most popular girl in school. Pretty. Athletic. Bright. Perfect. God, if I hear one more thing about how wonderful Madison Taggart was, I'll puke all over myself."

Not too broken up, was she? "Wasn't she your friend?"

She narrowed her dark eyes. "Why did you think that?"

"I thought she was friends with everybody."

The words tumbled out. "Friend? She was so stuck up. She thought she was better than everyone. She was mean to everyone. I hated her. A lot of kids did."

Miranda kept her face expressionless. The Taggarts' perfect little girl was mean? Kids hated her? That was a new twist. "I didn't mean to—"

She wasn't listening. "We used to be friends." She turned and picked at the plaster between the bricks with her dark fingernails. "Best friends. Then she decided I was weird." She wiped her face. Was she crying?

Miranda reached out for her, lightly touched her arm.

She pulled away, glaring at her. "Now Tiffany Todd is the most popular. She's even meaner." She pointed out toward the courts. "See how stuck up she is? She wouldn't let me play on either team. Not that I wanted to."

Miranda watched Tiffany Todd prancing around on the pavement. The girl did look like she owned the place. She thought of the night she saw the other two girls taunting Wendy. Did they do that all the time? "Can't your parents do anything about it?"

Wendy laughed out loud, almost tearing up again. "Man, what planet did you come from? Parents can't do anything. Especially not my parents."

"Why not?"

She hugged herself tightly and stared down at the ground, her dark hair covering her face. "They're never around. My mother's always working. My father's never home. Even when they are home, they ignore me." She looked up, her face full of pain.

Miranda stared into those dark eyes and felt a knife go through her chest. *My mom's an executive and my dad's always away. They are never home*. Automatically, her gaze went to Wendy's neck. She couldn't see anything beneath the choke-collar necklace.

"Most of the time, it's just me and the cook at home. She's sort of my nanny." Wendy dug in her pocket and pulled out her cell phone. "Tiffany Todd, I hate you," she said to the phone.

Miranda waited for her to explain.

"I asked her to come to my house after school today. Look what she texted me." She held up the phone.

Miranda squinted at the tiny screen. Huh? "'idhwm.' What does that mean?"

Her voice nearly broke as she answered. "'I don't hang with morons.'"

"Morons? That is mean." She suddenly felt defensive of the strange girl. She thought a minute. "Hey. Ask her how she looks in the mirror then?"

Wendy stared at her, then smiled. It was the first smile Miranda had seen from her. "That's really good." She punched at her phone.

They both turned toward the yard and watched Tiffany Todd reach for the cell in her pocket. She read the message. Her face turned beet red. She looked across the yard and glowered at Wendy. Quickly, Miranda turned her head so she wouldn't be recognized.

Wendy laughed. "She's really mad now."

Miranda got an idea. "Hey, I just got a new cell phone. Maybe you can text me sometime."

Wendy looked at her, her lip curled again.

"I mean, if you want to talk about anything. Or if you need a good comeback."

She studied her a little while as if weighing the pros and cons of being friends with an adult. At last she shrugged. "Sure."

Miranda gave Wendy her number and watched her carefully punch it into her cell phone, feeling concerned that the girl was giving in to her request so easily.

"What's your name?" she asked.

"Miranda. What's yours?"

"Willow," she said without looking up.

Inventive little thing. "Is that your real name?"

She finished with the phone and put it back in her pocket. "That's the name I go by this week."

Miranda nodded. "All right, Willow. How about giving me your number?"

She rolled her eyes, but started to answer. "It's six-seven-eight…" Her voice trailed off as her attention focused on something near the street. Suddenly, she seemed nervous. "There's that guy again."

Miranda turned and saw a black sedan pull up along the fence near the pavement. The sight of it made the hair on her arms stand up. The car had tinted windows. She couldn't see the driver. Someone spying on the kids? A weird feeling pulsated through her. Like an echo from another life. Cold. Frightening.

Suddenly, she remembered Tiffany Todd and Ashley talking about a strange man hanging around the schoolyard the night she went to Mockingbird Hills. They said Wendy had been talking to him. And Madison. "Do you know that guy?"

Wendy's defenses were back. "Why should I know him?"

"You've seen him before."

She shrugged. "A couple of times. I think he sells books or something."

The tinted window lowered about an inch. She couldn't see inside. What was the driver looking for? A little girl to prey on? Miranda turned back to Wendy, maternal instincts belting her. "Maybe you shouldn't hang around here by yourself."

Wendy rolled her eyes.

Miranda kept her eye on the car. He rolled past a group of girls, moving closer to the building. Was he headed for the parking lot? "You don't talk to that guy, do you?"

A bell rang.

"I gotta go."

"You shouldn't talk to him. Hey, you didn't finish giving me your number."

She shrugged and walked off.

"Call me sometime."

Wendy didn't answer.

"Nice talking to you," Miranda muttered to herself.

She watched the girl amble toward the area where the teachers were lining up the students. Her head down, Wendy shuffled to the back of the line. Miranda's heart went out to the strange kid. All her parents' millions couldn't buy her what she really wanted. Friends. The esteem of her peers. Most of all, her parents' attention.

The Van Aarles were her real parents. Had to be.

Miranda turned back and saw that the black sedan was gone. She had to find it again.

She scooted around the front of the building. Didn't see the car on the street. She hurried to the other side and came around the far corner just in time to see a man strolling up the sidewalk from the parking lot. The black sedan sat in the row of cars. This guy had to be the driver. Quickly she crouched behind a thick bush and watched him.

He was tall, lanky, with curly red hair. He carried a box and had a big smile on his face. Not the way she'd imagine a serial killer, but then she'd never seen a real one this close. As he reached the side entrance, he shifted the box with a grunt. It must be full of books. A serial killer selling textbooks? Well, it was one way to get to kids. It would give him a chance to pick out his targets. He opened the door and slipped inside.

As soon as it closed behind him, Miranda stepped out from behind the bushes and strolled over to the entrance as if she did it every day. When she got to the steps, she put her hand on the metal door handle, hesitated. If he'd seen her, if this guy was a killer, he could be waiting on the other side, ready to smack her with a two-by-four or a tire iron. On the other hand, if he was the strange man Madison Taggart had talked to before she was murdered, Miranda wasn't about to lose him. She'd take her chances.

Bracing herself, she took a deep breath, and pulled on the handle, trying not a make a noise.

The hall was deserted, silent. Where had the bookselling killer gone? A sign overhead told her this area was for grades one through three. The rooms were dark. Nobody was around. She glanced at her watch. It was late. The younger kids must have gone home.

Slowly she tiptoed down the corridor alongside the small lockers, past the classrooms, the walls decorated with colorful crepe paper and cutouts. At last she reached a door that was half open.

Muffled voices drifted out from behind it. Miranda's heart began to pound. Flattening herself against the wall, she listened hard. Laughter echoed softly, dreamlike. A feminine giggle. A masculine chuckle.

At last, she pushed herself right up to the doorpost and dared to peek inside.

Luckily, the salesman had his back to the door. He also had a teacher sprawled across the desk, her skirt hiked up to her waist, her legs in the air. He was nestled between them, his pants loosened.

"Oh baby," he moaned. "There's no one like you."

A pair of full lips smiled up at him. "What took you so long to get here?" The teacher whispered.

"I had appointments. I'm a busy man." With their accents, they sounded like a bad, x-rated Southern soap opera. He uttered a low groan as he took his pleasure. "But my mind was on you all day long. And the Biology lessons you like to give me."

Biology lessons? Gross.

The teacher sighed. "I think you learned about the birds and bees a long time ago. Mmm. Do that again."

He chuckled again. "This?"

"Yes. Oh, yes."

"Am I your man?"

"Oh, yes. You're a wild man."

"Say it. Say I'm your man."

Jeez. Where was your barf bag when you needed it?

"How can you even ask, when you make me feel like this?" The teacher laughed giddily in the throes of orgasm. "Of course, you're my man. You're my only man, Dexter Hinsley."

Miranda shot back against the wall, her heart hammering in her chest. *Dexter Hinsley? Coco's* Dexter Hinsley? The one who didn't want her looking for a job as a singer?

That sonofabitch. Miranda wanted to march straight into that love nest and bloody his nose and maybe a few other body parts he was using just now.

But that wouldn't be smart.

Instead, she forced herself to think of what the pretty blond singer who'd given her an alibi in court had told her about him. She'd said Dexter sold textbooks. That he worked late a lot of the time. That he had a bad temper.

What did Parker say about the typical serial killer profile? Abusive childhood, violent history, belief in their own supernatural abilities, a need to dominate their prey. She didn't know anything about Hinsley's background.

What about the ritual? The seasoned cooking oil? The ribbon on the neck? Did that fit with being a philanderer? She wasn't sure, but Wendy had recognized him. He could be seducing teachers to get information about their students.

She heard shuffling inside the room. Footsteps. The lovebirds were getting dressed. Uh oh.

Her breath hitching, she looked around for a place to hide. Across the hall was another classroom. Hoping they didn't see her, she counted to three and sprinted across the corridor as fast as she could go. She reached for the doorknob, found the room open, bounded inside, just as Hinsley stepped out into the hall.

She slapped a hand over her mouth to still her panting as the blood rushed through her brain. She listened hard as his footsteps clicked down the hall, waited a beat, then slowly opened the door and peeked out. The door to the "Biology" room was shut. Thank God.

She stepped out and rushed down the hall to the entrance she'd come in, burst through the door, spotted Hinsley heading for the parking lot. She raced over the lawn, ducked behind a pickup as he climbed inside his black sedan.

He drove off. Madly, she groped inside her pocket for the notebook and pen she'd been trained to keep with her. She yanked it out, scribbled down his license plate just before he was out of sight.

Gasping for breath, she stared down at the pad. She got it.

Now what? She had a suspect but not much proof. Time to call in the big guns. Hurrying, she headed for her car and back to the office.

She couldn't wait to see the look on Parker's face.

CHAPTER SEVENTEEN

Miranda screeched into a parking spot outside the Imperial Building, jumped out of her old jalopy and raced to the back door. Good thing Parker had showed her this way in. No hard looks or questions from the nosey receptionist. She took the stairs two at a time. When she got to the fifteenth floor, she hurried over to Parker's office.

A minute later, she stood puffing in his doorway. Where was the boss man? The space was empty. She turned around. His assistants' desks were vacant, too.

She took off down a hall. Rounding a corner near a cube bank, she nearly collided with Becker.

"Steele, what are doing here?" he said in his nasal Brooklyn voice. "I thought you were sick."

"Quick recovery," she said. "Have you seen Parker?"

"Yeah. Funny you should ask. We just had an Aikido session with him in the gym. It was way cool. Did you know he has a fourth degree black belt?"

"Gym. One floor down, right?"

He nodded. "The fourteenth."

She turned and ran all the way to the elevator.

By the time she slammed through the double doors of the gym, Miranda was out of breath again and her T-shirt was sticking to her. Panting, she looked around the room as the heavy metal clanged shut behind her.

Half gym, half dojo, like everything else in the Parker Agency, the hall was huge and opulent. Mirrors lined one of the walls, expensive-looking exercise equipment on the other. Colorful mats covered the floor. Punching bags in assorted sizes hung from the ceiling. More mats were wrapped around a row of posts. A boxing ring stood in the far corner. Everything was sparkling clean. It smelled more like a spa than a gym.

So this was where Parker trained his army of IITs for combat before he unleashed them on the world. She remembered it from the tour Detective Judd gave them on her second day here. He said they'd have a class with Parker here this week. She'd missed it.

She noticed steady breathing coming from the far corner and spotted Parker.

He was alone, lifting free weights, with his back to the door. Gingerly, she stole across the floor until she stood behind him. He had on a pair of long gray sweat pants and was shirtless. Her blood pressure spiked. And here, she'd imagined him giving an Aikido lesson in his business suit.

She stood watching him a moment, admiring his shoulder muscles as he worked them, the sinews of her stomach clenching in time to his reps.

Finally, he finished, put the barbell down and turned around. He hadn't been looking in a mirror, but somehow he'd known she was there. "Miranda," he said in his dignified way. "What are you doing here?" His smooth voice had a touch of disappointment and anger in it that made her feel a little guilty.

She gazed at the black hair scattered across his chest and her mind went blank. "Huh?"

He crossed his arms over that delicious torso. "I thought you called in sick today."

She watched a drop of sweat trickle over his firm pectoralis major. Man, he was in good shape. "Yeah. I did."

His face grew hard. His deep gray eyes scolded her. "Then what are you doing here?" he repeated.

"Uh, I played hooky."

He gave her a dark look. "Hooky?" He took a towel off a rack and draped it over his neck.

She shook herself, took a deep breath. Back to business. "For a good reason. I went to Dogwood Academy."

Darkness turned to shock. "You did what?" He put his hand on a stretch bar along the wall as if to steady himself. Letting her words sink in, he wiped the sweat off his face with the end of the towel. "Please explain."

Excited, she paced a little as she talked. "Friday night I went to see a friend and found out his mother works at the school. I asked her for a temporary job in the kitchen. She got me in today. You know, to snoop around."

An eyebrow rose. "Snoop around?"

"Yeah. Undercover. To see if I could find out anything about Madison Taggart. So I went there and washed dishes."

"Dishes."

"Yeah. Some of it was pretty gross. Anyway, during a break, I went out to the schoolyard where the kids were playing. I talked to Wendy Van Aarle."

"You did what?"

"I talked to Wendy Van Aarle," she repeated. "She was hanging around and we struck up a conversation."

Slowly, he exhaled and leaned a foot on a weight bench. She watched the expression on his face turn from anger to intrigue. "What did you find out?"

"For one thing, Wendy hated Madison Taggart. She told me Madison was mean to everybody, especially her. A lot of kids disliked her."

He nodded, taking in her words.

"Now Tiffany Todd has taken her place as the top dog at school. She's nasty, too." She stopped. He'd already questioned everybody several times. "Maybe you already know all this."

"No, I didn't."

Parker stared at the woman before him. The past two weeks, he had forced himself to stay away from Miranda Steele. Gen had been right. It wouldn't be fair to his new recruit to keep her out of training. And working on the Taggart case, he'd decided, would be too much emotional strain after what she'd been through. Evidently, he'd been wrong.

He rubbed his chin, his mind racing. "Childhood rivalries aren't usually a motive for this kind of murder, if that's what you're thinking."

Miranda blinked at him. Did he think she thought Wendy…? "No." She shook her head. "I'm just worried about her. You know Wendy's parents aren't home very much. She's kind of a loner." She had bonded with the girl more than she realized.

Parker picked up the free weights he'd been using and put them back in the rack along the wall. "That's understandable. I'm concerned, too. But, unfortunately, there's little we can do for her. Is that all you learned?"

She shook her head. "No. I'm getting to it. While we were talking in the schoolyard, a black sedan drove by. There was a man in it. It made me remember something." She rubbed her arms as she recalled the strange chill the sight of that car had given her.

"What?"

"The night I went to Mockingbird Hills, I heard Ashley Ingram tell Tiffany Todd that a weird man had been hanging around the schoolyard. That Madison and Wendy had talked to him."

He blinked. "Are you sure?"

She nodded. "The guy I saw today might be him. Wendy recognized him and his car."

He leaned forward, his gray eyes intent. Now she had his undivided interest. "Go on."

"Wendy said he was a textbook salesman. She acted like she knew him, then denied it. She's a strange kid."

"She is. Did you get a license plate?"

"Yeah, right here." She dug in her pocket, handed him the scrap of paper she'd scribbled it on. "Pretty good, huh?"

He studied the paper and slowly nodded. Was that a grin he was hiding?

"I followed him inside the school building."

His grin disappeared. "You did what?"

She blew out a breath. "I found him making it with one of the teachers in an empty room."

His brow rose. "Do you mean they were having sex?"

"Uh huh. It was pretty gross. There were no kids around, though."

"That's some comfort. Did he see you?" Alarm was in his voice.

She shook her head. "I stayed out of sight and just listened. It got pretty hot and heavy. After awhile, the teacher said his name. I recognized it, the cheating bastard."

He tucked her scrap of paper in the pocket of his sweatpants. "You know this man?"

"Remember Coco? The singer in The Gecko Club? The one Estavez got as an alibi for me?"

He nodded. "Cora Beth Hinsley."

"The sleazy textbook salesman is her husband."

He frowned. "Are you certain?"

"Coco said his name was Dexter. Her last name's Hinsley. That was the name the teacher uttered in the throes of passion. *Dexter Hinsley.*"

Parker stood silent for several minutes. His face took on a strange look she didn't quite understand. "I'll have to look into that," he muttered half to himself. "Good work."

A thrill shot through her. She hadn't realized how much his approval meant to her. "Thanks."

He wiped his face and tossed the towel in a nearby hamper. "However, in the future, don't go off on your own. Any work you do for us must be under supervision."

Well, that was a kick in the head. She pursed her lips. That glory was short-lived. "Sorry. I thought you'd be pleased."

He crossed his arms again. "I'm impressed. But the Agency is responsible for you."

"You sound like Gen. I thought you didn't like being hemmed in by rules."

He frowned.

"You said that was why you quit the police force."

He nodded. "Ah, yes. But sometimes rules are necessary. What if you had gotten hurt today?"

Why was he being such a stickler? "Uh, I think you know I can take care of myself."

"Can you?"

Was he trying to piss her off? "You bet. And I think I did great today." She turned away with a shrug.

His low voice came over her shoulder. "Don't get so cocky. I haven't forgotten that you missed my class."

She turned back, put a hand on her hip. "So what you gonna do, boss? Give me demerits?"

Parker inhaled, trying in vain to control the raw animalistic urges Miranda Steele stirred in him. Impressed was an understatement. She'd gone undercover on her own initiative and found out more from Wendy Van Aarle than he had after three interviews. She'd discovered facts about this Dexter Hinsley that could be a significant lead. And she'd only been here two weeks. She had even more talent than he'd realized. With a little training, she could be a full-fledged investigator in six months.

She needed discipline. Reining her in wouldn't be easy. Nor would reining himself in. Or trying to behave like a professional, like some semblance of an employer. He really shouldn't let himself get close to her. But she had the most expressive blue eyes he'd ever seen.

He took a cocky step toward her. "You need to make up the time you missed."

She wanted to laugh. Was he serious? "I'm already pretty good at martial arts."

"So there's nothing new to learn?" He gestured toward the mat.

He wanted to spar? Now? Here? Alone? And what was that funny look in his eye? She wasn't sure, but it was making her blood pump with the thrill of a challenge. "Okay, boss man. I'm game." She half laughed as she kicked off her shoes and stepped onto the soft surface. "Let's see what you've got."

He chuckled confidently.

She turned and watched him bow to her. A traditionalist. Nice. They had a few weaknesses. She did the same, then squatting down into a back stance, turned her hips and chest, so she could strike at will. She spread her arms protectively.

He took a similar position. His eyes boring holes into her, slowly he moved to the left, panther-like.

She watched the sheen on his muscled arms as she moved away in the same direction. Suddenly, she remembered Becker saying he had a black belt. She'd never stayed with any martial arts school long enough to get past the second or third level. Her preference was breadth rather than depth. Maybe she was a little out of her league. Still, she'd picked up tips in barrooms that martial artists didn't know. She could hold her own.

Easy, careful. He'd make his move any second now.

There it was. His arm shot out, reached for her face. She grabbed it, turned it over her shoulder. He broke free and smiled. Pleased with her response? "Your *fudoshin's* a little off."

She gritted her teeth. "Can't admit I surprised you, can you?"

Fudoshin, huh? Her first sensei, an old guy who gave classes out of his garage, had been the first to teach her about *fudoshin*. Calm despite the storm. Emotional control. Not her strong suit.

She kicked out at his leg. His split second retreat made her miss. She stumbled just a tad. His reflexes were pretty good, too.

"Center your *chi*," he said quietly.

Chi. Life force. Energy flow. He was really asking for it, wasn't he? "My *chi* is just fine," she sputtered. It wasn't her *chi*. It was his chest. Bare and glistening. Strong and darn distracting. She sidled away from him.

With lightning speed, he charged toward her, reached for her wrist.

She pulled out of his grip with a twist.

"Not bad." He exhaled, fascinated by her skills. Her technique hadn't been molded in formal schooling as his had been. Instead it was a conglomeration of styles and tactics, mixed with street skills. He could only imagine where she'd learned them. "That day I saw you go after your boss on the road crew, I noticed your footwork could use some improvement." It was a lie. Provoking her ire would show if she could control it.

He really knew how to push her buttons. Miranda took a step back, took control of her breathing and relaxed. That was better. Unlucky for him, since her bout with Fat Mama, she'd been practicing her *kata*, her martial arts forms, at home every night.

His fist came for her again.

Quarter turn backwards. Double block. "How's that for footwork?"

"Better." Admiration sang in his heart.

"Really? How do you like this?" She took a few steps back, steadied herself, came toward him. She spun around with a flying kick, brushed him on the chest.

The force pushed him back two steps. He stopped to wipe his mouth and grinned again. "Excellent."

"Yeah, it was, wasn't it?" She didn't care what her teachers said. Rage fueled her. And about now, his smug attitude had her royally pissed. She let out a cry and lunged toward his face.

He caught her by the arms, blocked her. They were close, both breathing hard. He wasn't getting the best of her. With one swift, sudden movement, she butted her head against that powerful chest and down he went.

"Outstanding," he laughed as he hit the mat.

But he still had her hands. As he fell, she tumbled down on top of him. The next instant, he surprised her, grabbing her arms and turning her over on her back. "But calm control always trumps rage, Miranda."

She looked up into that gorgeous face. He was on top of her, had her wrists pinned to the mat. They both panted in each other's face. She should be panicking about now. Feeling those old emotions of helplessness and fear.

Instead, all she felt was passion.

She stared at his luscious mouth, longing to pull his lips down to hers and find out what they tasted like. He must have had the same idea. With a single move, he bent his head and devoured her mouth.

She squealed beneath him as desire burst inside her. She fought his grip holding her down. She wasn't afraid, wasn't panicking. She wanted to touch him, run her hands over those lovely muscles of his. As if sensing her need, he let her go, her fingers flew immediately to his smooth back, rippled sensuously over those amazing shoulders.

The well of desire inside her was deep. She pressed back hard, brutally against his mouth. Her hands moved to his chest. She felt the firm muscles, gloried in the touch of his moist flesh. She lingered another moment, then pushed fiercely, turning him over until she was above him.

She ran her hands over his biceps, down to his wrists. It was her turn to hold his arms to the mat. He fought back with his mouth against hers. She thought it was cheating when he slipped his tongue inside her. She went mad. Let his arms go and threw hers around his neck.

They tumbled over and over, their kisses growing more potent, more violent with each turn.

He had her down again. As his tongue worked the inside of her mouth, fanning her flames to a brilliant fuel, his hands began exploring her body. Her arms, her stomach, her breasts.

She groaned beneath him at his touch. He was making her long for more. For him. Was she out of her freaking mind? What were they going to do? Make love right here in his dojo? He was her boss, for God's sake. Before she could voice her protests, they extinguished into thin air as his hand captured her breast, worked her nipple, flooded her with unbearable pleasure.

Filled with desire and ecstasy, she closed her eyes and exhaled in a wordless moan.

Across the room, a latch turned. Steps sounded on the wooden floor. Was that who she thought it was?

Over her, Parker's body stiffened as a female voice materialized in her ears.

"Oh…my…God."

Yep. With a gargantuan effort, Miranda broke free of Parker's hands. She sat up, gasping for breath, looked up at the figure standing over them.

Gen.

She'd never quite seen that expression on anyone's face before.

She uttered a cry like a wounded hyena. "What in the hell is going on here?"

Parker sat up and wiped his mouth. "I thought I taught you to knock before you enter a room."

Gen stared at her father a moment with a ferocious look, then decided to lash out at Miranda instead. "What are you doing here, Steele? I thought you were sick."

Miranda started to get to her feet. Now she was really in hot water. Pretty dicey, messing around with the boss. "Look, lady—"

Lightly, Parker laid a hand on her shoulder to stop her from saying any more. He stood in one graceful move, then pulled her up. He wasn't about to be shamed by his own daughter. Or let her embarrass Miranda. "Ms. Steele and I were sparring."

"Sparring? That's not what it looked like to me. Where was she today?"

"On assignment for me."

Miranda stopped brushing off her clothes and stared at Parker. He was sticking up for her?

"Dad. Didn't we already decide—"

"*I* make the decisions in this company, Gen." His voice was strong, firm, very much the Commander in Chief. Miranda's heart did a little dance. He gestured toward the papers she had under her arm. "Do you have something for me to sign?"

Her eyes blazed. "Darn right, I do. Steele's dismissal papers."

Dismissal? That bitch wanted to fire her? "Listen, you—"

Sharply, Parker raised a hand. "Why do you think she should be dismissed?"

"Besides this?" Gen put a finger against her chin. "Oh, let me think. She cut class early last Friday, her clothes barely make the dress code, and she skipped work today for no reason. Oh, and I found out today she's got a record."

"I'm aware of that. It's only misdemeanors."

Miranda stared at Parker. He'd known all about her background and had hired her anyway. Had pursued her as an employee.

Gen hissed aloud. "Only? She's a liability to the firm."

He shook his head and chuckled, tenderly. "You'll indulge me if I use my own judgment on this one, dear?"

Rage flamed in her eyes. "Dad, I just can't handle her."

Parker looked Miranda over. Her thick dark hair was tangled around her intense face. Her sweatpants and tank top were still awry from their wrestling match. His blood still ran hot from the taste of her. A hundred times over the past two weeks he'd told himself his interest in her was merely professional. That he would let others handle her training. That it was best for both of them if he kept his distance. Who was he kidding? She was his recruit. He wasn't going to miss the opportunity to watch her grow, guide that talent, help her hone those instincts. And after what had just happened, he knew she was more than a recruit to him.

He turned back to his daughter. "Very well, Gen. I'll take over her training."

Miranda watched Gen's chin drop to her chest. "That's not what I meant."

"But it's what *I* meant."

"What about morale? The other trainees?"

"I occasionally take a promising new hire under my wing. They'll have to understand that."

"Promising? Dad, she's not licensed. She's got to go to class."

"Oh, she will. Part time. I also want her help on the Taggart case."

She was back on the Taggart case? Miranda wanted to shout and prance around the gym in triumphant glee.

Parker reached out a hand to her. "Shall we?"

"Sure." As Gen stood speechless, she took hold of it and let him lead her right past the stunned young woman.

"Thanks for saving my hide," she whispered to him as they crossed the gym.

"Don't mention it." His steel gray eyes took on a mischievous glow. "And what a lovely hide it is."

She had to laugh.

Gen found her voice. "Dad," she cried out in exasperation.

"Don't worry, dear," Parker called out to his daughter, his eyes fixed on Miranda. He chuckled as he opened the door for her. "Ms. Steele won't be carrying firearms."

CHAPTER EIGHTEEN

"I called you three times this morning."

"You did?" It was Tuesday morning and they were crossing the Imperial Building parking lot, heading for Parker's silver Mazda. Briefcase in hand, Parker was dressed in a navy suit, matching silk tie, and crisp white dress shirt, looking as GQ as ever. Miranda was in one of her new, tough-looking outfits. A short, low-riding dress skirt with a dark lace-up top that had made her boss's eyes light up when he saw her.

When they left the gym last night, she'd half-expected Parker to ask her to his penthouse, or wherever rich Atlanta investigators bedded their women, but he'd only dropped her off near her cube and said he'd be in touch tomorrow.

She'd told herself that was the way she'd wanted it, though she'd have preferred to be the one to say, "not tonight, honey." But she had to admit that her heart had done a little flip when she got back to her desk this morning and found a phone message from him telling her to meet him out here in the lot. She could just imagine the look on Gen's face when she found out she was off with dear old Dad today.

She pulled her cell out of her pocket and turned it on. It jingled and beeped, showing her the other messages he had left. Oops.

"Sorry. Didn't have it on."

"Why not?"

"The battery runs low."

"You were provided with a charger, weren't you?"

"Yeah. So?"

Beside her, he stiffened. "So use it. Communication is important. Check your messages several times a day. And put the phone on mute. You might not want to be heard."

She pressed the button to turn off the sound, hoping she'd hit the right one. "Jeez, what a hard ass," she muttered under her breath.

He stopped in the middle of the aisle and turned to her. "Excuse me?"

"I mean, yes sir, Mister Boss Man." She put a hand to her forehead in a salute.

He sighed. "I'm not pulling rank, Miranda. It might save your life some day."

Save her life? A cell phone would make a nice impromptu weapon, but she wasn't in the habit of calling for help. If it meant that much to him, fine.

"Okay, I'll try to get in the habit." She stuffed the thing back in her pocket.

He nodded and continued on.

So it was going to be all business. That was fine, too.

Last night, she'd gone home and tried to practice her *kata*, but she couldn't concentrate on her stretches and kicks after that lust-ridden smooch-fest. Talk about *fudoshin*. She'd sure lost control with Parker last night. And she wasn't thinking of the match. The thrill of his fiery kisses, the lusty touch of his hands, the scent of his body, all replayed in her mind, making her shiver so hard, she gave up on the exercises, got a beer from the kitchen, and sat down to sort out her feelings. And sort them, she had.

Wade Parker was just about the sexiest man she'd ever laid eyes on. As a PI, she was beginning to admire him as much as Becker and Holloway did. She'd realized how much she wanted to work with him, how lucky she was to get the chance. She was even starting to see why Fanuzzi was so gaga about him.

But that was as far as she would ever let it go. She didn't dare let herself sink any deeper in the pool of his charms. That would be way too dangerous. She didn't believe in serious relationships. She'd had one once and had vowed never to have another. She definitely didn't want a man in her life. Not permanently. A man in your life ruined everything.

Not that Parker wanted to get serious. He'd given her no indication of that, and besides, why should he, when he could have any woman he wanted for the asking?

Right now, all she cared about was finding Madison Taggart's killer and the girl who'd written the letter from The Seekers. Parker had put her back on the Taggart case and she was determined to take advantage of the opportunity. Right now, that meant doing something about Dexter Hinsley.

"Today, you'll be introduced to mobile surveillance," Parker announced as they reached his car.

That sounded good. "Trailing a suspect?"

"Precisely."

"Cool."

He reached for the handle on the driver's side. "Get in. You're driving."

"You want me to pilot?" She grinned, a little surprised.

"Do you think you can handle it?" There was a note of amusement in his voice.

She narrowed her eyes and let out a huff. "I won't even dignify that with an answer." But she smiled as she slipped inside and onto the soft leather seat.

With a smug chuckle, he closed her door, came around the passenger side and slid in beside her.

She touched the padded steering wheel, ran her hand over the expensive leather of the interior. This was too cool. The vehicle was immaculate and smelled new. But it was still kind of plain for a man of his means. "How come you don't drive a fancier car?"

He reached for his seatbelt. "It's important to blend in. Look ordinary."

She clicked hers on, too. "Like you're supposed to be there."

"Correct." He gave her that sexy, wry smile of his. "Of course, I had the engine replaced with a BMW V-8."

Chill bumps danced up her arms. "Oh, yeah?"

He nodded. "In addition to anonymity, you need speed."

Squirming in her seat with excitement, she turned the key in the ignition. The powerful engine came to life with a smooth purr. "I've got a need for speed."

"Only when necessary," he warned.

"Okay, spoilsport." She'd see if they agreed on what was "necessary," she decided, pulling out of the parking spot. "Where to, boss?"

He smiled at her, as if he finally had her where he wanted her. "Head south down I-85. Do you know how to get there?"

"I think I remember." That was the way to her old work site.

"In case you need help," he pushed a button on the dash and a small screen appeared. A map flashed on it. "Here's a good route."

"Wow." Delighted, Miranda wanted to stop and ogle the screen. "My old clunker doesn't have a GPS. I never bought one." In her travels, she usually just followed her nose.

As she headed for the exit of the parking lot, a female voice with a British accent sang out, "Dunkin Doughnuts, I-85. Estimated arrival time, thirty-eight minutes."

"What?" She stepped on the brake and the car made a little screech.

Parker caught himself on the dash with a scowl. "What's wrong?"

Her temper spiked. "We're making a doughnut run? I thought we were going to look for Hinsley."

He turned and studied her with that penetrating investigator's look, the corner of his mouth turned up in a half-grin. "The bloodhound has caught the scent, hasn't she?"

"Woof. But you know my bite is worse than my bark." She hoped she didn't sound as disappointed as she felt.

He was silent for a moment, as if centering himself, then he spoke in his quiet, steady voice. "Dunkin Doughnuts is merely a point of reference. I'm hoping we'll pick Hinsley up there on his way out of town."

Her heart jumped again. "Really?"

"If we stop wasting time."

"Why didn't you say so?" She took her foot off the brake.

He sat back again. "I just did."

"Turn left, twenty feet," the British lady said.

"Right on, sister." Miranda turned and headed down Piedmont.

"Turn left onto Lenox Road, zero point three miles."

Miranda scowled. The British lady was getting on her nerves. "Can you turn her off?"

Parker chuckled. "So soon?" He pressed a button and Miranda exhaled. She was on her way to catch a killer. Nothing could dampen her spirits now.

The temperature had cooled off a few degrees, and the Mazda's air conditioning was cranked and comfortable, but it was still bright and sunny. She pulled down the visor as she took a turn onto the Buckhead Loop then spun onto GA-400 where they cruised past tall, sleek office buildings, each built in a different shape, as if each builder was in competition with the other for the most imaginative design. They went through the tollbooth and traffic got heavier. They slowed, coasted under a few bridges and as they emerged, another row of tall buildings, these encased in checkerboard glass, rose above them and over the green trees like sentries. She thought nothing could match Parker's building for class and style, but these structures were impressive.

The traffic sped up. She pressed the accelerator just a tad. With a smooth hum, the Mazda zoomed forward. That BMW engine could move. Fanuzzi would go ape doo-doo if she could see it. "This cruiser handles a whole lot better than my old jalopy."

"I'm glad it meets with your approval." Parker paused, then as casually as if he were talking about the weather, he said, "I checked with Hosea last night. There are still no leads on the murder."

Which was why they were out here, she supposed. "Did you mention Hinsley?"

He shook his head. "Not until we have something solid." He reached for his attaché case, opened it, and pulled out some papers. "I did a little homework on our textbook salesman."

"You did?"

"Just a bit of research." He opened a folder.

Chill bumps went down her spine. Parker really must have thought her visit to Dogwood Academy yesterday had turned up a decent lead. For the first time in her life, she felt like she'd done something worthwhile. From the corner of her eye, she watched him scan over the stack of information.

"Dexter Xavier Hinsley. Age twenty-eight. Married to Cora Beth Hinsley, age twenty-six. Residence, Doraville."

"Never heard of it."

"It's a town just northeast of here."

"We're headed in the other direction."

"Correct," he murmured, lost in his data.

She glanced at the file's thickness. "You do all that research on Hinsley in one night?" Or had he had as restless an evening as she'd had?

"I had help. My chief assistant ran some reports for me. I did the rest."

His chief assistant, Noreen Tan. A tough Asian woman who'd been with Parker for years. Miranda had heard Becker and Holloway talk about her, but she'd never seen her. They said she was married to a high-up on the police force. A mutual friend of hers and Parker's. That's where he got a lot of his clout with the police department. So they said.

He continued to summarize his findings. "Middle class background, average earnings. Dexter and Cora are from the same town. They went to grade school, high school, and college together. They've been married five years."

"Childhood sweethearts. Precious."

"Dexter has worked several sales jobs. Cora Beth is a homemaker."

Miranda thought about the night she met Coco. "She wants to play piano. Dexter won't let her."

"Hmm. That fits the profile," he said half to himself.

"Which profile?" Didn't sound like a serial killer's.

"Two years ago Cora filed a domestic abuse charge against him, then dropped it."

"Oh, that profile." Miranda squeezed the steering wheel with both hands as anger rippled inside her. She'd suspected that's what Coco meant when she said Dexter had a temper. That bastard.

"Hinsley works for Boozer and Big, a company that sells textbooks and other supplies to middle schools. He has the southeast territory." He pulled a paper from the stack. "I have a list of possible destinations for today."

"You know where Dexter's going?"

He gave a hopeful shrug. "Patterns from the company's financials and recent sales figures on their website indicate the schools he might be visiting today."

"You got all that from financial reports and a website?" Parker was something else.

"We'll see how accurate my deductions were. Apparently, Hinsley is good at what he does."

She smirked. "So the teacher at Dogwood Academy thought."

His chest rumbled a bit. "I mean, he's one of Boozer and Big's top salesmen."

"Guess he's got a persuasive style."

"Apparently."

"Hey, maybe we can sneak up behind him and rough him up a little."

For a second, Parker looked as if he'd enjoy that idea. Then he cleared his throat. "Let's stick to the task at hand."

"Okay, party pooper."

With a scolding look, he adjusted the now silent GPS and gazed out at the cars surrounding them. Miranda did the same. The map indicated heavy traffic. It was right on. Three lanes of solid bumper to bumper surrounded them. Miranda had seen rush hour snarls in a lot of cities, but Atlanta's took the cake.

At this time of day, the city's interstates turned into giant parking lots of metal. Every imaginable vehicle from tiny Kias and Bugs to monster Hummers and SUVs crowded onto the pavement. Every now and then, the mechanical landscape intensified with the loud, grinding axles of a smelly eighteen-wheeler.

Traffic from hell.

Miranda gripped the wheel and hunted through the sea of cars for the black sedan she'd seen yesterday. Suddenly, a familiar-looking vehicle came into view. Her heart hopped into her throat. "There he is. Midnight black Grand Prix in the far right lane."

Parker shot up in his seat. "Can you see the license plate?"

She inched up until the plate came into view, but it was too far to decipher. She couldn't see the driver through the tinted windows. Parker reached for the binoculars in the glove compartment, read off the digits. "That's the number on your paper."

A thrill shot through her. "Guess it was a good thing I took it down." The right lane sped up. She stepped on the accelerator, flipped on the blinker. "I need to get over."

"Stay where you are for now. Changing lanes suddenly could attract his attention."

"We can't lose him."

Parker's voice was calm and steady. "What do you imagine the first rule of mobile surveillance is?"

She thought a moment. "Uh, don't get made?" She knew that from movies and crimes shows.

"Correct. And how does one do that?"

"Don't follow too close?"

"Excellent response."

Frustrated, she turned off the blinker. Of course, she didn't want Hinsley to see them, but part of her wanted to drive right up behind the jerk and ram him in the ass. A big, chili red Grand Cherokee took a chance on the space she'd left and shot in front of her, then zipped into the right lane.

"Hey, jerkoff."

"Easy," Parker said.

She waved her fist at the driver. "He took my spot."

"It's a public highway. How much coffee have you had this morning?"

"None," she growled. "Wait till you see me after a cup or two." She squeezed the steering wheel and muttered under her breath. "These drivers in this town really get my goat."

"Take it in stride. It's merely part of the job."

Easy for him to say. She glanced over at the black Grand Prix. It was getting farther away. "Damn." The traffic slowed again, came to a halt. The right lane kept moving. A noisy semi rolled up and blocked her view of Hinsley's car entirely. She squirmed in her seat. "Double damn."

"Take a deep breath. Relax."

"Sure. Right," she grumbled. "The zen of surveillance." But she inhaled anyway. Didn't help much. "Your big V-8 engine doesn't do much for us now."

He put the binoculars away and sat back with his easy confidence. "It will."

At least the little yellow Audi in front of her was small enough to see over.

The vehicles in front of it started to move, but the Audi stayed put. The driver was on a cell phone.

"Hey," Miranda slammed her palm on the steering wheel. "Move it," she yelled. "Man, I hate it when these Atlanta drivers sit there with their fingers up their butts."

The Audi driver got his head out of his ass and zoomed up. But before Miranda could close the hole he'd created, a huge Suburban jumped in front of her.

"Asshole," she cried. She raised her hand, about to jam it into the horn.

Parker reached up and caught her wrist just before her palm hit the rubber. "Remember the first rule."

Goose bumps shot over her skin at his touch. Confusion peppered her mind. Damn. She thought she'd flushed those feelings last night. With a grunt she twisted out of his grasp. "I know. I know. Don't get made."

"Don't do anything to attract attention."

This was a lot easier on TV. She took an exasperated breath. "Fuck!"

"You curse a lot when you're upset," he observed.

She turned up a lip at him. He was studying her with that telepathic look of his. "Am I offending your Southern gentility or something? I thought you'd be used to rough language in your job."

"I am, but profanity mixed with anger often indicates…"

"What?"

He turned his head away. "It may indicate…issues."

"You a psychologist, Parker?"

He kept his eyes on the traffic. "Understanding of the human psyche helps in this work."

She straightened her shoulders. "Oh yeah? What do you do? Keep psychological profiles on your employees?"

"If necessary."

She didn't like that answer at all. "What are you? The Personnel Nazi?"

Turning back to look at her, he chuckled. "I seem to have hit a sore spot."

She held on tight to the steering wheel and stared at the back of the Suburban. Parker was pissing her off more than the traffic. She blew out a breath. "Everybody cusses. Especially in traffic like this."

"My wife didn't."

Miranda looked over at him. He had a faraway look in his eyes. "Oh, yeah?"

"Sylvia rarely used bad language."

"I find that hard to believe."

"Other than a few vulgarities from Chaucer, the worst I ever heard her utter was when she dropped her wedding ring down the drain once."

Wedding ring. Miranda bristled at the mention of the sentimental symbol. She'd pawned hers after she left Leon. Didn't get much for it. "What did she say?"

"She said 'Poop.'"

Miranda snorted, shook her head. Hah. A sweet, genteel Southern belle. She hoped Parker wasn't making a comparison. She could never live up to that woman. Good thing she'd decided her relationship with him was just professional. "Your wife must have been a saint."

"She was," he said softly.

"Well, sorry. No saints here. Just us sinners."

He looked at her with a strange, half-tender look that made her wonder what he was thinking. "Present company included."

She brushed her hair back and studied the traffic. "If you say so."

Parker eyed the sharp look in her deep blue eyes, her thick black hair, her smooth skin. What was this power she had over him? She was about as far away from Sylvia as a woman could get. How could he be so attracted to her? He had always felt, with her demure ways, Sylvia lived on a plane somewhere above him. Miranda was just on his level. Her raw, unbridled temper was very human. It amused and aroused him. Sinners, indeed. He had a sudden flash of that wild temper, as they lay tangled in the sheets of his bed.

After their bout in the gym yesterday, that vision had been in his head more than once. And yet, he felt more toward her than mere lust. Just as he'd noticed last night, he could see there was more to her anger than simple frustration. More to her. She had secrets. Hidden pain. He wanted to help. To reach deep down inside and sooth whatever hurt tormented her. Perhaps it was time to look deeper into her background.

Uncomfortable with Parker's silence, Miranda drummed her fingers on the steering wheel. "I think we've lost Hinsley."

"No, we haven't. He's right up ahead."

The semi pulled off onto an exit revealing the black Grand Prix purring along.

Before Parker could react, she saw a free spot and scooted into it. She pulled up right behind him. "Got you, you sonofa…uh, you sucker."

He cleared his throat. "Is this really what you want?"

Crap. She was too close. Hinsley might be able to see them in his rearview.

"Slow down and let someone in."

She did. Luckily, it was a little blue Saab that broke in front of her this time.

"One more."

"What?"

"Two vehicles between you and the target is the minimum."

She rolled her eyes, but eased off and let a beige Toyota in.

"Excellent."

She frowned. "You sure about that?"

"Absolutely. You're doing well."

Glad he thought so. They'd better not lose him.

After another half hour or so, they made it to the I-20 exchange and followed Dexter as he took the exit. All the way down the interstate, Miranda kept the right number of cars between them. Old Hinsley didn't suspect a thing.

A few miles past the west leg of the perimeter, the Grand Prix took an exit onto a surface street. She followed him, staying well behind. They headed through a rural area toward a town the sign said was Mableton. A spot zoned for twenty-five miles an hour made her hit the brake, but she recovered nicely and cruised slowly past the lanes of doublewide trailers, a KFC, and a Kwik Way convenience store. After a few more lazy turns, Dexter pulled into a middle school parking lot.

"Bingo," Miranda grinned, ready to move in for the kill.

"Drive past the entrance," Parker said.

Huh? "Won't we lose him?"

"He'll be there a while. He'll notice us if you pull in behind him."

"Good point." Forcing herself to go slowly, she drove down to the next street. "Let me guess. Find a place to turn around and go back to the school?"

"You're catching on."

She lifted a shoulder, trying to imitate his casual air. "Nothing to it." She pulled into a driveway, turned around and headed back.

"Park along the street. Here will do."

There was a nice spot behind a green Honda along the curb. Oak trees and bushes provided enough coverage for a little camouflage. She stopped the car and turned off the engine. "Now what?"

Parker opened the glove compartment, took out his binoculars and handed them to her. "Now we watch."

She lifted them, adjusted the focus. She saw Hinsley get out of the car, straighten his tie, grab a box from the backseat and head inside the school.

"What do you see?"

"The cat going for the canary."

"It could be just a legitimate sales call."

"He's peddling something."

"Objectivity, Miranda. It's unwise to convict without evidence."

"Okay," she sighed. But soon her instincts proved out. After about fifteen minutes, Hinsley exited the building with a lady on his arm. A cute little blonde with short hair and a pert walk. Another teacher? "What did I tell you? This guy sure likes playing school." She reached for the keys.

Parker touched her hand. "Don't turn the car on yet." He opened his attaché case and pulled out a second pair of binoculars. This one sleek and silver.

"Thoughtful of you to bring two."

"This one has a camera."

"Don't our cell phones have cameras?"

He nodded. "They do, but this one captures more detail. High-speed shutter, 8X telescopic lens, stores several thousand images in high resolution, downloads to a computer, of course. You'll learn to work with digital photography in your classes." He raised it to his eyes, adjusted the lens.

Dexter and the woman crossed the lot and headed for her car, a little lemon-colored Camry.

Parker snapped a shot just as Hinsley opened the door for his prey and gave her a pat on the ass. That would be an incriminating close-up. Damn, Parker was good.

The lovebirds shot out of the school's entrance.

"Now," Parker said.

Miranda turned the ignition and pulled onto the road.

"Easy," Parker reminded her.

But he didn't need to. She kept her foot steady on the accelerator, making sure there was plenty of room behind the Camry. A silver pickup truck pulled out in front of her. This time she was glad for the cover. Parker's Mazda blended right in. He was right about looking normal.

They followed Mr. Textbook and his personal tutor to a Days Inn down the street and sat across the lot as the couple got a room and went inside. Parker took more pictures.

"Wonder what kind of private lessons she's giving him," Miranda muttered. "Sonofabitch."

"Not the kind you win a scholarship for." Parker uttered a low growl that she'd never heard from him before. He sounded mad. Real mad.

Mableton was only Dexter-Boy's first stop. They followed him to a school in Villa Rica where he met a lanky brunette, then across the Alabama line where he stopped for lunch at a drive thru. Parker and Miranda grabbed some sandwiches and tagged along to Anniston where a petite, dimple-cheeked redhead was waiting, then on to Talladega where there was a thin, freckle-faced blonde.

It was late afternoon when Casanova ended his tour outside of Birmingham. Here, he altered his pattern a tad. He got in a car with a sultry-looking black-haired woman and they drove to her house.

For several hours, Miranda and Parker sat outside watching. It turned dark and Dexter was still in there. So this was an example of one of Dexter's overnight business trips Coco had mentioned. By now, Parker had enough snapshots to fill the family photo album.

Miranda thought she heard a soft moan come through an open window where the lights were off. "Bastard."

"It seems you were right about Mr. Hinsley's sales technique."

"I'd like to give him an order he'd never forget."

"Likewise."

"What are you going to do with all those pictures?" she asked.

"Have them printed and keep them on file."

She turned to him. "You can't do anything more?"

Grimly, he shook his head. "Unfortunately, no. They aren't strictly legal, since a client didn't request them."

"What if we showed them to Coco?"

He seemed to consider it a moment, then frowned. "I've worked quite a few divorce cases over the years. It usually backfires when you get involved uninvited."

She knew that but didn't want to let it go. "We could try."

He shook his head. "Coco has to ask for help first. Then we can do more investigating."

She sighed, dissatisfied with his answer. More noises came through the window. If she could catch Dexter alone some night…

Parker blew out a breath that sounded as frustrated as she was. "As reprehensible as it is, I don't see anything in Hinsley's behavior that links him to Madison Taggart's murder. Do you?"

"No," she admitted. Dexter's prey were willing. As far as she and Parker knew, he hadn't talked to a single child all day. He didn't look like a serial killer. Just a horny, cheating SOB. Poor Coco.

But Wendy had recognized him. Had she been mistaken? On second thought, the kid was the type to make things up.

The voice through the window grew louder, shot through the still night air. "Dexter. Oh, Dexter."

Miranda rolled her window down all the way.

"I'm coming, baby." It was Hinsley's husky drawl. "I'm coming."

The female giggled. "You're coming on Tuesday, but will you come again on Friday?"

"Of course, baby. Haven't I come on Friday for the past three months?"

"Oh, yes you have, Dexter Wexter. Every Friday. Oh, yes. Yes!"

Miranda wanted to lean out the window and woof the burger she'd had for lunch. Instead, she turned to Parker and they spoke the word at the same. "Alibi."

Shit. They'd spent the entire day driving and sitting around and had come up with zip. "Damn."

"Damn, indeed."

She slammed her hand on the steering wheel. "I want to catch that killer, Parker."

He smiled at her with tenderness and pride, stirring something deep inside her she didn't know was there. He felt exactly the same way, didn't he? On that one point, they were just alike.

"We will," he said. "Eventually. You did well today."

His compliment consoled her a little. "Thanks. Except that we wasted a whole day."

"You usually have to go down a few dead ends before you find the street you're looking for."

She groaned and wiped her eyes. "You know, detective work can be pretty frustrating. Not to mention monotonous."

Parker gave her his famous wry half-smile. "Hours of boredom interrupted by moments of sheer panic."

She hadn't seen any panic yet. Hinsley and his faculty members were the only ones getting excited today. She opened her mouth and let out a yawn.

"Let's head back." He looked at her tenderly, then got out of the car. "You're tired. Slide over. I'll drive."

She did.

He got in, started the car and quietly turned out of the dirt drive and onto the road. "Are you hungry?"

"Not really." Watching Dexter boink his way through middle school teachers all day hadn't done much for her appetite.

"If you can hold on until we get to the city, I have a place I'd like to take you. You're dressed well enough."

What did that mean? She was too wiped to ask. She leaned back in the comfortable seat and closed her eyes. "Sure."

CHAPTER NINETEEN

The sound of cars along a busy street buzzed in her ears. With a start, Miranda raised her head and frowned. How'd her head get onto Parker's shoulder? She rubbed her face and yawned. The Mazda was stopped. They were in the city somewhere. It was dark. "Where are we? My place?"

"Mine, in a manner of speaking."

He got out of the car and handed his keys to a red-suited valet. Another one opened the passenger door and helped Miranda out. Parker came around, offered his arm and escorted her across a sidewalk, through a set of shiny glass doors, and into a tall building.

He led her through a lobby filled with big, beautiful paintings, antique vases, oriental rugs and European-style furniture. Soft harp music filled the air. For a minute, Miranda thought she'd been transported to the eighteenth century.

They were on the elevator before the softly lit signs outside registered in her head. Parker Towers. Did Parker live here? As the car rose, a funny sensation roused below her navel. It wasn't from the elevator. Where were they headed? And did she really want to go there?

On the top floor, the doors whispered open and Parker led her down a short hall to a doorway where a man in a starched white coat stood behind a podium.

He greeted them with a bow. "How are you this evening, Mr. Parker?"

"Excellent, Jorge." He turned to her. "My associate, Ms. Steele."

"Pleased to meet you," he bowed again.

She nodded. "Likewise." She guessed.

"Your usual table?"

"That would be fine."

"This way."

Miranda exhaled in relief as she followed the man into a wide room and a barrage of delicious odors accosted her senses. Maitre d'. Restaurant. That was right. Parker had said something about food. She'd thought he'd meant IHOP.

She ran her fingers through her thick hair as they passed rows of linen-covered tables decked with candles and fine crystal, where finely clad guests sat. She guessed she looked okay in her black skirt and lace-up top. She remembered Parker said she was dressed "well enough." Guess Gen's dress code was good for something.

Jorge seated them in a quiet spot next to the window with a breathtaking view of the city. After gawking a bit, she turned and took in the inside.

Under muted lights, more paintings graced the walls. Hunting scenes and dreamy, old-fashioned landscapes hung in elaborately carved frames. Tasteful hunter green wallpaper and golden sconces echoed the color scheme, as did the tablecloths and upholstery of the high-back chairs. The whole room had a quiet, gilded look. It smelled of gourmet food, wealthy patrons, and old Southern money.

Miranda laughed self-consciously. "I don't think I've ever been in such a fancy eatery."

He reached across the table and touched her hand softly. "Then it's my pleasure to introduce you to it."

Sounded like that wasn't all he wanted to introduce her to. A sexy strand of hair fell over his forehead. She watched those kind but naughty gray eyes drinking her in. After their long day, his navy suit looked as clean and pressed as if he had just stepped out of a haberdashery.

She cleared her throat, pulled her hand away and opened her menu. She studied it a moment. *Aquitaine Caviar*? *Veal in Aligot and Brie Cream*? *Langoustine*? She laughed. "I don't think I can read this."

He chuckled and took her menu from her. "I'll order for you."

A waiter appeared and Parker murmured some instructions to him that she didn't understand, spoke a little French to him, which she also didn't understand. Might have thrown in an Italian phrase or two. Whatever he'd said produced a stunning feast.

Before she knew it, waiters brought bread, wine, and an incredible salad with blue and purple garnish. Hoping she'd grabbed the right fork, she tried a bite. The fresh greens bathed in tangy vinaigrette dazzled her tongue. This was a salad? She'd never had one this good. Before she knew, it was gone and a hand reached for her empty plate.

At the same time, another hand laid another dish before her. A huge, artfully designed mound of glistening morsels laced with colorful, exotic vegetables, and ladled with a creamy sauce over a bed of wild rice. Her stomach grumbled and her mouth watered.

Gingerly, she took a bite, closed her eyes as the rich flavors snapped in her mouth. She'd never tasted anything so heavenly. "I don't know what this is, but it's out of this world."

He smiled tenderly, enjoying her pleasure. "It's lamb and pheasant in a wine sauce with fennel and chestnuts. An interesting combination." He took a bite of his own dish. "It is quite good. Oh, I had the chef add extra spice to yours."

He'd remembered the peppers they'd shared at Ay Chihuahua. She grinned and popped another forkful into her mouth. She couldn't hold back a sigh. "I didn't know food could taste this good."

He couldn't stop grinning. "I'm glad you like my selection."

She really shouldn't make a pig out of herself but she couldn't help it. She dug in.

Just as she finished the last bite and wiped her mouth, a waiter brought another plate. She was about to protest. Then she got a look at it. Flames danced over an ice cream concoction smothered with coconut and almonds, and dotted with dark chocolate truffles. Now that was decadent.

Miranda blew at the flames, nibbled at the ice cream and groaned with delight. "It just keeps getting better."

His eyes twinkled at her reaction. "I've always considered Chef Basardi a true artist."

"Is that the cook's name?" She raised her wineglass, which was filled with something expensive and delicious. "My compliments to him."

She finished the whole thing. After all, she'd had a hard day. She made a mental note to do some serious weightlifting when she got home.

She pushed the plate away as waiters cleared the dishes and brought coffee in fine china cups. She sat back with a sigh and looked out over the twinkling sight below. Atlanta lay spread out beneath them, shimmering like jewels. Parker's city.

"This town belongs to you, doesn't it?"

He thought a moment, sipped from his cup. "I'd say it belongs to my father."

"I thought you knew everybody." And probably had dirt on most of them.

"I know the people, but my father owns the real estate. This is his hotel."

"Yeah. Parker Towers. I saw the fancy sign when we came in. You live here?"

He shook his head. "No. I don't live in my father's buildings."

She remembered he'd said his father had disowned him when he became a cop. It sounded like they still didn't quite get along.

He scanned the skyline. "Actually, Parker Towers is only a fraction of his holdings. Over there is Wade Plaza." He gestured toward a tall, needle-like building that shimmered like a long, narrow diamond. Then he indicated another monument, dark in the shadows. "The Russell Financial Center. That's his, too. It's named for me."

"Your middle name."

"Yes." He gestured down below to a small, quaint-looking building with lighted Grecian columns. "There's La Maison de Julia, named after one of his lady friends."

"Lady friends?"

"My mother passed away when I was young. My father never remarried. Since then, he's become something of a player."

"I see." She took a sip of her coffee. That was interesting, especially the part about the gene pool.

He indicated a squarish edifice beyond the dome. "Parker Station."

She held up a hand. "I get the idea." Like Fanuzzi had told her once, Parker's family was loaded.

He leaned forward and stroked the handle of his cup. "Now you know a bit about my background. What about yourself? You're such a mystery, Miranda."

She smiled in surprise at his remark. "That's your business, isn't it? Solving mysteries."

"It is. But perhaps tonight you'd just like to talk."

She shifted her weight, remembering she was sitting across from a man with some of the best interrogation techniques in the business. "What do you want to know?"

"Whatever you want to tell me."

She looked down at the dark liquid in front of her. "You've already done a background check on me."

"Background checks reveal only superficial details. They don't tell you about the person."

Oh, yeah? He already knew more about her than she wanted him to. Confession might be good for the soul, but it drew people together. She didn't want to get any closer to Wade Russell Parker than she already was. She'd stamped out whatever spark that had ignited last night in his gym. It would stay out.

She shrugged. "Can't think of anything in particular."

He laid an arm on the table, leaned near her. "Why did you never marry?"

Her gaze shot to his eyes. His look was steady, immovable. His background search hadn't gone back that far. The news filled her with relief. "Never wanted to," she lied.

"Was there never anyone special?"

She tensed, searched his face. He'd assumed, like everyone else, that she'd been an unwed mother who'd given her daughter up for adoption then changed her mind. That explained why he wasn't in a hurry to help her find "Someone Else's Daughter." But she knew finding Madison Taggart's killer had to come first.

"I don't need someone to look after me." *Or telling me how to live my life.* "I can take care of myself." She looked at her watch. "Hey, it's getting late. I have to get up early tomorrow. My boss is a stickler for punctuality."

He sat back with a knowing look. "You can come in late."

A waiter placed the check on the table.

She eyed Parker with suspicion. She knew his game. Soften her up with fine food and wine, make her feel all feminine and pampered, pepper her with personal questions, then move in for the kill. Like father, like son. She didn't want to be pampered. She certainly didn't want to be his conquest. "You don't have to give me special favors. What do I owe you for the fancy grub?"

He looked hurt for a second, then resolve took its place. "Nothing."

"You don't want to take it out of my pay, along with everything else I owe you for?"

His jaw stiffened at her remark. The only reason he'd asked for repayment of her advance was that he knew she'd be too proud to take the money as a gift. He laid a card on the table. "Tonight is my treat."

"Okay. Thanks. Next time will be mine. It might be a hotdog at the Varsity, though."

He chuckled and eyed her as if he could see right through her façade.

She didn't care. She wasn't going to give. And yet, those sexy lips of his seemed to call to her. If she could just taste them one more time. Nope. Not gonna happen. She didn't want a handsome prince to take care of her. She sure didn't want to get used to a lifestyle like this.

In the hotel lobby there was a vendor selling roses. Parker selected a red one, gave the man a few bills, and held the flower out to her.

"What's this for?"

"Peace offering. In case I offended you upstairs with my questions. Force of habit, you understand."

She eyed him with caution. He was so smooth. But the sentimental gesture touched her. "Sure. I didn't mean to snap. I'm just...private."

"You're entitled." He reached for the door.

So this was a new tactic. Act disinterested, aloof, even apologetic, but stay hard on the trail of what you want. Give it up, Parker. It won't work with me.

A valet brought around his car. They drove silently down Peachtree. It wasn't the right direction. They were heading for her apartments. "Aren't we going back to the office?"

"I knew we'd be back late. While you were asleep earlier, I called and had someone bring your car to your place."

Had it all planned out, didn't he? He was in for a rude awakening.

After a few minutes, they pulled into the Colonial Towers parking lot. She looked around. Sure enough, there was her old jalopy sitting in a space. She swallowed. If he had any ideas about spending the night, he'd better revise them.

He parked near her car, got out and opened the door for her.

"You don't have to be so chivalrous. I work for you." Get the hint? Our relationship is purely a business one.

He leaned on the door in that sexy way of his and held out his hand. "It's my raising. Indulge me."

She took it and got out of the car, but dropped his hand as soon as she was on her feet. This was awkward. "Like I said upstairs, I can take care of myself."

"Duly noted. I'll walk you to your door."

Man, he was stubborn.

"You did extremely well today." He smiled when they got to the front door of the apartment building.

"Did I?" Her heart did a flip, despite her attempt to sound aloof.

"I'd give you an A. You displayed good instincts, persistence, and intelligence." He was sure laying it on thick. He leaned in a tad. "You're also damned attractive."

She smirked. "Beauty and brains. That's me, all right."

"You sell yourself too short."

"Do I?" His intense gaze roved over her, tempting her to give in to his charms. Time to change the subject. "Uh, what about tomorrow?"

He inched a little closer. "Tomorrow?"

"Work."

"Of course. Back to classes. I have to be out of town for few days."

For some reason, her heart sank at that news. She forced herself to shrug it off and sorted out her keys. She found the right one this time. She reached for the door, turned to him briskly. "Well, thanks for a wonderful meal."

"My pleasure." Instead of leaving, he moved a little nearer. She felt his warm breath on the back of her neck. The wistful smell of magnolias was in the air. Must be his cologne. "I was wondering if there was anything else I could do for you?"

Oh, that was good. So this was an offer of Southern hospitality. "Nothing I can think of. Like I said, I can take care of myself. I don't need a man." She meant to be firm, but her voice broke. Her heart was doing double-time. The key was slippery in her palm from sweat. Damn. She couldn't lose control. She couldn't let things get out of hand the way she had last night.

"So you said before." In a bold move, he took a step and blocked her from the door. A wisp of hair fell sexily over his forehead as he bore into her with those Magnum-gray eyes.

She twirled the rose in her other hand. It was just as damp. Other parts of her were getting there, too. "Excuse me." She pushed past him and shoved her key in the door. "I don't mean to make a case out of it, but I meant what I said."

He chuckled softly. "But you have made a case. Your Honor, let the record state Miranda Steele does not need a man to take care of her."

She turned the key and yanked the door open. "You making fun of me, Parker?"

He pushed it shut again. "Not at all."

She ought to level him right here and now. "I'm fine. I can take care of myself."

He took her chin in his hand. "So you said. And since you've made it so abundantly, so unabashedly clear that you don't need a man, I just have one question for you."

"What?"

Bending his head, his face almost touching hers, his eyes filled with desire, he whispered, "Do you want one?"

"Huh?"

Before she could answer, his lips were on hers. Hot, furious. She kissed him back just as fiercely, as if her mouth had a mind of its own. She hadn't squelched those sparks last night at all. They'd just been smoldering under the embers all this while. Now they flared up, engulfing her in hot, scorching flames, as if an army of waiters from the restaurant was pouring brandy over her and tossing in lighted matches.

She grew dizzy, limp as her arms went around his neck. That aggressive tongue of his fought its way to the soft inside of her mouth. They spun, shuffled backward, as if caught in some erotic waltz, and landed against the Southern-style column of the porch. He pressed her against the rounded surface. Trapped. His hands moved over her body. She moaned as she felt his arousal. Her heart ached for him like it would bleed. She held onto his neck for dear life and surrendered to the flood of passion ripping through her.

What was he doing to her? He was scaring the bejesus out of her. Part of her brain woke up, demanded, "What are *you* doing?" Good point. With all the strength she had, she broke free of his kiss. He held her tight as she gasped for breath in his arms. "I'm not in the mood for a one-night stand, Parker."

His eyes glowed in the moonlight. "That's not what I had in mind."

She froze. "What did you have in mind?"

"Definitely more than one night." His lips found her cheek, gently played over her skin, making her long to give up, give in. "Why don't we just see where Fate takes us?"

Fate? He wasn't talking about Fate. He was talking about something long term. He was talking about a relationship. That idea scared her more than the one-night stand.

She shook her head, forced out a laugh. "You don't want to get mixed up with someone like me, Parker."

"Why not?" he murmured, working his way to her ear, as if she didn't have a say in the matter.

She smirked. He wanted the truth? She'd give it to him. "Because my personal life's a fucking mess." She sucked at relationships.

"I'm good at straightening out fucking messes." He captured her mouth again, sent delicious, heady sensations down her spine with his tongue.

His hands moved over her body, making her shudder with something very close to surrender. His fingers teased at the laces of her blouse, caressed her breast. She couldn't let him go on. She couldn't make love with him. It would only mean pain. For both of them.

Parker drank in the taste of her lips, so alive with passion, the feel of her firm curves beneath his hands, even as she resisted him. Why, Miranda? Why fight so hard? What happened to make you so terrified of closeness? He didn't ask. He knew she wouldn't answer. But he could make her feel.

He reached beneath her skirt, ran his hand up her thigh. She sucked in her breath as his fingers touched her softness. His palm rocked gently against the sensitive place between her legs. She grew wet with desire.

Miranda shuddered, her mind going blank at his merciless touch. The magic of his lips, his tongue, his fingers, lured her, mesmerized her. Stop him, she thought. Stop him.

But she had to let him linger just a little while, stroking her, teasing her, fanning those flames ever higher. She wanted him. What if she gave in to him? Just for one night? He wouldn't be satisfied with one night. Then where would they be?

Her own weak, foolish desire suddenly enraged her. What the hell was she doing? She used her anger to force herself out of his spell. She put her hands against his chest and gave him a hard shove. "I can't do this."

Parker stepped back, stared into that expressive face. Serious, intense. Her hair awry, her lips red and swollen with passion.

His head cleared. She was right. He'd gone too far. He'd been lured in by that siren song. Those mindless, powerful urges he couldn't get control of. Not like him at all. She turned him into some sort of beast.

"Forgive me. Things got out of hand."

Miranda watched him pull himself together stiffly. He was angry, hurt. She could see it in his eyes. She couldn't let that get to her. "I'm sorry," she whispered. "I didn't mean to…"

"It's all right."

He straightened his suit coat, ran a hand over his hair as if he were reconstructing his masculinity. Then he turned to her with those deep gray eyes. "You made your feelings clear. I'm the one who should apologize." He stepped toward the door and opened it for her. "It's time we said goodnight."

Miranda stepped inside her apartment and closed the door behind her. She looked around, feeling very alone. The place seemed dull and tiny compared to the elegance of Parker Towers. So what? That swanky hotel, or anything like it, wasn't her life. Never could be. She crossed to the kitchen, found an empty beer bottle, ran some water and shoved Parker's rose in it. She set the bottle on the counter and went to the living room to roll up the exercise mats she'd left on the floor last night. She put them in the closet.

No *kata* tonight. Or weightlifting. She was bushed. Besides, it was late. She pulled off her clothes, took a shower, put on a T-shirt and lay down in her rented bed. After a minute, she got up, went to the kitchen and retrieved the beer bottle with Parker's rose.

She put the bottle on the nightstand and lay back down.

As soon as she closed her eyes, she could feel Parker's lips against hers again, his hands roaming over her body. Damn. She sat up, punched at her pillow, lay down again. *Do you want a man?* Parker had made her want one. Him. But only for sex. Not for a relationship. She didn't have relationships. Not with anyone. She should have opted for the one-night stand and kicked him out in the morning. With a grunt, she turned off the light.

She'd had sex after she left Leon. An occasional coworker she'd become friendly with, whose medical history she'd checked out first. Rarely, she drank too much and went home with someone in a bar, dangerous as that was, as empty as that left her. But it was just to quench a temporary thirst, like taking a drink from a public water fountain. Not anything serious. There was never a relationship.

She rolled over, stared into the darkness.

Relationships. Shrinks had told her she needed a good relationship. A new relationship to overcome the lousy one she'd had. They were full of crap. Relationships weren't an option for her. Her brain was too jumbled, her heart too numb. She'd had her fill of that kind of bullshit a long time ago.

And yet as she closed her eyes, Parker's sexy smile haunted her. None of the forgotten men she'd slept with had ever made her feel the way he did tonight. A relationship with Parker? Something inside her seemed to awake, like the first bud of spring breaking through hard ground. Or a dog sitting up for a biscuit.

Bullshit. She rolled over, gave her pillow another sock, pulled the sheet up to her chin. A relationship would only make her relive her past, make her deal with it, dredge up old memories. That was the last thing she needed. Her mind churned with restless thoughts, but at last it tired, relaxed. The thoughts melted away. And she fell asleep.

The cold air whistled through the trees high overhead. Their bare limbs etched jagged black streaks across the night sky. Walking. Cold. Frost snapped at her legs. Ice crunched under her feet as she made her way along the sidewalk.

She had to be someplace, but she couldn't remember where. She had to keep moving. Moving. Her breath made smoke in the air as she walked. How far was it now? It was so dark. So cold.

Then she heard that sound. Slow crunching behind her on the ice. Footsteps.

He was there.

Now she remembered. It was her car she was trying to get to. If she could just get to her car, she'd be safe. She hurried along the sidewalk. It wasn't in this block. She crossed the deserted street, trudged through snow. The crunching was still behind her. Getting closer. She tried to go faster, but it was hard to move over the slippery surface of the icy sidewalk. She heard him breathing. Where was her car?

There. The silver door handle twinkled in the moonlight like a star. She reached out for it, but it was too far away. She stretched and strained her arm to reach it. Almost there. She had it. Just as her fingers touched its metallic surface, the handle disintegrated into cold dust, and he grabbed her from behind.

He jerked her arms behind her back. She cried out in pain, fear slicing through her like a knife. *No. Stop.* She struggled, but he was too strong. And she was weak, powerless. She'd never learned how to fight back, how to defend herself. She'd been hurt over and over and all she'd ever done was take it.

Forcefully, he turned her around. His face was a round knob of black wool, like a bizarre puppet. Ski mask. Don't hurt me. Please don't hurt me. *Don't beg. Why had she begged?* She twisted in his grasp.

He shoved her down, dragged her away to a cold, dark place, the sharp ice scraped at her back. His hands tore her clothes, forced her legs apart. *No, please no.* The pain was sharp, unbearable as he entered her. She shuddered, her stomach clenching in a hard heave. She was weak. Helpless. It was all her fault. Leon said so.

Leon.

Her hands balled into tight fists. Her arms flew at his face. Her fists pounded into the wool. She tugged it off and Leon's fierce black eyes glared at her.

She reached up. Her hand found a weapon. She'd kill him with it. She reared back, came forward with all her might. It smashed over his head and broke into pieces.

God in Heaven.

Miranda shot straight up in bed, the shatter of glass bursting in her ears, her heart hammering so hard in her head, she thought it would explode. Something had exploded.

For several moments, she sat on the corner of the bed, panting, hugging herself, shivering all over. Every part of her shook in terror and rage. At last, she wiped her face with a corner of the bed sheet. With a trembling hand, she reached over and turned on the light. She looked around the room. Her breath steadied. She was in Buckhead, in her apartment. The man in the dream was gone.

She was about to lay down again when she noticed the wall. Pulling her T-shirt close around her, she got up and crossed the room. She stopped when she felt something sharp under her feet. Glass.

Water stains ran down the neutral-colored paint to the baseboard. Dark brown pieces of a beer bottle lay shattered on the carpet. She glanced at the nightstand. Empty. She looked back at the floor, blinked.

There, in the middle of the shards, lay Parker's rose.

CHAPTER TWENTY

Alone in his hotel room, Parker stared down at the copies of crime scene reports scattered on the table. Two days ago, he had taken the three-and-a-half hour flight from Hartsfield to Pittsburgh International, where an old friend and former student had met him.

Frank Donaldson had left the Parker Agency several years ago to return home to Pittsburgh and go into police work. He was Assistant Chief now, and when he read about Madison Taggart's murder in the papers, he'd given Parker a call. He might have a connection, he said. After the dead end with Hinsley, after nearly two weeks of reviewing the evidence with Hosea and the coroner until his eyes were red, Parker finally had a lead. Of sorts.

At the Pittsburgh Bureau's headquarters on Western Avenue, Donaldson had reviewed the facts with him. The incident had occurred over a month and a half ago, and the case was growing cold.

The victim was Barbara Thomas. An older single woman who lived alone in an apartment building on the outskirts of the city. Facts were sketchy, but it seemed that she had gone out for a walk one night and never come back.

The victim's background was also sketchy. No close family, few friends. She was a teller at a local bank. When she didn't show up at her job the next day, her coworkers became concerned. They called the police, who started a search for her. A few days later, officers found her body in a wooden area about a mile from her home.

Parker picked up the photos of the dead woman. Small, short brown hair. The purplish marks on her neck made the continuous horizontal line of ligature strangulation with a rope. Similar to the marks on Madison Taggart's neck. Also, GHB had been found in Barbara Thomas's blood stream.

Was there a connection? Any rope of the same size used as a garrote would make such a mark. In the Thomas case, there was no seasoned cooking oil or ribbon around the neck. She wasn't a young girl. She was in her fifties.

He laid the pictures on the desk. Perhaps the killer's signature was evolving.

Parker thought about his recent visit to the crime scene and Shelby Van Aarle's reaction to his presence, his misleading statement that he'd canceled an event to come home and comfort his daughter.

Parker had done some checking into the golf pro's touring schedule. Van Aarle had been in town the day Madison Taggart was kidnapped. He'd also been in town the day of her murder. But he hadn't been at home in his Buckhead mansion. Parker had found records of a hotel stay at the Ritz-Carlton.

There was one more coincidence.

The day Barbara Thomas was murdered, Van Aarle had been in Pittsburgh doing a promotion for Yager golf shoes.

Parker put the photos and papers in his attaché case and snapped it shut. He poured himself a drink and went to his hotel window.

Over the years, he'd had occasion to speak with Van Aarle at a number of social affairs they'd both attended. He'd never cared for the man. He was arrogant and self-serving. From Jackson Taggart and other neighbors, Parker had learned that both Van Aarle and Iris had neglected their daughter. But he'd never thought the golf pro capable of murder.

What could his motive be? A burning rage inside? A hatred for women that made him strike out randomly? Was that the reason he avoided his wife and daughter? Van Aarle had no criminal background. No record of abuse in his family that Parker knew of. And why not hide the body better? Why risk his career? The pieces didn't quite fit. That indicated Parker didn't have them all yet.

He stared out the window.

Pittsburgh's magnificent skyline lay before him, the Allegheny River shimmered in the city lights below. It was a town built on iron and steel, while Atlanta, his city, had been built on finesse and Southern charm. The contrast reminded him of Miranda and himself.

Miranda Steele. A woman vastly different from any he'd ever known. Nothing in the least like Sylvia.

He thought of the fire in her kisses on her doorstep Tuesday night, the softness of her skin, her wetness on his fingers. Her hard shove against his chest that pushed him away. He wasn't used to being rejected by women. His pride had been shaken a bit but only momentarily.

Sooner or later, they'd end up in bed together. But what then? Tuesday night proved the trust he'd built with her was tenuous, fragile as a spider's web. He'd have to tread carefully so as not to disturb it.

She was so special. Unique. Her mind was sharp, her fighting skills surprising, her instincts rare. Her lead on Hinsley had been a good one, even though it turned out to be a dead end. She would make a superior investigator. That promised a bond with her that he'd never had with Sylvia.

He wrestled with the gnawing need to classify his feelings for her. He wanted to say she was a passing fancy. That his fascination with her was temporary. But that would be a lie. What he was afraid to admit, even in the dark recesses of his mind, was that his feelings for Miranda Steele had burrowed deep into the pit of his gut and refused to let go. Every thought of her rang with solidity, with permanence, with happiness. Was this...love?

The very idea seemed a sacrilege to Sylvia's memory. She was his wife's exact opposite. Brash, tough, independent. Mesmerizing. Never in his life had he had such intense feelings for such a woman.

He finished his drink and got ready for bed. As he unbuttoned his shirt, he thought of the feel of her lean body in his arms. She was raw, wild, instinctive. She had secrets. He'd just begun to unravel them.

He strolled over to his laptop, reviewed the data on the screen.

After researching Van Aarle, he'd dug deeper into Ms. Steele's background this week. He'd discovered she'd lied to him. She'd been married for seven years to a police officer with a bad record named Leon Groth. Groth had filed for divorce ten years ago on the grounds of willful desertion, acquiring all marital assets. The facts had raised more questions than they answered.

With a sigh, Parker turned off the laptop, lay down and switched off the light. He thought of Miranda's reaction to Dexter Hinsley's philandering. Her resistance to his probing. Her general tension, rage, fear, all the emotions that seemed to simmer inside her. What had her relationship with Groth been like to leave her that way after all these years?

He could speculate, but she would tell him. Eventually. He was a patient man. He could wait until she was ready. Until then, even a dysfunctional relationship with her was better than none.

Wishing for the feel of her hair in his hands, he closed his eyes. It was time to change tactics. His new strategy? Keep things professional. Distant. Reserved. He'd create a vacuum, a void between them. If Miranda Steele felt anything for him, the desire to fill that vacuum would gnaw at her just the way it did at him. It would break down that stubborn resistance.

Next time, she would come to him.

CHAPTER TWENTY-ONE

Blah, blah, blah.

Miranda slid down in her seat and crossed her arms over her stomach, wanting to groan at the big man with wavy gray hair in front of the classroom. Detective Hank Judd might have twelve years experience, he might be one of the Parker Agency's top people, but he was the most boring lecturer she'd ever heard. The cost of various database searches. The importance of double, triple, quadruple-checking your sources. Yeah, yeah. He'd already gone over this material twice. She knew it by heart.

When were they actually going to do a search on these super-duper databases? That's what she'd come to the Agency for in the first place.

She fingered the chains on her belt. Her outfit had really gotten Gen's panties in a wad this morning. It sported lots of black leather and was borderline motorcycle gang. After she saw it, The General had sent a ferocious email to all the newbies with the dress code attached. Miranda smirked to herself. Maybe she'd get a tongue ring next.

Blankly she glanced around the classroom. The small room held enough tables and chairs to accommodate the seven newbies that had started at the agency around the same time. The blinds had been drawn to reduce distraction, but it only added to the tedium. One student was doodling, another twirling her thumbs. On either side of Miranda, Becker and Holloway sat alert and attentive as soldiers.

The good news was that each table held several laptops, all wired into the Agency's network. It was about time they got to the lesson on record searches. But methodical old Judd had to repeat his lesson about privacy and keeping things legal before he let them loose on the keyboards.

As he droned on, she studied his long, oddly-shaped face, the lines that told a story of hard on-the-job experience. Twelve years. She could never stick with a career that long. A common name could yield too many matches, Judd warned. Big surprise. Information could be inaccurate, out of date. Nobody knew that better than she did. Everyone who was dead might not be in the Death Master File. Duh.

Okay, okay. When do they get to use the computers?

Miranda closed her eyes and let Judd's monotone voice lull her into a zen state. Her mind wandered to her dinner with Parker a few nights ago.

She thought of those steamy kisses of his on her doorstep. The passion they'd shared. The nightmare he'd given her. Being with Parker was a trauma trigger. He stirred emotions in her that should be kept buried. She'd had bad dreams before. She'd lived with nightmares for years after she left Leon. All the more reason to keep their relationship strictly business. Solving Madison Taggart's murder was the only reason to be around Parker now.

So why couldn't she stop thinking about him? She'd stop that right now.

She was still pissed Dexter Hinsley had turned out to be a dead end, frustrated she couldn't work the case while Parker was out of town. Hinsley must have been the weird man hanging around the schoolyard Ashley Ingram had mentioned. But why would Wendy and Madison Taggart talk to a textbook salesman? If Hinsley wasn't the killer, her money was on Van Aarle. She wished she could ask Wendy a few more questions. Maybe she could think of an excuse to drop by the mansion.

Beside her, Holloway gave her a nudge.

"Ms. Steele?"

She looked up. Detective Judd was staring down his long, irregular-shaped nose at her. "Would you like to participate?" He held out a sheet of paper.

She swallowed and sat up. "Uh, sure." She took the paper and he moved on.

On the other side of her, Holloway shook his head. Becker leaned over and whispered. "I know this is probably old hat for you, but we're supposed to be doing these practice problems." He pointed to his sheet.

"Thanks," she whispered back and glanced at the title of the paper in her hand. "Skip Tracing Exercises." She grinned. Hot damn.

While the class turned on their computers, Detective Judd pointed them to a couple of sites to get them started on the exercises. Most seemed pretty easy on the surface. Miranda read the paper. The first problem was to google a name of someone you hadn't seen in several years and see what you could find, then use that information in one of the databases.

"My ex-wife's got a new boyfriend," Holloway cackled beside her. "I want to see if he's got a record." He attacked his keyboard. Holloway was divorced?

Miranda sat back and crossed her arms. She'd waited for weeks to learn how to do this and she couldn't think of anybody to practice with. She didn't dare start with Amy. If Gen got word she was using the company's computers for personal reasons, she'd boot her out on the street before Parker came back. She'd have to wait till after hours for that.

She thought of the high-school friend she'd said she was visiting the night she went to Mockingbird Hills. She'd do. She entered the name "Jane Anderson" and clicked a button.

The computer worked a minute before it spat out a response. Miranda looked at the screen. Five thousand, three hundred and twenty-five hits. Sure were a lot of Jane Andersons in the world. Maybe she should narrow it a bit. She entered Oak Park, Illinois. That produced Four hundred fifty-three hits. Sifting through them would be a lot of work for someone she didn't really want to find.

Holloway grunted beside her. "The boyfriend's record is squeaky clean. Better be." He sounded serious.

"I'm looking for a girl I dated in high school in Brooklyn," Becker said. "Not getting much, though."

At least he had somebody to look for. Miranda thought a minute.

Now what. How about Fanuzzi? What was her first name? Joan. She knew her phone number. She typed it in, pressed the search button and waited. That was pretty good. Miranda got Fanuzzi's old New York address, along with the name of her ex-husband.

Now she was feeling cocky. She glanced over at Holloway, then at Becker. They were both absorbed in their own searches. Why wait till after hours? She could do a little work now.

She went to one of the best sites Judd had recommended. Holding her breath, carefully she typed in the name "Groth" and pressed Enter. The site shot back a long list with birth dates, death dates and last known residence.

None of them matched Amy's birth date. That was a relief. This was a death register, after all. She clicked a genealogy link. Then another. It would be easy to get lost in this stuff. After a few more clicks, another name popped up on the screen. Irma Groth.

She knew that name. Leon's mother. Miranda remembered her as an angry, critical woman, who had little to do with her after she and Leon married. Especially after his bout with measles that left him sterile. Leon was an only child, and his mother had wanted grandchildren. She wasn't too happy about that turn of events. Miranda got the impression the woman blamed her for it.

She looked at the birth date. Yep, that was her. She remembered Leon going to her house every year on that day with a gift, like he was paying homage to some saint. Once Leon told her when he was little, his mother would fly into a rage and beat him with a belt when he did something she didn't like. She was the only person he was terrified of.

She clicked another link. There was a death date and last residence. Denton, Texas. A chill went down her spine. Leon owned the house.

She stared at the date. Four years ago. That was when she had been in Texas, working on an oil rig. Outside Denton. Leon had been in the city with his mother then? That strange, eerie feeling she'd been having lately came over her. Like the feeling you got when you were home alone after you'd seen a scary movie. Like long, bony fingers reaching out from the past.

"Time for lunch," Judd said.

She cleared the history and closed the browser.

The students turned off their computers, gathered their things and began shuffling out of the room.

Lost in a daze, Miranda followed them.

"Have you checked your cell phone today?" Holloway reminded her as they headed down the hall to their cubes.

She snapped out of her funk. "You're such a nag, Holloway," she told him with a grin as she reached into her pocket and turned it on. She'd never needed a cell phone before. Never had anybody to call. It was hard to get used to it.

It jingled and beeped. A message. Parker? Her heart stood still as she checked it. No, a text message.

"OMG. You won't believe what she did now. G2R." It was from Wendy Van Aarle.

"You wanna try that new spot down the street?" Becker offered as they reached Miranda's cube. She'd had lunch with the Bobbsey Twins twice already this week.

She stared down at her phone. "Not today, guys. I've got an errand to run." It was time to do some follow-up. Just the opportunity she'd been hoping for. She grabbed her bag from her desk and took off down the hall, leaving her two buddies scratching their heads.

No one was in the schoolyard at Dogwood Academy when Miranda pulled up in her old blue jalopy. It was lunchtime. About now, Mama Ruby and her crew were feeding the hungry student body.

She drove down to a narrow side road and pulled over to a spot well away from the school where no one would notice her, just as Parker had taught her the day they tailed Hinsley. She rolled down her windows to let in a breeze.

The street was in a quiet, lush green area, typical of Buckhead. Willow and oak branches rustled overhead, casting cooling shadows over the pavement.

Miranda reached for the pair of binoculars she had snatched from Parker's supply room. Nobody would notice them missing by the time she got them back. She scanned the school building, the gymnasium, the cafeteria. No movement. Not a soul was outside.

She'd been hoping Wendy would be out somewhere, lurking around. Guess the girl was sticking to her schedule. If Miranda waited long enough, she'd see her when she came out for gym class. Or she could just text her back. But she wouldn't get the nuances of seeing the girl in person.

She reached for the spicy chicken sandwich she'd grabbed at a drive thru. It would be another hour or so before gym class. She wrinkled her nose. The chicken was too greasy and not nearly hot enough, but it was something to put in her mouth. As she munched on it, her mind played with possibilities of what she might do if she saw Hinsley lurking around the school again. Like tell the jerk she was on to him, and if he cheated on his wife again, there'd be hell to pay.

She finished her sandwich, put the wrapper in the bag and sat back with a sigh. This waiting was godawful boring. She should have brought something to read. She laid her head back and closed her eyes. The seats in her old Chevy Lumina Z34 weren't nearly as comfortable as Parker's car. He was spoiling her. Not good. Once more, she thought of the sexy look in his eyes the night she'd almost hopped into bed with him. Parker was really getting under her skin. Also not good.

She started to drift off. It wasn't just Detective Judd's lecture this morning that made her so drowsy. She hadn't slept well since her nightmare about her attack, the man who had turned into Leon. As she thought of it, that strange, eerie feeling began to creep over her again. Like a ghost from the past. Like she was being watched. Maybe Wendy Van Aarle had put some kind of hex on her. Seemed like the kind of thing she'd be into.

Her eyes still closed, she shook off the feeling. It was daylight, for Pete's sake. Just a warm afternoon in the sunny South.

Suddenly, an engine roared behind her. She shot up in her seat. *What was that?* A shiny black car surged past her and squealed onto the road in front of the schoolyard. She glared at it. It was a Pontiac, but it didn't look like a Grand Prix. Dexter?

She grabbed for the binoculars. The plates. Get the plate number. Too late. He was already around the curve. She fumbled for the keys, ready to tear after it.

"Hi."

At the voice, Miranda jumped so high, she nearly banged her head on the ceiling. She spun around.

In her usual dark makeup and clothes, Wendy Van Aarle stood leaning on the open passenger-side window, watching her with pre-teen disdain.

"You startled me," Miranda gasped.

"So I see," she said flatly. Today she had a neon red streak in her dark hair. She was dressed in a long brown satin top decorated with tassels and black straps. It had a mass of metal beadwork at the neckline and was topped by another choker necklace. This one adorned with tiny black hearts.

She pursed her dark-colored lips and shook her head. "You sure are weird. What are you doing here?"

Me, weird? Pot calling the kettle black. "I could ask you the same thing. Where did you come from?"

"I came around the front and through the woods." She gestured vaguely.

Miranda eyed the thicket of nearby trees she must have walked through. "Aren't you supposed to be over there." She pointed to the schoolyard.

Wendy shrugged carelessly. "What they don't know won't hurt them. I can go where I want. It's a free country."

Right. "Did you see that car that just went by?"

"What car?"

"That black Pontiac. Was that the textbook salesman? Were you talking to him?" Miranda studied her with suspicion.

She gave her an innocent look. "I didn't see anybody."

Maybe she was telling the truth. Miranda decided to change subjects. "I got your message."

She grimaced. "I sent it, like, hours ago. I almost forgot about it."

But she hadn't. " 'You won't believe what she did now.' What did you mean?"

She rolled her eyes.

"Is Tiffany Todd bothering you again?"

Her face grew sullen. "Every day. She makes my life hell."

Miranda's heart went out to her. "What did she do now?"

Wendy tapped her dark purple fingernails against the window rim a minute, as if deciding whether to divulge her secret to a grownup. Then she opened up. "I was talking to a boy. Gary Sullivan. He's in my Biology class. He's kind of nerdy, but cute, you know?"

No, but Miranda nodded anyway.

"He's the only one who talks to me in that class." Her voice started to break. "This morning, Tiffany Todd came over to our table and told him…I had *cooties*. He got his stuff and moved to another place." Hatred glowed in her dark eyes. "I want to kill her. I hate her. I hate her."

Miranda wished she could take Tiffany Todd by the shoulders and give her a shake. Who did she think she was?

She studied Wendy's troubled face. The weird getup didn't faze her. Kids dressed kookier every year. But Wendy Van Aarle's clothes and makeup were more than weird or kooky. They were a call for help. Alone and neglected by her parents and her friends, it was the only way the kid knew how to react. Compassion welled up in her and for a moment, Miranda wished this sad, angry young girl was her Amy.

She thought a minute. "When's your next Biology class?"

"Tomorrow."

"Okay, then. Tomorrow when you get to the room, go right up to Gary and say, 'I know I have cooties. I got them when I followed Tiffany Todd into the Girls' Room.'"

Wendy put her hand over her mouth and snickered. "I like that. How do you come up with stuff like that?"

Miranda shrugged. "Natural gift. Hey, are you sure you didn't see that black Pontiac?"

The smile disappeared as the girl froze. Miranda had caught her off guard. Suddenly she looked like she'd been caught with her hand in the cookie jar. She shook her head defensively. "I don't know what you're talking about."

Was she playing dumb? Afraid? This time, Miranda decided to sound like an adult. "Your parents might worry if you talk to strangers."

Her dark lip curled. "My parents don't care about me."

"I'm sure they'd care if they knew about it."

She scowled hatefully. "Are you gonna tell them?"

"Tell them what?"

Her dark-lined eyes glowed with resentment. "Nothing. There's nothing to tell." Across the street, a bell rang, calling the students back to their studies. "I gotta go."

"Wait." Miranda wanted to warn her somehow. "Be careful. Your parents care about you more than you know." She hoped so.

Her face turned more bitter than she'd ever seen it. "A lot you know."

"I do know." She didn't, but she had to encourage the thought.

"No, you don't."

"Yes, they do."

She was almost in tears. "They aren't even my real parents. I'm adopted."

Adopted? The word was like a knife stab in Miranda's heart. "How do you know that?"

"I just do." She turned away and shot under the trees and down the narrow road.

"Wait," Miranda called out of the window.

But Wendy didn't turn back. She ran across the street in front of the schoolyard. Her long dark skirt whipping around her legs, she slipped through the tall mesh gate and joined her classmates. At least, she was safe for now. If you could call it that.

Miranda squeezed the steering wheel, wanting to jump out of the car and chase after the girl. But she was too numb. Her head spun like a tilt-a-whirl, her eyes burned with tears. She wiped her cheeks with the back of her hand, then stared out the window, as the scene of kids playing in the schoolyard blurred.

Adopted? The word felt like a hard punch in the chest.

Miranda thought of Wendy's appearance, her attitude, her whole demeanor. She remembered her first impression of the girl with the dark hair and surly look in that picture in Parker's office. *My mom's an executive and my dad's always away. They are never home. I think I'm adopted.* Those words echoed the same loneliness and desperation she saw in Wendy. It couldn't be. It just couldn't.

Miranda pulled herself together and started the car. She had to get back to the office before someone got suspicious, but tears had welled up in her eyes again. Biting her lip, she fought them back. It couldn't be true. It couldn't be. By the time she turned onto Piedmont, she had given up the fight.

Something deep in her heart told her she was right, had always been right. Parker said she had good instincts. Right now, no matter how much she wanted to deny it, those instincts were screaming the truth at her.

Wendy Van Aarle was "Someone Else's Daughter." And if that were true, she could also be Amy.

CHAPTER TWENTY-TWO

When Miranda got back to the Imperial Building, her heart was still aching, but her head had cleared. She was supposed to be a fledgling detective. How many times had Parker told her to be objective? She needed facts. Cold, hard facts. And one fact she was sure of was Wendy Van Aarle told lies. Saying she was adopted was probably one of them. It would be natural for the girl to invent the idea because her parents neglected her.

As she reached her cube, Miranda decided she needed more time to sort things out. She stepped into the small space and stopped dead in her tracks.

A brand new laptop sat on her desk, a colorful screensaver tracing patterns on the flat screen monitor. Next to it was a pile of manila folders about a foot high. "What's this?" she said aloud.

"Homework," Holloway told her, as he stepped toward her cube. He and Becker sat a few desks away. "Client requests for background checks. I thought I'd come by and fill you in."

"Appreciate it." She guessed, eyeing the stack.

"Judd said now that us newbies have gotten our feet wet and are ready to use the equipment, it's time we started earning our keep."

"Oh yeah?" She gave a deep sigh and sat down. "Guess I'd better get to work."

"Need any help?"

"Naw, I'll figure it out. Thanks."

"No problem. Catch you later, Steele."

"Sure." She started to go through the stack.

What she really wanted was to get to those special databases she'd learned about this morning and search for information about Wendy Van Aarle. But she couldn't do that now. Not during regular hours. Not with Parker out of town. If Gen or Detective Judd caught her, she'd be canned for sure. She'd finally gotten what she'd been waiting for. She couldn't lose this job now. Trying not to think about Wendy, she pushed through the folders.

Just before five o'clock, Holloway and Becker stopped by her cube again.

Miranda looked up and saw their two eager faces.

"How are you doing on the assignment?" Becker asked.

"Not so good," she groaned. "I'm only about halfway through this stack."

"Half way? How'd you do that? I've only done five."

Wearily, Miranda frowned at them. "Weren't we supposed to finish by tomorrow?"

"Heck no," Holloway chuckled. "We've got till the end of next week."

"Oh." She sat back, embarrassed. She'd busted her ass for nothing.

"Hey, next week Judd's going to show us how to take fingerprints." Becker grinned, trying to cheer her up. "Won't that be cool, Steele?"

"Yeah, sure."

"She's bushed after all that work," Holloway said to Becker. "Glad it's Friday. Why don't you knock off and come party with us tonight? We're heading out to hit some Buckhead nightspots."

"Yeah," Becker said. "There's a new singer at The Gecko Club. The AJC's got a picture of her. She's a real looker." He held out a folded newspaper.

Miranda was about to push the paper away when she glanced down and did a double-take at the familiar face. Gorgeous, blond hair, perfect makeup, dressed in sequins. Coco. She read the ad. The Gecko Club? So Blondie had finally landed that job. Good for her. Miranda wondered if Dexter knew about it.

"What do you say, Steele? You wanna come?"

Miranda shifted her weight. She couldn't see Coco without mentioning Dexter's little escapade the other day. She thought about Parker's warning not to get involved. Besides, she had work to do. "I need to finish up here."

"You've already done more than me and Holloway put together." Becker sounded disappointed.

With a shrug, she turned back to the computer. "Maybe I'll catch up to you later. I want to finish up this last file."

"Suit yourself," Becker said with remorse. "Here." He laid the newspaper on her desk. "You'll need the address if you change your mind."

"Thanks."

"Don't work too hard," Holloway called out as they left.

"Yeah, okay." She was already lost in thought.

After about a half hour, Miranda took a break and got a drink from the water cooler. As she sipped from the paper cup, she surveyed the office, waiting for all the worker bees to leave. She had to fill the cup three times, but finally, the last hangers on shuffled through the exit. She glanced at the clock on the wall.

Quarter of six. At last, everyone was gone for the day. Time for her own agenda.

She returned to her desk and stared at the screen. Sucking in her breath, she thought of Wendy Van Aarle, so lost and alone, rejected by her parents and her peers. Was Wendy Van Aarle "Someone Else's Daughter"? Was she Amy?

Miranda was going to find out. She got out her cell phone, pulled up Wendy's number, grabbed her keyboard, opened a reverse number site and entered it.

The results flashed before her. No good. The site didn't record data on a cell phone. Wait. Wendy was Ashley Ingram's neighbor. She knew where they lived. She accessed the database she'd been working with earlier and entered the address, 112 Sweet Hollow Lane. Quick as a wink, the program returned a list of information. She scanned it. Not much there about Wendy. The house was in her father's name. He'd paid about five million for it.

She sat back and folded her arms. Background searches were about as aggravating as surveillance. All this going around your backside to get to your thumb was maddening. What kind of information could she dig up about Wendy with this database, anyway? She was just a kid. Think.

"Don't overlook the obvious," Judd had said in class today. Okay, what did she know? Shelby Van Aarle was a famous golf pro. Wendy's mother owned Iris Rose Cosmetics. Of course. Both of them had to have web sites loaded with personal information. Again, she attacked the keyboard. Start with Mama.

She entered the company name in her browser and clicked Go. Bingo.

A dazzling, sexy site materialized on her screen. Colorful beauty ads danced before her eyes. Glamorous skin lotions in pink pearl containers shaped like roses, a rainbow of lipstick tubes and eye shadows, elegant perfume bottles. She could almost smell the fragrances. Soft music played from her speakers while a sensual female voice invited her to explore the collection.

Enough of that. She stopped the audio, clicked the "Corporate Info" link. In the upper left a smiling, red-haired woman appeared. In a cobalt business suit and pearls around her neck, she looked like she'd just dropped by your living room for a cup of tea.

Miranda read the bio. Iris Rose had founded the company seven years ago in her kitchen. Since then, it had grown by leaps and bounds and was now worth several million dollars. The text babbled on about what an innovative visionary the CEO was. Didn't mention Wendy. Didn't mention Iris sucked as a mother. Miranda peered at the woman's photo, trying to see a family resemblance. Cheekbones, maybe.

Down at the bottom, the page was signed, kind of like a painting. "Designed by Out of This World—an Isaiah Todd company." Isaiah Todd? As in snotty little *Tiffany* Todd?

She clicked the link. Another web page opened, just as sleek and sophisticated. "Out of This World," it read. An advertising agency. A link read, "Who We Are." Just what she wanted to know. She clicked it.

Pictures.

A broad-shouldered man with a headful of thick sandy curls and a big smile appeared in each one. Miranda read the captions. This famous client. That celebrity. Accepting an award. Thanksgiving. Christmas. Down near the bottom was a shot of the man with a small, sharp-featured woman in a red suit, with short dark, auburn-streaked hair and flawless makeup. The same woman in the bio. Sure enough, the caption read, "CEO of Iris Rose Cosmetics."

The broad-shouldered man's smile was even bigger in this photo, and he had his arm draped around Wendy's mama in a casual way that seemed awfully chummy. Time for some confirmation.

With a huff, Miranda got up and went to Parker's office. She switched on a light and went inside. Files were stacked neatly on his glass table, depositions and interviews from the Taggart case that he'd showed her on her first day. She grabbed the first one and opened it.

It was the file on the Ingrams, Ashley's parents and Wendy's next-door neighbors. There was a photo of Ashley with her folks. Miranda didn't recognize them. She opened the next file. This was what she wanted. The Todds. There was Tiffany's picture in her blonde, superior loveliness.

She picked up a photo of a tall, elegant-looking woman with her brown hair in a chignon. Tiffany's mother? She looked at the next picture. The smiling, broad-shouldered man in the web site. She read the name. *Isaiah Todd.* Yep, that was him. She put the folders back the way she'd found them, and strolled back to her cube, deep in thought.

Three young girls who had been best friends. Tiffany Todd, Ashley Ingram, Madison Taggart. Wendy had been friends with them once, too. Ashley was adopted. Did Wendy get the idea she'd been adopted from her? She'd given Miranda a phony name the first time they met—Willow.

Miranda sat down and rubbed her eyes. Lightning fast computers, access to fancy professional databases, and she wasn't a whit closer. She drummed her fingers on the desk. Might as well check out Papa.

In a few seconds, she had Shelby Van Aarle's web site on her screen. Against a field of Kelly green, his name was scrawled across the page in large golden letters. She recognized his wavy, tinted hair and athletic body in a large picture of him taking a swing on some famous golf course.

The site contained his schedule, tips on improving your line drive and your chip shot, a list of every tournament he'd ever won. Ads for Yager golf shoes danced merrily in the margins.

Miranda exhaled and clicked "About Shelby."

Birth date, height, weight, residence, wife's name, Wendy's name.

She read the paragraphs below the data. He'd had a stunning career. Won several tournaments on the PGA Tour. Competed against Tiger Woods in the British Open. It went on and on. His amateur career, his first titles, his setbacks, his returns, his amazing feats as a golfer. Finally it got to the personal stuff. Talked a little about his folks. They seemed normal, supportive. His dad's dream was that his son become a professional golfer. How sweet.

Then she saw his birthplace. Poised over the keyboard, her hands trembled. Her throat went dry. Oak Park, Illinois. Miranda's hometown. Amy's birthplace. She and Shelby Van Aarle were from the same town?

She read on. Van Aarle had had a breakdown several years ago. The stress of the circuit had gotten too much for him. He'd decided against seeking professional help, but he'd had to miss a few tournaments. His father had been very disappointed. Shelby and Iris had left the Chicago area six years ago. To get away from the pressure from Shelby's father? Van Aarle didn't seem the type to have emotional problems.

There was a quote from Van Aarle. "It was hard to leave the place where I'd grown up, but I felt like I was following a higher calling. I'd wanted my daughter to grow up there. She was born in the same hospital I was. Oak Park General."

Miranda sat back with a thud. She ran both her hands through her hair. Her heart felt like it had stopped. Oak Park General Hospital? On Lake Street? Exactly where Amy had been born. Her mind raced. Would Van Aarle know that? Yes, she remembered. Adoptive parents could request that information from the state in Illinois.

She squeezed her eyes shut as she remembered that cold winter morning she'd stared at an empty crib. How she'd run through the house, screaming at the top of her lungs. Leon's quiet disdain. His blows. His rough hands grabbing her, throwing her out into the snow. Her long, slow recovery. Her search for Amy. And now…?

Was her own little girl, the child she'd lost that day long ago, the daughter she'd been looking for all these years…being cared for by a pair of neglectful millionaires?

Her hands still shaking, she pressed them to her temples and thought of Parker's words. Objectivity. Stay open. She hadn't really proven anything. She didn't even have the details of Wendy's birth. It could all be coincidence. Frustration boiled inside her.

She erased the history, closed the browser, and turned off her laptop. She'd had all she could take for tonight. Reaching for her bag, she caught sight of the newspaper Becker had left on her desk. She picked it up. Maybe she would stop by The Gecko Club after all.

As she headed out, she passed the photo lab and noticed the door was ajar. She stopped a moment, stood tapping her foot, then pushed it open. Coco deserved to know the truth.

It was easy to find what she was looking for. The pictures Parker had taken the other day were in a labeled folder on the desk. With a silent promise that she'd get them back before anyone knew they were gone, she slipped them into her bag. At least she could accomplish one thing tonight.

She decided to go out the back way. The lights were dimmed, not a soul was around. The office felt creepy alone at night.

Halfway down the stairwell, she froze as that strange, eerie feeling came over her. Like her dreams lately. She stood a few seconds, staring into the near darkness. A sweat broke out on her forehead. She shivered. What was the matter with her? She shook it off and moved on. She was just tired after the day she'd had. She left the building and headed for her car.

~

It was hard to wait. Hard to watch her, to follow her where she went. To hide in cold stairwells, in dark alleys, observing her, marking her habits, holding back the need to strike. Discipline. The divine task required the utmost discipline. Discipline had made him alter his schedule to monitor her movements, her travels back and forth from her apartment. In and out of that office. Her dealings with that investigator, Wade Parker.

And the girls. It was hard to watch them, too. They were so young. So pure. Artless, untainted, guileless. Such a shame they wouldn't remain so. No, soon they would grow into women. And women were a scourge, an evil to be beaten down, eliminated. Hadn't it been so from the beginning?

The girls, those he'd been watching, were just about to turn into women. Just on the verge of being defiled by the changes in their bodies. Even the one that was close to him. The one that belonged to him. It would happen to her, too, unless he stopped it.

He had to set them free before it happened. It was his duty. His calling. The sole, sublime purpose of his entire life. More sacred than anyone understood.

This he knew. He understood his calling. His existence had more meaning than it ever had.

She wouldn't stop him. Wade Parker wouldn't either. No, he would stop her. Once and for all. She was evil, too. But the timing had to be right, so he must wait. Her time would come soon. Very soon. There was one more task, and then it would be the right time. And when it came, at long last, the watching and waiting would end. It would all be over.

And so would her life.

CHAPTER TWENTY-THREE

The Gecko Club was even busier than Miranda remembered it. As she pushed through the throng of stylish partygoers and headed for the crowded bar, she looked around for Becker and Holloway but didn't see either of them. Probably had missed the pair.

She climbed onto a plush, shiny seat and waved down the bartender. She remembered the dude from her first soirée here. When she ordered a beer, he looked at her kind of funny, but didn't say anything.

Smooth-sounding tones came from the piano on the corner stage. Miranda looked out over the throng and saw Coco at the keyboard, all dolled up in red sequins and pearls. She was playing some old, jazzy tune. "I get no kick from champagne…"

Miranda smiled. The girl was good. Really good. She had a voice like velvet and she could really tickle the keys. Her soulful song could make you cry if you were the sentimental type.

She reached for some chips on the bar, dipped them into a fancy bowl of salsa. She scowled. "You got anything hotter?" she asked the bartender when he came by again.

He tilted his head for a second, like he was trying to remember where he'd seen her before. "Nope. That's our free picante sauce. Take it or leave it."

She shrugged and turned back to the show. The audience seemed to be eating up the retro stuff. Miranda watched some of the men in the crowd ogling the singer. Coco probably had no idea how many hard-ons she was generating.

After a minute, she crescendoed and ended the song. The audience applauded. She announced she'd be back after a break.

Time to move. Those photos were burning a hole in her bag. Miranda grabbed it off the bar and made her way to the stage.

Coco spotted her before she even got to the stage. "Miranda." She scampered down the short staircase. In two steps she was at Miranda's side, throwing her arms around her.

Miranda winced, resisted the urge to pull away. "Good to see you, Coco."

The girl squealed like a kid who'd just seen the ice cream truck. "How have you been?"

"Fine. And yourself?"

"Wonderful, especially now." She gestured toward the piano.

"Yeah, this is great."

Her blue eyes glowed. "I can't believe you're here. I haven't heard from you at all. Not since—"

Miranda held up a hand before Coco announced to the world that she'd been arrested for murder. "Sorry, I'm not good at keeping up relationships."

Coco smiled and shrugged. "Oh, never mind." She gestured toward a small table, hailed a waitress and ordered a cola. "Do you want anything? I get drinks for free."

Miranda took a seat beside her. "No, thanks."

"I can't believe you came to see me. How do you like the show? Do I sound all right?"

"You sound great. You're talented."

"Do you really think so?"

"Absolutely. You look gorgeous, too."

"Really?" She blinked self-consciously. She seemed genuinely stunned. Didn't she know she was a knockout?

"Sure. Is this your first night?"

She shook her head. "I've been here all week. But tonight's the biggest crowd I've had yet."

"Yeah. I saw your picture in the AJC. Guess that's what brought them in."

She rolled her eyes. "I wish they hadn't done that."

"Why not? Seems to have brought in a passel."

She lowered her voice to a whisper. "Dexter, of course. If he knew I was working here…"

"He doesn't know?"

She shook her head and bit her lip.

That didn't sound good. Miranda stiffened. "Uh, speaking of Dexter—"

Coco grabbed her arm. "I had to grab the paper this morning before Dexter saw it and pull out the entertainment section. Good thing he never reads that part."

He was pretty good at finding his own entertainment.

Coco lifted her glass. "So tell me what you're doing these days. Gosh, I don't even know what you do."

Miranda shrugged. "I've got a job here in Buckhead."

"Really? What do you do?"

"A little of everything."

With a confused look that stung Miranda's conscience, Coco nodded and sipped at her drink. "They're letting me play here for three weeks. That's pretty good, isn't it?"

"It's great." Miranda glanced around the room. How was Coco going to keep Dexter in the dark for three weeks? "Hey, I've got a cell phone now. You want my number?"

"Sure. I mean, if that's okay."

"Of course it is." She gave it to her. Coco wrote it down on a napkin and stuffed it in her pocket.

There was an awkward moment of silence. Finally, Miranda took a breath. "Look. I have to be honest, Coco. You're really good and all, but I didn't come here just to hear you."

She tilted her head. "Oh? What do you mean?"

Miranda played with a napkin on the table. "I need to tell you something."

Coco's big blue eyes grew round. "What?"

How was she going to say it? She was getting cold feet. "Maybe now's not a good time."

"You can't just say that and then not tell me."

She was right. Miranda's own foot didn't taste too good. "It's just that—"

"What?" She put her hand to her mouth. "You're not pregnant, are you?"

Miranda snorted. "No." God, Coco thought it was about her. "Don't you have to go back on in a few minutes? I don't want to upset you."

She reached across the table and grabbed her hand. "Tell me."

Why hadn't she waited until after the show? Too late now. "Okay." She freed her hand from Coco's grip and steadied herself. "I was doing some work at a local school a few days back and I ran into Dexter."

She frowned. "You work at a school? You saw Dexter?"

Miranda nodded. "Temporarily. Actually, I happened to see Dexter with one of the teachers."

She cocked her head. "Well, that would be normal. He sells textbooks."

"Yeah, I know. But it was a little more than a sales call."

The furrows in her brow deepened. "What do you mean?"

"I mean the teacher was a woman. She and Dexter were getting kind of chummy."

Coco's eyes grew watery. "Chummy?"

Miranda felt like a jerk. There was no sense drawing this out. She gritted her teeth and spat it out. "Dexter's cheating on you, Coco."

Her face went dead. "How can you say that?"

"I saw him with my own eyes."

"How do you know it was Dexter?"

"The teacher said his name."

"You were wrong. Or you're lying."

Damn, she was blowing this. "I wish I was. It wasn't the only time. Looks like it's been going on for a while. I have pictures." She reached for her bag.

"Why are you doing this to me? I thought you were my friend." She got up in a slow mechanical motion.

Miranda reached for her. "Coco, you've got to listen. Dexter's no good. You've got to get away from him."

"What do you know about Dexter?" She pulled away. "Leave me alone."

"You have a right to know what he's been doing, Coco."

"Go away."

"This woman botherin' you, pretty lady?"

Miranda turned and squinted into the face of a tall young man. He looked familiar.

"I have to go back to work." Coco broke away and hurried toward the stage.

The young man went after her.

Miranda grabbed his sleeve. "Leave her be. She's upset."

He spun around. Sandy hair. Thick, muscled neck. Baby face. She knew him now. The rich college kid she'd tangled with here before.

Recognition flashed on his face. "You," he growled. "Didn't I teach you a lesson the last time you were in here?"

"Other way around."

"You must be a slow learner."

Anger blazed inside her. She knew it was Dexter Hinsley she wanted to lash out at, but this guy would do for a substitute. Right about now, she was itching to give somebody a pummeling.

She put her hands on her hips, took a stance. "I think you're the one who needs a remedial lesson."

"Oh, yeah?" There was no warm-up tonight. With a sharp snap, his fist flew straight at her face.

Her arm shot up, blocking him in the nick of time. She flattened her hand and shot it towards his Adam's apple. Must not have his fill of booze yet. His reflexes were good. He leaned back just far enough to avoid the stroke and grabbed her arm tight.

"You sonofabitch." She twisted around, snatched his forearm, turned it over her shoulder and slung him into the table where she and Coco had sat, knocking it over. Noisily, drinks and chairs flew everywhere, clattering to the floor. Several women in the crowd screamed.

"You," Miranda heard the bartender scream. He knew who she was now.

Focus. Focus. Too late. The kid was already up and coming for her. She tried to sidestep him, but he grabbed her legs and down they went.

They tumbled around on the hard floor, arms flailing. Miranda got a couple good licks on his pretty face. That made him really mad. He jabbed at her, grazed her chin, then got a good one on her right cheek.

With all her might, she shoved him over on his back. She had him down now and was going to town on his nose when she heard a police speaker blare behind her.

"Two-four-oh. Assault and battery at The Gecko Club."

She shifted and saw uniforms. The barkeep must have wised up and called the cops right away this time.

One of the officers grabbed her and pulled her off the kid before she could break his cheekbones. A second policeman got hold of the kid.

She twisted to one side and glared at the dude who had her arms. Short curly hair. Wide-set eyes. Officer Chambers. The bull who'd nabbed her the night she went to the Ingram mansion. What was this? Old home week?

"What are you doing here?" she smirked.

He narrowed his eyes at her, as he realized who she was. "You. I thought I took care of you weeks ago."

"Didn't stick. I got out."

"Well, you're going back in tonight. If it weren't for you, I'd still have that cushy beat in Mockingbird Hills instead of pounding the pavement on Peachtree every weekend."

Guess they'd never be best buds. Her luck had run all the way out tonight. Miranda flinched as he shoved the restraints around her wrists and snapped them shut.

What in the hell was she doing in jail again?

Miranda sat on the mattress of her cell, her aching head between her hands. What kind of trouble was she in now?

But she couldn't think of herself now. Poor Coco. The girl was so upset. She shouldn't have told her about Dexter. She of all people should have known how a wife would react to the news. If anyone had told her Leon was cheating on her, she wouldn't have believed them either.

She'd been too needy. Too…addicted. She'd had such feelings for him. She could remember them, a little, in that jumbled up part of her mind. But she kept them stashed away in some corner of her heart like a pair of dirty socks stuffed in the back of the closet. Coco must really care for the lying philanderer she was hitched to. She was beautiful, talented. And look how that jerk treated her.

If only it had been Dexter she'd been pounding on tonight instead of that college kid.

"What in the world am I going to do with you?"

She winced at the sound of the voice. She looked up and saw Parker's handsome face with that sexy strand of hair falling over his brow. He wasn't in a tuxedo tonight. Just a charcoal suit. Probably Italian.

"You dressed down this time."

He didn't smile, just shook his head.

"You like hanging around jails, Parker?" she asked, wondering when he'd gotten back in town.

"I had some late night business with Lieutenant Erskine, lucky for you."

"Lieutenant Erskine. My best friend."

A jailor came and opened the door. "You're free, Steele."

That easy? She walked through the bars and followed the flatfoot down the hall.

"You have to shape up, Miranda," Parker murmured to her as they reached Processing. "You're giving the Agency a bad name."

"You post bail or something? What do I owe you now?"

That brought back his confident smile. "Nothing. I talked to Officer Chambers and the owner of The Gecko Club. It took some persuasion, but I convinced them of your character. He dropped the charges."

"You don't say. Guess it pays to have friends in high places."

The man in blue behind the counter handed her the bag she'd been carrying.

Parker studied it a moment. "I think there's something in there that belongs to me."

She stared at him. How did he know? Same way he knew everything. She opened the latch and handed him the pictures of Dexter.

He put them in his lapel pocket. "Did you show them to her?"

She shrugged as she turned and headed down the hall. "Tried to."

He opened to the heavy, metal door that led outside for her. "How soon will Coco be filing for divorce?" he asked wryly.

She stopped short and glared at him. Why did he have to know everything?

"I did warn you," he said softly.

She sighed and moved on. "You did."

After a few silent moments, they reached her car. "Do you know whom you were tangling with tonight?"

"Other than Office Chambers? Some arrogant college kid who's too big for his britches."

"A college kid by the name of Bobby Lee Ingram."

"Bobby Lee." That's right. She remembered his friends calling him by that name. "Ingram?" She came to a stop in front of her old blue jalopy. "As in Ashley Ingram?"

He nodded. "Her older brother. Their parents got him out half an hour ago. They're very upset."

A neighbor kid whose sister was best friends with Madison Taggart. "He's got a real bad attitude about females."

"Oh? He didn't get that from his parents. Lamar and Giselle Ingram are both professors at Agnes Scott College. Very forward thinking. Sylvia knew them well."

Another set of Parker's friends. She considered that a moment. "You don't think he could have had anything to do with Madison's murder, do you?"

"If I did, he'd be in jail for more than a fistfight. I've already questioned him. He has the same alibi you do for that night, if you recall."

Right. She rubbed her face. Ouch.

"You've got a nasty bruise on your cheek." He reached up, touched her so lightly she could barely feel it. He pulled away. "Better put something on that when you get home."

What? No, *"I've got a first aid kit in my car?"* No, *"Let me take you home and take care of that?"* That was certainly different. "Sure." She straightened herself. "So when did you get back in town?"

"Earlier this evening. I discovered some interesting details about Van Aarle on my trip."

"Oh, yeah?"

He nodded. "I've got people trailing him round-the-clock. How would you like to work this weekend?"

"On the Taggart case?" She unlocked the door of her car.

"Of course." He reached for the handle and opened the door for her.

She brightened as she slid into the front seat. "I'd love to." She didn't care if it was the weekend. It wasn't like she had a calendar full of appointments to keep.

He closed the door and she rolled down the window.

"I'll pick you up at your place at nine," he said. "I'll tell you more then. Oh, wear something nice." He hesitated just a moment as if he were debating with himself about something, then he turned and walked away.

Miranda blinked at his elegant walk and the straight lines of his fine suit as he crossed the lot.

No goodnight kiss? No clever excuses to follow her home and trap her at the front door in another sensual embrace? No elaborate scheme to get into her apartment and finish the job? Parker was certainly acting differently. His whole presence was reserved, distant. It made her kind of sad.

She cranked her car, pulled out of the parking lot, made a left onto Ponce de Leon. It was past midnight and the traffic was light. Maybe while he was out of town, Parker had come to the same conclusion she had—that it could never work between them. That would be a good thing.

She took the ramp onto I-85 and joined the party-going traffic heading home or to other nightspots. So why did she feel so uneasy? So vulnerable? So hungry for those delicious sensations Parker could produce in her? The ones she'd promised herself she'd never feel again?

She shook herself and thought about tomorrow. If Parker was going to be all business, she would be, too. She wondered what information he had dug up on Van Aarle. Had her first impression of the golf pro turned out to be right, after all?

As her old jalopy rumbled off the Buckhead exit and onto Peachtree, she told herself Parker must be tired from his trip. That's why he was a little cold. Maybe he was as disappointed in her tonight as she was in herself. Damn.

Wade Russell Parker the Third had some nerve messing with her head like this. Why did she have to wrestle with these feelings about him? Why was she letting him get to her? He was her boss. Period. Why couldn't they just have sex and be done with it?

She reached Colonial Towers, pulled into a parking spot, and got out of her car. She headed up the sidewalk to the tall white columns at the entrance. On the steps, she pulled out a key and told herself she was through thinking about Parker. Done. *Finito.*

Then she froze.

That strange, eerie feeling she'd been having lately slithered down her spine. The hairs on the back of her neck stood up. Sucking in a breath, she spun around and squinted into the darkness.

Nothing. Was she going crazy?

A patrol car glided past the parking lot on its way down Peachtree. She let out a sigh of relief, shook her head at her silliness. With a laugh, she reached for her door. Relieved at the sight of a cop car. Guess she must be switching sides.

CHAPTER TWENTY-FOUR

She didn't dream that night, thank God. Instead she slept like a rock, and her nerves and emotions were back under control when Parker showed up at her apartment right on the dot at nine the next morning. As she hopped into his silver Mazda and they headed north up I-85, she was convinced she could keep things professional.

They drove for almost an hour. Along both sides of the wide highway, urban sprawl gave way first to subdivisions, then to acres of lush forest that lined both sides of the road like a large green cave.

Parker wasn't his talkative self, at all. *Okay, be that way.*

Miranda sat back, stared at the fleeting scenery, and let her mind wander to Coco and her problems with Dexter. That triggered thoughts of Leon, which triggered the habitual need to find Amy. Her brain went back to her search on the Internet at the Agency last night and Wendy Van Aarle.

The more Miranda thought about Wendy, the more frustrated she grew. Was Wendy really adopted? She had no real facts. Only an angry comment of a kid who liked to fib, and what you might call "circumstantial evidence" on her parents' web sites. The best way to find out the truth, Miranda supposed, was to confront the girl with the letter from The Seekers and ask if she'd written it. She wasn't sure she could handle the answer. Besides, Wendy's father was a suspect in the Taggart case, wouldn't doing that cloud the investigation?

She glanced at Parker sitting stoically behind the steering wheel, dressed in his usual impeccable manner in a fine gray suit. She could use his help. He liked to help, he always said. Suddenly, it struck her that he'd probably been making his own inquiries into Amy's whereabouts without telling her. No doubt ever since she told him about Amy. That would be just like him. He hadn't come up with anything or he would have told her. The thought made her uncomfortable.

After all he'd done for her, she didn't want to owe him anything else. Especially not with the confused feelings he aroused in her. She'd handle finding Amy herself. She always had before.

She turned away and continued to stare out the window.

~

After another half hour, Parker turned off the highway and onto a long drive. Miranda peered out at a gorgeous pastel sky spread over rows of vegetation that stretched out forever, like a green ocean. In the distance stood a castle-like fortress, complete with flags waving from its cone-shaped roofs.

"Nice digs. What is that?" She pointed toward the fields.

"Vineyards."

"Wine country? I must have missed the turn to California."

He gave her a mock look of offense. "Georgia has its share of wine production."

"Guess so. What *is* this place?"

"Chateau Élégant. A luxury resort, complete with a winery, a spa, an art gallery, restaurants, and several golf courses."

"Ah, golf courses. Van Aarle's haunts." Now it made sense.

"Precisely."

Detective work could be nice if you were tailing somebody who had bucks. Working for Parker definitely had its upside.

He drove past the fortress until they came to the rolling hills of a golf course, where he pulled into a parking lot. As they got out and headed for the clubhouse, Miranda could smell the scent of grapes in the air.

"Are you in the mood for breakfast?" Parker asked, holding a door open for her.

After dealing with Wendy's announcement, Coco's anger, Bobby Lee Ingram's fists, and Parker's strange behavior last night, she'd been in too foul of a temper to slurp down her usual protein drink this morning. Her stomach was already growling.

"Sure," she said and stepped through the entrance.

~

The clubhouse restaurant was sedate and highbrow, with deep green tablecloths and contrasting saffron-colored napkins. Its walls and ceilings were made of glass so that the diners had a view of the green outside.

Parker asked for a seat with the best view.

The menu had categories like "In the Fairway" and "Off the Tee Box." Cute. Feeling adventurous, Miranda ordered strawberry pancakes.

While the waiter poured coffee into elegant china cups, she gazed out the glass window-wall at a few golfers who were playing on the lush green. The landscape was dotted with colorful trees, shrubbery and flowers, in the artful style she was getting used to seeing everywhere around Atlanta.

After a moment, a figure appeared over the far hill. As he stopped to take a shot, she recognized him.

"There he is," she whispered to Parker.

He nodded. "I know."

"You're not watching him too closely."

"I have a man out there on the green."

She looked off to the right and saw another golfer. Tall, big-bodied, gnarled face. Detective Judd. Nice to have staff at your command.

The waiter brought their breakfast. Parker had a simple plate of hash. Hers was topped with mounds of strawberries and whipped cream.

She looked up bashfully. "I don't usually eat like this."

His face warmed. "Should we ask if they have jalapenos?"

She grimaced at him and took a bite. The sweet, creamy morsel oozed in her mouth. "Hmm. It's fine the way it is."

With a satisfied look, he watched her a moment, then turned his attention to the green outside. Miranda did, too. Van Aarle was still adjusting his stance.

Parker picked up his coffee cup. "I learned several interesting facts about our current target on my trip to Pittsburgh this week."

She'd been dying to know since he'd mentioned it last night. "Pittsburgh?" she asked, taking another bite of the delicious fare. That was the town she'd worked in before she came to Buckhead. "Why'd you go there?"

"There was a murder there a few weeks ago that had some similarities to Madison Taggart's. A former employee of the Agency contacted me about it."

"Really?"

"An older woman in her fifties. Identical cause of death."

"You mean," she gestured toward her throat.

He nodded. "Ligature strangulation with a rope."

Holding her breath, she leaned forward. "Was there a ribbon? And seasoned cooking oil on the body?"

He shook his head. "No. But GHB was found in her bloodstream."

Another victim with the date-rape drug in her? What did that mean? She gazed out the window again.

Van Aarle took a shot, studied it a moment, seemed pleased with himself. He draped his club over his shoulder and headed for the clubhouse. After a calculated pause, Judd stuffed his own club in his bag and started in the same direction.

With a frown, she turned back to Parker. "So do those facts link the two deaths together?"

"Not by themselves." He paused and stirred his coffee. "However, I discovered that the target was in Pittsburgh at the time of the murder."

She put down her forkful of pancake with a clink. "No shit."

Purpose colored his good-looking features. "Do you remember that he told us he'd come back to town just for Wendy?"

"Yeah, when he kicked us out of his yard. What about it?"

"Not true. He was in town two days before we saw him. In a room at the Ritz-Carlton. He was also at the Ritz the day Madison went missing."

Miranda took a sip of water and swallowed it as a shudder went through her. "Why would he get a room at a hotel when he has a big mansion where he could stay?"

"Good question."

Didn't look good for the golf pro. She thought about the mention of his breakdown on his web site. Was he still having emotional problems? Problems that would drive him to kill a woman in Pittsburgh? "You think he didn't want anyone to know he was in town, don't you?"

"Possibly. But the timing of his trip to Pittsburgh and his stays at the Ritz aren't enough to link him to the murder. The police need more for an arrest. They can't do anything yet. But I can. If the target slips up and we witness it, we'll have probable cause."

"Do you have anything yet?" she asked cautiously.

"Tan is working on tracing the calls Van Aarle made last night. The calls he made at the Ritz were to an unlisted cell number." He shook his head. "So far our golf pro is clean as a hound's tooth. He's gone about his daily routine, such as it is for him. Last night Detective Tan followed him up here and reported that he checked into a room at the inn. Not that unusual if you have an early tee time in the morning. He had dinner alone and stayed in his room, again made a few phone calls. Judd took over this morning."

Miranda pondered the details Parker had given her. Her mind kept going back to Pittsburgh. Why would Van Aarle kill some woman in Pittsburgh? There was something funky about that, but she couldn't figure it out. She worried about Wendy. Van Aarle wouldn't hurt his own daughter, would he? But she might not be his real daughter. If he were going to do that, why would he kill her schoolmate first? There had to be a connection.

"There may be some link between—" Parker stopped talking.

"Well, if it isn't my old friend."

Miranda turned and looked up into Van Aarle's picture-perfect face, eyed his athletic body. Was this a cold-blooded killer standing before her?

The two men shook hands. Van Aarle turned and offered her his hand. "And you're here with your associate, Ms.—"

"Steele."

A thousand emotions went through her as she took his hand and gave it a shake. Once more, she thought about Wendy. Was this man her own daughter's adopted father? They might not be able to prove much about him, but she knew for a fact that he was a lousy father. The golf pro didn't even know Madison Taggart had been making Wendy's life miserable. That might be a motive, if he gave a damn about his daughter. But he didn't.

"What a pleasant surprise to see both of you."

His greeting was more of a question than a statement. She studied that phony smile, wanting to rip it off his face. But if they had any chance to prove he was the killer, she had to play it cool. She smiled back. "I heard Parker was coming up here to check out the sights, so I asked to tag along. You know what they say, 'Follow the money.'" She laughed. If Van Aarle thought she was a gold-digger, he might let down his guard.

"I see." He gave her a knowing wink. "What are you doing way up here, Parker?"

Behind them, Judd came into the restaurant and went to the bar. He acted like he didn't even know them.

Parker didn't flinch. He turned to Van Aarle with a casual air, leaned an arm over the back of his seat. "I wondered the same thing about you, Shelby, when I saw you out the window. With about a hundred golf courses in the Buckhead area, why come up here to practice?"

Van Aarle shifted his weight. He didn't like the question. After a second, he flashed a perfect set of teeth. "That's easy. Besides wine being one of my passions, and this place being one of the top ranked courses in the country, my father used to take me here when I was a boy, when I was first learning to golf. The place has a lot of fond memories for me."

Really? Miranda thought of the bio she'd read last night. Van Aarle's family wasn't particularly well off before he hit it big. How'd they afford trips to a place like this? Besides, Van Aarle had left Chicago to get away from his father.

"I didn't know you had a penchant for wine, Shelby," Parker chuckled.

"Oh, yes. I have quite an extensive collection." Van Aarle looked annoyed. He spoke before Parker could ask another question. "And you? What brings you here?" He wouldn't let the subject go.

Parker gestured toward the window. "Many things. The view. The company." He allowed his eyes to rest on her. As if on cue, he reached for her hand. She felt a chill go down her spine. She knew that look wasn't a hundred percent acting. "It's good to get out of the city once in a while. And my father has property up here he likes me to check on occasionally."

Van Aarle eyed their clasped hands. "Oh yes, the residential community. I hear they're selling like hotcakes."

"They are and my father is delighted."

His jaw clenched as he searched for another subject for small talk. He ground his teeth a little. "I suppose I'll be seeing you tonight, as well?"

Parker nodded in slight surprise. "Oh, yes. The Policeman's Ball. I attend every year."

"I'm glad I'm in town for it this year. It's such a worthy cause." Van Aarle glared at Parker. "Especially now, with a killer on the loose." He meant it as a jab. "Too bad our best detective is up here lounging around."

Carelessly, Parker allowed his gaze to linger on Miranda's fingers. "I could afford to lounge, if I were ahead of the police, couldn't I?"

Van Aarle froze. Miranda watched his fists clench, but he forced an extra-cordial smile. "Well, I'd better get back to the course. I look forward to seeing you two tonight. Have a nice day." He turned sharply and walked out of the place.

She looked at Parker. Their gazes locked. It was almost as if together they'd coerced an unspoken confession out of Van Aarle. He'd sure acted guilty of something.

Parker's face beamed with admiration.

"What?"

"You take to detective work like a fish to water."

"Do I?"

"Pretending we'd come up here for a liaison. That's good thinking on your feet."

"Thanks." She released his hand, which had lingered on hers, looked down and dug at her pancakes, trying not to admit how good his compliment felt. Smearing syrup and whipped cream around your plate was also a good way to evade the suggestive idea of coming up here for a "liaison."

"What was all that about the Policeman's Ball?" she asked after she had worked her plate into a gooey mess.

"It's tonight. A gala annual event. Ranges from five to fifty-thousand dollars a table."

"Whew." She put another bite in her mouth and decided it was too sweet.

"The donations are for a good cause. To support and honor our men in blue."

She took a swallow of coffee. "Sounds nice. Guess I've been getting pretty cozy with Atlanta's police force lately."

"I'd like you to come with me."

She froze. "I didn't mean it that way."

"But I did."

She narrowed an eye at him. She knew that standoffish act of his last night had been baloney. "Sorry, Parker. I can't even afford a twenty-dollar table."

He fixed her with that steel-gray gaze. "The Agency has a table reserved. A sizable annual donation helps to strengthen our relations with the force."

She cleared her throat. "You know, the gold digger thing was just an act."

"Of course. But I'd like you there."

"C'mon, Parker. Me? At a fancy party? In honor of policemen? I can just see me hobnobbing with all my close buddies at the station."

His face was intense.

She shook her head and pushed another syrup-drenched strawberry around her plate. "Like I said before. You and me—"

He raised a brow, stopping her in mid sentence. "Oh, did you think I was asking you on a date? I apologize for being unclear. This is business."

She eyed him with suspicion. "Business?"

"Among the other guests, most everyone in Mockingbird Hills will be there. There's much to be observed about people in a relaxed, social setting. Under certain situations, they reveal more than they would face to face. Besides, Van Aarle just told us he'll be there. We can continue our surveillance."

She put down her fork and pushed the plate away. "Okay, since you put it that way, I'll go." If she could work on the case, it was a different story. She'd make sure it was just business. And no monkey business.

"Do you have something to wear?"

She looked down at herself and shook her head. She'd worn the dark slacks and metal-studded navy top she liked to harass Gen with. "This is the best I've got."

He gave her that sexy, wry half-smile. "Then we need to go shopping."

They ended up, over Miranda's heated protests, at *Elegant Ensembles*, one of the ritziest dress shops along Peachtree Road. She was really pissed. She didn't want Parker paying for any more of her clothes, but what choice did she have?

Giving up the fight, she started trying on things. Dozens of them. Outfit after outfit. After a couple of hours, she must have put on every dress in the store.

Her tastes ran to dark colors, tight spandex, leather-and-chains. Parker's ran to pastels, ruffles, Barbie doll. Yuck. She hated every single one of his choices. Since he was footing the bill, she supposed she'd have to give a little, but come on.

The frazzled saleslady who had to haul the garments back and forth seemed at the end of her rope. Stoically she hid her annoyance behind a stiff, painted smile. Miranda had gathered from her remarks that Parker used to take his wife to this shop. That made things even more awkward. Miranda was certainly no clone of that saint. Not in clothes. Not in education. Not in speech.

Just when she thought her nerves couldn't hold out another minute, Parker held up his final selection.

Miranda felt the blood drain from her face. "You've got to be joking." It was a baby pink thing, so frilly and lacey, it looked like underwear.

He pulled out the full gathered skirt. "It's lovely. Very girlish."

She put a hand on her hip. "Just my point."

"Humor me?"

How did he always know how to get his way? With a loud grunt, she grabbed it out of his hand and stomped into the dressing room.

Inside, she yanked the thing over her head, fighting every inch of the way with the stiff, scratchy taffeta. When she looked in the mirror, she almost gagged.

She stomped out of the dressing room with a bitter scowl.

Parker tried to hide his smile. He couldn't really like this thing.

"No way, José," she warned.

With that sexy confident smile, he strolled up to her, turned her around, stood behind her in the mirror. She looked ridiculous next to him.

"You're lovely." His hands barely touched her arms as he held them out.

She shivered at the sensation. What was he trying to pull? "I look like a clown."

"You should get in touch with your feminine side."

"Hah." He couldn't make her wear this thing. There had to be some boundaries in the employer-employee arrangement. "Look, Parker, I—" What was he grinning about?

With a sly gleam in his eye, he reached out for another gown, held it up to her, so that it covered the pink monstrosity. "How about this one, then?"

Sucking in her breath, she beheld a stunning creation. A chic halter top with a bias-cut draped skirt in a shimmering burnt gold that faded to blue tones at the angled hem. It was gorgeous.

She smiled.

"Are we agreed, then?"

She turned around and gave him a smirk. "So the pink thing was a ploy?"

He shrugged. What a manipulator he was.

"Yeah, we're agreed." She reached out for it.

He pulled it away. "Next, we'll find you some shoes."

"Oh, brother."

Hours later, Parker dropped her off at her apartment with her packages and told her to take a nap before he picked her up for the party tonight. He didn't even try to invite himself up for a drink or anything. What was up with that? He was driving her crazy with this on-again-off-again treatment. His behavior infuriated her.

All business, her ass. That slippery detective was up to something, just like he had been with that dress. He was cagey. Secretive. And, she decided as she opened her apartment door, he was really screwing up her life with all this pampering and red carpet treatment.

He'd given her a job, trained her as detective, paid her rent, bought her clothes, bailed her out of jail—twice. The longer she knew him, the more she owed him. The more grateful she felt to him. She didn't want to feel grateful. She didn't want to owe anybody anything. She could take care of herself. She didn't need a man.

She put her packages down on the couch and rubbed her arms as she thought about the way he'd barely touched her in the dress shop. He was turning her on more than she could stand. It wasn't fair.

If she were a normal woman, she'd jump at the chance to get involved with Parker. Her old co-worker Fanuzzi sure would. Who wouldn't want to go steady with the wealthy, suave private investigator? But she couldn't take a risk like that.

Relationships didn't last. For her, closeness could only end in disaster. She couldn't take that kind of pain again.

She hung her new dress in the closet and got ready to lie down.

So was tonight really just about business? At her front door the last week Parker had hinted at a relationship. How could they have a relationship? They were worlds apart. She had too many issues. It could never work for them. She flopped onto the bed and closed her eyes. The sooner he got that through his head, the better.

If he was waiting for her to make the next move, he'd have a long wait.

Her mind wandered to Van Aarle. The golf pro had lied about his whereabouts the night of Madison's murder. He'd been in Pittsburgh when some woman had been killed. Both victims had been strangled. Both had GHB in their bloodstreams.

Parker hadn't seen Van Aarle following them on the way back from the golf resort this morning. He must have lingered around the course awhile. Why? She couldn't guess, but she knew Detective Judd was hot on his trail. He'd follow him back to Atlanta and the party.

The Policeman's Ball. Ironic event to catch a killer. Something was going to pop tonight. She remembered Judd telling the class that when a case is about to break, a good detective can feel it in his bones. She could feel it. Tonight was the night.

And after it was over, she'd get her chance at Wendy. The poor girl would have it even harder if her father went to prison for murdering her friend. Maybe Miranda could help her with that.

Maybe after tonight, everything would be different.

CHAPTER TWENTY-FIVE

In the downtown ballroom, sparkling crystal and fine china glittered like diamonds atop the rows of linen-decked tables set for several hundred guests. High overhead, blue-and-pink fluorescent lights stretched like a phosphorous sky, giving the place an artificial glow. Mingling about the wide, open space, men in tuxedos alongside women in silk, chiffon, and shimmering jewels filled the air with sophisticated murmurs.

The city's annual Policeman's Ball. Atlanta's elite honoring Atlanta's finest.

The fundraiser would have been a joyous event, if it weren't for the stench of recent murder that hung in the air.

In her new dress, Miranda stood studying the room on Parker's arm, butterflies mating in her gut. He'd surprised her when he'd picked her up twenty minutes ago in a midnight blue Lamborghini. Now that was the kind of wheels she'd expected him to have, rather than his plain old Mazda. She knew he'd been holding back.

But as she'd slid onto the smooth leather seat, got a whiff of his pricey cologne and an eyeful of his finely tailored tux and his perfectly styled salt-and-pepper hair, her nerves had spiked. Now standing with him at the top of the stairs leading to the dance floor, she felt like an uninvited guest.

This was Parker's world. The one he was born to. His friends, his compadres. This event only underscored the differences between them. His wealth, his connections, his success.

And what was her world? Road crews and oil rigs. Dry wall and paint. Endless, restless moving from place to place, punctuated by the occasional barroom fight and night in jail. What was she before he'd given her a job? An out-of-work construction worker with a record. A drifter. A woman with issues that would never go away. Standing here at this ritzy fundraiser on the arm of this elegant man, posing as his date, she suddenly felt like an imposter. Good thing it was only a cover.

She watched several bejeweled women turn their heads his way. Parker was something to look at with his fancy silk lapels, his satin tie, his to-die-for face.

Mature, stylish, wealthy. She'd probably be garnering cold stares from the ladies all night.

It didn't matter. She was here to do a job. And even if Parker had used the occasion as an excuse to be with her, she meant to do it. With determination, she straightened her shoulders as he led her over the blue-and-white terrazzo floor to a bar along the wall where cocktails and hors d'oeuvres were being served.

She wanted a beer, but he talked her into a glass of White Zinfandel. Sipping it, she tried to look classy as she studied the crowd. No sign of Van Aarle.

Parker let his gaze take in the length of her, pleased with the way her lean, muscular body filled out the golden gown he'd chosen for her. Wisely, she'd worn her hair down. Her dark curls circled her distinctive face, just touched the contours of her finely shaped shoulders. She was striking.

He picked up a glistening hors d'oeuvre from a server's tray and offered it to her. "I think you'd enjoy the Beef Satay with Thai Chili Sauce."

Miranda grinned at him suspiciously. "Charming me with gourmet fare, again?"

"Perhaps," he chuckled.

The morsel shimmered with red-colored sauce. It looked awfully tempting. She hadn't eaten since breakfast. She snatched it from his fingers and bit into it. The flavors snapped in her mouth. "Wow. That's good."

With the smile of a conqueror, he handed her a napkin.

"Thanks." She wiped her lips and eyed the serving platter.

"Would you like to try the Tomato Basil Bruschetta? A Miniature Cheeseburger?"

Tantalizing, but she shook her head. "I'd better hold off until dinner." There were only so many reps she could do with her free weights.

Parker waved the waiter away and turned his attention to the guests, pointing out judges, lawyers, business people, city councilmen. He indicated the Ingrams, who were at a table, talking with the CEO of one of the city's large corporations.

Ashley's parents, the mild-mannered college professors. Miranda remembered them from the photos in Parker's office. Lamar Ingram looked the role, with a balding head and thick glasses, but his wife Giselle seemed too glamorous to be a teacher, with her strawberry blond hair and low-cut, green silk gown strewn with pink flowers. The dress showed off her figure, which was rather buxom. She glanced around the room as though she were looking for someone, seemed a little nervous. Maybe she was an introverted scholar, despite her good looks.

Parker nodded toward a man with a loud laugh, joking with some friends at the bar. "That's Isaiah Todd."

Instantly she recalled the broad-shoulders, sandy curls and ever-smiling face of the dude in the "Out of This World" web site. The one who'd had his arm draped around Iris Van Aarle. "Tiffany Todd's daddy."

He nodded. "Over there is her mother, Wilhelmina."

She recognized the elegant woman from the photos, as well. Tall and lean, Wilhelmina Todd wore a stern black dress and simple pearls. Her dark brown hair was in a rather plain updo. She seemed the exact opposite of her husband. They seemed to be keeping their distance. Parker wasn't kidding when he said there was a lot to observe in a social setting. "They don't look too buddy-buddy," she said.

"They're professionals," Parker shrugged, "socializing with their respective colleagues. Isaiah's in advertising, while Wilhelmina's a very successful criminal defense attorney with Chatham, Grayson, and McFee."

She thought a minute. "Chatham, Grayson, and McFee…"

"Estavez's law firm."

"Right." So Parker's surrogate son, Antonio Estavez, and Tiffany Todd's mother were colleagues. She nodded. "Ambitious lady, huh?"

"You could say that. Wilhelmina and Antonio often compete over the high-profile cases."

And what was Isaiah Todd competing with Iris Van Aarle over?

Parker set down his drink. "There's Jackson. Come, I'll introduce you."

They crossed the room to a corner where a tall, thin man in a gray suit stood gazing out at the crowd. As they approached, he gave them a sad smile. "It's good to see you, Parker. I won't ask how you're doing with the case."

Warmly, Parker shook his hand. "I understand you want to know, Jackson. All I can tell you is that it's progressing. I didn't expect to see you here tonight."

He studied the floor. "I felt I had to show my support. I don't intend to stay long. Cloris is at home resting. These past weeks have been so difficult."

Parker laid a hand on his friend's arm. "It must be hard on her. Gatherings like this were always Cloris's specialty. I'm so sorry for both of you."

Miranda knew he wished he had answers for his friend. She did, too. For the thousandth time, her heart went out to him and his grieving wife.

Parker turned to her. "Jackson, I want you to meet my associate, Miranda Steele."

Taggart reached for her hand, gave her a sincere, friendly shake.

"I'm sorry for your loss," she told him. It was the standard line, but she meant every word.

"Thank you, Ms. Steele."

"Ms. Steele has already been a help to your case."

She blinked at Parker. Did he think so? She wished she could do more. She wished she could deliver up the killer tonight.

"I'm so grateful for anything you can do, Ms. Steele." Taggart smiled softly. "I would say that I'll be happy to return the professional favor, but I hope I'll never have to."

She cocked her head.

"Dr. Taggart is Chief of Staff of Saint Benedictine Hospital."

"Oh, yes. I remember Parker mentioning that," she laughed. "Thanks. I would like to stay out of there."

A rough, dark hand reached out for Parker's arm. "So glad to see you all here supporting our men in blue."

Miranda turned and looked into Lieutenant Erskine's black, marble eyes. They still unnerved her, but he didn't seem half as threatening dressed up in a tuxedo.

"Good evening, Ms. Steele." He pursued his lips at her as if he were about to interrogate her. "Nice to see you someplace where the bars are for serving drinks," he said under his breath.

"Likewise," she smirked and sipped her Zinfandel.

Dr. Taggart extended his hand. "Lieutenant Erskine, Cloris and I deeply appreciate what you and your men are doing to find Madison's killer."

Erskine's face grew stern. "We'll do everything in our power to bring the perpetrator to justice, Doctor."

Grimly, Dr. Taggart nodded. "I know you need to talk. Please excuse me." He stepped into the crowd.

Erskine stood silent, eyeing Miranda carefully.

"Anything you have to say to me, Hosea," Parker told him matter-of-factly, "you can say in front of my associate."

He moved his lips back and forth. He didn't like it. "If that's the way you want it." He leaned over and murmured in Parker's ear. "I managed to pull a few strings. We'll have a tail on your pigeon when he arrives."

"As will I," Parker replied smugly.

"So I expected." Erskine ordered a gin and tonic from a server. "I don't imagine he'll give us much tonight."

"One can never be sure."

Miranda glanced around the room again. Van Aarle hadn't shown up yet, but across the way, she saw Detective Tan all dressed up in a fancy red gown. Waiting to take over for Judd, she guessed.

She spotted a tall, handsome young man striding toward her group. Even without those sassy black eyes brimming with confidence and the long black ponytail, she'd have recognized Antonio Estavez, her one-time lawyer and Parker's surrogate son. He was stunning in his black tux.

"If it isn't the two hardest-working people in law enforcement," he said in his Hispanic accent as he reached the group. He held out both hands in exuberant greeting. "Good evening, gentlemen, Ms. Steele."

Erskine gave Antonio's hand a firm shake. "I'm all out of favors tonight, Estavez."

Antonio put a hand to his chest dramatically. "I want nothing more than to solidify my relationship with my colleagues. We are all working for the same cause, after all, aren't we?"

"Mm-hmm. Lawyers," Erskine muttered under his breath.

Antonio turned to her and took her hand with the air of a conquistador. "Ms. Steele, you're looking especially lovely tonight."

She raised a brow higher than Erskine's, even though the compliment felt nice.

Parker leaned toward her. "You must forgive Antonio. It's his nature to flirt with every female he sees. Something I couldn't train out of him."

Antonio laughed and raised his glass. "And all this time, I thought I was following in your footsteps, Señor Parker."

Erskine gave his glass to a waiter. "I'll leave you two to talk over old times." He nodded toward Parker. "I'll keep you alerted if I discover anything." He went to join some of the other officers.

Parker eyed Antonio. "Have you anything to tell me about Van Aarle and Oliver Chatham?"

Chatham? As in Chatham, Grayson, and McFee? That was right. Estavez's law firm handled Van Aarle's legal affairs.

Estavez showed a set of gleaming white teeth. "As I told you before, Señor Parker, I cannot tell you anything. I really don't know. You know I would help you, if I could." He reached for a glass of champagne from a passing server's tray, took a sip, looked thoughtful. "I will say Chatham mentioned Van Aarle has been making some big financial decisions, moving funds from one account to another, and so forth." He gestured with his forefinger.

Parker's face glowed with interest. "Like what you would do if you were intending to leave the country?"

He shrugged and nursed his drink. "Or planning to divorce your spouse. I really don't know any more than that."

Was Van Aarle preparing for a getaway soon? They'd better find something on him that would stick, fast.

"Is my colleague harassing you, Parker?" laughed a warm, female voice. Wilhelmina Todd strolled up to the group with a decisive gait. Close up, she looked stunning in her sparkling black dress.

Parker chuckled. "Actually, Wilhelmina, I'm trying to stop him from flirting with my new employee." He turned to her. "This is Miranda Steele."

The tall woman held out a hand. Miranda shook it with the same firm snap its owner gave her. "Glad to meet a fellow female professional. How do you like working for the Parker Agency?" She nodded toward Parker. "I hear this fellow's a real slave driver."

Miranda grinned, feeling a connection with the woman. "He's not too bad, if you know what buttons to push."

Wilhelmina raised a brow, impressed, regarded her with the piercing eyes of an attorney. "You'll have to fill me in on that technique next time he goes after a client of mine."

"I will," Miranda smiled. "And what's it like working at the law firm?"

Wilhelmina blew out a breath. "Busier than ever with my caseload and the girls' end-of-year school activities. It's so hard to juggle raising kids and a demanding career."

"Sounds like you have your hands full." Miranda wondered if she knew what a little snot her younger daughter, Tiffany, had become at school, or about her older one's late-night escapades with her boyfriend Jason.

Sipping her drink the attorney nodded. "My high school girl has been grounded more times than not this year. I've found the best way to handle her is to make her babysit her sister. She hates that. It's what I've got her doing tonight at the Ingrams." She shrugged. "It saves money and at least they're not with a stranger."

Miranda smiled, decided not to comment, but she wondered what sort of wickedness Ashley and Tiffany were cooking up right now. Not to mention Felicia.

Another hearty laugh came from Isaiah who sat farther down the bar. Wilhelmina didn't acknowledge her husband's amusement. Miranda wondered if she knew about that picture of him with Iris Van Aarle on his web site.

Wilhelmina gazed out over the floor where Dr. Taggart was talking to a city councilman. She gave a deep, anguished sigh. "I'm so worried for my girls these days. And I feel so sorry for him." She turned back. "Do you have children, Ms. Steele?"

"No," Miranda said flatly.

Parker leaned toward the pair. "Ms. Steele has been helping out with the Taggart investigation," he said, admiration in his voice.

She gave him a stern look. The compliment was nice, but he was rescuing her. She could handle a simple question without help.

Wilhelmina eyed them with discernment, as though surmising that there might be more to their association than work. "Is that your background? Criminal investigations?"

Miranda shrugged, twirling the wine in her glass. "I've worked a variety of cases." Sometimes her work had involved lifting fifty-pound cases. "I've traveled a lot."

"Interesting. Perhaps we can get together sometime and compare histories."

If only she had one to compare. "I'd like that." Good Lord, what was she getting herself into?

Luckily, the smooth tones of a piano distracted the persistent woman. From a stage off to the side, a soft, sultry voice fluttered over the speakers. Was that who she thought it was? She turned toward the stage and saw the blond head at the keyboard.

Yep, it was Coco. That girl got around. She was a vision of loveliness in a low cut, hot pink evening gown that shimmered like a star. At the white baby grand, she looked like an angel.

Miranda turned back to make a comment, but everyone was listening to the delicious music. She caught the look on Estavez's face as his black eyes drank in the singer. The handsome young man was moonstruck.

"What an exquisite voice. I never would have imagined she could sing like such a seraph." Of course, he remembered her. Very fondly, it seemed.

Look out, Antonio. You don't want to get tangled up in that marital mess.

He gestured toward her. "Perhaps we should say a few words to our mutual friend?"

Was that wise? But maybe it would be better if she didn't let him go alone. "Sure, why not?"

He gave his colleague a bow, then turned to Parker. "You'll excuse us?"

Parker raised a brow at Miranda.

She grinned back at him. "Mind if I go say 'hi' to my friend?"

Frowning, he leaned toward her ear. "Don't start with her—"

"I learned my lesson," she huffed back in a whisper. "I won't mention you-know-who doing you-know-what again. I just want to make things right."

He hesitated another moment, then gave in. "Just keep your eyes open for Van Aarle."

"Sure thing, boss." Taking a wary breath, Miranda slipped a hand through Antonio's arm and sauntered across the floor.

They reached the stage and stood at its edge waiting for Coco to finish her song. She turned around as she reached the last notes. When she saw Miranda, she started. Then she caught sight of Estavez and her eyes glowed with surprise.

Flustered, she blinked at them. "Hello, Mr. Estavez, Miranda." She said his name with gentleness, hers with a soft sneer.

"I'm surprised to see you here," Miranda said.

Coco didn't even break a smile.

Estavez glowed with charm. "We had to come tell you what a wonderful singer you are. What a talented musician."

That coaxed a smile from her. She blushed. "Thanks, do you really like it?"

"How could I not? It's lovely."

She let out a soft laugh. "I beat out a hot reggae combo for this gig. Of course, it's just during cocktails and dinner. They'll be a full band for dancing afterwards."

"I'm proud of you." Miranda told her.

Coco acted like she was deaf.

Estavez was hot on the trail. "Perhaps you'd be interested in playing for some of the affairs my firm sponsors."

"Sure, I'd love to."

"I'll give your name to our coordinator. I still have your card."

"Do you?" Her eyes glowed.

That spark between them shouldn't be there. Miranda worried about this girl. "Hey, maybe I could get you something." Parker's agency had to put on some fancy shindigs, too.

Coco ignored her.

Estavez sensed the tension. He looked like he'd like some time alone with Coco, but he was gentleman enough to realize the two women needed to talk. He looked around the room. "I see a client I need to speak to. If you'll excuse me."

Coco frowned, as if she didn't want him to go. "Sure. Thanks for stopping by," she murmured at last.

"Again, your performance is charming. I'll be in touch."

"Thanks."

He moved off.

Miranda watched Coco gaze after him. You're buying yourself a load of trouble, girl.

Coco turned and scowled at her as though she wished the ground would open up and swallow her.

Miranda took a deep breath. "I'm sorry about last night, Coco. I didn't mean to pry into your business."

She looked around but didn't say anything.

"I was just trying to be a friend."

She studied the keyboard.

Miranda was surprised at how much it stung to be snubbed by her. "You still have my number, don't you?"

She nodded.

Miranda fidgeted with the jeweled purse Parker had bought her. "If you need me, if you're ever in trouble or anything, don't hesitate to call."

She didn't move.

"Anytime. Night or day. Understand?"

She nodded and began the intro to her next song. "I'm working here. Do you mind?"

"Sure. I'll move on." She left her alone and found the table for the Parker Agency.

Miranda took a seat next to Parker at a fancy table, ignoring the curious stares of the top dogs from the Agency who were gathered around it. No doubt they were wondering what she was doing at this swanky shindig.

Parker leaned near her ear. "Friendship burgeoning again?"

"Like a bleeding ulcer," she muttered, glancing across the room at the piano player she'd just left.

He gave her a sympathetic look and turned his attention to Detective Tan who was seated on his other side. Miranda surmised she was catching her boss up on Van Aarle's activities earlier that morning.

Someone next to Miranda touched her hand. She turned and saw a middle-aged woman with a warm, round face and graying hair done up in curls. She said she was Detective Judd's wife and introduced her to the other spouses. Luckily, the lady was the talkative type. She chattered on about her husband's years with the Parker Agency, their second home in Miami, her grandchildren's honors at school, as if she didn't give a rip that the seat beside her was empty.

Judd must still be tailing their pigeon, Miranda thought, idly nodding in agreement to whatever his wife was saying at the moment. Was it common for golf pros to run so late to a party? Something didn't seem right. But Parker carried on just as happily as Mrs. Judd, casually joking with his employees and their spouses, as if there was nothing unusual about Judd's absence.

Miranda picked up a card printed in fancy script that had been laid against the centerpiece. It had tonight's menu on it. Wild Striped Bass, Filet Mignon and Lobster Tail with Horseradish Mashed Potatoes, Roasted Rack of Pork with Caramelized Maple Pearl Onions. Wow. At the moment, she couldn't eat a bite.

When the waiters began serving, she discovered Parker had ordered a special dish just for her—extra hot Szechuan Style Chicken with Wasabi Potatoes. So this dinner party was just for business. Right. He winked at her as she took a timid bite and savored the heat. Man, it was good, but she was too tense to do anything but pick at it.

The other thing spoiling her appetite was sitting right across the table. Gen.

Parker's daughter looked nice tonight. Silver earrings, a hint of glitter in her short platinum hair, a long silver pendant against a sheath of sparkling aquamarine blue. Her dress color made her eyes even darker and more intense than usual. Just now, they bored into Miranda like sharp drill bits.

Didn't take a crystal ball to figure out what the young woman was thinking. She hated the idea she was with Parker.

Miranda raised her wineglass toward her in a mock toast.

Gen's mouth twisted in a grimace.

Satisfied, she took another bite of the Szechuan dish and glanced over the diners. It was too crowded to see Van Aarle, if he'd finally showed up. Wouldn't Judd have joined them by now, if he had? Maybe not.

She kept hunting for him. At a table where some of the city councilmen sat, she noticed a pretty young woman in silver giving her an icy stare. Miranda eyed her angular face and frosted hair. A waiter poured champagne at a neighboring table. Sipping it, a shapely woman in teal, wearing an edgy hairdo curled a lip in her direction.

Miranda smirked. Guess being with Parker meant she had a regular fan club. Gen must be the president.

She turned her attention to the table of media folk next to her. An elegant-looking, long-necked woman with straight, shining black hair parted on the side gave her a bitter glare. Her distinctive face turned even sourer when her gaze moved to Parker.

Miranda stopped chewing. She'd been feeling smug until now. Somehow, the black-haired woman's look made her see reality. Not only were these people Parker's friends and associates. Some of them were probably his lovers. No doubt he'd had a pretty good track record since his wife died. These women weren't just jealous. They were guarding territory they thought was theirs. The thought hit her in the stomach like a chunk of lead. She put down her fork.

The black-haired woman raised a glass to her cohorts. "I know this is supposed to be a gala event, but isn't it ironic to be celebrating the police department when the neighborhoods of Buckhead are so unsafe?"

A few members of Parker's staff turned to glare at the woman. Miranda felt Parker bristle at her side.

Judd's wife leaned over and whispered to her. "That's Tanya Terrance. I'm sure you've heard her local radio talk show. Very controversial."

Miranda nodded. She'd caught snatches of it driving into work but hadn't paid much attention.

"Look at poor Dr. Taggart," she went on in a dark, articulate voice Miranda now recognized. "He's been so gracious this evening. I want to know why there's been no progress in his daughter's case."

Parker dabbed his lips with a napkin and cleared his throat. "Correction, Tanya. There's been no progress the police are willing to divulge to the media."

She turned and gave him a wicked scowl while her colleagues' faces went blank. "Is that so, Parker? What do you have to divulge?"

"Nothing to you."

"That's because you have nothing." That intense look had to be inspired by more than just the Taggart case.

"Rest assured, Tanya. As soon as I have a solid lead," Parker smiled, oozing Southern charm, "you'll be the *last* to know."

Cursing under her breath, the woman turned back to her dinner partners.

Parker concentrated on his meal.

"Sounds like she's got it out for you," Miranda whispered to him.

"I suppose she does. We dated for a while several months ago. When she began to use my clients' cases for fodder on the air, I broke it off."

No wonder the talk-show host had such a grudge. No wonder she'd been giving Miranda looks as dirty as Gen's. Parker had gotten around. Why should that fact bother her so much?

CHAPTER TWENTY-SIX

Miranda decided to forget about the women and concentrate on the fancy saucer of Kahlúa Cream Tiramisu a waiter had just placed before her. As she picked apart the coffee-soaked cake with her fork, a woman in a flowing red dress went to the podium and began a program of awards.

Local celebrities she'd never heard of gave speeches. Parker was among them. He spoke just before the mayor and told about the wonders of Atlanta and the progress in law enforcement he'd seen over the years, assuring the audience that keeping the town safe was a high priority for his Agency. He even made some sharp remarks aimed toward the media.

That should shut Tanya Terrance and her toadies up for tonight, Miranda thought with satisfaction. He got a rousing round of applause when he finished. Then the mayor took the podium and made a long, ass-kissing speech that made her yawn.

Once more, she looked around the darkened room and wondered where Van Aarle was.

Finally the program ended, the tables were cleared and the band set up. Music started to play and people swarmed onto the dance floor.

Parker appeared next to her, extended a hand. "May I?"

She looked up at his warm, handsome face and realized her heart was already waltzing. Still, she hadn't expected to be cutting rugs with him.

"I haven't been to a formal dance since high school."

"I'm sure it'll come back to you. Your footwork seemed pretty sure to me in the gym the other week."

She put down her napkin. "A *kata* isn't quite the same as a samba."

He took her hand and pulled her to her feet. "Just follow me."

He wasn't taking no for an answer, was he?

Parker made it easy. As the band started up with a soft, jazzy tune, he swept her onto the middle of the floor with a smooth, debonair move. Her steps mirrored his like water. She melted into his arms.

When they were lost in the crowd, she could no longer avoid his smoldering gaze.

"You look lovely tonight, Miranda. I should have said so earlier."

She shrugged, glad he liked her look. "You're not so bad yourself."

"You have excellent taste in gowns."

"You like it? Picked it out myself."

He chuckled.

She looked away. Business, she reminded herself. "I haven't seen Van Aarle anywhere."

He gave her a knowing look. "I checked in with Judd just before dinner. He still hadn't left his house."

She started. That was why Judd had missed dinner. "He made such a point about being here. Something isn't right."

"Not necessarily. What Tan and Judd have told me so far makes Van Aarle as innocent as a lamb."

"Or a wolf in sheep's clothing." She studied his face, tried to read his thoughts. "You're not a hundred percent sure Van Aarle did it, are you?"

"I never use percentages. Facts prove your case. Until they do, you don't have one. So far, we don't have enough to convict Van Aarle of jaywalking." He spun her around.

She cast a glance at the other dancers and saw several bejeweled women in silk and taffeta giving her death looks. They were getting on her nerves.

"You're making quite a stir tonight," he said.

"Yeah," she smirked. "Didn't know there were so many catty rich women in Atlanta."

"I was speaking of the men."

Huh? She looked at the dancers again. Sure enough, there were several nice-looking chaps in cummerbunds and diamond cufflinks giving her a hungry eye. She laughed to herself. She was used to getting looks like that in a bar. She'd never thought she'd get them in a fancy ballroom.

Parker's arm was firm around her. "As I've said before, you sell yourself too short."

She forced a laugh. "Guess this gold-digger act is going over pretty well."

His smile turned grim. He pulled her close. "You're not the only one who's been acting lately."

So he had been aloof on purpose, just as she'd suspected. She could see it in his face. Tonight his eyes said I want you and I'll have you, one way or the other.

Once more, he was making her long to give in to him. She felt her resistance weaken. He took her breath away. No one had ever made her feel the way Wade Russell Parker the Third did. She almost hated him for it.

"Excuse me," snapped a voice.

Miranda took a step back and nearly bumped into Gen.

In her long, sparkling blue sheath the young woman glared at Miranda, her dark eyes burning as hatefully as a troll's under the bridge. "I was hoping I could cut in. I don't often get to dance with my father."

And you'd like to keep me away from him, wouldn't you?

Miranda watched Parker stiffen. He didn't like the idea, but he could hardly refuse his own daughter. "If you'll excuse me." He let her go, reluctantly, it seemed.

"Fine with me, Gen." The young woman didn't realize she'd just rescued her. Miranda leaned toward Parker's ear. "Think I'll wander around and see if our pigeon's here yet."

His eyes danced with admiration. "Good idea. I'll catch up with you in a bit."

"Sure thing, boss." She was sure he would.

Parker took Gen's hand and pulled her into his arms. "It's been a while since I've danced with my little girl."

She gave him a snide look. "I need to keep you out of mischief. You've been getting away with murder lately."

"Always the administrator."

"It's a tough job, but somebody's got to do it."

He chuckled. "I think I'm old enough to handle myself."

Gen gazed across the dance floor where Miranda had disappeared into the crowd. Her face grew sullen. "I remember when you used to go to these affairs with Mama. She always had so much class."

Parker bristled. He could read her feelings, but she wasn't trying to hide them. "Things change, Gen."

"I know. But I don't have to like it." She turned back to him, smiled sadly. "Tonight makes me think of when I was a little girl sitting on the stairs watching you and Mama get ready for one of these affairs. I couldn't wait until I was old enough to go with you."

The memory she evoked touched his heart. "I believe you were fifteen when we first took you to a formal dance."

"The Piedmont Ball. It was beautiful. I was so thrilled and proud watching you two together. Mama was so gorgeous in her gown and jewels. You were so dashing in your handsome tuxedo. Just like you are tonight." Her eyes grew watery. Something rare for Gen. "I miss her so."

He stopped dancing. "Would you like to sit down, dear?"

She dropped her arms, took his hand and led him to a small alcove along the wall where she wouldn't be seen. She wiped her cheek against the back of her hand. "Things have changed, Dad. This past year, I've had to stand by and watch all kinds of women throw themselves at you. It's as if every available female in town has to have a chance at you." He reached for her arm, but she brushed him away. "It's hard to take. And now you're with *her*?" Her voice broke as she gestured vaguely toward the dancers.

"Ms. Steele is an employee. I'm training her for—"

"Don't bullshit me, Daddy. I know very well there's more than that going on. It's written all over your face."

She read him well. "I'm sorry you don't approve."

"I just don't like the woman." She hugged herself tightly. "Oh, Daddy. Losing Mama was so hard for me. I know it was on you, too. I worried about you for a long time. You kept to yourself, didn't speak. You spent so much time alone. I'd never seen you like that. And then all of sudden last year, you started dating everyone. Anyone. Women of all professions. Young ones, old ones. Widows, social climbers, seductresses. Tanya Terrance, for God's sake."

He'd done it to try to forget his sorrow, to snap out of his depression. But it had seemed as though the love he'd had for Sylvia, the memories of their years together would stay with him forever. He'd never get over her. Never find anyone like her.

"Life has to go on, Gen. And Ms. Steele—"

"She's not my mother," she snapped. Another tear ran down her pretty cheek. "She never will be. None of those women are. None of them could take her place. Least of all Miranda Steele."

So this was what had been bothering her all this while. He stepped beside her to block the view of her and pulled out a handkerchief.

She took it and wiped her eyes. "Oh, Daddy, what are you doing? How can you be so unfaithful to Mama's memory?"

What could he tell her? He barely knew himself. His emotions were just as confused as hers.

Tears glistened in her eyes, breaking his heart. She was right. No one could ever take Sylvia's place. A year of dating most of the eligible women in this ballroom had told him that. He'd been a fool to try to replace her. Sylvia was a unique jewel that had no substitute. Always lovely, sweet-tempered, feminine and graceful. She always knew just what to do and say. He'd loved her for it.

But it hadn't been complete bliss.

Gen didn't know the strain his work had put on his relationship with her mother. The quiet arguments they'd had behind closed doors when he took on a dangerous case. Sylvia had never comprehended why he had to take such risks. She had always tried to pull him away from the life that made him who he was.

But Miranda…

It wasn't only her potential to become a top investigator that excited him. It wasn't merely her street-smart fighting skills or her dead-on instincts. Miranda Steele understood the part of him Sylvia never had. She knew the burning desire to solve a case, even if it meant putting yourself in danger. The need to sacrifice yourself for the sake of another. She could look into his eyes and see his soul.

Gen stepped toward him, put her head on his chest and sighed so deeply he felt it go through him. "I just wish we could go back to the way we were."

"I know, dear. I know." Parker stroked his daughter's back gently, trying to comfort her. But his own thoughts consumed him. Could Miranda take the spot in his heart that had belonged to Sylvia so many years?

He was having as much trouble getting used to the idea as Gen was.

Out on the floor, dancers swayed to a soulful tune with a rocky backbeat. Miranda picked her way through the crowd, eyeing the euphoric faces. No luck. She couldn't spot Van Aarle anywhere. Maybe he'd told Parker he was coming to the party just to brush him off this morning.

She made her way along the perimeter of the room, back toward the bar, past the dancers. Just past the bar, she spotted an opening to a narrow hallway. Something told her to follow it.

The music died down as she stepped into the passageway. It angled back and forth until it opened up again into a small alcove. In the corner was a dark room labeled "Wine Tasting." No one was near it. As she approached the entrance, she heard voices. She stopped.

"You didn't come today." Her hair stood on end. It was Van Aarle's voice. "You didn't return my calls. I waited for you for hours."

"Shelby, please," a woman answered.

He wasn't alone. What was he doing with a woman in the Tasting Room?

"What's happening to us?"

"I can't do this anymore, Shelby."

"What do you mean? Have you stopped loving me?"

Good Lord, she'd stumbled into a love nest.

"Try to understand," the woman pleaded.

"Why are you doing this, Giselle?"

"Please, Shelby. You're a married man."

Giselle? Guess that ruled out Iris as the woman. She was still out of town, wasn't she?

"Married." Van Aarle's voice was bitter, harsh. "I have nothing but the shell of a marriage. A pretense. Iris doesn't care about me. Do you know how long it's been since we've had sex?"

"Seven months. Do you know how many times you've told me that?" Her voice was cultured, clear. It was Giselle Ingram. The college professor. Ashley and Bobby Lee's mother.

There was a pause. Miranda could feel her heartbeat in her neck. She heard pacing. Holding her breath, she flattened herself against the wall and looked across the way at a dark corner. Judd stood motionless in the shadows.

He put a finger to his lips. Her palms growing moist, she nodded.

Van Aarle grunted. "Ever since she hired Isaiah Todd to design her website, we hardly even speak. I know they're sleeping together. He takes as many trips abroad as she does. What business does a web designer have in Paris? I can just see them together in some slimy hotel on the Seine."

"It wouldn't be slimy with Iris's tastes."

Good point.

"Giselle, have a heart," Van Aarle cried out. "Can't you see how broken I am?"

Her voice broke with emotion. "You still love her, don't you, Shelby?"

"I love *you*, Giselle. Why didn't you come to me today?"

So that's what Van Aarle was doing at a golf course fifty miles to the north. Waiting for Giselle Ingram. Bet those phone calls he'd made went straight to her cell number.

"I told you, Shelby. I do love you. But I can't risk my family, my children, my professional reputation."

Miranda's mind raced. Poor Lamar Ingram. He'd seemed so meek and quiet. But what if he wasn't? Maybe he drove Giselle away. He was Bobby Lee's father, after all. Maybe the spoiled college kid had gotten his opinion of women from dear old Dad. What about little Ashley? God, the couple had been friends of Parker's wife.

She glanced at Judd, saw he was wondering the same thing she was. What did this steamy rendezvous have to do with Madison Taggart's murder?

"Think of what we've had together. Ever since I saw you sunbathing near your pool that day…" She thought of Giselle's buxom figure. Bet he got an eyeful.

"Don't remind me of that, Shelby. I can't hurt Lamar like this. He's been a good husband. He doesn't deserve it. I just can't do this any longer." She started to cry.

"Come here. Now, now. No tears."

Their voices hushed to murmurs. Miranda heard soft kisses. She swallowed hard. Pretty soon, they'd either get it on or come out of the room. She'd better get lost. She'd heard enough.

As she turned to go, Judd came up behind her. "You need to report this to Parker," he murmured.

"Just where I was heading," she whispered back.

Her heart pounding, Miranda made her way back across the dance floor. Things were getting lively. The drinks flowed while the crowd gyrated to a hot, sassy number with a beat so loud, Miranda felt it in her solar plexus.

She scanned the faces. At last, she spotted Parker off to the side talking to Estavez. She headed for him, but just before she reached him, she heard a blood-curdling scream over the band.

The music stopped. The whole room went silent. Everyone looked toward the bar.

Isaiah Todd was bracing himself on a barstool with one hand. With his other, he held onto his wife Wilhelmina, who was sobbing. Lieutenant Erskine had a strong hand on her other shoulder and a dark look in his eyes. A uniformed officer stood next to him.

Alarm streaking through her gut, Miranda ran toward them. The next instant, Parker caught up to her. Estavez was just behind.

As she approached, she saw Wilhelmina Todd put her long, thin hands to her face and wail loudly. "No. Please, God. Tell me it isn't true."

"You have to be wrong, officer," she heard Isaiah grunt. "Lieutenant, there's been a mistake."

Erskine shook his head grimly. "I'm sorry, Isaiah. There's no mistake."

The crowd started to murmur.

Parker reached the party just before Miranda. "What's going on?"

Wilhelmina's elegant shoulders shook. "It can't be true. It can't be. My baby. My little girl."

"What happened?" Miranda asked as she stepped to Parker's side.

The woman stared at her blankly, reached out for her arm and squeezed like she was drowning. Miranda didn't know what to say to her, but she read the message in the woman's eyes. She knew that panic. That bewilderment. That pain.

Another mother had lost a child.

Isaiah grabbed Parker by the hand. "You have to help us, Parker. It's happened again. The same place, or near it. Out behind the Ingrams' house."

"What's happened, Isaiah?"

Miranda could hardly stand to hear his answer.

"Our little girl. Our Tiffany. Lieutenant Erskine just told us—." His voice broke. His eyes were wild with grief. "She's dead."

CHAPTER TWENTY-SEVEN

Miranda never saw a man drive so fast. It wasn't fast enough for her.

When Parker's Lamborghini squealed up to the curb outside the Ingram mansion in Mockingbird Hills, she threw open the door and was the first out and up the hill. Lieutenant Erskine was just ahead of them, already to the top. Parker caught up to her. They were side by side for a moment, but she fell behind.

Damn these heels. She kicked them off, hiked up her skirt and shot past him, sprinting over the crest that led to the Ingrams' backyard. Behind the swimming pool, the grass sloped down steeply, ending at the familiar tree line. She slowed as the lurid scene came into view.

Against the black sky, the ghostly silhouette of swaying oaks and tall Georgia pines was streaked with flashing floodlights. Bloodhounds bayed in the distance while cicadas chirped a mournful dirge, a tragic chorus to the studied murmur of police meandering about the yard.

Dark uniforms huddled around a spot where the trees met the lawn.

Miranda pushed her way through the officers. When she looked down at the scene, her blood ran cold.

Blond hair tied back in a ponytail. Hands and feet tied with rope. The pretty, young face, now wearing a still, serene look instead of her usual sneer. A white ribbon around the neck. Miranda could smell the faint scent of rosemary and sage.

Just like last time.

Parker came up behind her, put a strong hand on her shoulder. "Don't look."

It was too late. She touched his hand and shivered. Why couldn't they stop this?

With a growl, Lieutenant Erskine reeled toward the man in charge. "Norwood, I had double patrol in this area. I want those officers' reports."

"Yes, sir," answered a thin man with an intense face. "We got a call from one of the neighbors. The Oglethorpes." He pointed toward the Oglethorpe house down the street. "Their two teenage sons had gone out to look for their cat and came across the body."

"I know that," Erskine barked. Then ran his hand across his brow. "The call came in about half an hour ago, right?"

"Correct." Norwood raised his hand toward the Ingram mansion. "There were several juveniles home at the Ingram place tonight. Their daughter, Ashley Ingram, age thirteen. The victim's sister Felicia Todd, age sixteen, and her boyfriend Jason Sullivan, age seventeen."

Jason? Miranda wrapped her arms around herself and dug her fingers into her arms to keep from screaming with rage. Wilhelmina's disciplining strategy wasn't worth squat.

"Walsh has already questioned them. Ashley Ingram claims she and the victim were studying for exams and had an argument over clothes. The Todd girl left the house in an angry huff about three hours ago, saying she would walk back home."

Miranda held her breath. Three hours ago. Was that just the time Van Aarle was getting back from the vineyard?

The radio on the officer's hip squawked. He picked it up and spoke into it. "The Ingrams just arrived home. Walsh is questioning them now."

Erskine nodded.

Norwood glanced down. "The body was wrapped in a blanket that was covered with leaves. We bagged the cover and sent it to headquarters already. The hounds are following the scent. They've trailed it back up there." This time he pointed past the Ingram house. "To the Van Aarle place. Walsh reported that Mr. Van Aarle just arrived home from the party."

"Good work, Norwood. Let's go talk to our man."

Erskine and the officer headed off up the hill toward the Van Aarles' just as Miranda saw Detective Judd coming over the crest.

"Van Aarle just arrived home," he said to Parker as soon as he was at his side. "Tan is still on him."

"Fine job," Parker told him. "Erskine just went to question him."

Judd looked down at the body. Forensic officers were finishing up gathering evidence, bagging it, taking photos. His face grew even grimmer than usual.

"When did Van Aarle arrive back from the vineyard?" Parker asked Judd.

"About three hours ago."

Three hours ago, Miranda thought. "The same time Tiffany left the Ingram house."

Parker nodded. "Did you see anyone walking around the neighborhood at that time?"

"No one."

"Did Van Aarle leave the house? At all?"

Judd folded his arms. "No, sir. I was out there watching him all afternoon. He didn't leave the house."

Parker persisted. "Are you sure?"

"Of course I am. I would have seen him."

"Unless you missed him."

His voice grew stern. "I don't miss, sir."

The officers finished with the body and got a bag to take it away. A man came up behind them. "Is there anything I can do?" It was Dr. Taggart.

"Stand back, Jackson," Parker said.

Too late.

"Oh, my God. Oh, poor little Tiffany."

Parker grabbed hold of his friend and pushed him back from the murder scene. "You shouldn't have come."

"I want to do something. I hate this feeling of helplessness."

Miranda watched the officers zip up the bag and lift it onto a gurney for transport to the morgue. Helpless. Dr. Taggart hit the nail on the head.

Parker let go of Taggart and peered off into the distance toward the woods. Miranda followed his gaze. He sensed something. She did, too. That strange, eerie feeling she'd been having lately. It came over her dark and empty, like a deserted house. Like a single pair of eyes were focused just on her. She had no idea what it meant.

"Get a light," Parker said to Judd. "Come over here." Miranda followed him for a few steps.

"I have one," said an officer.

Parker pointed down. "All right, Rawlings. Shine it here."

The bright flash illuminated the ground, which was half dirt, half grass, dotted with the start of the undergrowth that led to the trees.

Miranda looked at the spot. Her heart raced. Large, irregular indentions marked the ground where the grass gave way.

"Shoeprints." Parker said.

"A man's," Miranda whispered. It wasn't raining this time. There was more evidence left at the scene. "This is the proof we need."

Parker studied the ground. "Perhaps."

She hoped to God it was enough to convict the bastard who did this.

He looked up again, pointed into the woods. "There's a creek behind these trees."

"Yes, sir," Rawlings replied. "Runs behind all these properties. Through the entire subdivision."

A second officer began taking photos of the prints.

"Keep shooting, Yeoman," Parker said. He waved them on as Rawlings followed the marks with his light. They ran along the tree line for several feet.

Miranda followed Parker as he and Rawlings moved into the woods. Several other officers and Dr. Taggart were right behind them. The farther they went, the closer the prints got to the water. Finally, they ended along the creek bank.

Judd stood, scratched his head. "He must have gone this way to hide his trail."

"But it's in the opposite direction from the house," Miranda pointed out.

Parker shielded his eyes and peered into the water. His gaze ran along an imaginary path that the killer might have taken.

Miranda felt his body tense. He took a deep breath and stepped into the waters.

"What are you doing, Mr. Parker?" cried the officer with the camera.

"Hunting evidence, Yeoman."

Miranda knew exactly what he was doing. Thinking of the pain on Wilhelmina Todd's face, she plunged into the water behind him. "I'm with you."

Parker turned around with a snarl. "Go back, Miranda. I don't want you getting hurt."

She had to help. "I can take care of myself."

"Do as I say."

She ignored him. Who did he think he was, her boss or something?

With an annoyed huff, he turned around and took a few more steps. She followed him, peering into the muddy water, looking for anything. It gurgled and splashed under their steps.

"Careful for moccasins, Mr. Parker." Yeoman called out nervously.

"Moccasins?" Miranda said.

Slowly Rawlings ran his lamp over the water's surface. It was dark, murky. "No moccasins in these parts."

"Course, there are," Yeoman insisted. "This ain't no time to go proving our manhood, Mr. Parker."

"Moccasins?" Miranda asked again. "Why are they worried about shoes?"

Parker turned back to her, but kept his eyes straight ahead. "Not shoes. Snakes. Poisonous ones."

Miranda sucked in her breath. That was right. These woods were full of them.

"Moccasins don't usually inhabit neighborhood creeks, Yeoman," Dr Taggart offered. "But they are semi-aquatic. We do treat an occasional snakebite at the hospital."

Miranda swallowed. "That's great news," she muttered under her breath.

The water splashed as Parker took another step. It was almost up to his knees now. "The snake we're following went this way."

Miranda waded behind him, shivering. Hell, she wasn't afraid of a little reptile. She'd tangled with enough of the human variety. She'd face a hundred snakes if it meant bringing in that killer. She squinted hard at the water. There had to be something. Somewhere.

Then she saw it. "Look," she cried. "Under the water."

Parker stopped. "Looks like we have something." He waved. "Rawlings. Over here."

Miranda took a step closer as Rawlings' floodlight flickered over the dark shimmering ripples where Parker pointed. A patch of white poked out of the shadowy water.

"There it is," she whispered. Just what they'd been hunting. What was it?

Parker put a hand in his pocket, drew out a handkerchief, wrapped it around his hand. Then he reached down into the water, grabbed onto the patch.

"Watch out," Yeoman cried.

"Parker, be careful," Dr Taggart said.

He gave it a yank and pulled up an object. "Here we are."

Rawling's light revealed a soggy, dripping white mass.

Parker chuckled to himself smugly. "Not a moccasin. A Yager golf shoe."

"Van Aarle's brand," Miranda murmured.

After a stunned pause, Yeoman started snapping photos.

"Get a bag," Judd shouted to another officer on the bank.

Miranda came closer.

Parker scowled at her. "I told you to get back on the shoreline."

Now he was pissing her off. Hadn't she just helped spot that shoe? "I'm fine," she snapped. But just as she took a step toward him, she felt something slimy slide under her toes. She sucked in her breath.

"What's the matter?" Parker said.

"I don't know. I felt something—" She opened her mouth. All at once, sharp teeth grabbed onto her flesh. "Aaahh." She lifted her foot. A slimy, grotesque creature had latched onto her ankle. It swung back and forth like a miniature circus artist on a trapeze.

"My God." Parker handed the shoe to Yeoman, grabbed the thing with both hands and pried open its jaws.

As it came off her ankle, Rawlings focused the light on the creature. It was about a foot long, with a green, scaly body, a long tail—and teeth like tiny daggers.

The officers were fascinated. "What is that? A snake?"

"It's a baby alligator."

"Can't be."

"But there it is. It's rare, but I've heard of people seeing them things in their backyards once in a while."

"Yeow, that hurts." Her ankle was throbbing like hell. For an instant Miranda watched the ugly little creature wriggling in Parker's hand.

Its red eyes glowed, fixed right on her. She shivered all over with repulsion and humiliation. She'd never known how terrified she was of such creatures. Suddenly, there was a sharp pang of nausea in the pit of her stomach. The voices around her became tinny. The lights grew fuzzy.

Then suddenly went out.

"Miranda." Parker reached for her and caught her with one arm before her body hit the water.

"Gimme that thing." Rawlings took the baby alligator out of his hand.

Parker grasped her with both arms and lifted her up.

"Is she hurt?" Jackson asked.

He turned her foot toward the light. Her ankle was bloody and mangled. "She's been badly bitten."

Jackson looked at her foot. "It's nasty, but it looks like mostly superficial wounds. We can take her to the hospital."

Parker thought a moment. She'd hate that. "Can you treat her here?" he asked his friend.

Jackson rubbed his chin. "Maybe. I've got my bag in the car. I'll see what I can do. Can we take her somewhere nearby?"

Parker thought a moment. "I know a place."

CHAPTER TWENTY-EIGHT

When Miranda opened her eyes, a strange, giddy feeling rippled through her. Slowly she became aware of low lights from a fancy chandelier sparkling overhead. Was she still at the ball? Hmm. She didn't make a very good Cinderella, did she? Though she'd lost a slipper…or something like that.

She blinked. Long, gray gauze curtains played in a soft breeze from tall arched windows somebody had left open. The sound of cicadas accented their dance. The smell of something Southern sweetened the air. Magnolias, maybe. Or jasmine.

She exhaled, closed her eyes. She was lying on something very large and very soft. Hmm. She could sleep forever. Then she moved her foot and felt stabbing pain.

"Ow!"

"Don't move."

She lifted her head and saw Parker crossing the room, a glass of water in his hand.

She raised up on her elbows and found she was lying on the hugest bed she'd ever seen, atop a comforter of soft, silky, pure white. Her foot was wrapped in a bandage.

"Jackson said you need to be still and rest." Parker handed her the glass.

He had the lights turned down low, but Miranda could see that the room dwarfed the bed. It was much more than just a bedroom.

Walls of soft designer blue, art deco paintings, and furniture providing cherry-and-plum accents. In a corner sat an expensive-looking chair arrangement, like a small living room, waiting for some wealthy pair to park their butts for a little seduction. In another corner, a brass bamboo fountain gurgled as water cascaded down its sculpted lily pads, while a naked Grecian statue looked on. Parker had brought her here for…what reason?

"You're lucky St. Benedictine's Chief of Staff was at the crime scene tonight, or you'd have to go to the hospital." His voice was flat, weary with exhaustion.

She swallowed a sip of the water. "No. No hospitals."

"I thought you'd feel that way." He took the glass, set it on the table, crossed the room to what looked like a humongous walk-in closet. "There might be something in here you can wear."

Wear? She looked at herself. The expensive dress Parker had bought her was ruined. "Oh crap," she whispered quietly. But her dress was a small tragedy compared to the one they'd seen tonight.

She lay back down and stared up at the huge chandelier overhead. It was suspended from a domed ceiling of pure white with sculpted molding that reminded her of a wedding cake. She felt like she was floating up to lick the icing. Dr. Taggart must have drugged her. She wondered if Parker had added anything to the prescription.

She rubbed her head. "Where are we?"

"My father's place."

"Your what?"

"This is the house I grew up in. It's mine now, really. He wanted me to have it. He put it in his will."

Will? Suddenly, the luscious bed seemed a little creepy. "Uh, your father didn't die here, did he?"

"No. Why do you say that?"

"You just mentioned a will."

"Oh. It's not in effect yet. He's quite alive. He checked himself into a nursing home a few months ago because of a heart problem. He wants me to move in and take care of this place, though he has the regular staff still on duty." His voice got clearer as he emerged from the closet holding some folded things. She looked at him. His tux wasn't in much better shape than her dress. His five o'clock shadow was going on midnight.

He held up the stack and a pair of tennis shoes. "Just what we need. Ladies clothes. I thought he'd have some things around." He brought them to her. "My father is quite the ladies' man."

"So you mentioned. And he kept extra clothes around for them?"

"Exactly."

The seductiveness of the décor took on a fresh interpretation. She raised a brow. "Like father like son, huh?"

Parker chuckled. "That comment would make him laugh. He always joked about my preference for the married life."

Until Sylvia was gone. Hard to believe that was still true after the women she'd seen ogling him tonight.

He set the folded clothes on the bed. "These might fit." His gaze ran over the length of her. His probing look was darned evocative.

When he got to her foot, he shook his head. "I won't say I told you not to follow me into the creek bed."

She smirked. "Then I won't say I wished I had listened." She raised her chin. "But I did see Van Aarle's shoe first."

He nodded. "You did. That was good work. However, you also need to learn how to take orders." He gave her a sexy half-grin that produced an involuntary rush of titillation.

She saluted him. "Yes sir, boss man. But I saw the shoe first."

He shook his head at her. His sad smile and the fatigue lines around his eyes told her his mind was still on tonight's heartbreak. Despite his natural charm, he wore the look of an investigator who'd been up half the night hunting down a murderer.

She gestured toward the room. "What am I doing in the house where you grew up? In your, uh, father's bedroom?"

"I didn't want to carry you a long way. This house isn't far from the Ingram mansion." He tore his gaze from her, moved to the window, drew it shut, leaving the curtains open. "If you look hard, you can see its lights from up here."

From the bed, she shifted her chin, peered through the trees. Small dots twinkled in the distance. A view overlooking a crime scene. Lovely.

"Jackson patched you up, gave you an antibiotic and a sedative."

No wonder she felt so funny. And her foot was going numb. Right. She'd been bitten by an alligator. "Thanks for reminding me," she muttered. Not to mention how embarrassing it was to pass out in front of Parker and half the Atlanta police force. She reached for the T-shirt he'd put on the bed and held it up. It looked like it might fit. "What happened?"

"The police arrested Shelby Van Aarle."

She put the shirt down. "What about Wendy?" She was worried about her.

"She's at home. The cook who usually takes care of her is there, of course. Erskine left a guard at the Van Aarles' for her as well. Iris is on her way back from Paris."

"It takes a murder rap to get the woman to come home."

"Apparently."

Poor Wendy. She'd been through so much. What a father she had. If he was her father. As soon as this was all over, Miranda vowed she'd get to Wendy and show her that letter from The Seekers. She'd get the truth out of the girl. But that conversation had to go on the back burner for now.

Miranda thought of Tiffany Todd's cold, lifeless little body. "We blew it, didn't we? If only we could have stopped Van Aarle before he struck again." She sat up on one elbow. "Hey, why aren't you down at the station grilling him?"

His gray eyes met hers. He moved to the side of the bed, sat down next to her and shook his head, bitterness in his movements. "No one can. He's lawyered up."

"Bastard." She thought a minute. "Let me guess."

"Right. Estavez."

"Guess Chatham, Grayson, and McFee is a full-service law firm."

He grimaced. "Antonio will have Van Aarle out by Monday morning. He'll make it hard to make anything stick. Even with that shoe, the evidence is inconclusive so far. Van Aarle swears he doesn't know how it got in the creek. It was the only statement Antonio let him make." He rubbed his hands over his eyes. "I spoke to the Todds on the phone just now. They're beside themselves, of course."

"That poor family." She thought of Wilhelmina's death grip on her arm tonight. The shock and pain and terror in her eyes. Miranda's heart went out to the poor woman. And to Parker.

Now he had two sets of friends grieving over the loss of their young daughters. And his surrogate son was the one who had to defend Van Aarle. "Guess being the top gumshoe in town isn't always all it's cracked up to be, huh?"

He grunted a humorless laugh. "No, it isn't." He stared off in the distance. "Detective Judd swears Van Aarle didn't leave the house until he went to the ball."

"Maybe he went out the back door. You can't see over that hill from the street."

"Judd's the best man I have. He never misses."

She didn't know what to say. She shrugged. "First time for everything."

Parker was silent.

Did they have the wrong guy? "You don't think Van Aarle's innocent, do you?"

"I didn't at first, but the evidence is inconclusive. Usually the façade starts to break apart at this point."

"The police haven't processed everything yet," she offered. Her mind went back to the ball. She sat up. "I just remembered something."

"What?"

"At the dance. Just before Erskine told the Todds about Tiffany. Remember, I was wondering around looking for Van Aarle?"

He nodded.

"I found him. Overheard him, really. In the Tasting Room."

"Oh?"

She inched over next to him, kneeling beside him on the comforter. "He was alone in there with Giselle Ingram."

He raised a brow. "What was he doing with her?"

She tapped her fingers against her lips. Parker and his wife had been friends with the Ingrams. He wasn't going to like hearing this. "From the sound of it, they're having an affair."

He stiffened. "You must be mistaken."

She grunted in frustration. "Judd was there. He heard them, too. Giselle was supposed to meet Van Aarle at the golf resort this morning. Didn't show."

His look grew more intense.

"Sounded like it's been going on for quite a while. Van Aarle thinks Iris is sleeping with Isaiah Todd. He told Giselle he loved her."

She watched his eyes glimmer with shock. Then the wheels in his head turned as the implications sunk in. Giselle Ingram might give Van Aarle an alibi. Not to mention it didn't make much sense to have an affair with your neighbor while you're murdering young girls. Though it could be revenge against Todd to kill his daughter. And if he were that unstable, he might have killed Madison Taggart for Wendy. Maybe the girl had mentioned to her father how Madison tormented her.

Parker stood up and straightened himself. "We're both too tired to think straight tonight."

Okay, she'd drop it for now. It was a lot to process. "You're right." Think positive, she told herself. The police got their man. They would get enough evidence from the crime scene to put Van Aarle away. Van Aarle had to realize that sooner or later. He might even be confessing the truth to Estavez this minute.

"We'll sleep on it."

"Sure." Wait a minute. "We?" She didn't want to admit she felt a shiver of arousal go down her spine, in spite of tonight's grim events. "And where are you going to be?"

He rubbed the sexy stubble on his chin. "This house has ten bedrooms, as I recall. I should be able to find somewhere to sleep."

He didn't leave. He stood there staring at her, his gray eyes drinking her in, his breathing steady, a stray wisp of hair falling over his forehead. It must have been the drug Dr. Taggart had given her. Almost involuntarily, she reached up and undid the button of his shirt. Before she could get to the next one, he snatched her by the wrists.

"Don't tempt me, Miranda."

She gazed into those knowing, deep gray eyes. "Why not?" she murmured. "You've been tempting me since the first night I saw you."

"Your foot's been hurt. You're drugged."

It didn't really sting much anymore, but his intense expression told her what he really meant. *Don't write a check with your body that your heart can't cash. Don't get started if you don't want more than a one-night stand.*

What did she want? Outlandish feelings tumbled in her. Tender, sensitive feelings she didn't want to admit to, couldn't sort out. She didn't want to think about them. Or about tomorrow. All she knew was she wanted Wade Russell Parker the Third tonight.

She wanted him now.

"I don't care," she whispered.

He didn't need any more of an invitation. He pulled her hands apart, leaned in. His mouth hit hers with an aggressive force that pushed her backwards. She dug her hands into his hair and pulled him down onto the bed.

He caught himself with both hands, then without leaving her lips, began to explore her with them. She drank in his heady kisses like a drunkard swigging down his last bottle, a parched desert castaway guzzling from a pool of water he'd just found. The sheer skill of his persistent tongue shot thunder and lightning bolts straight through her as he tortured the inside of her mouth with it.

She grew wet, needy, wild with greed. She pushed him back with her mouth, until they were both kneeling upright on the bed.

His hands stroked her sides as she struggled under the domination of his mouth to get her own hands back to his shirt. Before she could undo another button, he surprised her by turning her over on top of him and grabbing for the zipper on the back of her dirty, ruined dress. Oh, yeah. She was supposed to change her clothes.

She heard the zipper come down, struggled to her knees again. She tried to wriggle out of the material, but it wedged around her waist He rose to his knees once more as she reached for his shirt. She was mad to touch that wonderful chest of his.

His hands met hers at his collar. They fumbled together a moment. Finally he sat up and yanked the thing open. Buttons flew everywhere. She lifted her arms and let him pull the nasty dress off of her.

He ran his hands through her thick curly hair and plundered her mouth. She felt one hand move to her back, struggle a moment. Her bra came loose. He pressed her to himself. The feel of his chest against hers thrilled her. Lower down, his arousal made her shudder. Oh, she wanted him.

He laid her down again. Now his touch grew softer, slower. His fingers slid over her skin, her nipples like a gentle breeze. She shivered with delicious chills.

Parker smiled at her intense face, the wild mass of long dark curls spread across the bed, as free and untamed as their owner. He let his fingers roam over her skin as he explored the length of her, taking in the feel of her firm, lithe body beneath his hands. Her muscles were womanly, despite their fitness, despite her efforts to mask her femininity.

He ran his fingers up the soft flesh of her inner thigh until they reached the warm folds of her womanhood. He lingered there a moment, teasing her, then slipped inside her, felt her moisture. He worked her slowly, easily, then quicker, gradually increasing the strokes until she gripped the sheets and began to groan.

To hell with self-control. To hell with waiting and holding back. He'd had his fill of it. Tonight he'd take his fill of her. He would take what he could get and use the opportunity to give her pleasure she'd never known. An experience that would be difficult to shrug off later. He'd make her need him. As he needed her.

"You're driving me insane," she whispered.

"Just my intention."

His hands were relentless. She felt herself soaring toward the edge. The idea of being conquered by him, of his bending her will to his with his fingertips should have infuriated her. Instead, she was mesmerized by the erotic thrill of it. What a master of seduction he was.

She let out a long, low growl. The sensation ceased.

"Do you want me to stop?"

Her breath ragged, she stared at his eyes glimmering in the low lights, anger flashing like a lightning bolt inside her. Was this some kind of trick? If she didn't want him to touch her, one swift kick to the gut would make him quit. No, he wanted to underscore the fact that this was her choice.

She blinked up at him, gazed into that delicious face, so full of emotion. A warning bell went off in her head. What were these feelings growing between them? Until now, she'd been in control. Until now, she had refused to allow herself to get emotionally tangled up with Parker. All that could ever mean was pain for both of them. Pain and loss of self. What they were doing could be a dangerous mistake.

And yet, at that moment, she couldn't make herself care. She was at the mercy of his touch. "You got a condom?" she murmured.

He grinned. "I'll take that as a no."

He fumbled with a drawer in the nightstand a moment, retrieved the target. As soon as he'd positioned it, she reached out for his hand, drew it to her breast. "Glad that's settled," she sighed as he attacked her again.

Slowly, his maddening fingers stroked her breasts, drifted down her stomach, over her thighs, between her legs. He lingered there an excruciatingly long time, working that magic of his. She was definitely under his spell. She was almost ready to beg. It seemed like an eternity before at last, he plunged into her. He began so slowly, she wanted to bite his shoulder.

She did.

"What an animal you are." But his movements became quick, aggressive strokes.

She laughed. "Worked, didn't it?"

Her head hung over the side of the bed now, her hair sweeping the thick carpet. The gurgling bamboo fountain was upside down, it's liquid flow reversed. He was turning her whole world upside down. His strokes grew harder, stronger. She grabbed onto the mattress, the bedpost. Their hips danced as though together, they would shake the whole earth.

Just as she reached her peak, she gasped out loud, wondering if she'd ever catch her breath again. Was this *real* sex? God, what had she been missing all her life? She'd gone through the motions, felt the tension, the mundane spurt of occasional release, but she'd never even imagined such...ecstasy. She wondered if you could die from making love.

With a cry that was half agony, half pleasure, Parker emptied himself.

She felt him come. Hot, furious, as if he had touched her very soul with his own life force. Never in her entire existence had she felt such power, known such bliss.

He pulled off her, lay beside her. In unison, they gasped for breath, a duet of sated lust. She stared up at the frosted dome and the chandelier overhead and thought about the women at the party who'd eyed her with such disdain tonight. She grinned. She'd trumped them all. For now, anyway.

Then reality set in.

"I should go," she whispered when she could finally speak.

There was silence for a moment. "You don't have a car."

Right. She was dependent on him for a ride. The regret started already.

He turned over, his look stern. "I'll take you home." From where he lay, he reached for his shirt that was strewn on the floor along with its buttons.

Parker watched the irritation color her cheeks. She didn't really want to leave. It was just a matter of waiting for her to realize that.

She lay there, staring at his chest. Didn't make a move to get going. There was a possibility she couldn't get up. Her legs probably couldn't hold her just now. His own felt fairly wobbly.

He dropped the shirt and leaned on one elbow. His hand reached for her. Slowly, he circled her nipple with his fingertip.

She arched her back and moaned softly. Arousal burst inside her again. Oh, God, there was more? He wasn't finished, was he?

"Shall I get my car?" His finger didn't stop.

"Yeah," she breathed, wondering how she could form the word. "I'll wait right here for you."

She melted as his mouth took her lips once more.

It was still early. She couldn't leave right in the middle of this artistry. She owed it to herself to stay a while and find out what else he had in his magical arsenal.

Her arms went around his neck. Her heart leapt as he rolled her over and once more, began to work his spell.

CHAPTER TWENTY-NINE

In her dreams she heard a jingling. The soft song of happy music. Childhood. A moment of joy when her father gave her a music box and hugged her. Another life, another place.

She opened her eyes. She was in the huge bed, a satin sheet covering her. She tried to move. It wasn't easy. Her body was numb after such intense lovemaking. Was it five times? She'd lost count.

She looked up, blinked. Parker was moving toward her, still naked. Something was in his hand.

She sat up. "What is it?"

"Your cell phone. I charged it earlier." He handed it to her. It was ringing.

"Nobody calls me." Groggily, she took the phone and glanced at the time. Two a.m.? She punched the button. "Hello?"

Sobs. Heavy sobs. "Oh, Miranda—"

She froze. It was Coco. "What's wrong?"

"I'm just…I need…help. Oh please, Dexter, don't. No!" As her cry pierced Miranda's ear, the phone went dead.

She shot to her feet.

"What's the matter?" Parker asked.

"It's Coco. She needs us."

Miranda never saw a man dress so fast. Somewhere, he found a new set of clothes, while she hopped out of bed and madly gathered up the things from his father's closet, which they'd strewn all over the floor. She yanked on the T-shirt, jerked up the jeans, jammed her feet into the tennis shoes. Her ankle was starting to smart again but she ignored it.

Thanking God that everything fit, she followed Parker through the hall and bounded down the huge mahogany staircase, barely taking in the expanse of the mansion.

They jumped into the Lamborghini and took off.

In a few minutes, the sports car was blazing down I-285 to Doraville, the GPS pointing the way, but as they squealed onto the exit ramp, reaching Hinsley's street in what seemed like a NASCAR record, she wondered if they'd be in time.

Lit up by landscaping lamps mounted near the garage, the Hinsleys' house on Hickory Lane was a homey, two-story frame in a quiet, tree-lined subdivision where all the homes looked about the same.

Parker screeched to a stop in the driveway. They got out, scrambled up the walk to the porch. There were shadows in the window. Miranda heard a man shouting. A woman crying. Coco.

She climbed the steps to the front door. Parker reached it the same instant she did. They pounded on the door in unison.

"Open up," he shouted.

The yelling inside stopped.

After a minute, Dexter's voice came through the closed door. "Who is it?" He didn't sound friendly.

"Roto-Rooter man," Miranda yelled. "Open the door now."

"What do you want?"

"Sir, we received a complaint about a commotion," Parker said with the sternness of a cop. "We're here to investigate."

Slowly, the latch turned and the door cracked open. Disheveled red curly hair appeared in the gap. "There's nothing to investigate." Dexter Hinsley eyed them with suspicion. Miranda saw his shirt was half open. "You're not the cops. Who are you?"

"Friends of your wife." Parker shoved the door open, forcing Hinsley back. Shock colored his face.

A weak voice came through a door that led to a living room. "Who is it, Dexter?"

Miranda stepped through the opening. On the floor, in the middle of the beige carpet, Coco sat. Her pretty hot pink gown torn down the front. When she saw Miranda, her eyes grew round. She tried to pull the tatters of her dress around her. Finally, she just covered her face with her hands. But Miranda had seen how her makeup was smeared. She'd been bawling her eyes out.

She spun around, snarling at Dexter. "What did you do to her, you fucking bastard?"

"None of your goddamn business. Get out of here. This is trespassing."

She rushed at him, her hands ready to gouge out his eyes.

Parker grabbed her arms before she got to him. "Let me handle him."

"But—"

"I know how not to leave evidence. Go take care of Coco."

Blinking, she wondered what he meant. Then she saw Hinsley's face go white, as Parker grabbed him by the collar. "Where's the back door?"

Feebly, Hinsley pointed over his shoulder. "What are you going to do?" he chirped.

"You'll see." Parker's eyes narrowed as his voice took on a deep Southern tone she hadn't heard before. "I believe it's time you toted a whoopin', boy." He half-dragged him down the hall.

Her heart still pounding with rage, Miranda turned back to the living room. Coco hadn't moved. She crouched down beside her.

"I'm so ashamed," Coco moaned, her face still in her hands.

"You didn't do anything to be ashamed of. Let me take a look at you."

Miranda coaxed her to lower her hands. There was a cut across her forehead.

"God, what did he do to you?"

She looked down at the carpet, unable to answer.

Don't you dare say it was your fault. "You got a first aid kit?"

She waved a hand down the hall.

Miranda got up and found the bathroom and a small white box in a cabinet over the sink. She came back to the living room and sat down on the floor beside Coco. She opened the box, found some cotton, poured peroxide onto it.

"Hold still." She pressed it to Coco's forehead.

"Ow." She cringed.

"I know this hurts. I'll be quick."

It must have been the sting that got her talking. She started to chatter. "After the party, I went to my gig at The Gecko Club. Dexter said he had to stay over in Birmingham tonight. But when I got home, he was sitting here in the living room. Right in that chair." She pointed to a corner.

The black-haired teacher in Birmingham must have cancelled class.

"He demanded to know where I was. When I told him, he was so angry. I've never seen him that mad."

But she had seen him mad before.

"He told me I could never play in public again. He took my keyboard and said he's selling it. He threatened to break my fingers if I tried to play again."

"God." Miranda glanced down the hall, hoping Parker was stuffing Hinsley's balls down his throat.

Coco started to sob. "I don't understand what's happened to us. My momma always told me just to smile and be polite, learn to make good fried chicken and sweet tea, and you'll have a happy marriage. What did I do wrong?"

Why do we always blame ourselves? Miranda had blamed herself for years. "Nothing," she said sharply.

"I just wanted to play piano. Why did I think I could keep it from him? I'm so stupid."

"You are not stupid. You're just afraid. For a good reason. Hold still." She daubed at the cut until it quit bleeding. "Did he hit you with something? We'll need it for evidence." She would have thought of that, even if Judd hadn't spent all week drumming the importance of preserving evidence into her head.

"Just his fist. Evidence?"

"You're going to press charges, aren't you?"

Coco stared at her with her round, helpless blue eyes.

Anger bubbled up inside her. "You need to learn to defend yourself."

"What?"

"It's mostly attitude. Never plead or beg. Demand. Tell him to leave you alone. If he doesn't, attack."

"Attack?"

"Use anything you can grab." She held out the first aid kit. "A pair of scissors, a cell phone, a remote control. Just jam into it an eye or the Adam's apple or—" She stopped talking.

Coco's mouth hung open in shock. It wasn't sinking in. This was no time for a crash course in self-defense.

The girl's eyes filled with tears. "Oh, Miranda, what am I going to do?" Suddenly, she threw her arms around her neck, held onto her as if for dear life and sobbed.

Miranda resisted for a second, then let her arms wrap around the poor weeping woman. She stroked her back, hoping to give her a little comfort. She knew what she felt. She knew what it was like to feel helpless and alone.

Dexter's muffled shouts came from outside. "Leave me alone. You've got no right to—aah! Quit, I said."

"What's going on?" Coco pulled away, got up and ran to the back door.

"Don't go out there," Miranda said, but she was already in the yard.

Miranda sprinted to the spot where Parker stood over Dexter, who was on the ground moaning. She'd never seen such a pained look on a man's face before. "Stop it. Leave me alone." There was begging in his voice. About time he had a taste of his own medicine.

"I'll call the police," he threatened, guarding his crotch, trying to crawl away on his back.

"Too late," Parker said. "I just called them." He slipped his cell phone into his pocket. "I have a witness that saw you lurking near Dogwood Academy at the time of the Taggart murder. The police will want to talk to you about that."

"What?" he gasped. "That little rich girl who was killed in Buckhead? I didn't have anything to do with that."

"She was a student at the school. We'll see what the authorities think. There was another murder tonight. Another student at Dogwood Academy. Perhaps you can tell them about that as well."

"There was another murder? I don't know anything about it." He looked like he was about to pee in his pants.

Miranda stared at Parker, her heart filled with admiration. She knew what he was up to. A domestic abuse charge might not even put Dexter in jail for the night, especially if Coco didn't want to press charges. Suspicion of murder, on the other hand, would keep him locked up until Coco could get her head together and get away.

He turned to her and murmured softly. "This is one reason I gave up police work. Too many restrictive rules and procedure."

She nudged him. "Gosh, Parker. And all this time I thought you were a wuss."

He gave her a cocky half-grin.

CHAPTER THIRTY

The police came and took statements. When they were done, they took Dexter away in a patrol car while Parker tried to convince Coco she needed someplace to stay for the night. It wasn't easy. She was flustered, disoriented, came up with a slew of excuses not to leave her house.

Finally, Miranda packed a bag for the stubborn girl and told her to get in the car with them.

"We can take her to my place," Miranda whispered to Parker as he pulled out of the drive.

Parker shook his head. "Too small for the three of us."

"Three?"

"I'm not leaving you alone tonight."

She was too spent to fight him, so it was back to his dad's place in Mockingbird Hills.

It took another hour to get Coco settled in one of the mansion's bedrooms. When she was finally asleep, Miranda came back to the master bedroom. Parker was waiting for her in one of the chairs in the corner. With the lights on, the room looked even bigger than before.

She pointed to the stretch of carpet between the bed and an ornately carved armoire. "You could install a small swimming pool over there."

"I think my father was planning that." He looked around with a sigh. "This house was an old Southern mansion that he restored for my mother when they first married. His hobby was equipping it with the latest gadgetry. The master bath has heated floors, a state-of-the-art sauna, a steam shower with programmed pressure and temperature settings." He looked like he could have gone on, but he stopped. "My father has elaborate tastes."

"So I gather." She wasn't really listening. Her mind was on Coco.

Restless, she started to pace. She couldn't shake the jittery feeling. Like something evil was closing in on her. She thought about the way Coco looked tonight in her torn dress. Her fear, her humiliation.

She stomped back and forth, muttering to herself. "How could that bastard do that to her? Why didn't she stand up for herself?"

Parker interrupted her jabbering. "How's your foot?"

She stopped and looked down at it. Oh, yeah. The alligator bite. "I don't feel anything right now."

"It's probably numb. I should redress the bandage." He stood.

"It'll be okay." She paced some more. "If only I could have a moment alone with him." Parker had stolen that from her. He'd taught him a lesson, but Hinsley's type never really learned. "I'd smash his face. Make him sorry he ever—"

Parker caught her by the arms. "Calm down, Miranda. It's over for tonight. Let me have a look at your ankle."

She sat down on the bed. He kneeled on the floor and gently lifted her foot. "Does that hurt?"

"Uh-uh."

He lifted the bandage, grabbed a kit from a drawer, and started to redress it. "I'm feeling like a medical intern tonight. Perhaps we should turn my father's house with all its gadgetry into a hospital."

Ignoring him, she rubbed her arms, suddenly feeling a chill. "She'll go back to him. You always go back."

He finished with the bandage and sat staring up at her. "Did tonight bring back bad memories?" he asked softly.

She froze and looked down at him. "What do you mean?"

His face was intense. That direct look he wore when he asked a question he already knew the answer to. "Why did you never mention that you were married before?"

She stood up. "If I wanted to be interrogated, I could go to the police station." She walked away, stopped before she got halfway across the room.

He came up behind her, tried to put his arms around her. "Miranda."

She pushed away his embrace. "You been snooping into my past again, PI?"

He stopped trying to touch her. "A little. Why don't you tell me about it."

She spun around. "Why should I?"

"Maybe I can help."

He always wanted to help. "Nobody can help. Besides, it was a long time ago."

With a determined look, he took her chin in her hand. "Then it shouldn't hurt to talk about it. But obviously, it still does."

She hated it when he saw through her. She despised it when people tried to make her face her past, her feelings. The shrinks did that. It never did any good.

She shook him off, went to the rose-colored wing chair with the ottoman in the corner and plopped down. She stared out the window and thought of tonight's crime scene. No solace there.

She turned away. "So you want me to 'begin the healing' by baring my soul to you?" She made quote marks in the air with her hands.

"Not unless you want to."

What a crock. He was going to persistently badger her in that quiet way of his until she told him everything.

Parker moved toward the wall, pressed a button and a wet bar appeared. He selected a bottle, opened it and poured two glasses. Crossing the room, he handed her one. "This will help you relax."

"And loosen my lips." Oh, he was good. She took the glass anyway and took a sip. Expensive brandy. Didn't help a bit. She glared at him. He just stood there looking at her, waiting. Why not tell him everything? See what he'd think of her then?

"Okay. Yeah, I was married once. Up until about thirteen years ago. To a cop. A real pillar of society."

He took a seat on the opposite chair. "Leon Groth was hardly a pillar of society. Not a good cop at all."

Her breath caught. How much had he found out? She set down the expensive drink on the fancy table with a slap. "If you know so much, why don't you tell the story?"

His face was a rock.

She rose, paced back to the middle of the floor, feeling like a tiger trapped in a cage. Even if it was a large, luxurious cage. She looked down at the huge bed where they'd made love a few hours ago. Black satin sheets tangled with the silky white comforter.

Her mind blurred, she twisted her hair in her hands. "No, Leon was not a good cop. He wasn't a good husband, either. He was a lot like Dexter, though I don't think he ever cheated on me. He was too self-righteous for that. He thought women were inferior to men. Physically, mentally, morally. His favorite part of being a cop was busting whores. He said they were evil, a scourge on society."

Parker waited patiently, silently.

She went back to the chair and took a gulp of brandy. Still didn't help. "You just get used to it after awhile. The belittling, the yelling, the fits of temper." She took another sip, sat down on the ottoman. "You learn how to hide, how to be quiet. You learn to just swallow it when you're told how stupid you are, how ugly you are. How no one would ever want you, so you'd better not—"

She reached for the arm of the chair, squeezed it tight. He touched her hand. This time she let him linger.

"I was too weak to leave him. Too needy, too dependent. I hated being that way. I'll never be that way again." She looked at Parker.

His face was hard as iron. It was the same look he'd had tonight when he took Hinsley outside. He remained silent. He knew there was more.

"All right, you want everything?" She drained her glass and began.

"It was a night in February. Leon had gotten home around ten and didn't like it that he had a reheated supper. He was in one of those moods of his. I was scared, but I didn't know what to do about it. He went to the fridge and started yelling about ice cream. He wanted Rocky Road. I'd gotten vanilla. He grabbed me by the arms, shoved the car keys into my hands and told me I'd better go to the store and get him what he wanted or else."

She ran a hand through her hair. "So I did. I was glad to get out of the house, to get away from him. It was cold. There was ice and snow on the ground." She thought back, remembering the details she'd tried to shut out of her mind for so long. "The regular store was closed, so I drove around awhile looking for a place that was open and would have Rocky Road. I ended up in a bad part of town."

She smirked. "Who the hell eats ice cream in the middle of February? Leon did. I knew that. I was mad at myself for getting the wrong flavor. Guess I was thinking about that when I got out of the car."

She paused and looked down at her glass. "Got any more of that stuff?"

Without a word, he rose and retrieved the bottle. He filled her glass. She took another swallow, stared off into space.

"What happened when you…got out of the car?" Parker asked gently.

Miranda drew in a ragged breath. "Someone grabbed me from behind. I never saw who it was. He was wearing a black ski mask. He dragged me back behind the building. I tried to fight, but I didn't know how. All I could do was beg and plead, like a weak, sniveling, helpless…" She took a breath, set down the drink. "It didn't stop him." She put her head in her hands. "I couldn't stop him."

Parker reached for her. "That's enough," he said. "You don't have to say any more."

But there was more. "A few weeks later, I found out I was pregnant. Things got worse. Leon couldn't have children. He was left sterile by a bout of the measles. He said he couldn't bear the thought that I was carrying some creature that was half his wife and half some monster. He hated the way Amy was conceived, hated that a rapist could do what he couldn't. He said the thing growing in my womb was evil—produced by an evil act I had brought on myself. He wanted me to get rid of it."

"But you didn't."

She shook her head. "I don't know where I got the nerve, but I refused. I couldn't get rid of an innocent child. What happened to me wasn't her fault. Then Leon wanted me to give her up for adoption before she was born. I couldn't do that either. In spite of everything, I…loved the child. But Leon wouldn't listen. He said I was dirty, ruined, too filthy to be in his sight. The only thing that could purify me—was death." Her voice trembled. She felt a tear go down her cheek. Damn. "I guess I should be grateful he didn't kill me."

Parker squeezed her hand. "What did he do?"

"Nothing. After awhile, he stopped all the badgering. The months passed. I went into labor. He took me to the hospital, and I had Amy. After a couple days, we brought her home. I thought he'd gotten used to the idea. That he'd decided to try to be a father to the baby. That we could be a family. He might have. But I think when he saw it was a little girl, he changed his mind. That must have been when he started to formulate his plan."

Parker stiffened. "What plan?"

Miranda took in another breath. She let go of Parker's grip, reached for another drink. Her hands shook. She took a swallow and set the glass down. She pressed her hands together. "Leon never looked at Amy or held her or even touched her. It was as if he was just letting her stay there in his house awhile. He demanded his shirts be ironed, his meals cooked, everything, just like always. Like Amy wasn't there. I was exhausted most of the time, trying to take care of both of them, or maybe I would have seen it."

"Seen what?"

She groped at the arm of the chair. "What he intended to do. It was three weeks after we brought her home. I woke up one morning and…" she closed her eyes tight and squeezed Parker's hand as the vision of that empty crib materialized in her mind. "Amy was gone."

"Gone?" Parker's voice strained with tenderness and outrage.

"Leon had taken her to some agency he knew while I was asleep and given her up for adoption."

"My God, Miranda. How could he get away with that?"

"Leon had connections. He knew powerful people. At least powerful enough to cover it up." She wiped her face. The tears were coming harder now.

He stared at her openmouthed. She'd never thought she'd see such shock on the ace investigator's face. He'd assumed she had given Amy up for adoption. She'd let him believe that.

She watched his eyes dart back and forth. She knew what he was thinking. That he could pull some strings, too. That he could find a way to get Amy back. And she saw it in his eyes when he realized it was too late for that. Way too late.

She went on. "I was so angry when I found out. Leon was so cold. He didn't care what I felt, what I wanted. Then I did something really stupid."

"What?"

"I attacked him. I lost control and just lunged at him." She swiped at her face, trying to stop those damn tears. "That was when he beat me up and threw me out of the house."

Parker shot out of his chair and crouched before her, holding her arms with both hands. "What?"

"He threw me out," she said. "Told me he never wanted to see my face again."

"My God, Miranda," Parker said again. "What did you do? Where did you go?"

She shook her head. "I don't remember. I guess I found a hotel room and tried to commit suicide. Some strangers found me wandering around on the highway. I don't think it was that night. It might have been a few nights later. I'd tried to slash my wrists. They took me to a state hospital. I fell apart."

He stroked her hair so gently she barely felt it. "Oh, Miranda."

Her shoulders began to heave. "We were married seven years. Leon was my whole life." She choked back another catch in her throat. "He was a jerk. A bona fide number one asshole. And I still stayed with him. I still loved him. Why couldn't I have left him before he took Amy away from me? Why wasn't I strong enough? What does that make me?"

"Loyal."

"Weak. Stupid. Needy." She shuddered at the words. "I'll never be like that again."

"No, you won't. I promise you that."

How could he? It was up to her to make sure of that. She'd survived. She would continue to survive. All on her own.

She slapped herself on the chest. "I made myself strong. I learned to fight. I vowed to myself that no one would ever hurt me like that again. Never," she shouted at him. "Do you hear me? Never."

His arms reached for her. His hands went around her with such compassion they took her breath away. No man had ever touched her with such gentleness. She couldn't hold back any longer. She broke down and bawled against his shoulder like a baby.

Her head throbbed, her heart ached. Why had she gone and spilled her guts like this? Baring her soul to Parker was like being skinned alive. Would she never escape these memories? These terrors? She wanted them out of her brain now. Out of her heart.

She lifted her head. "I'm getting your shirt all wet."

"I welcome your tears," he murmured.

His kisses fell soft against her cheeks, melting her. There was such soothing in his touch, it made her long for the warmth of his body against hers. She wanted to feel the sensations he made her feel hours ago. The ecstasy that made her forget everything. It was a powerful drug. The only thing she could think of to drive out the demons.

"Make love to me," she whispered to him.

Parker rose, lifted her up, carried her to the bed, slowly began to undress her. He kissed her cheeks, trying in vain to extinguish the tears that wouldn't stop. For a long while he held her trembling body.

Her story had demolished his heart, but at last, he knew. He understood. He saw the truth. This was the reason for that simmering rage that lay just beneath her surface. This was the terror that haunted her, made her obsess about staying fit and physically strong. This was the fear that kept her from intimacy.

And yet…never in his life had he felt so close to a woman.

He wished with all his heart he could erase all that pain. Every last bit of it. He wished he could go back in time and change her past. But he couldn't. Not her past. Not his past. All he could do was make her forget. For a little while.

He ran his hand over her breast, watched her succumb to the waves of passion.

Oh, yes. He knew it all. He knew cruelty and hate and violence. He knew despair and anger and grief and helplessness. He'd learned it all first hand long ago when he'd lost Laura.

Laura. His first love.

Her brutal rape and murder so many years ago had been like his own death. Only in solving her case had he been born again. Bringing her killer to justice couldn't bring Laura back, but it had given his life meaning again. Set it on its present course. Yes, Parker knew what it meant to turn your life around after devastating tragedy. Just as Miranda had done.

With the horrors she'd endured, she might have turned inward. She could have grown sullen and morose, thought only of herself, turned to destruction, used unbridled violence against others. But instead, Miranda Steele had fought for others. For the innocent.

He thought of the day he watched her defend a coworker on the road crew and get fired for it. He thought of the morning she went to Dogwood Academy to investigate the Taggart case and risked her job with the Agency. He thought of tonight, when she'd plunged into the creek bed to help find a killer without thought for her own safety. And a little while ago, when she'd attacked Hinsley for his abominable acts to protect a woman who had snubbed her.

She was a selfless fighter, her soul bent on defending the weak and needy as much as his was. Yes, she had made herself strong. Yes, she had fought back. She was no longer a victim. But her purpose now was to help other victims out of their misery. And her purpose echoed his. She was a kindred spirit. A warrior.

She pulled him close. He slipped inside her, watched her eyes glow with desire.

As she moaned beneath him, all doubt fell from his heart. He was certain that he loved her. More than Laura. More even than Sylvia. And he knew why. In their heart of hearts, they were just alike.

Their iron wills had been forged in the same fiery furnace of pain and cruelty and injustice. They were one. They were avengers.

CHAPTER THIRTY-ONE

Somehow, Miranda fell asleep. Wrapped in Parker's arms, caressed by the soft satin of his huge bed, she should have felt safe and secure. But her dreams haunted her.

Her stomach clenched and trembled with that horrid, sick feeling. That strange, eerie sensation she'd felt at the murder scene tonight. In her slumber, she fought the sharp teeth nipping her ankle. The hands reaching for her, grabbing her, forcing her down. The glazed bloodshot eyes, full of murder. The bizarre images gnarled together in her brain until they woke her with a start.

She sat up. Blinked.

The room was dark, except for the moonlight flooding through the tall windows. Parker lay beside her. He murmured, reached for her in his sleep. Their lovemaking had been bittersweet. Intense, but reserved. He must think she was fragile now. She wasn't. But she suddenly longed for him to hold her again.

She didn't like the feeling. She couldn't let herself need him. And she couldn't disturb him, he must be exhausted.

She got up and went to the window.

She pulled back the curtain and peered into the darkness. There were still a couple lights on near the Ingram place. It must be almost morning.

What atrocities she'd seen tonight. Coco, attacked by her husband in her own home. Tiffany Todd, murdered and left in a neighbor's backyard. Once more, Miranda began to sift through the details.

A second little girl was dead. Her body left only several hundred yards away from the spot where Miranda had found Madison Taggart three weeks ago. Her neck tied with the same white ribbon, her hands and feet bound in the same way, her skin and clothes covered with the same seasoned cooking oil.

Madison Taggart, Tiffany Todd, Ashley Ingram. Friends. Three popular preteen girls who hung out together. Now two of them were dead. Had Shelby Van Aarle killed those girls? All they had was his golf shoe and his recent itinerary to prove it. And Antonio Estavez was about to get him off.

She peered through the darkness, but couldn't make out the Van Aarle mansion.

Wendy. Miranda's heart ached for the girl.

Iris was on her way home, but tonight Wendy was all alone. She was used to it, Miranda told herself. Her parents, if they were her parents, had left her alone to fight the horrors of the preteen jungle at school. But she'd never had to face something like this. What she must be going through. All by herself.

Did Wendy write the letter to The Seekers? Had Miranda's only daughter been given to such a family? The thought made her want to take Van Aarle by the throat and choke him.

Suddenly, she had to know.

She found the clothes she'd worn earlier on the floor. She put them on, found the jeweled purse she'd carried to the banquet and tucked The Seekers' letter into her pocket. Then she tiptoed out the bedroom door. She made her way down the long hall, down the massive staircase to the foyer at the bottom. Opposite the stairs, stood the front door. She crossed the floor, opened it, stepped outside, got her bearings.

Van Aarle mansion. To the right.

The huge house stood in its gray-stone European grandeur, its arched white sashed windows illuminated by ground lights, just like the first night she came here.

Miranda stood on the sidewalk on Sweet Hollow Lane and stared at the police car in the drive next to Van Aarle's Jaguar. The golf pro wouldn't be driving it to any fancy hotels or lush courses for a while, would he?

She sighed. How was she going to get into that house?

She took in the Ingram place with its off-white stucco and sweeping drive and thought about the night she'd met Tiffany Todd and Ashley Ingram here. They had thrown a rock at a window. Wendy's bedroom.

She stepped over the shrubbery and crossed the lawn to the side of the house. She peered up at the round-topped window on the second floor. A light shone inside. Was Wendy still up? She was probably having as hard a time sleeping as Miranda was, the poor girl.

Suddenly a silhouette appeared.

Miranda's breath caught. She stepped into the light and waved an arm.

After a minute, the casement opened. "Who's down there?" It was Wendy.

"It's me, Wendy. Don't be afraid."

The girl seemed bewildered. It was hard to make out her face, but her eyeliner was so dark, even from this distance Miranda could see it smeared down her cheeks in long black marks. She must have been crying all night. "Who is it?" she hissed.

"Miranda Steele." She stepped closer to the light.

"Miranda? What are you doing here?"

Might as well confess. "I'm helping to investigate Madison Taggart's murder. And Tiffany's."

"Investigate?" Her voice was shaky. She hugged herself and looked around the yard. "They say my father did it."

"I know."

"The police took him away tonight." She started to cry.

"I'm so sorry." Miranda grabbed at her hair in frustration, longing to comfort her. "Look. Can I come in and talk to you?" All she wanted was to hold her in her arms.

"He didn't do it."

"Oh, honey." What could she say to her? She touched the letter in her pocket. She'd have get the girl to settle down before she showed it to her. Even then, it would be bad timing.

"He didn't do it," Wendy repeated. "I know he didn't."

"If he's innocent, the police will let him go." If there wasn't enough evidence, they might do that if he was guilty.

"He didn't do it," she screamed.

She raised her hands. "Okay. Calm down. Everything will be fine."

"Fine? You don't get it, do you? You don't understand at all."

"What don't I understand?"

She looked around, rubbed her hands together in agitation. "Meet me at the front door." She disappeared.

She was in. Thank God. Without trying to figure out the girl's behavior, Miranda jogged around the house to the front porch. As soon as she got there, Wendy opened the door. She must have run down the stairs.

Wendy snatched her hand. "Come with me."

"What about that officer?" She didn't see him anywhere. Might be taking a nap on one of the sofas.

The girl yanked at her arm, ignoring her question. "I have something to show you."

I do, too. But she'd wait her turn. Wendy led her down a long hardwood hall, its walls covered with golf awards and pictures of her father. When they got to a huge ornate door at the end of it, Wendy reached for a carved brass knob. The door squeaked as she opened it. She switched on a light and started down a stairway. "Down here."

Miranda followed her down stone steps that wound around like a medieval castle. The air was cool, just a bit damp.

When they reached the bottom, she gazed around in amazement. Hundreds of dark-colored bottles were stacked along the walls in diamond-shaped racks of deep red wood. Glistening, long-stemmed glasses stood along a narrow counter that ran the entire length of the racks. Lit by sconces on the walls, fancy figurines decorated some of the shelves.

Miranda's sneakers squeaked softly on the stone floor as she stepped to an open door at the side. There were more rows behind it, arranged like aisles in a library. Must have been several hundred bottles in the side room.

A wine cellar.

Van Aarle said he had a passion for the stuff. This was more like an obsession.

She stepped back into the main area. The lights were low, eerie. A tasting table, of the same dark red wood, stood near the counter. A candelabra sat atop it. Right now, it reminded Miranda a little of a scene out of "Bride of Frankenstein."

Hugging herself, Wendy paced to the table, her face still streaked with dark makeup. "Don't you see?" she whispered.

Miranda looked down at her and shook her head. "Not really."

"Don't you get it?"

"Get what?" She wasn't making any sense.

She rolled her eyes in exasperation. "My father didn't kill those girls."

"How does this wine cellar prove that?"

She groaned. "He didn't do it. I did."

Miranda's heart jumped. The poor girl was hysterical. "No, you didn't." She reached for her.

Wendy backed away. "Yes, I did."

"You're just trying to protect your father. I know how you must feel."

"You don't know anything. Why are adults always so dense?" She pounded her chest. "*I'm* the killer. I killed Madison Taggart and Tiffany Todd. I hated them. They made my life miserable."

Miranda took a step toward her, held out a hand. "Aw, honey. You just wished they were dead because they hurt you. Nobody can blame you for that."

Wendy stamped her foot. "You don't understand. Why doesn't anybody understand? *I* did it. Listen to me." She held out her hands. "Take me in. Arrest me and let my father go!"

"The police aren't going to believe you, either." Her heart ached for the troubled little girl. If she'd just let her hold her.

"There's the proof." She pointed to the table. "That's where I tied them up. Like a human sacrifice."

"Right," Miranda said. "You've got a great imagination, kid."

"It's true. Why don't you believe me?"

Gently, she reached out, touched her dark, matted hair. "Look, Wendy. I know you're hurting. This night must have been terrible for you."

She shook away and went to a cabinet in the corner. She bent down and opened it. "Here's more proof. Here's the rope I strangled them with."

Miranda's throat went dry as she glared at the length of rope Wendy held out. About three feet, the right thickness, from what she remembered in the autopsy report.

"And here's the stick I used to tighten it with." She held out a dowel-like piece of wood. Where had she gotten that?

Ligature strangulation. She had to have heard how the girls had been killed. She was making it up. Had to be.

"And I made this for them. For the ceremony." She held out a bottle.

Miranda gasped. She closed her eyes and forced herself to breathe calmly. Wendy was holding a bottle of oil with spices and seasonings floating in it.

"Sea salt, rosemary, and sage. To purify them before their death. So they'd be happy in the afterlife."

How did she know the exact contents? Why it was used? That information hadn't been released. The pieces of the puzzle started to come together. The dark eye makeup, the red lipstick, the strange black clothes. It was more than just a fad. More than a call for help. It was a statement. What kind of weird shit had Wendy Van Aarle been into?

There had to be an explanation. "Wendy," Miranda said sternly. "You have to stop pretending. You'll only get yourself into trouble."

Wendy's eyes blazed. She growled with a voice of a wounded animal. "I am not pretending." She grabbed for Miranda's hand again and pulled her back through the side door, down a long aisle of wine bottles. "Here. Look at this."

There was a small alcove with a narrow door. She turned the knob and opened it. It led outside. "This is how I got them outside."

So that was why Judd didn't see Van Aarle.

The stone floor seemed to shift beneath her. That sick, queasy feeling roiled in her gut. She couldn't be seeing these things. Was she still dreaming? But she knew she wasn't. Oh God, it was true.

Her stomach clenching in spasms, Miranda reached into her pocket with a trembling hand. She felt paper. The letter from *Someone Else's Daughter*. No time for that now. Other pocket. As her fingers touched her cell phone, she blew out a soft breath, relieved Parker had slipped it in there. She scrolled to the numbers.

Parker's was the first one on the short list. He must have punched it in himself. Thank God. She pressed it.

He answered on the second ring. "Where are you?"

"The Van Aarle place. Get over here fast. There are some things here you've got to see."

She had to turn her in. What other choice was there? It was the right thing to do. The only thing to do.

But when Lieutenant Erskine and his staff arrived at the Van Aarle mansion for the second time that night, took statements and took Wendy Van Aarle away to the youth detention center in East Point, Miranda burst into tears.

She'd never felt so weary in her life. Her mind was a blur, her heart a pit of agony. Parker held her, tried in vain to soothe her, then he drove her back to his father's mansion and put her back to bed. The sun was coming up as he pulled the satin sheets over both of them and took her in his arms. She clung to his shoulders for dear life and again doused his chest with her tears.

Was that her own daughter who'd been arrested for murder tonight? Was that Amy? How could this be happening? How could her daughter be a cold-blooded killer? She was the spawn of a rapist, after all. What kind of genes did she have? Miranda wept until she had no more strength.

Tonight's images haunted her. The wine cellar, the rope, the bottle. Wendy's dark, pleading eyes. At last, they blurred in her brain and began to run together. As she fell asleep, she thought of Leon's words long ago. Filthy, vile, contaminated.

Had he been right?

CHAPTER THIRTY-TWO

Soft daylight streamed through the tall window, gently caressed her face. Miranda woke, sat up, rubbed her eyes. She felt stiff and headachy.

Parker was nowhere around. What time was it? She spotted a fresh set of clothes lying on the foot of the bed. He must have left them for her. Lord, he was thoughtful.

She got up, slipped them on and went down the hall. Halfway down the carved mahogany staircase, the smell of fresh coffee hit her. Her mouth watered, despite her headache.

She followed the scent down another hall at the bottom of the stairs. At last, she found a paneled door, pushed it open and saw a large kitchen. Parker was in dress shirt and slacks, leaning against a countertop sipping from a cup.

He greeted her with a smile that was as sad as it was warm and welcoming. It had been a rough night for both of them. "Good afternoon," he said in that low Southern tone.

She glanced at the wall clock. It was past one. She ran a hand through her hair. "Why'd you let me sleep so late?"

"You needed it." He stood watching her a moment as though weighing whether to kiss her hello or not. He opted for not. "Would you like some breakfast?"

"Some of that coffee sounds good."

He went to a cabinet, took out a teal china cup embossed with lilies and reached for the pot in a gourmet coffee maker. He poured a cup and handed it to her.

She took a sip. It was Heaven. "Man, this is good."

"It's St. Helena, from the island where Napoleon was exiled. My father's favorite."

Sounded outrageously pricey. "Nice of Napoleon to send it. Your family really is well connected."

He smiled tenderly at her attempt at humor, held her with his eyes.

Avoiding Parker's gaze, she glanced around. The room was an artfully designed mass of black granite, stainless steel, gleaming wood and antique brass fixtures. She took a seat on an iron-edged stool at the large stonework island. "Your father did a nice job on the kitchen."

"It was one of his favorite projects, though I don't know why. He never used it. It was the real estate developer in him, I suppose. Kitchens and bathrooms sell houses, he always told me. Even high-end ones." He went to the fridge and got out a carton of eggs. "The staff left some basic supplies. Do you like scrambled?"

"I'm not hungry."

"You should eat."

She shrugged. "Sure." She didn't have the energy to argue. She couldn't help a half-smile as he went to the stove.

He raised a brow. "You find scrambled eggs amusing?"

"I just can't see the CEO of the Parker Agency as a short order cook."

He nodded. "Unlike my father, I can make a few things." He reached for a skillet and got to work.

Miranda ran her fingers over the shiny counter of the island as she watched him. "Is Coco still asleep? Maybe she'd like breakfast, too."

Parker stirred the eggs, poured them into the pan. They sizzled on the heat and filled the air with a delicious odor. "Cora Beth woke up early and told me she decided to leave town."

"Leave town?" Miranda felt disappointed at the news.

He worked the eggs with a spatula another minute, grabbed a fine china plate from the cabinet and spooned his creation onto it. "She said she had an aunt in Iowa where she could stay for a while. I didn't want to risk her changing her mind, so I took her back to her place to pack, then to the airport."

He set the fancy plate in front of her, provided her with a fork and linen napkin.

She looked down at the steaming eggs. Miranda never let herself get close to anybody. But suddenly she wished she could have said goodbye to Coco. That's what happens when you get emotionally involved with people. They break your heart.

Parker reached for a piece of paper in his pocket, handed it to her. "She left you a forwarding address and said to tell you thank you."

She took it, looked at it a moment, stuffed it in her pocket. So Coco had enough of a head on her shoulders to get away from Dexter, after all. Good for her. She hoped it would last.

She took a bite of the eggs. They were good. "Not bad for a PI."

"I'm glad you approve." He went back to his original spot along the counter.

"I wish I could have seen Coco again before she left."

"I debated waking you, but didn't have the heart." He picked up his cup. "I called Judd to stand guard while I was away. He left about an hour ago." The PI sounded as casual as if he were talking about picking up the mail.

She poked at the eggs and frowned. So Parker thought she needed a bodyguard. The idea annoyed her. "Glad to see chivalry isn't dead," she smirked.

He ignored her tone. "On my way back, I stopped at the Ingrams'."

She stopped chewing. "Yeah?"

"I talked to Giselle. She confirmed what you and Judd reported about her and Van Aarle last night. They've been having an affair for several years." He exhaled slowly. "She begged me not to tell Lamar. She intends to break the news in her own way, as she put it." He looked at her. There was admiration for her in his gray eyes, mixed with sadness and regret for his friends. "Giselle swore to me that Shelby was innocent. She insists he isn't capable of murder, especially not a child."

"Of course, she'd defend him." Miranda put the last bite of food in her mouth and took her plate to the sink. She found a cloth and ran some water, deciding she'd pay Parker back for the eggs by doing the dishes.

He set down his cup and rubbed his eyes. "I also talked to Ashley."

She turned off the water. "Ashley was Tiffany Todd's best friend. She must be beside herself."

"She's traumatized. Lamar and Giselle are arranging private counseling for her. But she was able to tell me about Wendy. She said Wendy Van Aarle was strange. 'Weirdo' was the word she used. She and Madison and Tiffany avoided her. They didn't want to be friends with someone so bizarre."

"They hated her," Miranda murmured, wiping her hands. "She hated them back."

"Beside her manner of dress, Ashley said Wendy talked to odd people on the Internet. Erskine has already confirmed that from a preliminary scan of her computer."

Miranda remembered the cops had confiscated her things last night. "What has he found?" She was almost afraid to ask.

"A variety of things. Links to occult web sites. Scores of discussions with fad groups obsessed with morose subjects."

She winced. "Like?"

"Depression. Loneliness. Death. It's clear the poor girl is emotionally disturbed."

She nodded, rubbed her arms, thinking of the sad, lost look in Wendy's dark eyes. She was so alone and miserable. Hopeless, desperate. Had the poor child hatched a plot to kill her friends from talking to strangers on the Internet?

Miranda had to know the truth. "The rope, the stick, the seasoned cooking oil, the back door. Everything proves she murdered those girls, doesn't it?"

He paused a moment, as if wrestling with his own thoughts. "Not conclusively," he said finally.

She stared at him, her mind racing. "Van Aarle's shoe…"

"Wendy claims she took her father's shoes and wore them to make it look like he did it. She was angry with him for neglecting her and being away so much."

Miranda rubbed her head. Something wasn't right. "The bodies. Wendy couldn't have carried the bodies out to the yard by herself. You said that the first day we went to Madison's crime scene. They'd be too heavy for her. And what about the date rape drug? How could a thirteen-year-old get hold of that?"

Parker reached out, tenderly brushed her hair back from her face. "Even after the wretched night you had, your mind still works like an investigator's. You're a natural, Miranda."

She ignored the compliment. "Wendy's innocent," she murmured.

"The evidence says she was involved."

"But she could have read about everything in the paper. She has a wild imagination."

"She does. But why would she have assembled everything and put them in the wine cellar? And she showed you the back door. Erskine's men found shoe prints there that matched the ones we found near the creek."

She didn't want to hear it. "She has to be innocent."

He stepped toward her, his voice stern. "She had to have an accomplice, but Wendy was the principal. The one with intent. With the motive. The one who confessed."

She seized Parker by the arms. "Wendy has to be innocent," she said again.

His strong arms gripped her. "Miranda, you know she's not."

She let him hold her, though she couldn't bear his words. "Parker, please tell me she's innocent." Her heart was in shreds. She was coming apart at the seams. She started to sob. God, she was getting hysterical.

He steadied her, grabbed a stool for her to sit down on. "I wish you hadn't gotten so attached to the girl. She's bad blood."

"Oh God, Parker." She refused the chair, clutched him by the collar, nearly screaming in his face. "She's *my* blood."

His face twisted with confusion. "What are you saying?"

She almost gagged as she croaked out the words. "I think Wendy's Amy."

Shock made him go rigid. "What?"

Miranda put her hands to her cheeks and started to bawl. "She told me she was adopted."

He pulled her to him, held her close, stroked her tenderly as she drenched his shirt with tears. "Last night?" he asked softly.

Miranda wiped her eyes with the back of her hand and shook her head. "I went back to Dogwood Academy about a week ago. I talked to her then."

He lifted her chin, blinked at her, stunned. "You went back there after I told you—?" He stopped. "Never mind. What did she tell you?"

She pushed free of his embrace, tried to catch her breath. "At first, nothing I didn't already know. Her parents didn't care about her. They were never home. Then she announced she was adopted and walked away. That's when I started to believe Wendy could have written that letter I have from The Seekers. It sounds just like her."

He nodded slowly, reached for a napkin for her. "There is a resemblance to Wendy's situation in that letter."

She took the cloth from him, wiped her face, pushed back her hair. "There's more. That night, I used your computers to do some research. At first, I tried to trace Wendy's cell, but I came up with zip." She twisted the napkin. "So I researched the Van Aarles. I looked up their web sites. Van Aarle's bio said he moved here from Oak Park, Illinois. That's where I'm from. You know that. Van Aarle said Wendy was born there. In Oak Park General Hospital on Lake Street. Parker, that's where Amy was born."

He stared at her.

"Last night I was going to show her the letter from The Seekers and ask her if she'd written it. Before I could, she confessed to the murders."

"We can visit her in the youth detention center and show it to her."

Could they? She put a hand to her head. "How could I believe what Wendy says now? It wouldn't prove anything."

He thought a moment. "You're right. But there's a better way."

"What?"

"I'll ask Iris." Her heart jumped as he pulled out his cell, punched the pad. After a moment, he spoke. "This is Wade Parker. I need to speak to Iris Van Aarle about an urgent matter regarding her daughter. As soon as possible." He gave his number.

He'd gotten the answering machine.

He put his phone in his pocket, glanced at the clock. "She isn't home yet. I'll try again later." He ran a hand through his hair.

She stared at him. He'd move Heaven and earth for her, wouldn't he? But would it be enough?

"Iris might lie, too," she said. "And when she learns you and I had a hand in arresting her husband and her daughter, she'll probably tell you to go to hell."

"You have a point." His eyes narrowed, the wheels in his head turning. "There's another way. I can contact the hospital in Oak Park."

Her breath caught. Her stomach quivered in a spasm. "Can you?"

He nodded. "They should have back records. I can see if there's an original birth certificate for Wendy Van Aarle. And if not, it would indicate she isn't the Van Aarles' natural daughter. We could confront Iris with that and with The Seekers' letter. She'd tell us the truth then."

And if there was a birth certificate, they'd know for sure that Wendy belonged to the Van Aarles. Slowly, she nodded.

"It's Sunday. I'll call in the morning. It'll take a few days for the paperwork to get here."

Miranda pressed her hands against her face. After all this time, in a few days she might finally know who Amy was. "Oh, Parker. Thank you."

He reached out, pulled her to him. "You don't have to thank me. I want you to find Amy. I want to put this nightmare behind you." He kissed her forehead, gently stroked her hair. "Oh, Miranda. I want to take you away somewhere where nothing can hurt you again."

She touched his hand. It was strong, secure. "There's no such place."

"I know," he sighed. "I thought we could make believe there was today. Perhaps we could go somewhere. A ride in the country. The North Georgia mountains, maybe. We could stay the night."

A road trip? She tensed. "We have to work tomorrow. You have to call the hospital. We still have a murder to solve."

He sighed, touched her face, longing to take her pain away. Wendy's accomplice could have been anyone. A neighbor, someone she talked to on the Internet, some unknown stranger. A person they might never find. "We could come back early, then. Stop by your place and pick up some things."

She stiffened. "My place?"

He held her so he could look into her face, lifted her chin. His deep gray eyes pierced her down to the core. "I thought you might like to move in here with me."

"Here? In your father's mansion?"

"Yes. Here," he said in that low, magnolia voice of his.

She sucked in her breath. Grabbing at her hair, she pulled away from him, slowly moved back to the sink. "Gosh, I forgot to finish these dishes." She turned on the water, bent down to find some soap in the cabinet.

"There is a cleaning staff." Disappointment rumbled in his tone.

Guilt flooded her. "Oh, right. I usually give mine the weekend off." She found a bottle, shot some detergent into the sink. She shoved the water on full-blast, grabbed the gold-and-stainless-steel hose from the back of the sink and squeezed hard. It hit the plate at the wrong angle. Hot, soapy water splashed onto the fancy countertop, ran over onto the gleaming wood floor. God.

She put the hose back and grabbed a towel, letting out a hollow laugh as she wiped up the mess. "They call me the Domestic Goddess, you know."

"Miranda," Parker said in a low command. "Stop."

She rose, turned around. His intense look made her eyes water. "What?"

"There's no sense denying what we feel for each other."

Why was he doing this? She couldn't take it. Not now.

He took a step toward her. "I'm tired of holding back."

"Holding back?" She heaved a sigh as she rose. Why couldn't he leave well enough alone? "I didn't hold back when we made love last night. I didn't hold back when I told you about Leon and how Amy was born. I see now that was a mistake." Now there were feelings between them that shouldn't be. He knew too much about her.

"Mistake?" His voice broke.

She looked into those serious eyes. "Did you forget what I told you last night?"

"Of course not. Did you forget what we had together last night?"

Something too beautiful to last. She straightened her shoulders. "You know, it's pretty presumptuous of you to assume I'd want to move in here."

He folded his arms. "I didn't assume. I asked."

And expected a yes. She ran a hand through her hair and got it wet. She wiped it on her pants. "I don't think I could take living in a fancy mansion all the time."

His voice softened. "Would you like to move in somewhere else? My penthouse is—"

"No." She was on the verge of tears again. God, what was he doing to her? "What do you want with someone like me, Parker?"

He gazed at her for a long while. She'd never seen a more sincere look on a man's face.

"I'm falling in love with you, Miranda."

She turned back to the sink, unable to bear that look any longer. Not that. Anything but that. "Look, the sex was great. I owe you a lot. But I don't, I can't—" The tears came. Stop it, she told herself. But she couldn't.

Parker felt the anger flash on his face. It was as if she'd torn his flesh with her nails. Did she feel nothing for him at all? He reached out for her.

She spun out of his grasp. "Don't touch me." He was making her crazy. "I told you my personal life was screwed up. I have a nightmarish past I can't get over. My daughter could be a murderer."

"None of that matters."

"Yes, hell, it does." She glared at him. He seemed genuinely shocked at her outburst. Guilt stung her. She was hurting him. He didn't deserve that, but what else could he expect from her? "See? I suck at relationships."

"You can learn. We both can."

"You're not listening. When I was in the women's shelter, I made a vow to myself. I'd never let myself care for anybody again."

"For the rest of your life?"

She blinked at him. "I don't believe in love, Parker."

"Because of what happened to you years ago?"

"Because love isn't real. It never lasts. I don't believe in happily ever after."

He folded his arms and regarded her sharply. "Would you settle for moderately content for a lengthy period of time?"

Hell, he was stubborn. She grunted at him. "Parker, think. What kind of a couple would we make? Look at you. You're rich. Well-connected. The toast of the town. Everyone worships you."

"You're exaggerating—"

"Like hell I am. And now look at me. A restless loner with nothing. A head case with more baggage than the airlines."

There was fire in his eyes. "Don't make jokes, Miranda. You're far better than that. You're a talented investigator. You're a woman with noble passions. You're a fighter. Your past doesn't matter to me."

"Who's joking?" She wrung the dishtowel in her hands. "Maybe my past doesn't matter to you today. What about tomorrow? Next month? A year from now? You'd get sick of my problems sooner or later." If she let herself need him, what would happen to her then? She pointed a finger at him. "Gen knows who I am. And she hates me for it. But you know what? She gets it. She's right."

He reached out for her, groping for one last shred of hope that she felt something for him. "Gen can't stop my feelings for you."

"Then you'd better stop them yourself," she snarled, pulling out of his arms. "Don't you understand, Parker?" Struggling to get the words out, she waved her hand. "You and me…it could never work. Never. Not in a million years." She dragged her fingers through her hair. "I have to get out of here. I can't stay here another second."

She threw the towel on the glossy counter and headed for the door.

She stopped.

She didn't have her car. God, she hated being dependent on him. "Would you take me home now…please?"

CHAPTER THIRTY-THREE

On Wednesday the following week, Miranda sat at her desk at the Agency, poring over the latest news on her flat screen monitor.

Media coverage of Shelby and Wendy Van Aarle's arrests for the murders of Madison Taggart and Tiffany Todd went national. The famous golf pro headlined the evening news. His face appeared on the front page of all the papers and the covers of several magazines. Tanya Terrance, the controversial local talk show host, pressured the police for a personal interview with Van Aarle and his daughter.

At the Parker Agency, no one talked about anything else. Newshounds camped out in the lobby, and Gen instructed all employees to use the back entrance to avoid the maggots—her word. Miranda had never seen the fashion-model receptionist so frazzled as when she came inside for a break from the predators. No matter how many times Parker told those media ferrets he wouldn't comment on the case, they kept demanding to know the latest about the famous golf pro and his troubled daughter. It was hot news. They were mad for any new twist on the story.

They got it.

The next day, Giselle Ingram spoke to the newspapers and gave Shelby Van Aarle an alibi. She confessed they were downtown at the Ritz-Carlton the night Madison Taggart was killed. And she'd flown to Pittsburgh for a tryst with him the week a young woman, whose name was withheld, had been murdered in that city. She also mentioned her husband Lamar was filing for divorce. So were the Van Aarles. And the Todds.

A heyday for Estavez's law firm.

After Giselle's public confession, the judge reviewed the case and dropped the charges against Van Aarle. Now the focus was on Wendy. The little girl who had killed her schoolmates because they'd been mean to her. The judge ordered she be held for psychological evaluations. With luck, Estavez would get her released on bond later in the week. They hadn't decided yet whether to try her as an adult.

Parker kept Miranda updated on the events by email, but he didn't need to. The newspapers, the Internet, and Becker and Holloway had done that. Except for those emails, Parker kept his distance.

Gen seemed to sense there was tension between them and left her alone for once. She was probably having a private celebration in her office.

As Miranda started on another stack of background checks, she told herself it was just as well. It would be awkward to even talk to Parker now. It was over. There had never been anything between them anyway. Nothing that could last.

Her laptop beeped and she saw it was another email from Parker. Exhaling her annoyance, she clicked it open. In his terse manner, he told her that he'd tried to contact Iris Van Aarle about Wendy's birth again, but she'd hung up in his face. The next line caught her eye. As she read it, her throat constricted.

Oak Park General Hospital has cooperated enough to send partial records from the archives of their Maternity ward for the time in question, November, thirteen years ago. The information should be arriving soon.

And what would she do when it got here?

It was a week later that Detective Judd started a review of his lessons on fingerprinting. He'd covered the history of the method earlier in the week, beginning with the first case in 1892. As he rambled on and on about the effects of natural secretions from the eccrine glands including sweat, sebum, and certain lipids, Miranda yawned. They'd already been over this stuff. They'd practiced, too. She'd taken Becker and Holloway's prints so many times, she told them she could blackmail them for their paychecks.

She leaned back in the chair half-listening to Judd and wondered when the report from the hospital would get here. Would Wendy Van Aarle turn out to be Amy? What would she do if she were? Fight the Van Aarles for custody? Tanya Terrance would want an exclusive on that story.

Judd lowered the lights to display overheads of fingerprint samples. He compared several sets, pointing out the arch, the tented arch, the right loop, the whorl—the friction ridge patterns of various systems of classification.

Miranda wanted to put her head down on the desk. What was she doing here in the Parker Agency after all these weeks, anyway? She had stuck around to find Amy and to help solve a murder. She'd helped all right. She'd gotten a poor, troubled young girl arrested, while her accomplice was still on the loose. She wished Parker had never offered her this job.

Parker. She thought of the pained look on his handsome face when he'd dropped her off at her apartment Sunday afternoon. He must hate her after the way she'd treated him. He deserved better. All week, she'd wallowed in guilt, struggled with a deep sense of loss. She'd thrown away the best thing that had ever happened to her in her life. But what choice did she have? It could never work between them.

She felt that familiar restlessness in her gut. It was time to move on.

Judd announced he would liven things up. He put some famous prints up on the overhead and explained whose they were. JFK's. Einstein's. The last set evoked a round of oohs from the class.

Shelby Van Aarle's. Fresh from Fulton County Jail.

Miranda stared at the swirling circular patterns in the ridges as Judd pointed them out. All she could think of was Wendy.

Poor, troubled girl. She remembered when Wendy told her Madison Taggart used to be her friend. Her hurt look when she said everyone thought she was weird. The text message she'd sent her when Tiffany Todd told a boy she had cooties.

Miranda refused to believe it. No matter how much Wendy hated them, she couldn't have killed those girls. She wasn't the one who came up with the idea, as Parker had said. Someone else manipulated her. Maybe the prison psychiatrist would get the truth out of her. Wendy couldn't have gotten hold of a date rape drug. She couldn't have carried those bodies outside to the woods. Somebody else had taken those girls out there. Someone strong enough to lift a thirteen-year-old. A man.

Suddenly she sat up straight as a board. The second black sedan.

She looked up at the overhead. Fingerprints. Maybe she could figure out who that man was. When Judd broke for lunch, she asked if she could borrow one of the kits. She said she wanted to practice some more.

In broad daylight, the Van Aarles' gray-stone mansion had a cheery look that seemed glaringly out of place after Wendy's confession. As Miranda came to a stop across the street and shut off her old jalopy, she saw that Shelby's red Jag was still in the driveway. Must be a record for him to be home so long.

Suddenly, the front door opened and Van Aarle's tall, lanky figure shot out, heading down the walk. Right behind him was a woman who had to be Iris. She was screaming her head off. He shouted back at her. Miranda rolled down her window, but she could hear only snatches.

"My sales are sinking. You've ruined my business."

"The PGA Tour wants my head."

"Nothing but golf, golf, golf."

Something about "a damned obsession."

Van Aarle slammed the door of his car and sped out of the drive.

Iris marched back inside the house and slammed the front door with a bang.

Lovely couple. Their daughter was being accused of murder and all they cared about was their careers. Miranda waited a beat, then grabbed her kit, went up to the front door and rang the bell.

A tall, dark haired woman in a severe navy pants suit answered. Admin Assistant relegated to butler duties? "May I help you?"

Miranda shifted her weight. Admin Assistant on steroids. "I've been sent here by the Parker Agency, regarding our investigation." It was sort of the truth. And dropping Parker's name ought to open doors. At least this one, she hoped.

The woman raised a brow. "Do you have an appointment?"

"No, they told me to come right over." She took a breath. "We're working in conjunction with the police. You can call Lieutenant Erskine, if you'd like to verify." Miranda didn't want to think about the kind of trouble would she be in if the woman actually did.

She studied Miranda a moment, then squared her already square shoulders. "I'll see what Mrs. Van Aarle has to say. Wait here." With that, she turned and went up the stairs.

When she was out of sight, Miranda stepped inside, softly closed the front door behind her, and headed down the hall to the wine cellar. With any luck, they'd think she got tired of waiting and left.

Gingerly, she opened the heavy ornate door. Ignoring the squeak she stepped through and shut it behind her. She switched on the lights and descended the stony steps.

The place had that same spooky feel it had the other night. Even spookier after Wendy's confession. At the bottom of the steps, she looked around. Bluish gray fingerprint dust covered everything. The tasting table, the bottles, the shelves. Lieutenant Erskine's crew had demolished the place.

She stepped to the open door at the side and peeked into the room behind it. Had the cops dusted every rack? She found another light switch. Nope. Just the first aisle. There were about a dozen more aisles of bottles that hadn't been touched.

A good investigator thinks outside the box, Judd said. A good investigator leaves no stone unturned. Tiffany Todd's time of death could have given the killer several hours down here. How much at home would he have made himself during that time?

She took the brush out of her kit, dipped it in the graphite and went to work. She dusted every tier that Erskine's team had missed and examined each bottle. There were a lot of fingerprints. All Van Aarle's. She recognized their pattern from the print Judd had shown in class. Stubbornly, she kept going.

It took a long while. Several hours later, she was on the last rack in the very back of the room. Halfway through, she wiped her brow and stopped dusting. She'd come up with zip. The only fingerprints in the whole cellar were Van Aarle's. No wonder the police hadn't bothered. She pulled off her gloves, and with a sigh of disgust, bent down and packed up her kit.

Her heart heavy, she snapped the latch shut and rose. For a long moment, she stood with her hands on her hips, staring at the dark shimmer of the bottles. Wendy's future looked grim. If only she could prove the girl was innocent. For the thousandth time, Miranda's heart broke for her.

Then something caught her eye. Away up at the top, in the corner of the final rack, something glimmered. Not with the ruby glow of the dark bottles. This was lighter. Like clear glass.

She retrieved her gloves once more from her kit, grabbed the ladder she'd used to get to the upper racks and climbed to the spot. Carefully she pulled out the object so as not to smudge any prints. It was a wine glass from the cellar's main room. Slowly, she got down the ladder, opened her kit and gave it a dusting. She held her breath as she pulled off the cello-tape and placed it on a card. She held up the print.

This one had a distinct arch. Not at all like Van Aarle's circular pattern. The glass still smelled of the residue. DNA, too. She'd been right. Whoever manipulated Wendy Van Aarle into killing her friends in the wine cellar couldn't resist having a drink.

She put the glass in a bag, placed the print in her kit and walked out of the mansion without anyone questioning her. When she got back to the office, she dropped the prints and the glass off at the Agency's lab and went home for the day.

Not too shabby for an afternoon's work. She couldn't wait for the results.

CHAPTER THIRTY-FOUR

The next morning, Judd went on a rampage about accurate reports. He repeated the details of affidavits, formats, structure until Miranda thought her head would burst. She scribbled on a paper, pretending to take notes, but an hour before lunchtime, her stomach started to growl. She was wondering just how much longer she'd carry on the charade of being a trainee, when there was a knock on the classroom door.

"Miranda Steele?" an assistant said. "Mr. Parker would like to see you."

What did Parker want? Miranda grumbled to herself as she followed the woman down the hall. Had he found out she'd been to the Van Aarles' again yesterday? Was he going to chew her out for it? She hoped he didn't have any ideas about getting together again. A knock-down-drag-out in the office would be embarrassing. She didn't think she could take it.

When the assistant dropped her off at his office, she fidgeted outside a moment, then took a deep breath and stepped through the door.

Wearing his usual finely tailored suit, with his salt-and-pepper hair neatly groomed, he stood at the tall window looking out. The sun streamed in, lighting up the glass furniture with that heavenly glow.

He turned, nodded stiffly, gestured to a chair as he moved toward his desk. "Have a seat, Ms. Steele." It felt like the temperature had dropped twenty degrees.

He sat. She sat. "My, aren't we formal today?"

He ignored her and studied the papers on his desk.

Watching his handsome face, which was all business, she pulled at her skirt. She was wearing a new outfit. One she'd bought this week with her own cash instead of the money he'd advanced her. It was a nice, conservative long-sleeved white blouse and a straight tan skirt. No metal studs. She felt professional in it. Almost like a real investigator.

At last Parker spoke. "Wendy Van Aarle has been released on bond," he said quietly. "She's home now."

She blinked. "That's good. Are the charges still pending?"

He nodded. "The mayor wants the case wrapped up as soon as possible."

Politics. "Will she," she could hardly say it, "do time?"

He frowned with deep concern. "It's hard to say. Antonio is fighting for her to be tried as a juvenile. Her psychiatric evaluations clearly show emotional problems."

"Not much of a surprise there."

Parker stared at the woman before him, forcing himself, as he had over the past days, not to think about what there had been between them. What she had thrown away. She looked good in her outfit. Tasteful. She'd come a long way in a short time. He'd decided to continue nurturing her career from a distance, help her get her license and perhaps move on. It was the only type of relationship they could have now.

He leaned back in his chair. "How have you been?"

"Fine."

"Classes going well?"

"Pretty good."

"Is your foot healed?"

The alligator bite. She glanced down at it. "It's on the mend." She tapped her fingers on the arm of the chair. "Did you call me in here just to chitchat, Parker?"

"No, I didn't." Looking uncomfortable, he picked up a large envelope from his desk. "The information from Oak Park General has arrived."

She sat up, swallowed. So that was it. She'd thought that report would take longer to get here. For a moment she stared at the manila package. Funny. A single eight-and-a-half-by-eleven envelope could change her entire life. Would all those years of searching finally be over? She wasn't sure she wanted to know what was in it.

Slowly Parker opened the envelope and drew out the papers they contained. "I received this about an hour ago. I wanted to find a way to break it to you gently. But I might as well just tell you."

"Please do."

He took a deep breath, paused a moment, then spoke. "Wendy Van Aarle is not your daughter."

"She isn't?" She sank back in the chair, feeling like an anvil had hit her. She blinked, as her eyes teared up.

"Wendy was born to Iris and Shelby Van Aarle thirteen years ago on November twentieth. These are the records of the hospital stay." He handed her the official documents.

She looked over the scratchy writing, saw Iris's name, the weight, length of the infant, other details. They weren't the same as Amy's. She handed the papers back. What good were they to her? Numb, her throat constricting, she stared out the window at the cityscape. She'd been bracing herself to learn that her daughter was a disturbed child of a golf pro accused of murder. Now she knew…nothing. No more than she had when she first started to look for Amy.

She rubbed her arms and shivered, wiped at her nose.

"Would you like some time off?" he asked softly.

Time off? She sat up. "Hell, no." She still had a job to do. "Just because Wendy isn't my daughter, doesn't mean I don't care what happens to her. Or about the murdered girls. I want to find the real killer. The one who manipulated Wendy into doing it." She needed to catch him up. "I went to the Van Aarles' yesterday, and I—"

He scowled. "You what?"

"You heard me. I went to the Van Aarle mansion."

"Miranda," he said sternly. "Why do you keep going off on your own when I specifically told you not to?" He sounded more like a boss now, than the lover she'd known last week.

"Because I had an idea. When Judd talked about fingerprints, I—"

He held up a hand. "Do you realize you're guilty of gross insubordination?"

She curled a lip at him. "You sound like Gen."

"The Agency is responsible for you."

He wouldn't even hear her out. She didn't know him any more. "Look. You put me on the Taggart case. You said I helped."

"You did. But now I'm taking you off."

She was thunderstruck. "Because of what happened between us?"

"Because you're not ready. If there's a chance Wendy's accomplice is still lurking out there, it's too dangerous for a neophyte."

"*Neophyte?*"

"A newcomer, a—"

"I know what the word means." Anger flared inside her. "You thought I was ready enough when we trailed old Dexter boy. And when you took me to the golf resort and to the Policeman's ball to watch Van Aarle."

His jaw tightened. "That was different. You were under my supervision."

She stood up, put a hand on her hip. "Or maybe you just wanted to get in my pants."

His face flushed with rage. "You're dismissed, Ms. Steele."

"Fine." She stomped to the door, stopped in her tracks. She put a hand to her head.

Wendy Van Aarle wasn't her daughter. The letter she'd been carrying around for weeks was probably a fake. Amy could be anywhere in the world. She was back to square one. No closer than the day she awoke to find her daughter gone. What was the point of staying here and sitting through boring lectures and doing background checks?

She turned around and trudged back to his desk. "Do you mean dismissed from your office or from your Agency?"

He scowled. "My office, of course. I'm not firing you, Miranda."

"That's good, because I quit."

He got to his feet. "You can't quit.

"The hell I can't. From the way you're acting, Parker I'm not much of a detective anyway." The whole thing had been a colossal waste of time.

"Atlanta's been a dead end. I've been thinking that it's time for me to move on."

His face grew hard as flint. "Very well, if that's what you want." He put the envelope away. "Go ahead. Make a wreck of your life."

That did it. She shot toward him, put her finger in his handsome face. "Look, buster. My life was just fine before you came long. I don't need you and your fancy Agency. Like I told you before. I don't need a savior."

His eyes flamed, intense with the fury he held back. "Then you won't be getting one."

"Fine. You know, I really don't give a flying fuck." She turned and stormed out of the office, picked up her purse and headed for the elevators.

Her whole body shaking with rage and humiliation, Miranda drove back to her little apartment on Peachtree and yanked her suitcases out of the closet. How could Parker be so cold, so different from the sexy charmer she'd met weeks ago in that jail cell? She knew all those compliments, that encouragement, that taking her under his wing and all was bullshit. Just an excuse for his testosterone-ridden ulterior motives.

She shoved a suitcase onto the bed, began tossing clothes into it. She couldn't stay in this town. Not another minute. There were too many bad memories. Too many high hopes that had been dashed to pieces, like a jackhammer demolishing a sidewalk. Why did she let herself think she could solve a high-profile murder case? She was a construction worker, not a sleuth. She wasn't a detective any more than the man in the moon.

She went to the dresser, grabbed a rubberband and pulled back her hair. She was still in her work clothes. She'd change on the road. She had to get out of here.

Her letter from Amy lay beside her hairbrush. Her heart clenched at the sight of it. Why had she believed that letter? Why did she think she could find Amy here? It was an obvious fake. Why had she let herself think Wendy Van Aarle might be her daughter? She'd let herself care for the girl. And no matter how hard she'd fought it, she'd let herself care for Parker.

That's what happens when you start to care for people. You get hurt.

She grabbed the letter, crumbled it into a ball and tossed it in the trash.

It didn't take long to pack. All she had was a few bags and her laptop. But the tears in her eyes slowed her down. She wiped her nose with her arm as she forced the last suitcase shut and grunted at herself.

She had no reason to blubber. She'd never shed a tear before when she left a place. Atlanta, Buckhead, Mockingbird Hills with its fancy mansions, it was nothing to her. Just another blip in her monotonous, dreary life.

She'd lost some of her edge these past weeks. She'd have to work on getting it back. Dragging the suitcase to the door and down the elevator, she promised herself to sign up with a good martial arts school the next place she landed. And no more office jobs. Only physical work. She had to stay strong. Independent. Free.

In an hour, she had everything in her car, had things squared with her landlord and was ready to go. She climbed into the front seat and got out her road atlas.

Where to? Didn't really matter. She flipped through the pages. One place was as good as another. She'd liked her boss on that Pittsburgh job. Maybe she could get it back. On the other hand, she'd never been to Florida. Maybe she'd decide which way to turn when she got out on the highway.

She put down the atlas and started the car.

Parker didn't need her. She was just a charity case for him. And Wendy Van Aarle?

She pressed the brake as she came to a red light, stared up at it.

That poor little girl. All alone in that mansion with parents who didn't give a rat's ass about her. She was about to stand trial for murder. She could use a friend right now.

The light turned and she pulled around the corner. Suddenly, that strange, eerie feeling that had been haunting her for so long came over her like dark clouds before a thunderstorm. Like someone calling out to her from the past. What did it mean? She had no idea. But suddenly, it seemed to be saying that Wendy needed her.

Miranda didn't see the next light turn red. She jammed her foot onto the brake—just inches before she hit the car in front of her.

Those fingerprints. She'd left before they'd been processed.

She drummed her fingers on the steering wheel. She couldn't go back to the Agency and face Parker again. Besides, the prints themselves wouldn't tell the whole story. But she bet she could use them to get the truth out of Wendy.

She bypassed the exit to the interstate. As fast as she could, she turned around and headed for Mockingbird Hills.

CHAPTER THIRTY-FIVE

There were no cars in the drive when Miranda stopped along the curb in front of the Van Aarle mansion. She wondered if Iris or Shelby were home, if they'd even let her speak to their daughter. At the moment, she wasn't above begging.

She walked up the front steps and rang the bell. Nobody answered. Was anybody here? That would be just her luck. She reached for the door handle. It opened.

Strange.

She stepped inside the empty foyer and looked around. "Hello?" Her voice echoed.

No answer.

"Wendy?"

Nothing. Something was wrong. She should head upstairs, she thought. Try to find the girl's room. But instead, something drew her once more toward the wine cellar.

Slowly, she stole down the long hardwood hall toward the ornate door at the end of it. When she reached it, her nerves spiked as her spine went icy.

The door was ajar.

Determined, she slid it open—bit her lip at the squeak—and started to inch down the stone steps as noiselessly as she could.

She heard a groan and scurried down the rest of the way, trying to be quiet. When she reached the bottom, she stifled a gasp. The sight before her made her blood run cold.

Wendy Van Aarle was lying on the tasting table, her hands clasped together with thick rope, tied up just like the two murdered girls.

"Wendy." Miranda rushed to the table.

Groggily, the girl's eyes opened halfway. She'd been drugged. "Miranda," she murmured. "I tried to call you. You came to help me."

She glared at the ropes. There was no ribbon around her neck. The girl was dressed normally in jeans and a T-shirt. "What's going on?"

"You were right. I did talk to a man who was lurking around the schoolyard. I'm sorry I lied."

"It's okay. Did he do this to you?" She reached under the rope to untie one of the knots. It was tight. Miranda's fingers trembled.

"I lied about so many things. I'm not adopted." Her babbling broke Miranda's heart.

"I know. Just be still and let me get you out of here."

Wendy's eyes fluttered shut.

"Keep talking."

"Talking?"

She forced a laugh as she picked at the knot. "Keep me company while I do this." She had to keep her awake to fight off the drug.

"I wrote a letter to that agency about it."

"Agency?"

"The Seekers. Months ago. I'd forgotten about it until this morning."

Miranda winced at the girl's confession as she tugged at the fibers. Why wouldn't her fingers work? "This morning?"

"When Mr. Parker came to see me."

Miranda froze. "Mr. Parker came to see you?"

"Yes. This morning."

Parker had come to see Wendy Van Aarle? The idea made her want to weep.

"He told me about the letter. He said you were looking for your daughter. I said in the letter I was adopted, but I'm not. I'm sorry I was so bad."

Wendy had written the letter. And it was a lie. Right now, Miranda didn't care anymore. "It's all right. None of that matters now." She yanked at the rope. She had to get them out of here.

Wendy's eyes rolled back in her head. "I lied about Madison and Tiffany. I had to save my father."

"I know. I know." She knew the girl wasn't the murderer.

"It wasn't me who killed them. I just got them down here. For him."

"Him?"

"The man in the schoolyard. I thought he was my friend, but he's not."

"The man in the black sedan."

"Yes. It was all because of Madison and Tiffany. They were so mean to me. But I didn't think he would kill them. Really, I didn't. I just wanted him to scare them."

If she could just get the knots loose before the monster came back. "Be still, now. Don't talk any more. It's all right now."

"No, it's not," she squealed. "He's going to kill me, too."

"Who is?" Miranda glanced at the dark red wood counter and her mouth went dry. There was a spool of wide white ribbon on it.

"The man."

"What man?"

"That man. Right there."

Miranda's heart stopped. Slowly, she turned around and spied the dark figure standing in the doorway to the side room. Her chest constricted like a giant fist was squeezing the life out of her. *How long had he been watching her?*

"Hello, Miranda."

Her body went numb. Her gut hardened like cement. Her tongue went dry as sawdust. Her lungs burned, as her throat clamped shut.

She never thought she'd see him again. He looked different. Leaner. Older. Worn and world-weary. His black hair was long, instead of the regimental crew cut he used to wear. It fell in oily strings on either side of his head. Patches of a scraggly beard on his hollow cheeks were streaked with gray. But his eyes were the same. Those black, mean slits that made her feel like she was nothing.

"Leon," she gasped. "What are you doing here?"

A knife flashed in his hands. "Waiting for you."

CHAPTER THIRTY-SIX

Parker sat at his desk staring at the evidence before him. In all his years as a PI, he'd never had such a disheartening case. He turned the pages of the police reports on Wendy Van Aarle. Her statements, the psychiatric evaluations, reports from her teachers, schoolmates, the judge's comments. He thought of her demeanor this morning when he'd told her about the letter from The Seekers. She had finally told the truth about something.

He picked up her photo. The poor, disturbed child. So lonely and distressed she wanted to kill the girls who'd mistreated her.

He thought of Jackson and Cloris, Wilhelmina and Isaiah. They were good parents. But they had been oblivious to the fact that their daughters had been harassing a schoolmate. Like everyone, they were caught up in their busy lives. It was difficult to fathom the social inter-workings of young people.

He and Erskine had attempted to find Wendy's accomplice. They'd followed a score of leads from the girl's computer, run systematic background checks, searched airline reservations, bus terminals, credit card transactions. Parker had once again combed Mockingbird Hills, talked to the Oglethorpe boys who'd found Tiffany's body, as well as every person under seventeen in the neighborhood. His efforts had yielded nothing. Not a shred of evidence. Not even the slightest lead.

Who had helped Wendy Van Aarle kill Madison Taggart and Tiffany Todd? An older juvenile? An adult? They might never know.

Miranda still believed the girl was innocent.

He put down the photo, closed the file, ran his hands over his face. Miranda. His heart ached for her. He longed for her touch, her company, her bold audacity. Sternly he reminded himself her feelings for him were nothing like his. She had been too hurt, too wounded to let herself feel. She didn't believe in love, she'd said. There was nothing he could do to change that. It was a fact. He was used to dealing with cold, hard facts.

He had moved too fast. Pushed when he should have waited. But it wouldn't have made a difference. He should have known it would turn out this way when she told him about her horrendous marriage and how Amy was conceived. And how Leon Groth had stolen her daughter. Miranda had lost the ability to trust long ago.

Now she was gone from his life.

She had walked out of the Agency without a second thought. She wasn't the type to look back. She was a drifter at heart. A restless wanderer who could never know peace, like a cursed character in some myth he'd read about in school.

But how could he forget that thick dark hair? Her hard-to-coax smile? The softness of her skin against his hands. Her hungry moaning as he made love to her. Those dark, ebony lashes. The sea of emotion in those deep blue eyes. That warrior spirit he had felt so close to.

He would have to forget. He had no choice.

With a heavy groan, he got up and went down the hall to the cube bank. He found her desk and stared blankly at it for a long while. Might as well clean it off.

He stacked the folders she'd been working on, put the pens in a cup. He picked up some paper clips and opened a drawer. Her cell phone. He shook his head. She never did learn to keep it on and check her messages, did she?

He pressed the button. There was a message. From the other night? No. An hour ago.

"Parker, there you are. I've been looking all over for you."

Parker looked up into the youthful face of John Fry, the lab assistant who'd been at the Agency several years now. "What is it, Fry?"

"I just got these results. I thought you'd want to see them right away."

"What results?"

"Fingerprints. Ms. Steele dropped them off yesterday."

"She did?"

He nodded. "She said it was real important they be processed as soon as possible. Took me all day, but I finally got a match."

"Where were these taken?"

"At the Van Aarle mansion. Ms. Steele dusted the wine cellar yesterday afternoon. She gave it a better going over than the cops did. Look what she found."

Parker took the folder, opened it. His heart spasmed as he blinked at the name in front of him. How could it be possible? How could it be him? But he fit the pattern. Abusive childhood, violent history, the need to dominate.

Miranda had done it. She'd solved the murders.

He pressed the button for the message on the phone and listened. It was Wendy Van Aarle's voice.

"He's here. He's after me. Miranda, help me. Come help me. No." There was a sound of struggle. "Leave me alone. No, not the wine cellar. Please." Sobbing. Hysterical sobbing. "Please don't take me to the wine cellar." The phone went dead.

Parker stared down at it. Had Miranda gotten this message before she left?

He turned to Fry. "Call Judd and tell him to get to the Van Aarle place ASAP." He shoved the phone in his pocket and started for the door. "Call Erskine, too." As fast as he could go, he raced downstairs to his car, praying he wasn't too late.

CHAPTER THIRTY-SEVEN

"Don't come near me, Leon. I'm not the weakling I once was." Don't plead. Don't beg, she reminded herself.

The dark man tapped the knife blade against the palm of his hand and slowly shook his head. "I know that," he said with a sneer. "You've gone to martial arts and self-defense courses for years. I've watched you."

What had he said? She stared at him.

"I've been following you for some time." His cheek folded in a grotesque half-grin. "It wasn't hard. You made sure the post office had a forwarding address everywhere you went."

He'd been following her? For how long? "Why?" Shock choked the word in her throat.

"Because I want the same thing you do."

Cold fingers scraped down her spine. *He wanted to find Amy?*

His dark eyes bored through her like lasers. "You don't understand."

"Understand what?"

He moved to the corner where the spool of wide white ribbon sat on the dark red wood counter. He picked it up. "About three years after you left my home, I arrested a woman in the city. One of those worthless whores on Roosevelt Road."

So? He was always arresting streetwalkers.

He frowned darkly, as if wrestling with a painful memory. "It was a difficult apprehension. There was an altercation. The woman claimed I injured her. She insisted she wasn't a prostitute." He turned the spool, took the knife and cut off a length with a quick, vicious snap. "She was lying. I could see evil all over her. Smell it on her."

Miranda was inclined to believe the woman.

He turned the knife in his hand. "She had a family. They should have disowned the whore, but instead they took up for her. They brought a lawsuit for excessive force against me. Me." He hit his chest with the hand that held the ribbon. "They wanted a psychological evaluation. The stupid court gave in and ordered one."

He couldn't have passed it. "What happened?"

His eyes glowed red with hatred. "The unthinkable. They fired me."

Good for them. But Leon must have been devastated. The police job meant everything to him.

"I fell apart. I didn't know how to live, what to do. I had to move in with Mother."

"Your mother?" That couldn't have been pleasant.

He put a fist to his head, as if it ached. "I tried so hard. I tried to do everything just right, but it wasn't good enough. Mother said I lost my job because I was involved with wicked women. She said it was my own fault. Just like when I married you and got the measles." His voice took on a helpless tone as he brushed back an oily strand of his hair with his knife hand.

"That wasn't your fault," Miranda told him. That much was true. His mother was a bitch.

Lost in his own tormented thoughts, he took a step toward her, half-laughed to himself. "And then I remembered the child. She was the answer to everything. Finally I understood why I was being punished." He turned back to Wendy, slipped the ribbon around her neck, began to tie it in a bow.

She should try to grab his arm, but he still had that knife and he was so close to her. "You were being punished?" If she could keep him talking, maybe she could get him away from her.

"There was something evil that I had let go into the world. I would continue to be punished until I got her back. I had to find her. To do that, I knew I first had to find you. It was in Texas that I finally caught up to you."

Her mouth went dry. She could barely speak. "Denton," she whispered, remembering the records she'd found in Parker's database.

"Yes." He laid the knife down on the counter. It caught the light, glistening like a diamond.

Miranda released the breath she'd been holding. Could she get to that knife? She glanced at the hundreds of ruby bottles lining the walls in their slots of deep red wood. Or would a broken bottle be a match for it?

He took the ribbon and snapped it taut. "We moved in with a cousin there. In a house he was renting from me. Mother fell sick."

"She died there."

His eyes widened with surprise that she knew that. But he went on. "Yes. Just after she passed, I saw you in a diner outside of town."

Now it was her turn to be surprised. She recalled going to a greasy spoon with her coworkers on the oil rig. "You followed me since then?"

"I had to. How else could I fulfill Mother's last wish?"

Last wish?

"You were always looking for information. Talking to children, registering with adoption reunion companies. You hoped for a letter, an email, any kind of communication. Like the letter you got in Pittsburgh."

"Pittsburgh?" How did he know all that? Wendy must have told him.

He glanced away, muttered half to himself. "That stupid, vile woman."

He wasn't making sense, not that he had up to now. "What woman?" she demanded.

He bent down and picked up a cord that had been lying near his feet. He held it up. "I strangled her with a rope just like this one. She was my first."

Her mind raced. That friendly woman from The Seekers who had given her the letter? *She* was the unnamed murder victim in Pittsburgh? The women they thought Shelby Van Aarle had killed? Chills made her whole body shiver. "*You* killed her? Why?"

He screwed his face in a bizarre, quizzical grimace, as if he couldn't fathom why she cared. "Several reasons. First to make her tell me what she had given you. Then because I couldn't let her live after that. She would report me to the authorities. But most of all, because I felt her vile womanhood all over me. It repulsed me so, I couldn't let her live." He gazed at Miranda with a pitiful look. Then he moved behind the table where Wendy was, contemplated her almost lovingly.

The girl was still. The drugs had taken effect. "Don't touch her," Miranda said.

He ignored her. "When that woman told me what was in that letter, I knew you were close to finding Amy."

She gasped as she thought of the strange, eerie feelings she'd been having for weeks. They'd started in Pittsburgh. It had been Leon she'd sensed.

"I followed you here. I watched you apply for jobs in schools. The day you applied at Dogwood Academy, I sat watching the young girls playing in the yard. I saw this one, who looks so much like you. I lingered there. She saw me, came to the car. We struck up a conversation."

"You were in a black Pontiac."

His black eyes gleamed. "Yes, that was me." He moved closer to Wendy, raised a hand over her, as though he were blessing her.

"Leave her alone, Leon. She's not Amy." The knife was lying on the table, but close enough that he could grab it. She wanted to rush him, wrestle him to the ground. But she couldn't move.

"I know she's not Amy. I'll find Amy someday." He said it as if he were speaking to a small child. "In the meantime, she makes a good substitute. Like the others did. This one helped me. She understood the exalted purpose of my mission."

Mission? What did he intend to do? Rid the world of women one little girl at a time? "She was just angry at her schoolmates because they taunted her all the time."

He smirked. "Ah, Miranda. Your mind was always too small to grasp the deeper meaning of things."

"What deeper meaning?" She wanted to break his neck.

"They were so young. I saw I could rescue them."

Her voice broke. "Rescue them?"

"Mother said I had to atone for what I'd done. It was her last wish. But I had to find my own way to do it." He reached for a bottle on the counter behind him, where he'd laid down the knife. "Many cultures have purification rites for women. The Hindus, the Shintos of Japan. This one is mine. Wendy and I invented it together from rituals she found on the Internet."

Lovingly, he opened the bottle. "Oh, she didn't want to at first. When I brought the first girl to her after I had kept her alive in the trunk of my car for almost a week, she was fairly hysterical. An emotional, female reaction. But I persuaded her it was for the best." He began to pour oil from the bottle over Wendy's face and throat. She didn't move. She was under.

Miranda could smell the scent of sage and rosemary. Now. Jump him now.

"These herbs chase away the evil, the vileness."

He began to chant, like some sort of priest. "I consecrate you, purify you. I deliver your body chaste and pure to the universe. Before the men of earth defile you." He hummed to himself. "Don't you see? These girls are so young. Just on the verge of womanhood. If I catch them before they cross over that threshold, I can keep them pure. I can release them before they become defiled with femininity."

He was insane. "Stop it, Leon."

He glared at her. "Don't interrupt me. Wendy helped me with the others. Now it's her turn to be purified."

He returned to the ritual. She watched his hands caress the bottle as though it were more human than the girl before him. Strong hands. Too big for the rest of his body. Lumpy at the knuckles from too much joint cracking. She remembered how much it hurt when they smacked her face. The marks they made. The taste of blood in her mouth. She was still terrified of him.

Again she eyed the knife on the table. Insult and repulsion twisted in her gut, she took a step toward it, remembering at last, her years of training. She knew how to fight. She made her voice dark and gruff. "Get away from her, you prick. Now."

His eyes glazed over with that familiar, frozen look. The silence of a powder keg just before the explosion. "How dare you speak to me like that?" with a thud, he set down the bottle and came around the table. At least, she'd gotten him away from Wendy.

"You can't hurt me anymore," she sneered.

"Oh no?" In a flashing move, he raised back his hand and smacked her hard across the cheek.

She stumbled back and fell, her face stinging. Where were her reflexes? The instincts she'd honed for so long? Could Leon turn her back into the helpless, sniveling woman she once was?

She thought about how miserable he'd made her all those years. She'd been raped because of him and he'd blamed her for it. He'd taken her only child away from her. He'd killed that woman in Pittsburgh for trying to help her. He'd murdered two little girls and he was about to kill Wendy. He wanted to find and kill Amy.

No. Hell, no.

Slowly, she rose. Fury coursed through her whole being, bellowed up and gushed forth like hot lava spewing from a volcano. But this time it wasn't blind frenzy. It was focused. Parker's words rang in her head. *Calm control always trumps rage, Miranda.* But what if they merged together?

With a cry from some deep chasm inside her, she rushed at him, her arms outstretched. Before he could move, her palms hit his chest with the force of a locomotive. He fell back, smashing into the rows of bottles. With a brilliant crash, half a dozen broke open, spilling their red liquid over him and onto the stone-tiled floor. The air filled with the smell of expensive wine.

He staggered as he struggled to regain his balance.

Miranda tensed. Calm control. Parker was right. She'd be spent soon if she fought with all her anger. She took a deep breath.

Leon had recovered. His eyes glowing like a possessed maniac, he came back at her.

She was ready when he reached her. She grabbed his wrists, spun him around. He hit the opposite wall, stunned. Wine glasses shattered on the floor. Bewildered, he clawed at the counter to keep from falling. She saw her opening.

One, two. Now.

She came at him. As if released by a torsion spring, her foot flew up and caught him hard in the balls.

He cried out in shock and pain, his awkward steps zigzagging toward the table. The knife. He was going for the knife. Panic flooded her. She ran for it, tried to grab it. But he beat her.

As his fingers clutched the handle, he lashed out at her chest, slicing her best white blouse wide open.

Sharp pain flashed across her skin. She stumbled back, struggled to get her footing. He swung the other way and got her again. She gasped with fiery pain. Back again. This time, he nicked her chin. And again. She angled away. Missed. Again. She threw up one arm in defense. The knife sliced into it before she could step back.

"Yow!" That one wasn't deep, but it stung like hell. "Stop it, Leon," she screamed at him. "The police will get you for this."

"But you'll be gone before they catch me." He slashed toward the table with his blade. "And so will she. I'll release both of you. I'll bury your bodies in the bed of the creek behind the house."

She glanced down and saw his feet. Golf shoes. He was wearing Yager golf shoes.

He smirked. "That's right. They belong to her father. She brought them to me. The first and the second pair. I lost the first escaping those teens in the creek, as you know. The night the alligator bit you."

Dread hammered through her chest. He'd been watching her that night. Hiding in the woods somewhere when she and Parker found that shoe. He was a maniac. A monster. She had to stop him, even if he killed her.

Again, she lunged at him.

His thick hand reached out, grabbed her cut arm. She yelped in pain, but kept her head. With a turn, she yanked her arm away, trying to loosen his grip, but he held tight. He flailed with the knife in his other hand, now slashing near her face.

She ducked, twisted, bobbed. Just when she thought she had enough power to toss him over her shoulder, she stumbled over his feet and slammed to the ground.

He came down on top of her so hard, he nearly knocked out her breath. Her body ached from the fall on the hard floor.

Inches away from her face, he turned the knife.

Her blood hammered through her body, as cold as water from a frozen lake. Her chest constricted with rib-cracking terror. She'd lost. He had her. The room, reeking with wine, took on a, dreamlike feel. How could this be happening? How could this monster be here after all these years? How could he have resurrected from her ancient, buried memories? How could he be about to kill her?

His horrid face hovered over her, his filthy breath fanned her smarting cheek. "Now, I'll give you the fate you so deserve, you whore, you."

His insults meant nothing to her now. "You're going down, Leon," she spat through gritted teeth. "They'll fry you when they catch you."

He didn't answer. He was in a world of his own. He held up the knife, laid it across her chest and ripped open the rest of her blouse.

She cried out. "What are you doing?"

"You'll see."

Oh, my God. He was going to rape her. "Leave me alone."

"You don't understand, Miranda. It's an act of love. As much as my ritual is. It's for love that I'm releasing these girls. I'm saving them before they can be contaminated. When I'm through with you, I'll release you, too. And Wendy. And then I'll find our daughter."

Daughter. Amy wasn't his daughter. She'd die before she let him touch those girls. "Get off me, you bastard."

He didn't hear her. "Don't you see, Miranda? I want to free you of your pollution." He reached down with his free hand to loosen his pants. "Despite all you've done, all your evil, I still love you."

With a gargantuan effort, she grabbed his wrist, tried to push the knife away, but he held it to her throat with the force of a demon.

He struggled with his belt. His sharp, ugly nose bobbed over her like a crow's beak. If she could just get to that nose with her teeth, she could take it off in one bite and put him into shock.

His belt came loose. "Don't struggle," he commanded.

She strained under his knife, Her heart hammering so hard, she thought it might burst on the spot. But she refused to die before she had her chance. If she could just get to his nose. Just turn her head the right way.

"I don't want to kill you yet," he pleaded. "It'll be so much easier if you don't fight."

His knife cut into her flesh, she felt the blood ooze down her neck. If she could just get to his nose before it hit the jugular vein.

"I want to love you, Miranda," he whispered in a raspy voice that sounded like it came from the pit of hell. "Give in to your fate." His face twisted in a repulsive, contorted grimace.

And then she saw it. Not the nose. The wrist. With her last bit of strength, she shoved his wrist up and sank her teeth into it.

He shrieked as the knife fell from his grasp. "No, Miranda, don't spoil it. I have to love you."

"Oh, no you don't."

Huh? Miranda blinked.

Leon's face went white with shock. Suddenly he rose up off of her, as if she'd wished him away. There was a cloudy vision standing behind him. A tall man had him by the scruff of the neck.

Parker.

He held Leon suspended above the floor, while the crazed man beat the air with his arms and legs like a trapped lobster. Then Parker set him down, reared back and gave him a wallop. Leon fell backward, knocked over some figurines. But Leon wasn't done yet. Straining, he pulled himself up and swung at Parker's head. Missed.

In a daze, Miranda watched the two men duke it out. Leon threw another wild punch and missed again. Parker jabbed with his right, hit him dead on. Leon tottered for an instant, then came back with a furious uppercut that caught Parker on the chin. Parker recovered, she thought, but the struggling images began to blur. Her stomach pulled up and down while the fuzzy figures danced strangely, like an out-of-focus movie.

Miranda tried to shake away the wooziness, suddenly wanting back in the fray. Why should Parker get all the fun? She struggled to her feet. The floor tilted.

She attempted a step toward the men. The room shifted the other way. She caught herself on a shelf and looked down. Her shirt was covered with blood. Nausea rose in her windpipe. She stood, staring down for what seemed like an hour. Then she saw it. A glint. On the stone floor near the table. Stained with red.

The knife.

There was banging. Loud, guttural grunts. She looked up and nearly vomited.

Somehow, Leon had Parker pinned against the wall. His large hands were around his throat. Parker's head bounced against the wine bottles like a basketball. If those bottles broke, the spikes would pierce right through his skull and kill him.

"No," she heard herself scream. She didn't know how she picked up the knife, but the next second, she had it in both hands and was lunging at Leon's dark frame. Raising the blade overhead, she took aim, plunged it into his back as hard as she could.

Leon's head rolled back on his neck. He opened his mouth wide and let out a cry like a demon from hell. He shoved her off, fell to the floor in a heap.

She looked up and saw Parker's bruised and bloodied face staring at her in amazement. "I think you killed him."

Her knees grew wobbly, the room fuzzy again. "Did I?"

It was the last thing she remembered.

CHAPTER THIRTY-EIGHT

Somebody must have called the police. Cops were swarming all over the place. EMTs, too.

Miranda came to on a gurney just as they hoisted her into an ambulance. A cute guy in a white coat with a smart haircut leaned near her face and mumbled some bio-techno-gibberish. Something about losing a lot of blood. Then he hooked her up to an IV.

She closed her eyes.

They took her to Saint Benedictine's, gave her blood, worked on her in the ER for a couple of hours. For a little while they thought they might lose her.

The lacerations along her chest were deep, requiring twenty-five stitches. The nick on her chin would heal by itself. The cuts on her arm and along her neck also needed some darning. The neck wound was just millimeters away from the interior jugular and carotid artery. She'd been lucky. A nurse told her all about it when she woke up in a room hours later.

Sitting up, she looked at herself and found that, sure enough, they'd cleaned her up, put her in a gown, treated her gashes. Twenty-five stitches. That was a record for her.

Seemed fitting, for the fight of her life.

The nurse said they'd keep her a few days to monitor her progress. The doctors checked on her often. So did a small army of nurses and the staff psychiatrist.

Funny, she told the woman after they'd talked a while, she didn't feel much of anything. Just numb. The shrink said she was still in shock, and that response was normal. Sure, Miranda understood. Typical reaction after discovering your ex-husband was a child murderer and then killing him for it.

The shrink added that stronger feelings might come out later. She gave Miranda her card and told her to give her a call when they did. Another card. Miranda put it away in a drawer.

Lieutenant Erskine came by and got her statement. He was soft, even gentle. She wondered how he managed to pull that act off. But she also saw admiration gleam in his black marble eyes. It felt kind of good.

Jackson Taggart stopped by to check her stitches. She wondered why he had come until she remembered he was Chief of Staff at the hospital. She thanked him for letting her stay and for taking care of her foot the other night. She joked that the bite from Leon's knife made her forget all about the bite from the alligator.

But Dr. Taggart was truly grateful. He wanted to thank her for all she'd done to stop Madison's killer.

She told him not to mention it. She was sorry for his and his wife's loss and only wished she could bring back their daughter. He wore his grief so graciously.

A few days later, they said she could go home.

Home? Where was that now? Miranda wondered as she eased into the jeans and blouse Dr. Taggart had dropped off for her. She'd figure something out. She always did.

There was a soft knock on the door. She looked up.

It was Parker.

He had a small bandage above one eye. His right cheek looked a little swollen, but he was still as handsome a devil as ever.

They stood staring at each other for what seemed like an eternity.

"I stopped by to see how you're doing," he said at last.

She shrugged. "Pretty good. How are you?" she gestured toward his brow.

He grinned, touched the adhesive strip. "Oh, I'm fine. I didn't sustain the injuries you did," he said in that fine Southern drawl of his. "I'm glad to see you well."

"Thanks." She looked around the room. "Well, I'm discharged. Told the nurse I didn't need a wheelchair. I was just leaving."

He seemed to know that. He held the door open for her. "I'll walk you out."

"Okay."

As they headed down the corridor a nurse started for them. But Parker fixed her with a stern gaze and she stopped in her tracks.

"I've got her," he said. "You can speak to Dr. Taggart if you have any questions."

She just stood there with her mouth open so they moved on to the elevators.

Parker pushed the button.

Miranda resisted the urge to look at him. "Dr. Taggart's been watching over me. He stitched me up."

"Twenty-five, I heard."

"Plus five on the throat," she said proudly.

"That's right. Can't leave those out."

She had a feeling Dr. Taggart hadn't been the only one watching over her. "So, uh, what happened to…?"

He read her thoughts. "Leon Groth? He's in the intensive care unit down at Brandywine-Summit Memorial Hospital. The doctors worked on him after the EMTs brought him in, but he lost even more blood than you, after that wound you gave him. It punctured a lung. They don't expect him to last long. He's in a coma."

"I see." That cold, dead numbness still gripped her when she thought about the encounter with him. She pushed it out of her mind.

The elevator doors opened. They stepped inside. Parker pushed the button for the ground floor.

"What about Wendy?"

"She's fine, physically. Once the drugs Groth gave her wore off, she couldn't remember anything that happened."

She nodded. "What about the murder charges? Her role in Madison Taggart's and Tiffany Todd's deaths?" She braced herself to hear bad news. How long would they keep Wendy in the youth detention center, she wondered.

Parker paused a moment. She tried to read his face. He smiled. "Antonio got her off."

She let out the breath she'd been holding. "Really?"

He nodded. "He convinced the judge it was all Groth's doing. He'd conceived the idea. Wendy had only told him how much she hated Madison Taggart and Tiffany Todd. Groth did the rest."

She put her hands to her face as relief washed over her, then shook her head. "She's a long way from being normal."

"True. One of the conditions of her release was continued therapy."

She hoped it would help the poor, lonely little girl. And her dysfunctional family.

"Oh, I almost forgot. She wrote you a note." He took a piece of paper out of his pocket, handed it to her.

Gingerly Miranda opened the paper and read the handwriting that was so familiar.

Miranda,

I'm sorry I messed up so bad. Thanks for rescuing me. Thanks for being my friend.

Wendy

She smiled, folded the paper and put it in her pocket. The best thing she ever did.

The elevator doors opened and they walked through the lobby, past a marble fountain and a large reception desk.

"The Van Aarles and the Ingrams are postponing their divorces. Both couples are opting for family therapy."

She smirked softly. "It'll take a lot of head shrinking to straighten out that mess."

"You're right. Wilhelmina Todd insists she doesn't need therapy. She's divorcing Isaiah and taking a long sabbatical in Rome with Felicia to get over the loss of her younger daughter."

Miranda barely knew the woman, but she felt for her. Leon had no concept of the terrible pain he'd inflicted. She imagined him lying alone in intensive care about to die. She wondered if there was a hell and if he was on the verge of burning in it.

Parker held the entrance door open for her. "You, on the other hand, have become something of a folk hero in Mockingbird Hills."

"Me?"

"Everyone is talking about how you rescued Wendy. They're grateful to you for stopping the killer."

All in a day's work, she guessed. But that news felt good. They moved out onto the street, crossed the parking lot. The warm Atlanta sun shone brightly.

"Looks like it's going to be another scorcher today." She shielded her eyes as they reached her old blue Lumina. It sat in a spot where somebody had parked it for her, still packed with all her stuff.

Parker folded his arms. "So where are you off to?"

She shrugged. She was supposed to check in with a doctor in a week, but she could do that anywhere. "Not sure." She had no idea where her search for Amy would take her next.

He studied her a moment. "You know, just because that letter was a lie doesn't mean Amy isn't here in Atlanta. It's a big place."

Huge. The whole country was huge. "Amy could be anywhere."

"You certainly can't say you've searched every inch of the town." He waited another moment, shifting his weight.

Her heart warmed as she looked into his handsome face, meeting his gaze. In the charm of the laugh lines around his Magnum-gray eyes she caught the gleam of his spirit. Defender, rescuer, Southern gentleman. She'd miss him.

She turned and stared at the handle of her car door. At last, she reached for it.

Parker let out a long sigh. "I don't know how I'm going to fill that vacancy at the Agency. The last employee left me high and dry."

She tapped her fingers on the handle. "That's too bad. Maybe you wouldn't have had so much trouble, if you'd let her have some freedom once in a while."

For moment, he didn't answer. She turned and watched him slowly stroke his chin. "Maybe her old dog of a teacher has a few things to learn."

His words humbled her. She pressed her lips together. "Guess she could be pretty hardheaded at times, too."

"Just passionate. It was one of the things I admired most about her."

"Yeah?" His words made her smile. "I think her last adventure taught her to listen better and not go off on her own without backup." She looked him in those sexy gray eyes. "I guess a man comes in handy once in a while. Like when your ex-husband wants to kill you. Thanks for saving my life, Parker."

He grinned. "Likewise."

She squinted at the buildings surrounding the parking lot. "You know, this detective thing has its advantages. I guess I could give it another try, that is—if my boss would lighten up."

"I promise he'll try." He nodded toward the street. "There's a nice bistro around the corner. Maybe we could discuss it over lunch. I think they serve jalapenos." He took a calculated step toward her. "Actually, that boss of yours…?"

"Yeah?"

"He just wants to be your friend." He extended his hand.

For a long while, Miranda stared at that hand. Elegant, yet rugged. Firm and powerful. She thought of its touch, its vigor, all that it had done for her. Slowly, she inhaled and reached out for him. She wrapped her fingers around his palm, felt his strength. It felt good.

She looked up into his kind, patient face. Maybe this could work out. She caught the gleam in his eye. If they could both keep their libidos in check. "I guess I could use a friend once in a while."

He gave her that sexy, wry half-smile.

They turned and slowly walked hand-in-hand across the pavement together toward the bistro.

Suddenly, lunch sounded pretty good.

THE END

ABOUT THE AUTHOR

Writing fiction for over fifteen years, Linsey Lanier has authored more than two dozen novels and short stories, including the popular Miranda's Rights Mystery series. She writes romantic suspense, mysteries, and thrillers with a dash of sass.

She is a member of Romance Writers of America, the Kiss of Death chapter, Private Eye Writers of America, and International Thriller Writers. Her books have been nominated in several RWA-sponsored contests.

In her spare time, Linsey enjoys watching crime shows with her husband of over two decades and trying to figure out "who-dun-it." But her favorite activity is writing and creating entertaining new stories for her readers.

She's always working on a new book. To keep up with her releases feel free to join Linsey's mailing list at linseylanier.com.

For more of Linsey's books check out her website at **www.linseylanier.com**

Edited by

Donna Rich

Editing for You

Second Look Proofreading

Gilly Wright
www.gillywright.com